3-14-10

Dan -

Thanks for your interest in Grey Pine. I hope the story works for you.

All the Best,

T. Lloyd Winetsky

Grey Pine

Grey Pine

T. Lloyd Winetsky

Mill City Press, Inc.

For more information contact :
Mill City Press, Inc.
212 3rd Avenue North
Suite 570
Minneapolis, MN 55401
or info@millcitypress.net

www.millcitypress.net

ISBN - 0-9799120-1-6

ISBN - 978-0-9799120-1-6

LCCN: 2007927120

Cover and Interior text Design by Elizabeth Wargo

~

To Sol and Mary, who had everything
and nothing to do with this story.

~

~

Acknowledgements

Chapter Twenty-five uses a few words similar to some terminology in *Feeling Good,* by Doctor David Burns (Morrow/Signet). I submitted this chapter a few years ago to Doctor Burns for his comments or concerns. The vague terms did not require permission; he only wished me good luck with the novel. More importantly, Doctor Burns has given inspiration to untold thousands of people, myself included. Instead of easy answers from dogma or drugs, Doctor Burns offers intellectual tools we can use by ourselves, if we so choose. He helps us look at our own decisions, not to cast guilt, but to see if at some point we stopped telling ourselves the truth.

My thanks to Victor West, who very professionally critiqued and edited *Grey Pine,* and to Tom Clayton, for introducing me to the work of David Burns. Kudos to the staff of Mill City Press for patience in dealing with the novel's "interior monologue." I will always appreciate five real teachers who encouraged me to write: Cliff Claycombe, Julia Wheaton, Lydia Broyles, Nancy Hansen-Krening, and most of all, Kathleen Ruth Nelson.
TLW

~

~

Part One

...And there, there overhead, there, there, hung over
Those thousands of white faces, those dazed eyes,
There in the starless dark the poise, the hover,
There with vast wings across the canceled skies,
There in the sudden blackness the black pall
Of nothing, nothing, nothing — nothing at all.

- Archibald MacLeish
The End of the World

1

The seventy year old cab driver had taken a liking to his steady new customer; it didn't matter that Phillip was forty years his junior and seriously ill. On their return trip from a clinic in the city, Freddy was trying to make the ride comfortable. After he passed the small town of Ponderosa, he maintained his slow speed, wisps of volcanic ash eddying behind the cab's tires.

"Could you step on it, please?" Phillip said to the back of Freddy's grey head. "I need to get home." *To my carpet.* The taxi accelerated past alfalfa fields recently baled only the second time that unusual summer. The last mile seemed endless to Phillip as he tried to hold off the chill in his head by focusing on the diamond shapes woven into the seat covers. *No good, it's worse.*

Freddy hacked out a smoker's cough and turned into the rural housing development where Phillip lived. "Your appointment go okay?" he asked, his bloodshot green eyes checking his fair-haired passenger through the rearview mirror.

"What?" Phillip asked, annoyed by the interruption. He had one hand over his eyes. "Maybe you'd be better off if you didn't worry about me." *Crap, stop barking at him.* The taxi turned down Phillip's street and sped up to his garage.

Just get out. He climbed down and walked stiffly as if it were his leg, not his arm, in a cast. Every muscle in his slight frame seemed to ache.

"You need anything, call me," Freddy offered from behind, but Phillip was already moving slowly toward the garage.

All I need is my damn carpet. He wanted to hurry, but the house seemed to be agonizingly distant. In his languid daze, he forced himself to make one step at a time through the garage and into the kitchen.

When he finally got to his bed, Phillip tried to rid himself of the chill for the third time that day. Over the tip of his nose he traced the carpet pattern below scores of times, then fell into an agitated slumber that brought him an encore of a familiar nightmare. He watched a white cougar attack his father while a distorted caricature of their next-door neighbor laughed at the slaughter and said, "Me and your ol' man was peas in a pod."

Shut up, prick. The images faded and Phillip opened his eyes, realizing right away the chill hadn't completely subsided. *Get rid of it.* He sat up, stared at the carpet again, but found only slight relief. *Damn, now what?* Phillip staggered out of the room and tried his father's door. It didn't open; he dug into his jeans pockets with his good arm, but the sluggish efforts were fruitless until his third attempt. The keys hefted like iron, blurring together in his hands until he finally opened the door.

He approached his father's bed. *Maybe here.* Phillip sat on the edge, leaned sideways and drew his index finger slowly along the pile labyrinth in the ash-dusty yellow chenille bedspread. *This has to work — down, around, to the right, out, and in...* On his knees and one elbow, he traced the thin pathway until the chill receded some. Phillip became drowsier with each loop and a murky vision of the neighbor materialized again. *Screw him; keep going — up, over, around, and in...* After several more seconds, his finger came to an obstruction, an old army revolver. *I shouldn't have left this thing here.*

Phillip picked it up to get it out of the way, but he held on to the loaded weapon and stared at it. *I never shot one of these. Just pull the trigger, idiot. He'll be out there sometime today, half-hammered, fooling around in his yard, nonchalant as hell. I wonder how cool he'd be if I—* The chill rallied at full strength; he put the firearm behind and returned to his course in the bedcover.

...up and over, around, and back again. Keep going — left and down again, back and around... In a couple minutes, the track brought him back to the pistol. ***There's*** *an omen for you. Such BS, Phillip. No, no it isn't; find the prick.* He grabbed the gun and left the room. The chill was there, but somehow he moved more quickly than he had for hours.

On a pastel spring morning, months before he met the cab driver, Phillip watched pink and tangerine clouds retreat and scatter from the sun, dissipating in the powder-blue sky. Taking advantage of his father's absence, Phillip sought some serenity in their expansive back yard. This was his time to enjoy the day — the early quiet, the crisp air, and the shade from the house over their open patio. Most other residents of the Ponderosa vicinity would wait for church to end or for the chilling influence of the mountains to burn off so they could begin sun-worshipping activities later in the day.

In ragged jeans and a faded green flannel shirt, Phillip stretched back in an aluminum chaise, his wool slipper-socks resting well short of the end of the furniture. His new black and white Ponderosa Panthers baseball hat was tilted back, and a swatch of dark blond hair spilled over his forehead, tickling his fair eyebrows.

Phillip swept the strands to the side and settled in with the thick Sunday paper, a cup of hot cider, and two plain cake doughnuts. Under his chair, rock music from a transistor radio thumped away in a soft, regular beat. He wedged a pillow gingerly behind his weathered, slightly sunburned neck.

After reading the headlines then starting on the sports, Phillip heard squawking from one of the flowering bushes that lined their back fence on both sides of a crabapple tree. He looked up to see a fat robin perch precariously on a lilac branch, bending some lavender blossoms to the ground. Phillip returned to the sports but decided he'd read enough of another "Miracle of Lake Placid" story. He began an article about his favorite team, the Portland Trailblazers, and their chances of winning the NBA championship as they had three years before, in 1977. Phillip lost his place moments later when an orange blur streaked by above the bill of his cap. Lifting his head too late to see the robin clearly, he noticed that the steady finches had abandoned his birdfeeder in the crabapple tree.

What's the deal? The cat must be around. He squinted at the tree and then reached over to a nearby chair for the bulk of the Sunday paper and plopped it onto the ground next to him. Recalling his father's decree to spray off the furniture and the patio, he brushed the chair's plastic straps with the ends of his fingers and then checked his hand.

It's hardly even dirty. So? He didn't want to anger Stephen and give him an excuse to cancel a doctor's appointment when he returned from the convention back in Chicago. Phillip had finally convinced him to have a mole on his neck checked and to get a physical while he was at it. Since he had failed for years to get his father to find help for his alcoholism, Phillip felt little compunction from a covert phone call he made to fill in the doctor on Stephen's addiction.

The chairs can wait till tomorrow. He finished one doughnut, sipped some cider, and then reached down for the front page.

Thank God there's only a month left. He would only have to steel himself from Stephen until the end of the school year and the beginning of his summer plans.

Phillip was finishing his sixth year of teaching science, health, P.E., and coaching basketball at Ponderosa Junior High. The week after school was over he would be off for the mountains as a low-wage research assistant on a summer project to investigate the population and range of the Canada lynx in the Northwest.

The news about the research came before Thanksgiving just after another development, Phillip's new relationship with Guadalupe Rosendall. He couldn't decide which was more unlikely, being hired for the project or having a girl friend like Lupe, whom he considered "out of his league" when they met. Taken together, his new girl friend and the lynx research allowed him hope that the balance of events in his life had taken a positive turn, but his optimism struggled against an underlying dread that Stephen waited at some sort of imminent fulcrum with an anvil in each hand.

Phillip caught himself in thought, still reading the news but not processing the words. *He'll pull something for sure to avoid the doctor. You've got two more days; don't even think about him.* He let the paper drop to his lap, drank more cider, then put his head back again and tapped his calf to the beat of Neil Young's "Heart of Gold." Enjoying one of the song's harmonica riffs, he was surprised to see a bank of steel-grey clouds blotting the western sky. The music cut off on the radio and he sat up, expecting to hear low rumbling in the distance.

The weatherman's wrong — he said hot and dry. Good deal; bring on the rain. Phillip stood up to scrutinize the dark front. There was still no thunder; it was completely quiet for several seconds until one of the robins screeched and then a high-pitched voice began stuttering on the radio.

"...uh, we're breaking in — yes, for some, uh, news — no, a news bulletin." The young disc jockey, apparently trained only to deal with pre-recorded programming, continued to speak incoherently and seemed to doubt what he was reading. He finally got it across that Mount Saint Helens in the Cascades had a massive eruption and the ash was heading their way.

Phillip immediately rechecked the menacing clouds; they were already closer and darker, stitched with white heat lightning. *Good God, get the camera. Wait, who should know about this? Lupe — no, she's in town.* Feeling like he had to share the startling news with someone, Phillip moved toward the house, his head turned back to the looming gunmetal-grey horizon as if it were chasing him. He heard the whine of a grass trimmer next door; Phillip stopped and decided that even his father's obnoxious drinking crony would want to know.

2

The five thousand or so residents of the Ponderosa area had no medical specialists and no taxis, so, like Phillip, they sometimes found themselves with no choice but to hire a Four Rivers cab for a doctor's appointment in the city, forty miles away. Such inconvenience was anathema to a powerful faction who had pined for years for Ponderosa to become "a bustling small city." It drove them nuts that so many fellow citizens said things like, "This is a nice little farming town; folks around here would just as soon keep it that way."

Back in 1966, after the long-awaited arrival of their only fast-food chain restaurant, the boosters' pride in the new chicken joint spurred them on to new projects, starting with a motto. Since the valley was located an hour's drive from a small skiing resort, the local chamber of commerce began promoting Ponderosa as "The Aspen of the Northwest." A few irked citizens pointed out that it was pathetic to pretend to be some other place.

Undaunted by the criticism, the chamber decided they needed an attraction that was somehow related to the trees for which "the growing city" was named, though most ponderosas had long ago been removed from the valley. The stalwart western pines were still ubiquitous in the nearby hills and riparian zones, and a few survived on the ridges of basalt escarpments east and west of town.

After greasing the wheels of progress, the boosters and investors began planning for The New Ponderosa Ranch to be constructed southeast of town on the road to Ski-Eden. More than a dozen people spoke against the project at a hearing before the Redfield County Planner, who, to no one's surprise, summarily decided the "Ranch" was approved.

Not long after that, two new signs went up at the city limits. One said, "OPEN NEXT SUMMER: THE NEW PONDEROSA RANCH - STATE RD 39 - MILE 21," and the other, "WELCOME TO PONDEROSA - THE ASPEN OF THE NORTHWEST," the latter with a logo of a pointy Christmas tree that resembled neither a ponderosa nor an aspen.

So, scores of pines were removed and underbrush was cleared from the land. Without consulting the owner of the rights to the TV western, the developers created a mini-version of a cattle town and the famous family's spread, carefully avoiding use of the words, *Bonanza* or "Cartwright."

The mock homestead even had sculpted dummies of the TV characters with trumped-up but unmistakable names like "Horse," instead of "Hoss." False-fronted shops on Main Street hawked cowboy trinkets and apparel; you could buy "Pa's Mint Moonshine" ice cream at the Sarsaparilly Saloon, and there were other attractions like The Ol'Timey Arcade, Hop Wing's Restaurant, and The Cattle Drive Miniature Golf Course.

They advertised throughout the West, once on national TV, and every visiting vehicle was decorated with "SEE THE NEW

PONDEROSA RANCH" bumper stickers. Most of the businesses ran only in the warmer months and by the second year they started going belly-up. The boosters couldn't fathom why the world didn't beat a path to the gates of *Bonanza* redux, and the grand scheme was abandoned. They kept Main Street as a ghost town and scaled back the enterprise to two active buildings: the Chinese restaurant and the Ponderosa Ranch Gift Shop and Museum — "ONLY ONE BUCK TO SEE 'PA' AND ALL THE OTHER DUMMIES UPSTAIRS."

The vicinity's only modern subdivision, predictably dubbed Ponderosa Estates, was to be the second jewel of local expansion. Two miles past city limits on the road to the ill-fated Ranch, the housing project covered most of an entire rural section and was divided into one-and-a-half-acre parcels — just enough room to convince prospective buyers that they would be in for some natural country living — but the elderberry, serviceberry, bitterbrush, bunchgrass, sage, cottonwood, willow, and the coyotes, prairie dogs, porcupines, jackrabbits, falcons, meadowlarks, pheasants, quail, rattlesnakes and skunks soon gave way to the bulldozers.

At first there were only a few models — three-bedroom ramblers with sprawling lawns to blend in with a planned three-par golf course. The next homes sprung up one by one with unrolled turf, spindly foreign trees, and great slabs of pavement. That initial energy was followed by years of declining sales, and the subdivision stabilized with as many empty lots as homesites. Sage gradually reclaimed the unsold acres, cheat replaced bunchgrass, and small critters and coyotes again made themselves at home.

Soon after the original "ranch homes" in Ponderosa Estates went on the market, Stephen Stark told his son that he'd asked for a transfer and they would be moving from Seattle, across the mountains to Ponderosa. Phillip was seventeen and reeling from his first experience with an immediate death — his mother's — a few weeks before, but he didn't complain about changing schools for his senior year. On a July weekend in 1968 they moved into one of the last models built in the development. Phillip soon found work in town at the market and on days off he sought refuge from his father's worsening drinking habits by exploring the mountains.

As a child, Phillip Stark was Rockwell material for the Saturday Evening Post — thin and towheaded, with a mask of freckles beneath his azure eyes. By the time his senior year began, his face was free of maculation, his thick hair had darkened some, and he was in top shape from all the hiking.

He conformed enough to get along during his one year at Ponderosa High, but Phillip stuck mostly to his own interests and made few friends. His reasonably good looks and even some unexpected celebrity in basketball couldn't save him from occasional ridicule. Phillip's main "offenses" were reading unassigned books about animals and bringing in his collections of natural specimens to Advanced Biology, his only "A" subject.

In the eleven-plus years after the Starks settled into Ponderosa Estates, the land for the doomed golf course gradually turned even wilder than the vacant lots, and the subdivision eventually became a patchwork of tract homes, a few two-story places and, most recently, some doublewide modulars. Some of the newer landowners ignored the development's covenants for tidiness, which angered Stephen, who frowned upon anything less than a fairway-perfect yard.

It was Stephen's immaculate lawn that made Phillip hesitate after he heard the frantic announcement about the eruption. Before heading for the neighbor's fence, he recalled one of Stephen's parting edicts: "Remember to walk around to your damn birdfeeder." He had planted a long strip of new grass to replace one of the garden beds.

"Screw it," Phillip said, separating two of the chest-high manicured arborvitae that surrounded the patio. As if crossing a creek, he long-jumped Stephen's precious seedlings and then turned back to discover that his heels had trampled a few lime-green blades of grass.

Too bad; they'll grow back. He rolled up his sleeves on the way to the fence then climbed up on a pile of old steppingstones his father put there to provide a boost over the planks. It always bothered Phillip that Mick Lewis, who was six-foot-four, could snoop into their yard any time he wanted. Like Stephen, Phillip was five-eight, and now his eyes, nose and mouth just cleared the top of the boards. He checked Mick's nearby patio and pool, then scanned the half acre of weedless lawn until he spotted him trimming around his garden shed, unclothed down to the waist.

Though Lewis was slender below the midline, his shoulders and arms were burly, and his beer belly protruded over the front of the baggy swim trunks he liked to wear night and day. His black body hair made his tanned skin seem even darker, and from a distance he could pass for a tall, portly aborigine. Phillip didn't know and didn't care what Mick looked like face to face; he avoided and despised him for starting up drunken binges with Stephen, who once told his son that Mick referred to Phillip as "Steve's fuckin' ol' lady."

Lewis turned off the trimmer, walked across the lawn to the patio and picked up a beer. His two-story colonial with the forty-foot pool was custom built a few years after the Starks moved in. Now in his mid-fifties like Stephen, Mick was divorced with no kids and could afford the home because he and his siblings inherited a local dairy, though Phillip was sure he made a negligible contribution to the business.

"Mister Lewis," Phillip called. ***Mister?***

Mick took a swig from the can and looked at Phillip. "What do you want, kid?" Not caring if Phillip answered, Lewis put down the beer and glared at a black stinkbug drowning in the shimmering blue water.

Kid *— shit. Well, you had to tell somebody; what did you expect?* "Those clouds up there." He pointed over the wooden shingles on Mick's roof. "It's ash from the volcano."

Not even looking up, Lewis turned away. "It's a storm — see the damn lightning?" he said, reaching for a pool skimmer.

Asshole, suit yourself. Phillip jumped down and rushed to the house to retrieve a camera. On the way back out he stopped briefly to check the news on TV. They were showing the spewing volcano and talking mostly about mudflows and casualties, not the ash fall. By the time he came outside, the sky was still a brilliant spring blue to the east, but the oncoming iron-grey ash moved in from the west like a slow curtain of turbulent dry fog. He sat on the back step and hurriedly put on his shoes, watching the spectacle as he tied.

Phillip finished off the film with shots of the ominous slate clouds and the mute lightning, knowing the latter wouldn't turn out. He inserted his only spare cartridge and cursed himself for putting off the repair of his old thirty-five millimeter camera. Next door, Mick's lawn mower roared to life and then idled.

Idiot — screw him, it's almost here. This'll be incredible.

3

Violating Stephen's new grass more than once, Phillip moved around the big yard for some different angles and took another half-dozen shots of the billowing black and grey ash above. "Should save some of this for later," Phillip said to his camera and aimed it up again, but a few dark specks landed on the lens. He wiped the glass with his shirttail, forced the small camera into his back pocket then looked up and saw the charcoal clouds were losing their sharp definition, like a monochrome TV picture going out of focus. The creeping dusk had finally extinguished all the direct sunlight.

My God, this is it. He turned east again where the jet-black front was overtaking what was left of the sky, now a milky false dawn. He flattened his hand and held it out, the way you check for rain. His skin tingled from a fine shower of hard granules, and he brought his palm up for a look.

Man, it's like ground pepper. He walked back to the patio, turned up the radio and sat on the edge of a lawn chair. *Now what? Just watch for a while.* The disc jockey had been replaced but the news was similar to what he heard on TV, so he shut off the radio after a few minutes and just attended to what was happening.

Phillip extended his palm again until his arm fatigued and his skin turned sooty. He got up, brushed his hands, and then pushed his way through the cypress and onto the lawn. Turning back toward the house, he saw that only a strip of sky remained, the dusk thickening even more. He dispatched two last-chance photos of the midday dawn; then stood still and listened. *Mick's gone, no machines anywhere — nothing, not even birds; they must be fooled into sleeping.*

Phillip waited and watched for several more minutes, until the very last of the light was gone. Particles of ash tickled the hairs of his exposed wrist and he tried to inspect his skin but couldn't even see the outline of his arm.

Head in, I guess. He smacked his baseball cap on his knee and brushed off his back and shoulders as he returned to the patio. After tripping over the chaise, Phillip pulled open the sliding glass door and tossed the three pieces of aluminum furniture into the dark den. He felt around for the radio and also found the doughnut and the cup before stepping up into the house. Phillip put everything on the floor, then turned back to the yard and switched on the patio floodlight. Leaning out the doorway, he watched the flecks of ash fall like steady snow caught in a car's high beams.

Man, it's just amazing. Mesmerized, he stared into the ersatz storm until a troubling sensation surfaced into a clear thought. *This could screw the research.* Phillip glared at the ash and then turned off the patio light; it was pitch-dark inside and out. *God, not another damn summer with him.*

He slid the door shut, then stumbled in the blackout over the patio furniture. "Shit," he said, and swept his hand along the wall until it clicked the inside light switch. Phillip sat to remove his shoes, as was Stephen's rule, and saw the doughnut on the floor, powdered with dark-grey ash.

Yum. He noticed his grimy footprints on the carpet. *Vacuum that or he'll have a cow.*

Stephen kept the house spotless, including the large den they called "the poolroom." A full-sized billiard table and a pinball machine, both now rarely used, took up half the space. They kept a small desk cramped into a corner for the extension phone and one of Stephen's large glass ashtrays. Two of the pine-paneled walls were bare; the third was half-covered with a sheet-sized *yin* and *yang* South Korean flag Stephen brought back from the war.

Phillip climbed the two steps into the dining room, which deserved that name only in the sense that they usually ate there in front of the television. Like the den and hallways, the TV room had been matted on Stephen's orders with dark-green indoor-outdoor carpet to make things "easy to clean."

They each had their own recliner. Phillip's was an old brown Naugahyde with two positions, all the way up or all the way down. It used to be his father's, rejected years before in favor of a new model with motorized reclining, vibrator, and a drink holder/ashtray built into one arm. In a back corner next to a rack of metal TV trays, two folded up director's chairs waited for infrequent visitors. The single amenity in the room was Stephen's framed photo of Ingemar Johansson on the wall above the TV. Gloves held high in a pugnacious pose, the former heavyweight champion reigned over the sports, news and situation comedies that emitted from the RCA below.

Phillip walked over to the room's only window and lifted back one side of the thick curtains Stephen installed to keep sunlight off the TV screen. *Geez, it's like midnight outside, but no lights.* He let the curtain go, switched on the TV and backed up a few steps to his chair. Before he could sit all the way back, he was startled slightly when his cat materialized in front of him, its claws digging into Phillip's knees. Every inch of the feline was white as an albino rabbit, and its eyes, one blue and one gold, darted toward some enigmatic disturbance. The cat was the sole survivor of the menagerie of dogs, cats, rodents, rabbits and birds they had when Ellen Stark was still alive.

"What's wrong, boy?" he asked, stroking its short fur. The old rangy cat twitched its head, glanced at Phillip, then stood tentatively on his lap, tail bottle-brushed, reluctant to sit down. As quickly as it arrived, the cat jumped to the ground and disappeared through the pet door into the garage.

The darkness must be freaking him. Phillip returned his attention to the TV, but it was a national broadcast again. He got up and twisted the dial to check each channel. They all had special reports with news he'd heard repeatedly, so he left it on the last station. He sat down and reclined the chair to wait for some new information but was soon asleep, napping for most of an hour. He woke up to a news telecast from Four Rivers, the hub of the television market in their part of the state.

"...though there's no end in sight, the ash is just falling lightly in Four Rivers," the announcer said.

How could that be?

"...results of the ash analysis are not yet available; there is concern about the possibility of glass particles, so please stay indoors if possible, or find some sort of mask if you must go out."

Glass particles? I doubt it. How do you know, Phillip?

"...update you again at the hour on the ash fall. We return you now to network coverage of the eruption and..."

Falling lightly, *maybe it's not as bad as you thought. One way to find out — let's see, painting masks.* Phillip rushed into the garage and moved in the dark easily since Stephen always kept everything in the same place. He came to the doorless portal to the shop and turned on the light.

Except for a line of ash near a door to the yard, the shop was immaculate; not a wood curl or bit of sawdust defiled the table saw, lathe or workbench. Phillip opened a painting drawer and found a half-dozen white particle masks, precisely stacked like the perfectly cut potato chips that come in a cylinder. He hung one of the crisp new masks on his neck then hurried back into the house and down to the den.

He switched on the patio light; the beam was completely clotted by the dry blizzard. *My God, total whiteout* — ***grey****out, I guess.* He removed his cap long enough to pinch the mask's aluminum strip over his nose and then snap the elastic band behind his head. Without sitting down he put on his shoes and tried to watch the falling ash at the same time.

Phillip went out, stopped, and felt particles whisk across his forehead like gnats. His trapped breath recirculated in the mask and he began to sweat around his mouth. He stepped off the single stair, bent over and scooped up a handful of soot.

"Man, at least an inch already," he said, his voice muffled. Phillip stood up into the strong light, rubbing ash between his fingers. *It's softer now.* His shadow should have stretched across the yard, but it didn't even reach the end of the patio where it faded into the opaque air. The shrouded arborvitae resembled enormous licorice gumdrops, and the settling dust completely cloaked the lawn except for a few long blades of edge grass.

Stephen'll have a damn fit. His peripheral vision picked up some movement; he turned toward it. A mouse, grey as the ash, held still, as if aware of its camouflage. Amazed that the rodent stood its ground, Phillip stooped and leaned closer, within a couple of feet, before the mouse scurried into the dark, leaving behind delicate forked footprints. Phillip squatted to check the tiny tracks, the only imperfections in the uniform layer that covered everything.

He let me get so close. He stared at the prints for several moments until they were obscured then erased by the unrelenting ash fall. Phillip stood and turned toward the floodlight to gauge how hard the ash was coming down. *It's not letting up at all.* He pulled the mask away a moment for some air.

Phillip sat on the step beneath the light and took off his cap. Earlier it was white with a black "P," but now he saw it was dark grey, the capital letter barely visible. He smacked the hat on the side of his leg and put it back on. From Mick's yard Phillip heard the report of a metal pole clanging on concrete.

"Goddamn it to hell," came sputtering out of the pall in an even, matter-of-fact tone.

Gee, Mick, what's wrong? He got up and brushed off his rear. *Crap, see if the jerk needs help.* Phillip walked a few feet onto the patio and turned back to the light to examine his footprints, each one so precisely molded it cast its own small shadow. *Man, so incredible. Yeah, if some of it went north, you're screwed. People are dead over there, Phillip, like you've got problems.*

Stepping backwards several more times, he watched his tracks and the floodlight fade into the pitch. He stopped, listening to the midday nightfall. *No noise at all on the block.*

A mumbled oath drifted in from behind: "Damn shit."

Except Mick. He turned around, stepping through the cypress into total darkness. As if blind, Phillip walked with his arms out until the bill of his cap finally bumped into a branch of the crabapple tree. After two more steps he made out the top of the fence; a dim horizon created by Mick's high-wattage patio lights. He felt around for the craggy steppingstones and climbed up.

"Son of a fuckin' bitch," Lewis said, cussing so blandly he could have been saying, '*Son of a gun.*' The strong floodlights exposed the flittering particles and Mick's silhouette, a stage performer surrounded by a fake storm. Less than twenty feet away from Phillip, he peered down at the detritus that was quietly descending into the deep end of his kidney-shaped pool.

The ever present can of beer in one hand, Mick folded his long legs into a squat and directed a flashlight into the surface of the water. "Fuckin' mess," he said, his voice muffled by the unseen cigarette Phillip knew was hanging from the side his mouth.

I warned you, idiot. "Need help with the cover?" Phillip called after lifting his mask.

Lewis continued to glare at the water. "You again? It's too damn late, it's floating to this end. Worst is over anyway."

"Not what I heard."

Mick stood and looked toward the fence, though Phillip was practically invisible. "And what did *you* hear, kid?"

Shit, it won't matter what I say.

"Well?"

"They said no end in sight."

"Bullshit; it's slowing down." He turned back to his pool and beamed the flashlight into the water again. "Tell your ol' man to call me when he gets back."

"Yeah." *Like hell I will.* "It's falling hard. You sure you don't want to keep some of it out of there?"

"I'm sure, goddamn it."

Screw it. Phillip started to turn around, but he stubbed his foot on a board.

"Why don't you take off; mind your own fucking business," Lewis said, emotionless.

As much as Phillip hated him, he was still struck by the remark. He said nothing, stepped down and sat on the concrete slabs, the fence blocking the light from the other side. *He can wipe his ass with the damn pool cover — be more useful that way.* Phillip stood up. *Tell him. Yeah, be just like him, like Stephen. They deserve each other.*

He started back into the dark toward the house. When he came into the faint light on the patio, Phillip discovered that the steadily falling ash had already rounded off the molds of his initial footprints. *Worst is over, huh? Plastered ol' prick, I hope it fills your damn pool.*

At the back door, Phillip stopped to brush off the ash and shake his hat. He tapped each of his heels to dislodge the grime and then entered the den. After he closed the door and turned on the light, he pulled off the mask and removed his shoes again. As he walked through the den, Phillip noticed the pool table's snap-on black vinyl cover was dusted with fine grey powder.

It's in here already. He gazed back at the falling ash. *A lot more to see outside, not with frigging Mick in his yard. Maybe go out front. No, see if Lupe's back.* He picked up the poolroom extension and punched in the numbers for the long-distance call to her parents in Sageview. Phillip listened to the clicking pulse from Stephen's new touch-dial phones.

How is this crap better than dialing? After a few rings, he got a "circuits are busy" recording. *Call the apartment.* Phillip tried her number in Masonville, same result. *Try later — check the volcano news.*

In the TV room, he walked in on a live telecast from the west side of the mountains. A middle-aged reporter wearing brand new neon-orange outdoor gear was speaking from some small town upwind of the eruption. Over his shoulder they had a clear shot of Mount Saint Helens in the distance, continuing to release thick leaden clouds.

Daylight over there, dark over here — wild. The ash, the announcer said, was being carried to the northeast by the prevailing winds. *Crap — north-northeast or east-northeast?* When the man started discussing mudflows, Phillip sat in his chair and waited for different information. Several minutes later, the cat jumped back up on Phillip's lap, its claws dug slightly into his jeans again.

"Where've you been?" he asked, half expecting the animal to speak right up. "Easy," Phillip said as he petted. His sixteen year old cat finally sat all the way down, but his dissimilar eyes kept exploring all corners of the room.

He senses we're right down to it; the earth's running the show. "Ready to eat, Ali? Past your lunch time." When Phillip was thirteen he found the white kitten scrounging in a dumpster not far from their old house and later named his pet for a tiger in a children's book that Ellen Stark used to read to him.

On TV, two studio reporters were transposed over a different live shot of the volcano. The man was listing damage statistics but he stopped and yielded to the female announcer. "We're getting some interesting reports now from the other side of the mountains," she said, and then paused.

All right, about time.

"We're told that the ash clouds in much of the central and eastern part of the state have turned day into night, and there's heavy ash fall in many towns, and lesser but significant amounts in the cities of Guthrie and Four Rivers. At this point, there seems to be no letup, and the ash continues to..."

Hear that, Mick?

"...few cars have been able to enter or leave a seven-county area since the ash started to come down. Travelers are stranded in schools and Red Cross shelters, and commercial airports are closed indefinitely. Health officials are asking the public to..."

The airport — God, Stephen will be stuck back there. Yeah, in seventh heaven, pickling himself in the hotel bar. Damned if he won't miss his doctor's appointment — you get to start all over.

The female reporter on TV accepted a hand-delivered note. "Bill, this just in: In at least these four counties: Redfield, Four Rivers, Chief Joseph and Guthrie, most government offices and schools are closed tomorrow and until further notice..."

You're kidding. Easy, it's probably just a couple days. "Well, we may as well get comfortable," Phillip said, reclining the chair slowly so he wouldn't disturb the cat. He returned his attention to the TV and stroked Ali, who began to knead lightly on Phillip's legs.

"...we've been so focused on the catastrophic destruction over here, and now these serious new complications are developing on the other side of the state."

"Yes, Diane, and I'm sure everyone over there has witnessed right along with us the heroic stories touching us all so deeply over the last few hours. Hopefully, that will help them a little as they deal with their own situation."

"You're so right. It's truly amazing how a tragedy like this brings people together. The impersonality of modern life seems to disappear, and we're neighbors again, neighbors helping neigh— "

"Well, Diane," Phillip said to the TV, "over on this side we're cleaning our swimming pools and minding our *own fucking business.*" Ali leaped to the floor, ducked through the cat door into the garage and didn't return for the rest of the evening.

4

When Phillip and his older sister, Joann, were children in Seattle, Stephen was only a weekend drinker, smashed on Friday or Saturday night with his friends. The few times he drank at home, he was so irritable that the family would just try to ignore him until he fell asleep or passed out, and the next day it was forgotten or even joked about.

After Ellen Stark was hospitalized with lung cancer, Stephen started to drink on weekdays, and Phillip sometimes had to dry him out for hospital visits. After her death, Phillip thought it was understandable when the drinking worsened, but after a year or so he began thinking of his father as two different people: his "real" dad, and Stephen the drunkard. It eventually became so difficult to communicate that Phillip had to surreptitiously trap Stephen's attention when he wasn't having one of his crapulent hangovers.

One morning, several months before the volcano, Phillip shut off his alarm early, got some juice and waited in his bathrobe for Stephen in the kitchen. His father came in wearing navy-blue chino trousers and a white shirt with "STEVE" monogrammed on the pocket, the uniform for his job as a hardware stock supervisor in Four Rivers. He was "Steve" only at work and to Mick, as far as Phillip knew.

"Can we talk a minute?" Phillip asked, as if such a proposal was an everyday occurrence, but Stephen just poured some coffee and sipped it. His face still tan from summer yard work, Stephen had just trimmed his modest sideburns and shaved. His Brillcreamed dark-brown hair, not a strand out of place, was parted on the left to form a straight scalp line. Besides their identical height, Stephen shared few physical attributes with Phillip, whose pyramid-shaped nose and blue eyes were in complete contrast to his father's flat pug and green irises.

"Dad, you pulled an all-time first the other night, you threw one of your big ashtrays at me." He chuckled as if it was funny.

"I think you're exaggerating, Phillip."

"Okay, let's say it was flung in my general direction. I've told you, you don't always remember what happens when you're drunk. Will you think again about talking to someone?" he asked, but Stephen just cringed, so Phillip continued. "If you get some help, who knows, you might end up seeing someone again. It's been over ten years."

Stephen surprised him by speaking right up, somber but direct. "It's *twelve* years, but that isn't your business. People don't have what your mother and I did," he said, looking away. "I don't want to see anyone else; that's just the way it is."

"Dad, you're still young, you— "

"Stop, Phillip, and don't bring it up again."

"All right, sorry, but the point is your drinking," he said, and Stephen put his cup down, turned away and walked to the garage.

Phillip tried to lighten the moment before Stephen got to the door. "Hey, I saw you working on your car the other day — running okay?" he asked.

"Yeah, just cleaning."

Scolding himself for being tactless, Phillip watched him go out. He knew the repercussion would be a binge when Stephen got home, probably leading to some kind of hassle between them.

Not long after that failed intervention, Stephen cornered his son on Halloween night after Phillip hung up the phone. He was in the habit of calling Lupe as if they lived next door, though her apartment was more than thirty miles away. Phillip rolled up the sleeves of his flannel shirt, took an unsatisfying sip of room-temperature beer and glared at some smoke that scudded up to the doorway. His disdain for cigarettes was intractable since his mother's cancer and because Stephen usually smoked when he drank. So he knew it was Stephen coming in, not his dad, who had returned sober that evening from work.

Stephen stepped down into the den, the cigarette, as always, burning toward his palm. "Just like Mick, the Marlboro Man," Phillip once told him and then added, "Do you realize how much smarter you are than that jerk?" Another squabble ensued and Stephen got in the last words: "Between the goddamn Okies across the street and the nosy old fart next door, Mick's the only good neighbor I have — just keep your clever little mouth shut."

Now Stephen cradled a bowl of trick-or-treats in one arm; the other hand held the cigarette as well as one of his "tall boys," which, as always, was preceded by a shot of bourbon. He had been watching a *Gunsmoke* rerun between surly trips to the front door to satisfy the neighborhood goblins.

Stephen Stark's inebriation never compromised his neat attire; he was wearing pressed slacks, a fresh short-sleeve sport shirt and shiny loafers as he approached his son. Phillip was thinking that the dime-sized black mole below Stephen's ear looked like a hole in his neck, just right for Halloween.

Stephen put down the miniature chocolate bars on the desk. "Jesus, you were on the phone with her again?" he asked, snarling his nose and squinting his blood-shot eyes, a circus-mirror visage of his sober self.

"Yup, every night," Phillip said, turning away from the cigarette. "So why wasn't it a problem yesterday?" he asked, knowing full well Stephen wasn't drinking the night before.

"You weren't on there for two goddamn hours." He placed a coaster on the pinball machine, set his beer on top, and then intentionally left the ashtray and the burning cigarette next to Phillip, who moved it right over to the pool table.

"It was barely more than an hour." Phillip faced the door, already planning to get out of there.

"Bullshit." Though Stephen was riled, his eyes sagged.

"How would you know? You're already wasted."

"Wasted my ass. Don't talk to me like that."

"Fine, did you need the phone?" He pushed it toward him.

"No, that's not the damn point..."

Seeing that a lecture had begun, Phillip slumped down into the chair while Stephen leaned on the pool table and kept talking.

"...and you should've got this kind of thing out of your system in high school."

"What's that supposed to mean?" Phillip asked, trying mid-sentence to mitigate his defensiveness.

"You're mooning around here with a stupid-ass teenage crush. How much younger is she?"

Phillip wondered how he knew that. He put his elbows on the desk and massaged his temples with the ends of his fingers and thumbs, staring silently at the trick-or-treats below.

"Well, how old is she?"

Phillip unwrapped a candy. "Almost twenty-three," he said, inserting the entire little bar into his mouth, still looking down.

"Friggin' cradle robber, I suppose you don't want to tell me her name, either." Stephen quaffed two gulps of beer.

"Why d' ya' ev'n care?" Phillip said, his words garbled by the candy.

"I don't, but tell me anyway. Look at me, goddamn it."

Phillip licked the last of the chocolate from his teeth, raised his head and resignedly pronounced her first name correctly, as Lupe preferred.

"*Loopy*?" Stephen said. "Jesus Christ, I didn't believe it."

"Believe what?"

"What a little turd told me in town. So she *is* a fu— "

"Stop, damn it," Phillip broke in. "Her name is Guadalupe Rosendall," he said, seething. "Her mother immigrated from Mexico. You happy now?"

That sent Stephen into a roar of derisive laughter and a racial snit about Mexican farm workers. "...and I bet the ol' lady probably sorts fruit at— "

"What if she did? She's been here forty years, she's a teacher, but you've got everybody pegged." Phillip grabbed his half-full can of beer and got up again. "Damn Kurt," he mumbled. He was sure that Kurt Raihofer, an ex-schoolmate in Ponderosa, was the "little turd" who gossiped to Stephen.

"Hold it, you're not getting off that easy. Her ol' man's name is Rosenthall?"

"Rosen*dall*." Phillip stopped at the door to the TV room.

"Don't tell me he's a kike."

He turned back to Stephen. "That's your ignorant word."

"I'll be a son of a bitch; and I suppose he runs a bank?"

"He's a commodities trader in Four Rivers."

"Same damn thing."

"Why don't you stop? This is none of your business anyway."

"Shit, leave it to you to find a half-kike, half-Mexican beadsnapper," he said, picking up the treats.

"Right, she's part Mexican, so she must be a Catholic. She's a Methodist."

"You can bet she was raised with Mary and the Pope. What a match — the beadsnapper and the pagan."

"Yeah, at least I went to some of Mom's big deals."

"Bullshit." Stephen wanted no mention of his wife. "Jesus, when the shit hits *Loopy's* fan, don't say I didn't warn you." He wrapped a hand around the neck of his beer and held up the candy. "You take charge of this crap; I'm going over to Mick's to watch the fight on the dish."

Phillip was asleep in his recliner where he had watched volcano reports for hours, occasionally measuring the accumulation outside with a ruler. The last time he checked the ash it was more than two inches deep, and coming down steadily. Local TV and radio information was still sketchy and uncertain; mainly they kept warning people to stay inside and not to drive except for real emergencies. Before he fell asleep, Phillip tried again to reach Lupe, but the circuits were still down.

Now he was attempting to turn on his side to get more comfortable in the chair, but a sharp pang grabbed his intestines. Phillip opened his eyes to jittery TV shadows on the ceiling. *Late show, I guess.* He looked down and saw it was the national network, their regular early morning program.

"What the hell?" he said. *It's the smile-until-it-hurts-show.* As if on Phillip's cue, the glib weatherman yielded to two grinning hosts who joked around in front of a backdrop of the smoking volcano. Phillip focused on the glow of the electric clock on the bar between the TV room and the dark kitchen.

Eight forty? God, sleep of the dead. He craned his head toward the kitchen window. *Still no daylight — unbelievable. How much ash? At least three inches, I bet.* He listened for a few seconds to the morning-show talking heads and realized they weren't even discussing the eruption.

"Who shot J.R.?" Phillip asked, incredulous. He moved his line of sight down to the TV tray next to him. His neglected dinner from the previous night looked like it was staged for pop-art: a red apple with one missing bite turned putrid brown, an untouched candy bar, and a partially unwrapped and nibbled bean burrito; all of it on a soiled white paper plate. At the side, a full glass of cola had lost its carbonation.

Guess I wasn't very hungry. Still bleary-eyed and stiff from sleeping in the chair, Phillip got up with the food. His gut still bothered him as he shuffled into the kitchen, turned on the lights and set the plate and soda by the sink.

Wonder if Ali's back? He picked up his prescription from the counter then swallowed a pill with the flat cola and saw his movements reflected in the dark window. Diagnosed with a bleeding duodenal ulcer at fifteen, just months before his mother died, Phillip never told her about it, and Stephen just paid the medical deductibles without comment.

Between his thumb and forefinger, Phillip pinched a stack of sandwich cookies from a package on the counter. He ate one in two bites, taking a closer look outside. There was no hint of morning light, and the dry ash-fog hid all the shapes normally visible at night.

Let's see, it was dark by noon. God, that's more than twenty hours. He glanced over at the TV and heard an announcer react with near titillation to his partner's sensational facts about the eruption. *Clowns, tell me about the ash fall.* He leaned over on the bar, ate part of another cookie and watched the program. They finally came up with a map that graphed the prevailing wind; the ash had been carried much more east than north.

It's nowhere near the project. All right! Phillip tossed the remaining piece of cookie in the air, caught it in his mouth and then made a quick trip down the hall to his bathroom. On the way back he saw a small, disemboweled creature and streaks of soot on the kitchen linoleum. *Ali's back.* During Phillip's brief absence the mouse was left for him on what had been Stephen's spick-and-span floor.

No more little prints in the ash for that rodent. Phillip found the dustpan, swept up the tiny carcass and some of the grime, and dumped it all in the trashcan. *Ashes to ashes.* Ali sauntered in through the flap in the garage door and stopped to sniff the spot where he dropped the mouse. Leaving that, he started making circle-eights around Phillip's legs, his purr rattling.

"Well, you're a changed man this morning. Thanks for the gross little gift," Phillip said and leaned over to pet him. Though Ali was neutered, he was a territorial prowler, gone sometimes for more than a day, the scourge of any unwary rodent or bird. A vacant lot north of the Starks was actually a finger of land from the defunct golf course, easy access for the cat to some relatively wild sage country. As soon as the petting stopped, Ali went right back out; he would return around noon meowing for canned food, a schedule Phillip attributed to the cat's nightly hunting.

Ruler in hand, Phillip headed straight for the poolroom and the sliding glass door. He flicked on the porch light and looked out. Like tiny scattering moths, just a few particles floated in the artificial light, but the beam still petered out in the haze at the end of the patio. *It's almost over.*

Phillip turned on the poolroom lights and looked down. "My God," he said out loud. The ash from outside was up against the glass, forming a nearly straight line across the door several inches above the ground. He cast the flimsy patio furniture out of his way and got down to his knees to check the depth; it measured just over five inches.

"My God," he repeated. *It must be even deeper away from the house.* He touched the glass to inspect the cross-section of ash, and it reminded him of the ant farms he used to make. The quarter of an inch nearest the bottom resembled minute black gravel, and the layers above changed from black into shades of grey like a test pattern on fifties TV.

Poor Mick — what a shame. Guess he'll have to dig it all out of there. He laughed out loud; then cause and effect dawned on him.

What do you think ***you'll*** *be doing?* He stood up to peer into the yard, agonizing between the good news about the path of the ash fall and the complication of having to deal with the profound mass of volcanic debris right in front of him.

Can't be all that bad. Phillip put his nose right on the glass and both hands around his eye sockets to cut the glare from behind. He could just make out that there were no demarcations between the patio and the arborvitae; everything buried under a level overlay of ash. He noticed one barely perceptible lump a few feet away. *Crap, the Sunday paper.*

He thought about sliding the door open, but decided a ton of ash would probably tumble right in. He walked back up to the kitchen, tucking in his tee shirt and rolling down the sleeves of his flannel. *Now what? Kill the lights.* He hit the switch, moved over to the sink and vaulted back onto the counter. Turning around on his knees to the window, he cupped his hands next to his eyes again. He could almost distinguish the silhouettes of the two trees in their front yard: a twenty-foot Asian ginkgo from the original landscaping and his ponderosa. Phillip thought about how Stephen still wanted him to get rid of the tree.

He had found it three years before on a logging road in mixed forest on the way up to a hiking trail. The pine was about three feet tall then and most of its needles seemed dead or pale in the shade of a Douglas fir. It took Phillip almost an hour to painstakingly unearth it from the hard dry ground. He cut the top off of a plastic water jug he kept in his truck, made a bed of loose damp soil inside and put in the ailing tree.

"What the hell is that you planted in the yard?" Stephen asked the next evening, a beer and a shot on his TV tray.

"Pinus ponderosa," Phillip said.

"It's a penis, all right. I try to make this place look right, and you stick in a dying piece of crap like that. Jesus, they must've spent twenty years getting them out of this valley."

"All the more reason to plant it."

"Spare me the ecology BS. It'll brown up and die anyway."

"I think it'll make it."

"Twenty bucks says it doesn't."

"Okay, twenty bucks," Phillip agreed, knowing that a wager was one way to postpone an argument with Stephen. Phillip nurtured the tree and watched it struggle until the previous autumn when its resting buds bulged noticeably. It burgeoned with lush green needles in April, but when Stephen noticed the fresh growth he said, "It still looks like a sick piece of crap to me."

Soured by the recollection, Phillip looked down from the window, a pain clutching his intestines. *Take another damn pill.* He opened the bottle, ran some water into a small cheese glass, took the drug and looked out again. Beyond their two trees he saw the very dim outline of the Watson's old pickup that hadn't moved for years from its spot on the other side of the street.

It's starting to lift — maybe the phones are working. He tried Lupe's number on the kitchen phone, but it was answered by her roommate's voice on their new answering machine: "...not able to come to the phone right now..." ***Not able*** *— sounds like the plague. Call her parents.* He disconnected without leaving a message then punched in the Sageview number but also got their machine.

Not able *again, it's a frigging epidemic. Guess I'm not able to talk on the damn thing.* Phillip roughly notched the receiver into the wall phone and then reached up for cereal.

He pried apart the top flaps of the new box then tried to pinch open the bag so it would fold up after he finished. Annoyed that the liner wouldn't separate, he stabbed the top of the package with a paring knife, ripped it open, and then accidentally overfilled his bowl with the sugary flakes. He scooped out some of the extra with his hand and tried to put it back in the bag, but a shower of cereal drifted to the floor.

More crap to clean up. He rolled up the bag and smacked the cereal box angrily onto the counter. Finally, he added milk to the bowl and sprinkled a few raisins on top. Breakfast balanced in his hands, he trudged into the TV room. *Now, Bozo, see if you can keep it off the chair.* He sat down, ate a little, and saw the morning show was replaced by announcers from Four Rivers speaking in front of a generic file photo of a volcano.

Great job; just stick up Mount Fuji or something. The reporters mostly repeated what Phillip already knew, then the background changed to a shot of ash clouds and they began listing accumulations in the vicinity. *About time.*

"...High Desert; Newbury and Sageview, about an inch; Masonville and Unger, two inches; and here in Four Rivers a bit more than an inch when it stopped falling hours ago. In neighboring counties..."

Amazing, that close and only an inch. Lupe should've made it back okay. He crunched on a mouthful of the hard cereal.

"...communities at the center of the ash fall's path. Some had nearly twenty-four hours of total darkness and are just seeing first light. Hardest hit were Saddle Lake with about four inches, Ponderosa and Simmons reportedly with six..."

***Reportedly**. They don't believe it. Man, six inches.*

"...and Lake Worth with about three. Though we have much less ash here in Four Rivers, the traffic is blowing it into the air, so everyone is encouraged to stay home if possible. Now, for the school closures; if you don't hear your schools mentioned, try your district number or you can call the Red Cross clearinghouse number listed below on your screen.

"Four Rivers Schools will be closed tomorrow and until further notice, probably two or three days. These districts are closed for at least today and tomorrow: Unger, Masonville, Mill Ridge, Otatop, Crofton, Stubblefield, Greenlee, and Wheaton, as well as..."

And us?

"...Mercury, Coyote Springs and Newbury. Saddle Lake and Onion Corners will be closed for at least the rest of this week. And so far, three districts in our viewing area have said they're closed for the rest of the school year. They are: Redfield, Ponderosa and Simmons. Parents in those..."

Though it was his first real sustenance since the previous morning, Phillip dropped his spoon into the bowl. *The rest of the year? The damn testing isn't finished; science fair Friday, and — this is bizarre, it's all just gone, a vacuum of everything that would've happened.* He looked back at the poolroom doors and the ash line on the glass. The phone rang, interrupting his thoughts.

Maybe that's Lupe — or him, from the hotel. He put the cereal on the TV tray and walked toward the kitchen. *God, Stephen stuck at a convention, fox in the chicken coop.*

5

Guadalupe Rosendall met Phillip the previous fall in an anthropology class that included weekend bus trips to tribal cultural sites. While many of the students complained about assignments or "boring Saturdays," Phillip and Lupe were enthused about the course. That commonality broke the ice for them and led him to believe there was some chance for a serious relationship, though he had long ago resigned himself to bachelorhood.

Phillip was convinced that women would always find him too peculiar or too cynical. He could accept the first of those judgments and go on his way, but the latter would win his accuser a pithy rejoinder about her naiveté. By his late twenties, Phillip thought he was ahead of the game if a relationship lasted long enough to allow him to get away from Stephen for a couple weekends. When there was casual companionship or sex, he considered it a bonus.

With Lupe, there were two firsts. Phillip actually shared some aspects of living with Stephen's alcoholism, though not to the point of explaining his father's divergent personalities. Lupe was also the first woman to remain with him more than a few weeks. She approved of most of her boyfriend's idiosyncrasies and especially admired what she said was Phillip's "maturity."

They thoughtfully weighed each other's opinions even when it came to religion. She spoke of her faith without proselytizing, and Phillip did the same with his agnostic views. It pleased him to disprove Stephen's prediction that their religious differences would be insurmountable. But Phillip admitted to himself that maybe there was something to Stephen's "high-school crush" tirades. Here he was, a teacher pushing thirty and smitten by a stunning woman who looked so young at twenty-three that she would certainly be carded at any tavern, if she drank.

The phrase "dark good looks" never meant much to Phillip before he met Lupe. She had the obsidian eyes and dark brows of both parents, and she could cascade her galena-black hair halfway down her back, though she mostly wore it in some kind of ponytail. Phillip believed Lupe's beauty was enhanced by genetically influenced Semite and pre-Columbian facial features, especially her arching cheekbones and a moderately prominent nose that lent character to her face and accentuated her flawless cocoa-milk skin.

In high school, Lupe was encouraged by her peers to go out for drill squad and cheerleading, but she chose student government and the tennis team. One hot day in practice she saw some boys clowning around by the drinking fountain, pouring water on each other. She continued working on her serve until a female teammate came over and said that Lupe's sweaty shirt was sticking to her breasts, causing the boys' amusement. Because she had dealt with "titty jokes" since she was twelve, Lupe dismissed it as "their usual childish behavior." She didn't date much until the end of tenth grade, and even then, always on her terms.

Lupe's one driving incentive during her teens was to graduate early from Sageview High, though she did have a passionate hobby. Lupe and her younger sister raised, cared for and exhibited their family's horses. She also took every available Spanish course in school, with the goal of speaking her mother's first language. When she discovered they taught mostly grammar, Lupe privately criticized a system that awarded her highest honors in foreign language yet offered scant opportunity to actually converse.

Lupe's family and close friends weren't surprised when she graduated after eleventh grade and went off on a one-year church mission to Central America. Her father traded commodities with prominent families there and arranged for Lupe to live with one of them. She turned seventeen during that year and fell out of favor with the evangelists because she spent most of her missionary time helping abused women rather than converting them. Lupe grew very close to her Costa Rican "family" and became an accomplished speaker of Spanish. She also found her eventual career, and was now a year away from her Master's of Social Work at the state university in Four Rivers.

Phillip reached for the wall phone in the kitchen. He hadn't spoken to anyone for a day and a half except Mick, who didn't count, and he felt strangely let down about ending his solitary experiences with the ash fall. He answered the call hesitantly.

" 'Lo?"

"Thank God. Are you okay?" Lupe asked, her tone anxious.

"Hi, Lupe, everything's fine. What about you?"

"Okay, now that we can talk. I'm at Mom and Dad's; I've been trying to reach you since yesterday. What a time for you to be all alone." Her words seemed to tremble through the static.

"Hey, don't worry, I'm okay." *Geez, why's she so upset?*

"Did you call a while ago? Someone hung up on the machine."

Crap. "I tried a lot of times; circuits were down. You can't believe the ash, half a goddamn foot, and— "

"Yes, Phil, I heard, but please."

I said **goddamn**. "Sorry." *Tell her about the clouds, the mouse, and the line on the door.* "Lupe, it was so incredi— "

"There's not even an inch here," she interrupted again.

"It's amazing. Probably smart to stay there a while."

"Oh I will," she said, still some panic in her voice. "My mom keeps saying He has certainly chosen to test us."

Let that one go. "Uh, did you get caught in the ash?"

"Yes, it was so scary. We were still in Four Rivers when it started getting dark; we left right away, and then we couldn't see at all. I thought we'd have to stop, but then it improved the closer we got to Sageview."

"Lucky you didn't end up in some cruddy school gym." He intended that to be a droll comment to help her calm down.

"It's not funny, Phil."

Jesus, okay already.

"Last night at church people were so upset, praying so seriously. I prayed for you there."

"Can't hurt, right?"

"I'm glad you accept that it helps me." Lupe waited for a response.

What can I say?

"Phil, give me a sec," she said, her voice faltering.

Man, not like her at all. He waited, staring out the kitchen window into the false dusk. The two trees and the junk pickup were now barely visible, no longer just silhouettes.

"Sorry, Phil."

"It's all right."

"They said there could be glass particles in the ash. You haven't been going out a lot?" Her voice was steadier.

"A couple times." *Liar.*

"I thought so."

"I have a mask, I'm fine."

"I was worried about you maybe getting too excited about something like this."

Something like this? "Jesus, Lupe, this is once in a lifetime." *Crap, now you did it.* "Sorry," he said again, scooting his rear end up on the Formica counter. He looked out, searching for some activity in the murk.

"It's my fault; I sounded critical." She had regained her usual confident tone. "I can't believe how it got to me, that horrible drive, and then not being able to talk to you. But now, just hearing how interested you are — it changes my perspective; makes it seem less frightening."

"That's good, but I didn't need to snap at you."

"It's okay. Phil, did you hear about your school?"

"Yeah, it's strange; we had so much left to do, and just like that, it's over. It's weird how it just isn't going to happen, all that activity waiting there like a void."

"I hadn't thought of that; it *is* strange."

"Just thinking out loud. Anyway, now I have three weeks until I start with Putman," he said, more upbeat. "I'll need the extra time to clear our yards."

"What about ash up in the mountains?"

"The project is north; we missed the ash, I think."

"Phil, you know I appreciate the importance of the research, but there's not much you can do if a volcano stops it. Sometimes we have to, well, leave things in God's hands."

Man, this really has her on a religious bug.

Don't say I didn't warn you.

Shut up, Stephen.

"Phil?"

"I'm here. I realize we're all limited, Lupe, but I think you know I'll do whatever I can to be ready to go, not to mention I need a break from Stephen."

"It's a shame you have to feel like that about your own father. You know, I do have background with some of his issues; I might be able to help."

No way. "Thanks, but that's just not in the cards," he said firmly, and there was dead air for a moment.

"Phil, maybe you should call and see if the volcano is going to affect your department."

"Yeah, that's a good idea." *At least I'd know.*

"If it doesn't come through, we'll make the best of it and have a great summer. I don't have a class, so we could kick back; take the horses up to the backcountry like I promised." Lupe had recently taught the reluctant "city boy" how to ride.

"You think I'm ready for that?"

"Gabilan took to you right away, you're a natural rider. Now if we could just dump that baseball hat for a Stetson— "

"No way, not in this lifetime."

"Okay, but you really do need boots. Anyway, we can float the river and..." She went on proposing summer activities.

Yeah, sounds good, but the project comes first.

"...for the co-ed soccer league. Phil?"

"Uh, yeah, soccer won't work, Lupe. Look, it won't take me three weeks to clean up." *I hope.* "We can do some things together before I go, and I'll be home a couple weekends; it'll go fast."

"Maybe you're right." She paused, and when she started speaking again, it was in a soft, almost seductive tone. "Shorty, you know what?"

You're up, Shorty. He didn't answer her. She came up with that name on their one semi-formal date — her friend's wedding. When he came by for her, Lupe called him "Shorty" because the low heels she was wearing made her a bit taller than Phillip. They laughed about it, and then she decided to change to some flats. When the name stuck, he wasn't especially thrilled about it, but she only used it privately, always in that intimate voice.

The nickname was sometimes her signal for ardor in their affair, and she liked him to call her "Lupita" in the same sense, though she established clear limits to their sexual contact. Phillip assumed she was a virgin and didn't push her at all, but it was Lupe who came up with what she called "our naughty little trick." It started with heavy making out until they shed half their clothing, and then she would wait for him to put on a condom. Following her rule of hands above the waist, they kissed some more and writhed together until he came. Phillip wondered if she was somehow getting off as well and ventured to ask her once, but she wouldn't talk about it.

"Shorty?" she repeated over the phone.

"Yeah, Lupita." *Good boy, Phillip.*

"Mmm, you say my name, so perfectly." She spoke with deliberate pauses. "There's going to be some, long, beautiful evenings, and we can relax, and well, you know."

Yeah, I know. His member crowded into the fabric of his jeans. "Lupe?"

"Just backup plans, Phil. They sound fun, right?" she asked, her voice normalizing.

Especially that last part. "Sure, of course, just don't count on all of it."

"Things will work out, I — ¡*Míralo*! There's the Suburban; I have to go help. I'm so glad you're okay. Call me tonight?"

"Sure, Lupe."

"Bye, Phil."

"Bye." He hung up the phone and shuddered, recouping from her provocative voice. He jumped off the counter, looked out again at the dull morning and saw the ash was all the way up to the bottom branches of his young tree. *Start right there.*

Phillip rushed into the TV room, past his soggy cereal and through the door to the garage. He turned on the light, glancing for a moment at his old Datsun pickup. *Lucky it wasn't outside —*

chalk one up for the good guys. He opened Stephen's winter cabinet and took out the sturdy metal snow shovel and a push broom.

On his way back through the kitchen he stopped for his mask, the ruler and a house broom before clattering his way down the hall with everything. After leaning the taller implements on the wall, Phillip sat on the inside doormat and chose his tennis shoes from the footwear on the floor. As he tied them he wondered if ash would cascade into the house when he opened the front door.

He reached up, carefully twisting the knob; the door opened a crack but all that fell through was a pale beam of light. *Dope, the roof hangs over.* He stood and opened the door all the way. *My God.* The small porch was eerily clean; the ash had settled an inch above its front edge, eliminating the one step drop-off to the ground.

Incredible; but get with it. He walked out, stood short of the ash and put on the mask. His baseball hat in hand, Phillip scanned the sea of grey powder before him and sensed an undulation above what he guessed was the curb. Farther away, past the old truck in the street, he detected a blurry rectangle floating in the dry overcast, the Watson's doublewide modular. Their other dead cars and the piles of tires and wood pallets were invisible, as was their neighbor forty yards away. It felt like being on an island to Phillip; the Watson's place was a boat and its weak porch light searched through the ash-fog for other vessels. He stood still to listen; the only sound was the lonesome drone of a distant motor.

Move it. He went back in for the yard tools, then returned to the front of the porch. Phillip stepped up, and when his leg came down his shoe and lower shin vanished into the ash. He strode forward twice, lifting his knees like a heron in shallow water, the front wall of each deep footprint collapsing as he lifted his feet.

Like pushing through wet snow. He stooped and stuck the ruler straight down until it hit the ground. *Man, six and a half inches.* Phillip stood up, took about a dozen more paces, and then gently poked the branches of his tree with the kitchen broom until most of the clinging ash fell below. With the snow shovel and push broom he began excavating furiously from the ponderosa's base. After several minutes his work formed an unintentional circle around the tree, about eight feet in diameter. He switched back to the house broom and attempted to sweep the remains out of the exposed grass.

No, it's in there for good. That'll just make the soil more alkaline; shouldn't hurt his damn lawn. Phillip plodded back to the porch, then turned around to check his tracks. *Geez, the Nazca lines — a jellyfish.* The circle around the tree now had four long legs drawn by the ruts he'd made going out and coming back. *Cute. Now get back to work.* He picked up the snow shovel and started plowing the walkway, from the porch toward the street, shoving the ash to the sides onto the lawn's accumulation. *You're not doing crap until it's carried out of here. Yeah, but you need paths.*

After a few more minutes he stopped when he heard some scraping noises in the neighborhood. *Finally, somebody's out there.* He forced his way down to the street and swept off the mailbox and the newspaper tube with the back of his hand. Out of habit, he checked for the morning paper.

Real smart; it couldn't be here without tire tracks. His proximity to the street allowed the Watson's undisturbed Jeep pickup to come into better view. A whimsical image came to Phillip of the disabled truck as a life-sized toy, replicated in thick grey frosting for a little kid's birthday cake.

Get going. He returned to the walkway and resumed his work. After a while Phillip noticed that his right hand was sore, but he kept on clearing. Halfway down to the street, his palm began to sting, so he stopped again and found a small broken blister on his hand, a larger one swelling next to it.

"Stupid shit," he said, and then stomped back to the house, angry about losing the work time. Although there was now ash all through the house, Phillip mindlessly followed Stephen's cardinal rule again and left his dirty sneakers by the door. After doctoring his hand in the bathroom, he found work gloves in the hall closet and returned to the porch to tie his shoes. *I'm not even to the side-walk — gotta be ready if Putman comes through.*

6

Regardless of Mick Lewis, the next sixteen hours of purging the ash made Phillip begin to feel differently about how people on his side of the mountains were responding to the volcano.

He worked another half-hour on the front pathway before finally breaking through to the sidewalk, which took more than an hour to scrape. To the north, Phillip only cleared a few feet past the driveway as there was no immediate need for access to the wild golf course land. More than a hundred feet in the other direction, he would connect with the property of Gil Beck, an elderly widower who, in Phillip's view, was their best neighbor. Stephen once cussed out Beck for calling the cops when he and Mick were shooting guns in the air at one A.M. Stephen avoided Beck when sober, like he did most everyone, but Phillip later apologized to the neighbor.

Visibility had improved by the time Phillip reached Beck's clean sidewalk, and he could see their neighbor working near the street corner. *Way to go, Mister Beck.* They waved to each other.

Phillip's next chore would be the wide driveway up to their two-car garage; he estimated it would require as much work as he'd already completed. While he slogged through the ash up to the garage, Phillip heard a large diesel engine rattle from somewhere in the haze.

The overhang from the garage roof had kept the ash from completely blocking the way, so Phillip only needed to scrape for a few minutes before he was able to open the double door. He walked in, turned around, and stood by his small tan pickup, contemplating the leaden sky and the grey expanse before him, still feeling very much like he was on an island. It was about two o'clock as he started in again, pushing ash toward the street, trying to take advantage of the gradual slope.

After a few minutes he heard the diesel engine clatter again, this time much closer. Phillip looked past Beck's where a fire truck, its redness blackened by the dirty air, slowly approached the corner, several men trudging behind its enormous wheels. They moved like ghosts through thick clouds of ash, one of them in dingy yellow garb like the driver. The truck stopped and a portly fireman climbed down with difficulty from the cab. They manned the hose in front of the dim headlights, opened the nozzle and aimed the strong flow toward the ground.

Phillip watched them turn the corner and start up the street. His spirits lifted by their industry, he flung the shovel toward the garage then took his paths down to the cleared sidewalk and jogged past the two front yards. At the corner he saw they had opened one lane from the highway, the muddy ash forced to both sides, sooty rivulets flowing away from the development. He watched the crew cut off the water and switch from the hydrant at the entrance to the one by Beck's house. Covered head to toe with ash, the workers in their particle masks looked like a team of surgeons in grey operating scrubs. They motioned for Phillip to join in, and he eagerly took a spot on the hose.

It took them fifteen minutes just to make it from the corner to the Stark's place. After Phillip ran up to move his tools and close the garage, the incessant force of the water pushed all the ash off the driveway and into Stephen's lilacs on both sides. When the stiff stream hit the young bushes a few of them snapped and most were half-buried. Though he knew Stephen would certainly fume over the ruined plants, Phillip turned with satisfaction to one of the men and they slapped a high-five.

For the next fifteen hours he stayed with the crew and its mission to free the cars and clear an escape to the highway. They liberated one block after another, and each fresh volunteer was as eager to help as the last.

The second fireman, about Phillip's age, barked instructions with a needless air of authority. Phillip decided the man was angry about being stuck on hose duty, although his much older cohort was in no shape to do anything but drive and supervise. After the young fireman taught new arrivals the basics of manning the pulsating hose, he sometimes left for long periods, and Phillip ended up explaining the procedures much of the time.

At about ten o'clock they took a long break when a Red Cross contingent showed up with sandwiches and drinks. Phillip chose the egg salad over the baloney, gulped it down with milk, and then scouted the next block while the others rested. By the middle of the night he'd lost track of time and didn't care that he and the two firemen were the only ones left from the original crew.

Shortly after a shrouded dawn they completed the last long block of Ponderosa Estates and were back near the entrance. The final group looked up at the grey-haired driver as the younger fireman climbed into the truck, scowling at his partner.

Still has a fork up his ass. He didn't do crap tonight. "Are we going to widen the lanes?" Phillip shouted over the knocking engine to the driver.

"Nope, next step is to scrape it and haul it," he yelled down to Phillip and the others. "It's back home for us before we meet ourselves coming and going," he said with a chuckle. "Our thanks to all you fellas, and good mornin' to you." He saluted the crew; most of them repeated the fireman's parting courtesy before they headed away in the sallow sunrise.

"So where's your next job for the rig, chief?" Phillip asked, his tone showing his readiness to keep working. The old fireman laughed, killed the motor, and Phillip saw the man's partner sullenly fold his arms and lean back.

"I'm not the chief, but I am the guy who's supposed to tell everybody to go home." His pink face was all the way out of the window. "You were a working fool out there, son, and I appreciate it. But after you sleep it off, you've got plenty to do at your place. I'd start with that roof if I were you."

"Man, I didn't even think about— "

"Yeah, you've got a load up there. Some of those farm worker shacks on the edge of town already collapsed." The other fireman had his hat over his eyes, trying to take a nap.

"I'd better get at it right away," Phillip said.

"As long as it doesn't rain, these houses here are okay. We heard it doesn't weigh much until it's wet."

"So scrape off the worst and take the hose to what's left?" Phillip asked.

"That's what I'd do after I got some sleep. You want a ride back?"

"No thanks, I'll walk."

"Okay, kid. Thanks again."

"No problem; it was great," he said, not caring that this man called him *kid*. The veteran fireman waved again, shook his head good-naturedly and started the engine.

Phillip watched the truck roll away then started walking up the cleared lane back toward his house. He felt a lump by his neck and fingered out a hunk of grimy material. It was the remains of the painter's mask he stopped using when the driver gave them the report that the ash wasn't harmful for most people to breathe.

He wadded the garbage into his pocket and began to check out the neighborhood. There was enough light filtering through for him to make out each house, and he was proud to see the exposed driveways as he strolled by. Though it was Tuesday morning when most everyone would usually be preparing for work or school, he didn't see much activity. Next to one of the few illuminated porch lights, a thick clump of ash remained on top of a large yellow bow displayed in honor of the hostages in Iran. Though that house was untouched, Phillip saw with satisfaction that most people had already been able to clear their paths and sidewalks.

By the time he got back to the house, the pall had lifted some more. Thinking he'd go right on working since he felt so good, Phillip went straight to the garage for the fruit-picking ladder Stephen bought at a farm sale. He carried it out front and then went back for his tools. The bulky ladder, narrow at the top and tapering to a very wide bottom, fit just right on the front porch. The brooms and snow shovel in tow; Phillip climbed to the top rungs and tramped through the ash up to the peak of the roof, which afforded him a view over the crabapple tree and into Mick's back yard. He knelt and held still when he saw Mick by the pool.

He heard Lewis cussing in his acerbic monotone, this time at two middle-aged Mexican men in straw cowboy hats and black aprons, conscripts from the dairy who often did his menial labor. While the men struggled to connect one of those barrel-shaped vacuums on wheels, they directed each other in Spanish, the muffled sounds of their conversation projecting all the way up to Phillip's elevated vantage point. Mick was in slippers and a robe, a beer can at the end of his fingers.

"Jesus Christ, wrong side," he said, deadpan, to the two men. "Put this end over there. No, goddamn it. Aw-kee — right there. You gotta know *some* fucking English by now."

What a prick. Phillip barely heard and didn't comprehend the workers' dialogue until one of them glanced at Mick and uttered,

"*Pendejo*," an expletive Phillip learned from one of the few Mexican kids at Ponderosa High in his day.

Mick didn't know or didn't care that he was just insulted. "About goddamned time," he said when the water spurted from the fat hose, but the men were aiming it at the lawn. "Jesus, not there, aw-kee. It's called a fucking drain. You boys learn that word."

Boys *— Jesus.* "Aim it right in the *pendejo*'s face," Phillip mumbled as they sent the flow to where Mick wanted it. For the first time since the previous morning, Phillip's intestines twisted, and then his enthusiasm for working ebbed like the water being sucked from the swimming pool. After Mick turned away, Phillip left his tools and slowly backtracked, descending to the porch. He idly brushed himself off, walked in and removed his encrusted shoes, leaving them with his hat and gloves by the door.

After a trip to the bathroom, he went in the kitchen for an ulcer pill and a cookie. In the TV room, Phillip ignored his old cereal and turned on the set. He leaned back in his recliner and bit off half the cookie. The local news was reporting emergency relief details, and he fell asleep after a few minutes.

The telephone woke him a few hours later, but before he could move, the ringing stopped. *Crap, you said you'd call Lupe.* Ali looked up from Phillip's lap, eyes half open.

"Hey, *gato*. What a couple of sleepyheads, huh?" He checked the clock. *Twelve thirty — could sleep some more — maybe go to bed for a while. No, enough sleep; back to the ash.* "You hungry, boy?" he asked, stroking his cat.

Phillip noticed the sunlight around Stephen's thick curtains was brighter than before. A quiz show yammered away on the TV. *Volcano, what volcano?* He snapped the recliner down to sitting position and the cat leaped off his lap, causing a puff of ash to float up from Phillip's jeans.

God, look at these clothes; you need a bath, too. He got up and took the rancid cereal to the kitchen and gazed out the window. His ashen jellyfish swam undisturbed in the yard, and the neighborhood was unchanged, except now there was enough light to give the impression it was just a very overcast day.

There's a lot more to do — the roof, then Stephen's lawns. He'll want them done yesterday, sure as hell. Wonder if Mick's still back there. Screw him; get after it.

Although it was afternoon, he began his morning routine and turned on the teakettle. As he petted Ali, Phillip's stomach felt hollow, but there was no sharp pain in his gut. He took another pill anyway, this time with a full glass of water, his thirst surprising him. Looking down toward the cat, Phillip saw a grainy mixture of pulverized cereal and tracked-in ash on the floor.

Later for that. "Got a new flavor for you to try; you've got to be getting tired of that tuna." The cat circled and rubbed while Phillip retrieved the can from the top shelf and opened it. He scraped the food down into the bowl, but Ali took a sniff of the meat conglomeration and sneezed as if he were allergic to it. He sat and then glared up at Phillip.

"You fart, Ali. Here, maybe this'll work." He dropped a couple of kitty treats into the bowl, but the old feline nibbled them up without even contacting the rejected food. Ali defiantly licked his shoulder, gave Phillip a dismissive look, and trotted through the TV room and out the cat door.

Some creature is about to be his lunch. Just stick with the tuna. The teakettle whistled, and he prepared some acid-free instant coffee, a brand he recently discovered. Phillip started to reach up for some cereal, but the phone rang right by his arm.

"Hello," he answered, before the first ring finished.

"Well whaddya' know."

Dad?

"I'll be damned, I finally got you."

It's Stephen. How drunk? "You've been calling?" He heard music, laughing and other tavern noise in the background.

"Three damn times yesterday," he said, his voice calm.

Mildly belligerent, two or three drinks so far. "The lines have been out."

"I heard they closed schools in Four Rivers. There too?"

"Yeah, rest of the year." Phillip opened the fridge, wedging the telephone between his ear and shoulder. "Where are you?" he asked, and added milk to his coffee.

"At the hotel. If the damn airport doesn't open tomorrow, I'll rent a car."

Phillip stirred his drink. "You've never driven that far."

Stephen's next words bristled. "How the hell do you know how far I've driven, or anything else for..."

You're wrong, Phillip, he's almost fried. He put the milk back, closing the door so hard it made the refrigerator wobble. *Easy, what did you expect?*

"...don't need *your* damn advice. Just tell me how bad the ash fall was."

What's he asking? "Uh, it was something," Phillip said, downplaying his enthusiasm. "Turned dark at noon; Ali was— "

"Whole state's in a disaster and he tells me about a damn cat he named after frigging Cassius Clay." Stephen was blustering, showing off for someone in the bar.

Asshole. Phillip took a sip of the warm coffee.

"Just tell me how many inches of ash outside."

"More than six."

"Hah, six damn inches! I knew it from that map on TV; hold on. Okay," he said, away from the phone, "pay up, dumb fucks."

No way he can drive. You say that, he'll freak. Phillip heard more ranting. *Nobody* ***there*** *is going to tell him.*

"Goddamn deadbeats." Stephen paused. "You there?"

"Yeah."

"They want proof. How can I prove we have six inches?"

"Shouldn't be hard. The Chicago library probably has the paper from Portland or— "

"Of course, the library, leave it to you; hold on. You damn cheapskates write down your room numbers. My son the schoolmarm figured it all..." His voice faded.

Shit. He waited, grabbed a cookie, dunked it and ate it.

Stephen finally came back. "We'll nail the sonsabitches now."

Three cheers for us. Maybe it'll pay the bar tab.

"You there?"

"Still here," Phillip answered, biting another cookie.

"So, did you start on the ash?"

"That's all I've been doing," he said around a swallow.

"Are you eating something?"

"Cookie."

"Figures; and they pay you to teach health."

"Don't start."

"You look like crap, too."

What? "Thanks. Anything else?"

"Stop feeling sorry for yourself. You're at that damn school day and night, then you come home and don't do shit around the..."

Phillip held the phone away from Stephen's housework diatribe and surveyed the pallid moonscape out front.

"...never do *any* damn work without me telling you. You listening?"

No. He moved the receiver closer. "Yeah, you finished?"

"When I'm damn good and ready. What're you using on the ash?"

"Brooms, snow shovel— " *Fire hose — no.* "I finished the walks and driveway; start on the roof today. I have to be ready to get out of here for the project."

"I forgot about the mountain lion bullshit; no wonder you're doing something. What about the house, you making a big damn mess?"

"Everything's dirty; ash comes right in." He glanced at the pile of dishes, then turned around to lean on the sink.

"Neat as a pin when I left."

No kidding. "I'll clean up before you get here."

"Sure, and don't forget to screw the Mexican maid."

"What did you say?"

"Relax, it's a convention joke; you wouldn't like it. My damn kid has no sense of humor," he explained to somebody at the bar again.

"This from the man who laughs at *all* of Bob Hope's jokes." Phillip sipped his coffee.

"Shit, the whole world laughs at his jokes. You wouldn't know a joke or an important man if you saw one."

"Our mailman is just as important."

"What kind of philosophical bullcrap is that?"

This is pointless, stop egging him on.

"Shit, tell me if you saw Mick," Stephen said.

I saw the prick. Mick the Prick — perfect.

"Answer me, goddamn it."

"Yeah, I saw him." With a thumb and forefinger, Phillip rubbed at the tension in his brows.

"So what's he up to?"

"Bossing some men to dig out the pool. He was too dumb to put on the cover. I offered to help him before it filled up, and he told me to fuck off." *If Lupe could hear me now.*

"Big deal. That's just how he talks."

"Sure." Phillip brought his hand down from his forehead.

"If he was serious, maybe you should've stood up to him." Stephen was chuckling.

Up yours. "I'm not afraid of your shitfaced friend."

Stephen laughed again. "Jesus, just stay away from him."

Stay away from dog crap. "Whatever you say, Steve."

"Don't call me that, goddamn it."

Sure as hell won't call you ***Dad.*** "Yeah, yeah," Phillip said. *Enough — convince him not to drive.* "I think you should stay there. They'll open the airport soon."

"And how do you know that?"

"They only had an inch or so of ash in Four Rivers."

"Either way, I'll probably go tomorrow."

"You can't drive in the shape you're in."

"Stop nagging me, goddamn it. Shit; look at that, one of those bastards just walked in. I'm going to get his number. Hang on," Stephen said and was gone again.

Phillip waited, pondering the comment about "nagging." Before his mother died, she made a point of talking to him about his father's drinking. She said he returned from Korea as a weekend drinker and wouldn't talk about it. Ellen confided she was thankful he didn't drink even more and wasn't physically abusive. She told her son to find his own direction in life, but Phillip was sure she also expected him to watch over Stephen. Near the end, when she hardly recognized him, Phillip made her that pledge. Stephen seemed to know some kind of promise had been made, but he never actually voiced a suspicion.

Why do you even care what he thinks? What's he doing?

Stephen came back. "Got it; that'll be ten more bucks."

"Congratulations. If you drive tomorrow, call me before you leave." Phillip sounded ready to hang up.

"You just worry about getting your ass out of bed and cleaning the house."

Shit. "I told you I'll get the worst of it, but I'll be outside mostly." His voice rose with resentment.

"That house comes first, then you're not going anywhere until we get all that crap out of my yards."

"That's what I *am* doing. What do you want, blood?" *Take it easy, Phillip.*

"I'm going to a meeting," Stephen said and hung up.

A meeting — bull. Phillip slammed the phone into the wall bracket and then stood next to the piled dirty dishes. *Same ol' shit.* He massaged the inner corners of his eyes until they hurt. *Maybe he'll sober up for the drive.* Phillip lowered his arm and stared at the ashen landscape.

Haven't talked to Dad for weeks; it feels like he's dead. Tears clouded his vision, making his view of the yard seem even more somber. *Cry about it some more, that'll bring him back. Get a goddamn grip.*

7

Though he had spoken in general terms with Lupe about Stephen, Phillip only had one real confidant, his best friend, Warren, who now lived in Seattle.

They met during preseason open gym basketball at the beginning of Phillip's senior year. Phillip had barely made the "C" squad at his city school, but he loved the game and decided to give it a last shot with the Ponderosa Panthers. When word got out that the new guy had written an essay about wild felines, a basketball letterman named Sam Fike began calling Phillip "Panther Pussy" regardless of his tough play at their informal workouts.

Warren Sims was a freckled six-foot-eight redhead who was finally going to be starting center as a senior after taking years of verbal abuse as the tallest, skinniest and smartest kid in town. He was a late-in-life only child of a local couple who had planned to leave him the family farm until it became obvious that their inheritor was destined for a different career.

One afternoon in the gym when a couple of players were harassing Phillip, Warren held the ball and told them to "shut up and play the damn game."

"*You* shut the fuck up," Sam Fike said back to Warren. Sam was a muscular six-footer whose role on the team was to rip down rebounds and immediately pass off to teammates who could actually dribble and shoot the ball.

"That's more than two syllables, ape; nice job," Warren answered, the others hooting in delight at the new nickname. "It's almost five," Warren added with a shrug, "I'm outta here."

"Shit, you and Panther Pussy must be in a hurry to go for a little sixty-nine," Sam said, and the players howled again.

"Fuck you, Fike," Phillip said calmly, catching the group off guard for a moment. Then they began chanting, "Fuck-you-Fike, fuck-you-Fike," pleased with the alliteration.

"Talk to me again, pussy," Sam said to Phillip, "and I'll kill a fucking cat for every word you say." A Phys. Ed. teacher at the other end of the gym moved toward them.

"Fuck you, Fike," Phillip repeated.

After the tussle was broken up, they walked away and Warren told Phillip that Fike was all talk. The next day at lunch hour Phillip had to hold back his rage when he found three mutilated cats in his pickup. That evening he grimly buried the scrawny feral animals in the foothills and plotted his revenge.

The police came to school on Friday morning to ask him if he knew anything about Sam's car. Phillip shook his head innocently, said he knew nothing about it and thought, "Three dead cats; four dead tires." At the next open gym on Monday, Fike called him "a crazy little queer" but let it go after that because their coach heard about the feud and threatened to cut Sam from the team.

Warren in math, Phillip in science, they were Mutt and Jeff with some smarts, though only Warren was an honor student. When basketball began officially, Phillip was adept at getting Warren the ball in the post; they both made starting five and became better friends than with any of the kids from their childhoods.

Phillip had no idea that his season in the basketball limelight would one day affect his career. After graduating, he didn't even get away from home for college. He entered the state university in Four Rivers and commuted forty miles to his classes for five years. He took prerequisites for a major in zoology and then switched to science education to improve his chances of obtaining a job not too far from his father.

His only long break from Stephen during college was working a five-week summer camp as a counselor in the nearby mountains. Even then, Phillip arranged to leave on Sundays to check up on Stephen and make sure he was taking care of Ali. The fledgling educator led the hiking and climbing activities at camp, and by his last year there he was teaching some environmental science.

A college advisor recommended that Phillip minor in physical education because school districts, she said, often gave hiring advantage to coaches. So he endured the tedious health/P.E. curricula and judged the courses in his science major to be watered down and pedantic. By the time he passed the required doses of educational theory and practice, Phillip decided that some of his professors hadn't set foot in a school for years, and only a few were the dedicated "teachers of teachers" he expected. He kept his dissatisfaction to himself, his grades were better than in high school, and he received good recommendations from student teaching.

Ponderosa School District, it turned out, was eager to hire one of its former basketball players for an opening at the junior high. As Phillip's astute advisor had foreseen, he was selected ahead of experienced science teachers who were not prepared to teach P.E. and coach boys' basketball.

Phillip felt challenged and motivated from the outset by his teaching at Ponderosa Junior High. He tried to organize field studies for his life-science classes, but the principal said the concept would be disruptive and that all trips had to be pre-approved before the school year. Phillip made due with the campus as his "natural environment" and decided he would wait until after the Panther Cubs basketball season to press the issue.

After both his teams played well for the first time in years, Phillip wrote a proposal for a hands-on project in fisheries management. Unaware of protocol, he showed up at a school board meeting with handouts and diagrams. When the agenda opened for community input, Phillip began his presentation, but the chairman politely interrupted. He said they would be delighted to consider the proposal when administration placed it on their agenda. Phillip's supervisor smirked and whispered a comment to his crony from the high school. Humiliated, Phillip sullenly took his seat and saw the two principals share a chuckle at his expense.

The day after the meeting he was called into the office before school. The principal sat behind his large desk as Phillip entered the room in attire that doubled for the classroom and gym, dark-colored jeans, sport shirt and sneakers. The principal, a grim sneer on his face, offered Phillip the black interrogation chair usually occupied by one of the school's bullies.

"Just another bad boy," Phillip thought. He decided to look out the window to show his disinterest while the principal wrote solemnly on some school form as if the world eagerly awaited his report.

Phillip's supervisor was in his late forties, a burly five-foot ten, flat-faced, his black hair chopped into a crew cut. He wore a brown tie and yellow shirt; part of a tattoo showed below one sleeve, enough to figure out the whole image was a blue snake and DON'T TREAD ON ME. The principal looked up from his desk.

"Mister Stark, tell me why you're making such a big deal out of our science curriculum," he said, his voice brusque.

"Like I said before, life science requires application in the outdoors, you can only do so much with a textbook." Phillip's tone was frank but not impertinent; he glanced at the kids in the courtyard. "We have no lab facilities, and we're barely allowed to go outside." He settled back into the stiff plastic chair.

"I think you're overstating things."

"Okay, we have a couple antique microscopes and we can go on the athletic field," Phillip said with mild sarcasm.

"You know, Stark," he answered, deliberately less formal, "if you hadn't made such a fool out of yourself the other night, you could've embarrassed us. Let's clarify a few things. We know you're a good coach, and you have potential as a teacher, but your final evaluation is coming up..."

To Phillip, that was a threat from a man who wouldn't know teaching potential "if it bit him in the ass."

"...assume that you've learned, Stark, that ambushes at board meetings are not the way we do things around here. Proposals have to be written and go through us, and we expect you to talk to us before you show up in front of the board."

Phillip faced him. "Would you approve a proposal?"

"Probably not." He tapped a pencil impatiently on his phone.

"What if some of us go to the school board to ask for better equipment?"

The principal shook his head. "I think I've made myself clear. Do you think you can live with that, Stark?"

"Guess I'll have to." He looked away again.

"That's right. Good, I'm glad you understand that." He smiled briefly as if there had been some mutual agreement.

"So that's it?" Phillip started to get up.

"There's one more thing. We're concerned that you're getting a little bit too close to your students."

"What?" Phillip said, standing up, managing to keep most of the indignation out of his voice.

"You're too personal with them. They're students, not your little buddies."

"No, I haven't crossed that line." The school district's 'dirty little secret' dawned on him. "Does this have anything to do with my predecessor being moved to the high school?"

"You shouldn't listen to rumors, Stark."

"Yeah, I'm sure it's less likely he'll diddle with kids over there."

"I suggest you drop it and think about *your* situation. You don't know these families. It's not like the old days when we could count on some respect. A lot of these kids would just as soon spit in your face as talk to you."

"That hasn't been my experience."

"Oh? So you're saying you know them better than I do?"

"No, I just don't agree with you."

"I suppose that's what they're teaching at that college."

"Can't say, but I'll tell you a quote I heard in one of my classes."

Nonplused by Phillip's response, the principal eyed him suspiciously.

"This isn't word for word," Phillip began, not sounding strident. "This famous guy said that our youth live in luxury; with bad manners. He said kids had no respect for their elders; that they're like tyrants. What do you think?"

"I'd probably agree with most of that."

For effect, Phillip waited, a sedate look on his face. "That was Socrates, about four hundred B.C., the good ol' days."

"For a quiet guy, you really are a smart ass, aren't you, Stark? I give you two years until you burn out."

Though Phillip's sixth year of teaching had come to an abrupt end two weeks early, school wasn't on his mind as he frowned at the pile of dishes in the sink. *Screw 'em; just get dirty again. How do you like that, Stephen?*

He saw his accidental jellyfish out front in the ash. *God, look at all that stuff. Call Lupe; make it quick, then get the roof.* He picked up the phone and punched in her parents' number. Phillip drank his cold coffee and listened to the irritating clicks of the dialing pulse. He remained standing and scanned the yard.

"Hello?"

"Hi, Lupe, sorry I couldn't call."

"Hi, Phil. I tried you this morning and last night a bunch. It would be nice if you had an answering machine. They're really very useful."

Not for me they aren't. "Actually, I was out all night."

"You were?"

"I was on a fire hose; we cleared driveways and made a lane through the whole development," he said, almost boasting.

"Sounds like you were working awfully hard."

"Didn't even notice it. I've never seen so many people act like that before. It was great."

"Act like what?"

"Everyone pitching in, cooperating; sounds corny— "

"Not at all. Church fellowship is like that sometimes."

"Everybody *wanted* to do this."

"That's not any different, Phil."

Drop it, now. "Anyway, you can't believe the mess out there, especially the roof. I can't talk a long time."

"Okay, I'll keep it short. Phil, I called about soccer..."

Great. He jumped back onto the counter, his heels banging lightly on the cupboards below.

"...they want you on our team, they don't care if you miss games."

"Lupe, I'd miss most of them. It's been a couple days; Putman hasn't called; I think we're on."

"You haven't called them?"

Don't want the wrong answer. "Been busy; I'll get to it."

She was silent a moment. "Phil, you worry me — working all night like that, and you haven't been looking well and..."

What? I get to hear this again?

"...you losing weight? I noticed when we were, uh— "

Eating? Doing our little thing maybe? She can't say it.

"Will you say something?" she said, a little bit cross.

"No, I'm not losing weight."

"When we go out, you mostly have French fries and pop."

Enough of this. "Lupe, I'm fine."

"Phil, I was too upset to talk about it yesterday, but your father agrees with me."

"About what? You talked to him?" He stopped swinging his legs and wound his ankles tightly together.

"Yes, last week. I called when you weren't home."

Shit! "When did you call? What day?"

"I called him on purpose," she said with self-assurance.

"For God's sake, why did you do that?"

"I can't talk to you if you're going to yell at me."

I'm not yelling. "I can't believe you called him."

"He was very sweet. He doesn't seem as bad as you say."

He's worse. "Lupe, you— "

"I had a very nice talk with him..."

Perfect.

"...he agreed with me that you aren't taking care of yourself."

Goddamn it, taking care of both of us. "If you wanted to know that kind of crap, why didn't you talk to *me*?" He angrily back-kicked his intertwined heels against the cupboard, causing an ear-splitting clap.

"What was that, Phil?"

"Nothing. Lupe, I'm pissed you spoke to him."

"When I mentioned before how tired you look, you wouldn't answer. I care about you, Phil, so I asked him. I'm sorry I've upset you; but you can't hide me from him forever."

The hell I can't; he'd ruin everything. Take it easy. "Remember what I told you he said about your parents?" he asked, somewhat calmer.

"Yes, but how can he get over that if he doesn't know me? Phil, you should've heard him the other night. You don't know how nice he was to me."

Phillip felt his calves fatigue so he unwound his ankles and slid down. "Yes, I do know; that was my dad you were talking to."

"Well of course it was."

"You don't know what I mean. Next time you try to call, he might tell you to go to straight to hell."

"I don't believe that, not for one minute."

Jesus. "I really have to get to work, Lupe."

"Even if he's drinking, I don't believe he'd say that. When does he get back from Chicago?"

She won't drop it. "He's stuck there, probably has to drive."

"Well, then the coast is clear for me to come over," she said with a hint of sarcasm.

I'll be on the roof. "Lupe, this end of the highway is closed." He exhaled a deep breath and stared out the window again at the untouched layer of ash surrounding the walkways.

"They said it'll probably open tomorrow — I can't come until then anyway."

"I thought driving in this stuff bothered you."

"Only in the dark. I'll borrow the Sherman tank." That was Phillip's name for her mother's Suburban. "I'll take it real easy," she said, now sounding covert, as if her sister was trying to listen in. "You've been alone for days, Shorty. I think you need some, uh, human contact."

Man, bringing out the big guns. He didn't answer.

She went on, very softly. "I want to see the deep ash and — we'll be all alone. Shorty, should I come over?"

Who do you think you're kidding, Phillip? No way you'll turn this down. "Uh, tomorrow's fine, Lupe," he said.

"Not much of an invitation."

He tried to sound more sincere. "Come on by, Lupita."

"I'll bring fresh corn, Shorty, and some home cooking. Get some meat on those cute ol' bones — sound good?"

Man-oh-man. "Yeah, sure."

"Okay, see you tomorrow about noon. I miss you, Shorty."

"Miss you too, Lupita. Bye."

"Bye."

Phillip hung up the phone, aware of his aching erection as he turned around. *Your brains are in your pants, Shorty; she thinks she can help Stephen, know him for God's sake. If she knew what he's really like.* He felt his arousal begin to slump. *What's this BS about my health — from both of them?*

Phillip whisked out white bread and peanut butter and reached over for a banana. He bit off the black nub, stripped the peels, and then hacked away at the fruit with a kitchen knife. *Shorty Stark, that's me all right, sounds like a cook on a friggin' wagon train. Rustle up the grub, Shorty; coffee tastes like piss, Shorty. Chop your damn banana, Shorty.*

After spreading great globs of smooth peanut butter on two slices of soft bread, he stuck the poker-chip-sized pieces of banana on both slabs and then triumphantly smacked them together. *Check this out, losing weight, my ass.* Like a character in an old black and white cartoon, Phillip chomped a huge half-moon out of his sandwich, then plopped it onto a paper plate.

He donned his flint-grey baseball hat, lifted a can of soda from the fridge and headed for the door, food in one hand and beverage in the other. He put his lunch down, slipped on his shoes, tied them, then stuffed the work gloves in his jeans and the pop can in the chest pocket of his flannel shirt.

Outside, Phillip circled the wide ladder and started up, balancing the plate on one palm like a ritzy waiter with a tray. At the edge of the roof he turned around, sat, and let his feet dangle while he took a second bite from his sticky creation. He panned across the barren block; Mister Watson was the only one in sight, his dim silhouette sweeping off junk in his yard. Phillip gulped some soda, twisted the can into the ash and perched the plate and sandwich on top.

If Lupe's coming tomorrow, you'll have to make up for it today. He got to his feet, climbed to the apex of the roof and picked up the snow shovel. Down at Lewis's, Mick was gone, and all Phillip could see of the two workers were straw hats and the grey mud they were heaving out of the deep end of the waterless swimming pool.

Good, Mick's sleeping it off. Do this side first before he comes out. After the first push from the top of the house, Phillip watched the massive bulk of ash cascade into the back yard, causing a cloud that billowed right back up to the eaves. Pleased that gravity made this part of the task so easy, he briskly shoveled off a ten-foot-wide swath, but after he went over it with the brooms he found the slits between the wooden shakes were still solidly packed with residue.

He went back down for the garden hose and hauled it back up to the top of the cleared area and turned the nozzle on full blast. Though he was eager to resume scraping, Phillip had to squirt the length of each vertical crack to force out the ash, and after a half-hour he hadn't even finished that one section.

When he was finally satisfied, Phillip turned off the nozzle and went back by the ladder to retrieve the snow shovel. He picked it up and didn't notice the little mess a few feet away. A breeze had carried away the paper plate, spilling the rest of the peanut butter and banana sandwich into the muddy soot.

8

Though Phillip was twenty-nine, his bedroom was both a boy's and a man's place. He still slept in the same bed that Stephen Stark built into a racecar frame when Phillip was eight. When he was ten, Phillip furtively sawed off the bumpers and fins and covered the hot rod flames with three shades of green paint. He soon added bushes, tree trunks, Tarzan vines and an ocelot copied from the encyclopedia. A few weeks later on a two-six-pack Friday night Stephen rebuked Ellen for allowing the boy to transform the frame. She quietly defended Phillip's right not to be enthused about racecars and suggested tactfully that Stephen should be proud to have taught him how to accomplish the remodeling. Reading a comic on the bed in question, Phillip heard his inebriated father retort with a half-hearted "Bullshit," the limit of disrespect he ever showed for his wife.

Stephen and Ellen were childhood sweethearts in the same Seattle neighborhood where Phillip and his sister, Joann, later grew up. Ellen was three fourths Scandinavian and was proud she knew a few Danish words and some old country cooking. After Ellen and Joann returned from Sunday services, Phillip's sister sometimes recruited him to help pester their mother for a batch of *Aebelskiver*, buttermilk-soured dough balls fried in a special cast iron seven-cratered skillet. Ellen insisted they eat the first ones traditionally with applesauce; then Stephen and the two kids would douse the rest with butter, powdered sugar, jam and syrup.

Ellen worked as a medical secretary, but she lived for her time at home with family, pets, the vegetable garden, and her artistry — sculpturing. Young Phillip was very impressed when she won awards for her striking fired-clay figures of animals. Long before Ellen was ill, he was convinced she regretted deferring her art for economic necessity. Weeks before her death, Phillip broached that subject on a drive to the hospital and was surprised when she explained how content she was with her life, "both its smooth strokes and its rough notches." Without self-pity, she said her only regret was smoking since she was fifteen. Ellen Stark continued her job and her craft until she was regularly hospitalized, and she managed to cook a batch of *Aebelskiver* for Phillip and Stephen a couple of weeks before she died.

The most prized possession Phillip kept in his room was his mother's sculpture of a life-sized manx she gave him after the piece won a blue ribbon at a county fair. He displayed the cat at the center of his oak desk, another old carpentry project of his father's. It pleased Stephen back then that young Phillip liked to draw and study at the wide roll-top. They were mixed, confusing realities for the boy: the flawlessly crafted desk and his dad, the racecar bed and Stephen the Friday-night drunkard.

After the bereaved Starks moved to Ponderosa, Phillip felt both resolved and doomed to honor his pledge to look after his father. It was around then that Stephen's housekeeping began to transform from orderly into compulsive. When there was any lull in his cycle of drinking, sleeping, and recovering, he would morosely clean the house or manicure the yard. Perfectionism he once had for woodworking was relegated to dustless counters and precisely trimmed grass.

Since tools and machinery filled their third bedroom, Stephen decided to build a shop on the back of the garage. Phillip encouraged the project, hoping it would rejuvenate his father's hobby. When Stephen's interest began to lag, Phillip would start difficult tasks or pretend to be stumped. Stephen figured out the ploy one day and, without a word, tied his apron to an unfinished truss and walked into the house for a nap. He was drunk a few hours later and told Phillip he was a "meddling little shit."

When the shop was finally complete, they moved the saws, lathes and drills out of the house, and Stephen told his son to take the large master bedroom with the half-bath because he had "so much crap." Phillip built ceiling-to-floor shelves right away, and by the time he graduated from college nearly half of the wall space was taken up with books.

He kept many old animal-related novels like *Sounder*, *Incredible Journey*, and *Incident at Hawk's Hill.* His library also included the family's encyclopedia, some children's science series, his texts and technical books, the first James Herriot novels, the works of Jane Goodall and Joy Adamson, and his expanding collection of publications about felines.

Phillip had everything from coffee-table books about panthers and mountain lions to the latest research on the lynx — anything that added to his knowledge of wildcats, especially those from the Western Hemisphere. Posters, drawings and photos of cougars, bobcats, lynx, jaguars and ocelots dominated the rest of the wall space along with some maps, charts, and yellowed newspaper clippings of the 1977 Portland Trailblazers.

On the oak desk there was also a recent picture of Lupe and a framed photo of his parents cheesing toward the camera without cigarettes or booze. They were at a fish and chips stand near a ferry terminal in British Columbia. As far as Phillip knew, it was the only real vacation they ever took.

He kept his typewriter and some reference books on an eight-foot worktable by the door, where he did research and lesson plans and listened to John Fogerty and Neil Young on his small stereo. A shelf over the table displayed framed specimens of insects and dried plants, a Y-shaped branch of petrified wood, and a softball-sized polished geode with a tiny crystalline white cave at its center.

The room's long walk-in closet was less than a fourth taken up by a small dresser and Phillip's pragmatic clothes. The shelf and floor space overflowed with science materials, collections, low-priority books, hiking gear, sports equipment and leftover junk from his youth, including one withering cardboard box filled with dozens of old *Uncle Scrooge* comics.

On Lupe's only visit to the half-empty bedroom he told her he liked to be able spread out, but she said the room was sparse, that he needed more furniture. She despised the brown and orange wall-to-wall low pile carpet and its monotonous, coiling *fleur-de-lis* design, but Lupe thought his bed was "cute," and they laughed about it while making out over his juvenile rendition of a wildcat in the rain forest.

For the first time in three days Phillip slept in his jungle bed instead of the recliner. After spending the rest of the previous day on top of the house and garage, it became too dark to finish the last row of ash, so he finally came in and took a shower. When his head began to nod halfway through a TV dinner and the rerun of *M*A*S*H*, he turned off the set and went to bed.

Now he was sleeping on his stomach, Ali by his head. The old white cat reached up and pawed some strands of Phillip's disheveled dark-blond hair, tickling his ear.

What? — Uh, Ali. The cat burrowed into Phillip's shoulder. "Morning, boy. What do you want? Too early to eat," he said, looking over at the clock on the shelf. *Man, eleven ten — slept twelve hours. I could sleep even more.*

"Okay, so it's almost time, let me wake up," he said, turning onto his back and closing his eyes again; but the cat activated his purring apparatus and parked next to Phillip's ear. Ali's rattle as well as a sibilant wind under the eaves overtook his consciousness.

"Geez, you're relentless," he said, and then sat up to pet the cat. "Bad hunting last night?" *Listen to it blow out there; it should be lighter by now.* He swung his feet down to the rough carpet, turned toward the flimsy curtains and watched them flap crazily in the air. Ali immediately ran for the door; but Phillip stood up to go to the dim window. He stopped after a few steps, stretched his stiff back and then moved on. He saw a dusting of ash on the floor, looked up and pushed the curtains aside, but couldn't even see the back yard. The strong wind had churned the ash into a thick grey storm.

"I'll be damned." *Looks like the first day.* Phillip slid the pane closed and went right back to the foot of the bed for his dirty jeans. He pulled them on and hurried to the chest of drawers in the closet for some more clothes. He sat on the carpet to slip on his socks, the cat peering at him from the door.

Check the front yard. Jesus, all that work. "Yeah, Ali, hold your horses, lunch will be a minute." Tucking in his clean tee shirt, he rushed to the bedroom door and then down the hallway, the cat running effortlessly in front of him. Phillip's stocking feet slid as they hit the cereal crumbs and ash on the kitchen floor, and he caught himself by grabbing the counter. He saw ash on the dishes as he closed the window, and out front the two trees were invisible in the turbid air.

Great. Ali rubbed Phillip's leg, impatient for his food. "Back in a minute," he said, and hastily shut two windows on the way to the front door. Phillip stepped into his bedraggled tennis shoes without tying them and spotted his flannel shirt and baseball hat clumped into a corner. He put them on, opened the door, and walked below the overhang, squinting. Like sand blowing into a windshield, the agitated grey sediment ticked against the exposed skin of his face, neck and hands.

Phillip turned his back to the gale, stepped off the porch and bent down to pull up his shoelaces. After tying the bows he checked his footprints. *Already an inch where I cleared. What about the roofs?* Extending an arm over his face, Phillip leaned into the flying grit and walked away to look for the ladder he left by the garage. He located it then clambered to an upper rung where the air seemed clearer than below. He inspected the shakes and found only a light dusting in the cracks. *All right, it's too heavy to blow back up here.* His intestines growled then gnawed into an ulcer pang.

Get a damn pill. Regardless of his sore back, he scuttled down the ladder and made it over to the front porch. His arm still over his eyes, he turned back to the walkway. *Shit, everything's buried again. If this wind ever stops, you get to do it all over.* He stomped into the house, slammed the door furiously, and stopped to remove his shoes. Standing on one leg, he pulled at the heel of a sneaker. *To hell with this, the house is already full of ash.*

Get those damn shoes off.

Screw you, Stephen. Phillip tried to forefinger the shoe back onto his foot, but the canvas was bent underneath, and he hobbled down the hallway.

"Damn it!" he yelled, and tugged on the fabric again, bracing himself on the wall with his other arm. Ali fidgeted and stared impatiently from the kitchen, showing no more rubbing or purring business. As Phillip stumbled on with a knuckle in his shoe, the cat howled; it would have been a roar in a larger feline's body.

Phillip yanked the sneaker off, stood straight up and shouted, "Shut the hell up!" He launched the tennis shoe, it smacked against an upper cupboard, and the cat jerked and watched it land on the counter. Not seeming to make the connection that the missile was meant for him, Ali looked hungrily toward Phillip, who was at the doorway gawking wide-eyed at the scene of his deed.

You crazy bastard, Phillip. He walked up to his pet. "Sorry, Ali," he said, trying to atone by rubbing the cat's ears, but Ali growled and pulled away.

"Okay, okay." Phillip grabbed a can of cat food from the cupboard and rummaged through the dirty dishes for the opener. *Last can of tuna, save half of it, jerk.* The cat changed his tune immediately and started to head-butt Phillip's calf. He mixed the canned food with some dry, put the bowl on the floor, and Ali began to purr as he gobbled his lunch.

He's so into eating maybe he forgot what you did. Phillip's gut constricted again, so he reached up for his ulcer prescription and a non-aspirin for his back. He took the drugs then watched Ali, who was consuming the tuna less ravenously. *What a prick; you could've hurt him.*

Goddamn worthless ghost cat.

Fuck you.

Ali stopped eating and looked up, licking his jowls.

"Sorry, boy," Phillip said, but the cat seemed to sneer before walking away into the garage.

He'll probably take off; he knows what you did all right. He faced the kitchen window. It was like an oversized TV telecasting grey and black interference; Phillip just stared into the void and would have been accused of daydreaming if someone were there. After a couple minutes he sensed some movement in the TV room.

Shit, wake up. He turned toward the back door and saw Ali settling into Stephen's recliner. *He didn't like the wind.*

Get him the hell outta my chair.

"Stay there all you want, Ali," Phillip said, "he won't be back for a while." He watched the cat curl up and go to sleep, then tried to decide what to do with himself.

Lupe won't know how bad it is here. He called her, but the circuits were down again. *She won't get here for hours, if at all. As soon as it stops, you can get back to work. Check the weather.*

He went to the TV room and petted Ali, but the cat ignored his touch. *Feels like somebody else threw the damn shoe. No, it was you, asshole.* Phillip realized he had been walking around with one shoe, so he took it off, tossed it into the kitchen and turned on the set. Glancing over at Ali, he twisted the dial through the channels. He came back to the first station. *God, quiz shows and soap operas, try the radio.*

Phillip walked through the kitchen then turned right and opened the sliding doors Stephen installed to partition off their living room. Since the doors were always closed, it seemed like they had one long hallway from the kitchen down to the bedrooms.

While Stephen's shop was testimony to a moribund hobby, the living room was his monument to Ellen Stark. He maintained her colonial furniture so well over the years that the wood finish looked showroom new. A red, white and blue afghan Ellen knitted for her husband was folded perfectly as a flag and lay unused on the long sofa. On an oak coffee table between the matching living room chairs, Bambi and Bashful and other glazed porcelain critters and gnomes grinned perpetually next to Ellen's sculptures of two small-scale bloodhounds, the only pieces she didn't give away.

Behind the sofa, a never-kindled white brick fireplace and a picture window to the back yard took up most of the long wall in the rectangular room. Ellen's sewing-circle quilt, each black square enclosing a bright butterfly, covered the far wall. The ladies in her group remembered Phillip as a boy watching the project take form, and they presented it to him after Ellen's funeral. Like the manx in his bedroom, the quilt was a valued memento, and Phillip made it clear to Stephen that it hung in there only on loan.

Stephen also saved his wife's family photos and displayed the framed ones in a long row on top of the secondhand Baldwin that Ellen bought for Joann when she quit high-school sports her senior year to play piano. Ellen had hoped she would go on to college and take music, but Joann got married and the only encouragement she had to continue studying died with her mother within a year.

Stephen referred to the room as "mother's parlor," but Ellen Stark, of course, was never in there. When Phillip once tried to stretch out to read on the couch, he felt uneasy around her carefully preserved things. The cloistered room also reeked of cigarettes notwithstanding Stephen's regular cleaning, so Phillip rarely stayed in the parlor for more than a few minutes.

Although he thought the memorial to his mother would be perceived by anyone else as morbidly sentimental, Phillip didn't criticize Stephen about it. He eventually convinced him to move the family stereo in there, but only because Phillip agreed to wire speakers into the poolroom, since no one would be allowed to "party" in Ellen's shrine.

Now Phillip moved by the piano and the furniture to the casket-sized stereo cabinet and wrote "P. S." with his finger in the film of ash that had sifted onto the polished wood.

He'll completely freak; better start cleaning. Dishes first, I guess. He opened one of the cabinet doors, turned on the radio and tuned into an AM station that always advertised itself as "The news leader for Four Rivers and beyond." Phillip listened to a caller who was ranting to the announcer.

"...that's all we ever hear about is how bad it is over on the west side. Well, people are suffering here, too..."

Who the hell is suffering? He sat on the arm of the couch.

"...people can't go to work, they're low on fresh food at the stores, and nobody's doing anything about the roads..."

Maybe in your neighborhood, lady.

"...now the wind is blowing it all back. This is a big disaster here, and nobody cares, I still say they should— "

"Excuse me, ma'am, how much ash at your place?" the host asked.

"Nearly two inches, and— "

"Do you have food, water and shelter?"

"Well, yes."

"Do you have anyone to help you with the cleanup?"

"My kids, but— "

"Ma'am, I know it's been difficult for everyone, but sometimes we need to count our blessings..."

Yeah lady, and shut up while you're at it.

"...out of time for your calls. Weather, news, just ahead," he said, and then a pre-recorded commercial came on. "Tired of trimming grass the old-fashioned way?"

Look outside, Bozo. He switched on the den speakers then backed out of the room, looking through the wide window at the airborne ash. *Doesn't seem any worse.* He closed the sliders, started up the hall and could hear the radio ahead.

"...accept no substitute, it's the Cadillac of weed trimmers..."

I'll take the Datsun trimmer, thank you. He returned to the kitchen while a new commercial harped on about the "ash cleanup sale" a car dealer was having at "the only clean lot in town."

He saw Ali was no longer in Stephen's recliner so he called for the cat and tried twisting the can opener. *Guess he took off — nice going, Phillip.* He cracked eggs into a bowl to start some French toast, listening to the speaker in the den.

"...that message brought to you by your friends at Four Rivers Dodge-Plymouth, who remind you that the big cleanup sale will resume as soon as it's safe again to travel.

"In case you just got back from Mars, we have a little wind in the Four Rivers basin today. It's gusting up to forty miles per hour and, as we feared, the ash isn't staying put. Hal's forecast will be up in just a minute. Visibility on most roads is nonexistent, and all major highways are closed again as of this hour. Except for emergencies, please don't attempt to drive. The airport, which reopened late last night, is closed again.

"Many services and businesses in Four Rivers County are closed for today; we'll list some exceptions later in the broadcast. In nearby Truman and Redfield counties the situation is even more severe. Officials there have requested all employers, except for basic and emergency services, to stay closed, and residents are asked to remain at home if at all possible until further notice.

"Once the wind stops, everyone in our broadcast area is asked to water down ash around your property. If you've already moved ash to your curb, please water that down too. However, residents of Four Rivers are not to wash ash into the storm drains. Now for the weather update, here's Hal."

"Thanks, Russ, we do have some good news. Winds are expected to decrease by midday to gusts of ten to fifteen miles per hour, decreasing even further this afternoon. By tonight it should be calm, and the front that's passing through will fortunately leave most of its moisture on the west side..."

"Fortunately?" Phillip said.

"...chance of showers this afternoon, mostly near the Cascade foothills. Temperatures remain comfortable, mid-seventies today, lower-eighties tomorrow — full reports at noon and five thirty. There you have it, Russ; decreasing winds and not much chance of any rain adding to the gloom," he said with the typical false cheerfulness of his profession.

"Maybe we'll take some of that rain, huh Al?" Russ said.

"Oh, right, heh-heh."

Heh-heh, what an idiot. Phillip finished making his French toast and ate one piece with peanut butter and jelly. He was nibbling on a plain slice and getting the dishes ready to wash when the phone rang.

Lines are open? It's Lupe. He picked up the wall phone. " 'Lo?"

"Hi, Phillip."

***Phillip?** — my God.* "Dad? Are you calling from Chicago?"

"No, left this morning," Stephen Stark said quietly.

Geez, it's really him. "Where are you?"

"Des Moines."

"Iowa?"

"Yes."

No, Idaho, dummy. Say something. "How's the trip going so far, Dad?" *Brilliant.*

"Fine. Be there in a couple days."

"Uh, what kind of car did you rent?" *Chevy.*

"Chevy."

"Same as yours?" *Dad?*

"Different color. Phillip, can you go and get my car?"

"No problem." *Talk to him!* "They reopened the airport last night; now it's closed again — the wind's blowing ash like crazy."

"It's good I got started then."

"Yeah." *C'mon, Phillip, maybe the ash bet.* "Uh— " *No, Dad won't talk about that.* "How'd you get this call through? We still can't call out."

"Lucky, I guess. The car's in J-7, Phillip, right in front; ticket's in the window. I'll square with you later."

"Sure, J-7, I'll find it." He jotted the number on one of Stephen's tidy note pads. *Quick, you're going to lose him.* "The wind is covering everything I already scraped."

"Is that right," Stephen said with no interrogative tone.

"Yeah, the highway's closed. When they open it, Lupe can ride in with me to get your car."

"Okay. My spare keys are in the usual place."

"Right." *Damn, what else?* "So you talked to her last week?"

"Who? Oh. Yeah, you weren't home. Phillip, I want to make South Dakota; I should get going."

No. Think! "Sure, um— "

"Call you tonight when I stop."

"Okay. Dad?"

"Yes."

I miss you. "Uh, drive carefully, okay?"

"I will. Bye, son."

"Bye, Dad." Phillip hung up. ***Son**, for God's sake — why didn't you talk to him?* Tears welled up in his eyes, and he ripped a paper towel off the dispenser and roughly wiped the moisture from his face. *Shit, stop bawling.* He stared again at the drab scene out front; a final tear slalomed down his cheek.

9

In the street, a car's dim shape crept from left to right in the grey pall; Phillip awoke from his daze. *Where does that fool think he's going? What was I just doing? Thinking about Dad, I guess — pull yourself together.* He put soap in one basin and started to run hot water for the dishes, then turned it off. *Crap, there's no hurry now, do it later.*

Since he couldn't work on the ash, he decided that reading was the only thing he wanted to do. Phillip went to his room and put aside a research paper in favor of one of his old novels, *The Yearling*. He stretched out on his bed and lost himself in the story of Jody, Flag and Fodderwing, protector of injured swamp animals. He got up occasionally to check the wind, but fell asleep in the early afternoon and didn't wake up until the hard-backed book thunked onto the floor. He picked it up, placed his marker and looked over at the clock.

It's after two; I don't hear any wind. So get to work. He put on his hat, hurried to the bathroom and tried to urinate quickly, but his stream seemed endless. He finished, then rushed back to open the curtains and check the yard. The wind had completely died down, and the deep volcanic powder was rippled with small-scale ash dunes. A forlorn-looking junco landed on the empty birdfeeder, its tiny black hood poking futilely for seeds.

Don't forget to feed them. He went right out to the hall, opened the front door and saw Gil Beck leaning into a push broom at the property line. Phillip looked at the accumulation on his own front walks.

A couple inches at most, could be worse — get going. He closed the door, searched for his shoes and spotted new wisps of ash on the hallway carpet. *It's creeping in everywhere. Your shoes are in the kitchen — and how did that happen, jerk? See if he came back.* Starting up the hallway to check for Ali, Phillip heard the phone.

It's her. No time for lunch, Lupe — gotta work. Just tell her the roads are bad, to wait a couple days. Phillip was almost at a full run when he entered the kitchen. To keep from falling, he extended his arms like a skater and skimmed halfway across the floor. Girding himself to be firm, he answered the phone and looked out. Only a ghost of the jellyfish survived in the yard, its long legs rounded into four gently rolling furrows in the ash.

"*Klaatu barada nikto*," said a contrived deep voice on the line trying to be the alien in *The Day the Earth Stood Still.*

All right, it's Warren. "Where are you, Big Turd?" His parody of *Big Bird* was a vestige of their schooldays repartee.

"Ya' little shit, how'd you know it was me?" A P.A. system blared in the background.

"C'mon, Warren."

"Phil, I figured out the other day why you always used to pass me the ball."

"I'm sure you did." He smiled and waited for the barb.

"It's obvious. I was the only one you could even see through all those knees and asses way down there."

"No, I was shooting, thought you were the pole." Phillip heard the P.A. again. "Where *are* you calling from?"

"Four Rivers airport no less."

"You are? It's open again?" He gaped at the street as if it might yield some sort of information about travel conditions.

"First plane in today."

"This is great — you need me to come get you?"

"No, Dad's here. We're waiting for the road to open, enjoying some fine cuisine. *Le bou terre fin guerre.*"

Hm, Butterfinger. "So you're here to help them dig out?"

"Yeah, took a week's vacation."

Phillip checked the grey sky. "What was it like up there?"

"We got a peek at Saint Helens; what a rush. It's still spitting; never saw a mountain with its whole top gone."

"Must've been something. What's it like on this side?"

"Hairy, like flying in fog. Man, this whole deal is wild; a week might not be enough. Dad still has more grass than a golf course and he said it's all a half foot under."

"Same here; I'll be lucky to get it cleaned up before I take off."

"Your project is still on?"

"I hope so. The ash fall didn't go straight north."

"Good deal. So tell me about when it hit there; my parents didn't even go outside."

Phillip described the clouds and his other experiences. Warren was duly amazed until he heard about Mick.

"That figures, Phil," he said. "Don't let that ol' wino bother you."

"Yeah, no skin off his nose." Phillip briefly told about the workers Mick brought in, and then he enthusiastically recounted his all-nighter with the street crew.

"So, except for Mick, you're having big fun with all this," Warren said with a laugh then paused. "Phil, Dad sold his big tractor — no luck renting one. Any ideas?"

"Wheelbarrows and shovels — afraid the fun's over."

"Guess I'll need to hire a couple guys, too."

"I'll be over when the road opens; no charge." *And what about Stephen?*

"No way; you've got your own mess."

Stephen can wait. "You can't keep me away, Big Turd." He peered out the window in search of his scraping tools.

"I said we'll handle it, ya' little shit."

"Man, it's good to hear your bossy voice."

"Now don't start queering on me. Wait, I forgot, *el navidad usted muy amigos con la señorita y el magnifico chi-chis.*" The butchered Spanish was further exaggerated by his rising inflections.

"That's bad, even for you." He jumped back on the sink.

"Oh, was I uncouth?" Warren said with feigned remorse.

"Yes, as usual. So what about you two? Hatching any kids?"

"Still thinking about it; we might wait for my first million."

"You'll be rolling in it," Phillip agreed without sarcasm. A draftee during Vietnam, Warren was an Army electronics whiz before going to college on the G.I. Bill to study business and computers. In just a few years he worked his way into administration for one of the new computer companies near Seattle.

"It's bigger than you think, Phil. When every science dork on earth has a computer, I'll be curious to see if you get on board."

"I will when they're more than a pain in the ass."

"Your enthusiasm overwhelms me. The time is here, my friend."

Phillip was watching another car escape the development at a slug's pace. *We might need the fire hose again.*

"Phil?"

"Yeah. So how's Marilyn?"

"She's fine; happy about finishing her degree next year. You haven't told me if you're still seeing Sophia Loren."

"Sophia's Italian, Bozo. Yeah, I'm still seeing her."

"Well, right arm and farm house," Warren said in their old sardonic version of *right on* and *far out*. "So, it's going okay, then?"

Phillip watched the car inch up to the corner to make the turn, a rolling cloud of ash behind. "We're doing all right."

"Doesn't sound like it. You're knocking on thirty my man; settling down does have plus sides, ya' know. *La chica es bonita*; but I think maybe she's *mucho* for you."

"Ha, ha. She's not into her looks at all; she'd rather be in old riding duds than a dress. She's a good person, intelligent and— "

"Okay, who are you trying to convince? So what's the problem?"

"Nothing major; sometimes we don't get each other very well."

"That's normal — news flash, pal, nobody ever gets you."

"Thanks a lot. You always do, somehow."

"Yeah? I bet you still don't own a friggin' watch. So how did you piss her off?"

"I didn't. She says she supports my project, but between the lines it seems more important to her for us to mess around all summer. I need to call Putman — sick of having it up in the air."

"Ahrrrrg, I swears to God almighty, I be knowin' it," Warren interrupted with his energetic if timeworn version of Long John Silver. "Matey, methinks ye have priorities that be with the wrong sort of pussies."

"That's terrible, but I should consider the source."

"Okay, Mister Wild Kingdom." Long John was already gone. "So the cat deal is the big touchy subject?"

"No, it's mostly Stephen. I've told her about some of his bad shit, but she doesn't get it. She wants to know him, try out social worker stuff on him." *Enough.* "So tell me how your parents are doing."

"Changing subjects are we? Well, Mom's a little freaked by the ash and Dad's too old for all this, but they're doing fine. What about your dad?"

He doesn't need more Stephen crap, either. Phillip stared at a towhee searching for grubs under the ponderosa, performing its backwards jump-dance to scratch away the ash.

"Phil? So what's going on with him?

"Same ol' deal." *Make it short.* "He's stuck at a convention in Chicago — plastered, of course. I pissed him off yesterday on the phone."

"You did? No more rolling with the punches?"

"I let him get to me — shouldn't have. Today he was sobered up; driving a rental back."

"Phil, I've never stuck my nose in this, but my God, you've got your own life. How long can you watch over him?"

I don't know. "Time to change subjects again."

"So you're mad at me for saying that?"

"No, I'm just tired of thinking about him."

"Okay, so what else is fucked up? We covered your love life, the ash and you-know-who."

Phillip chuckled at Warren's summation. "Your duty's done."

"Bull, all this crap coming down, you should've given me a call. Spit it out. What else?"

Phillip sighed. "I pulled one today that'd make Stephen proud. I got pissed about nothing; threw a shoe at Ali."

"That's pretty hard to believe. Did you hit him?"

He looked over to the TV room for the cat. "No."

"Now *that* I do believe. Look, everybody does something stupid once in a while. You know you didn't really want to hurt the cat; you couldn't hit the ocean with a rock, anyway, which is the real reason you always passed me the ball."

"Funny, Warren."

"Listen, Phil, since I'm hiring somebody I should be finished in a couple days, then I'll give you a hand before I take off."

"I don't want you to do that."

"You offered to come over and you're the one who's under all the pressure. Listen, I want to, so live with it."

"I just want to see you while you're in town."

"Fine, when we're working, if you don't queer out on me."

"You're beyond help."

"Yeah, at least I'm not bummed. Let's talk tomorrow."

"Okay." *I should have a lot done by then.*

"Take care, ya' little shit."

"See you, Big Turd." He hung up and grimaced toward the ash out front. *Do what you can, then help Warren. If Stephen doesn't like it,* ***he*** *can damn well hire someone.* Phillip started for the door. *Hang on; make sure she's not coming.* He phoned Sageview, and Mrs. Rosendall said Lupe was trying to call him before she left on a grocery run. Phillip made sure she understood it wouldn't be safe to travel for at least a day or two. While finishing the conversation, he located his shoes and told Lupe's mother he would call back later.

He tied his sneakers then checked for Ali in the usual hangouts, but he wasn't around. Phillip went out to inspect the ponderosa and was glad to find it wasn't encased like before, so he just shook off the branches and then turned on the sprinkler. He went out back to fill the birdfeeder and start the water there before returning to the front yard.

Phillip finished off the narrow row of ash on the garage and then re-scraped the walks in about an hour and a half. When he started on the driveway, traces of precipitation sprinkled his face. *Farm house — good ol' rain;* ***add to the gloom*** *my ass.* It turned into a steady shower, so he dropped the shovel and ran to turn off the hoses in both yards.

He returned to his shovel and found the wet ash easier to scrape, and there wasn't much on the driveway since the deep piles on both sides had served as barriers against the wind. As he finished the task, Phillip watched some people pass by in their cars almost at normal speed, no clouds tumbling behind.

Start under the eaves? No, better take a half-hour to join the parade before the ash dries up. Let's see, milk, fruit, bread, and cat food; another sprinkler maybe; and you can check out the highway.

10

Phillip left his tools on an ash mound and went in the house for his wallet and keys, then came back to the garage. Though it hadn't been driven in days, his little pickup started on the first crank of the ignition. He unconsciously buckled his seat belt — one of his mother's few rules, then backed down to the street and drove to the corner. Phillip turned right and tried to follow the cleared lane, but it was obscured by wet ash. He slowly approached the fake rock portal that once had PONDEROSA ESTATES across the top until the sign disappeared one Halloween, never to be replaced.

On the other side of the arch he turned left on the state road, where the ash blow-over was still settled, though the rain was letting up. Between the slow sweeps of his wipers, Phillip made out a peculiar truck coming toward him from the other direction. It was an ordinary farm pickup, but the owner had rigged the tail pipe to go up the side so it was actually venting its exhaust above the cab.

To keep from blowing the ash? Except for the road itself, the countryside hadn't been disturbed since the eruption; the drab sage and tumbleweed seemed to fit right in with the volcanic desolation. Phillip came to an alfalfa field where the bales lay interred in the ash at regular intervals like coffins after a battle.

After a mile of mostly sage and hay, the road notched through the basalt ridge east of town where a few wind-dwarfed, soil-deprived ponderosas looked as if they had been dipped in lead fondue. Phillip turned his head to see the valley, but the town was rendered invisible by a cloak of unsettled soot, regardless of the rain. He drove to the bottom of the steep hill, passed a quilt of ashen pear and apple orchards and came to the city limits sign. It read, W___OME TO POND__OSA - __E ASP__ OF THE NORTHW___ — its words and tree logo partially obliterated by splashed mud.

Asp of the north, Snaketown — makes about as much sense. Phillip went by some untouched potato and onion fields, thinking they resembled grey rice paddies, then he took the turn into town instead of staying on the road to the junction. As in most of Ponderosa, the first houses he came to varied from shacks to modest cottages to stuccos. He immediately took notice of the bright yellow streamers tied to many of the fences, doors and trees. Wondering why the ribbons stood out so much from the ash-blanketed homes, Phillip theorized that yellow was rarely matched with grey, making the contrast even more striking.

The rain had turned to mist, and most residents were out scraping roofs, walks or driveways; only a few had begun to reclaim their lawns. One man stood on a ladder with a long pole trying to knock ash from the branches of one of the mature elms that lined the block. Phillip turned off his wipers and stopped to watch a skip loader grating over the street, its massive tires mashing out eddies of pallid dust with each turn of the wheels. The loader's scoop dropped a load of ash onto a vacant lot with a dull *thump*, causing a cloud to ascend above the rooftops like the aftermath of a bomb blast. Phillip went on to the intersection and circumnavigated a pile of ash that was taller than the street signs.

He came to a block of venerable houses dating back more than a century, two of them with lofty old ponderosas in their yards. Phillip gawked at a three-story "mansion" with six-inch layers of undisturbed ash on every horizontal surface. Though the home looked somber, it reminded him of a holiday gingerbread house waiting for its perfection to be violated.

God, where are they going to put all of it? He drove slowly around more ash mountains and passed the city park near a cluster of three tall Protestant steeples and a small Catholic church. Across from Saint Inés, a corner grocery's windows were soaped with prices for *limón, cilantro* and three things Phillip never heard of: *chorizo, tripas* and *jícama*. The small market was shut tight, and ash had drifted all the way up to the mail slot in the front door.

He manipulated his way through busy neighborhoods onto Pine Avenue in downtown Ponderosa, only three blocks long but the hub of civic activity with the post office, city hall, and fire station. Like the handful of other drivers on the street, Phillip rolled by in low gear. Only the drug store, the hardware, and some government offices were open, their sidewalks cleared of residue. Other businesses like the taverns, the feed & seed and the barbershop were closed, as was the Sunshine Café, its gingham-draped windows dark and glowering behind a deep barricade of ash.

At the end of downtown Phillip passed by the defunct Ponderosa School, a square brick two-story, now the "Red Cross Disaster Relief Center," where numerous cars and trucks were coming and going. He came to the first of the town's two traffic lights, blinking red in both directions like it was three in the morning. Phillip yielded right-of-way to a station wagon and watched puffs of ash drift behind its tires. *It's drying up fast.*

After that intersection, the town gave way to a mile of orchards and fields up to a retail strip of gas stations, cafés, convenience stores, burger joints, fruit stands, bars, a motel, the fast-food chicken place, a bank and the market. They all prospered from the nearby federal highway, flashing their neon semaphores at night to entice travelers from passing by the town. As Phillip drove through, about half the businesses were open but only the convenience stores had a lot of customers.

He approached the second traffic light where Pine Avenue and the U.S. highway met the road Phillip could have stayed on to skirt the town. Cars streamed on and off the highway, ignoring a temporary ROAD CLOSED sign. *They're all chancing it before the ash dries.*

The market was right at the junction, its gaudy red sign, KURT'S, revolving above the jammed parking lot. Phillip passed a long line of vehicles at the main entrance and entered the back driveway. He saw that the lot hadn't been re-scraped but the customers were parking in almost the same spots they would have if the lines were visible. Phillip had to park at the back, about where he was supposed to during his days as a checker at the store.

It isn't this bad on Thanksgiving; must be a zoo in there. He walked across the lot and chuckled when he saw luxury cars and old beaters alike with grey mud up to their door handles. As Phillip headed toward the propped-open automatic doors of Kurt's Western Grocery, ash-dusty patrons hurried by in both directions, except for one man who pushed his cart off to the side.

"You stay here," he said urgently to his son, "I'm going back inside for another limit of bread."

Oh, what fun. Phillip went in and found all three check stands bustling, a long queue winding back from each one. Kurt Senior's usually cheerful and orderly displays were messy and depleted, his bright signage mostly old or missing.

Kurt Junior was at the nearest register, and Phillip walked toward him. Though Kurt played basketball in high school with Phillip and worked with him in the store for years, they were not good friends. After a long divorce and a short career as a car salesman, Kurt had moved back home from Four Rivers to take up his father's long-standing offer of partnership in the store.

Phillip walked behind the check stand as if he still worked there. The shiny toes of high-heeled cowboy boots stuck out below Kurt's green grocer's apron. Phillip believed he wore the boots all the time to compensate for his wiry five-foot-five frame. Kurt was also losing the latest battle in his perpetual war against acne. Constellations of inflamed red zits pulsed from the bridge of his nose up to his scalp, vanishing into greasy light-brown hair that some barber had chopped into a fifty's-era butch.

"Anything left in this place?" Phillip asked.

"What's up, Phil," Kurt said, not really asking, his overbite accentuating the perpetual *I-don't-get-it* look on his face. Though raised in the Northwest, he had developed a twang to his voice that sounded something like his favorite country music. "Ya' fell into the volcano, I guess," Kurt tried to joke.

What? Phillip looked down at his mud-caked sneakers. "Yeah, dirty stuff," he said, striking the front of his flannel shirt with his palm. Ash plumed into the air and some mud crust flaked onto the counter.

"Horseshit," Kurt mumbled, his usual response to any annoyance, but only Phillip detected the oath. Kurt wiped up the grime and returned to his groceries. "If we had another register, I'd hire you double pay right now."

Not for a million. "This is wild; any milk left?"

"Ain't seen any come through in a while. We put limits on everythin' fresh; should be some powdered, same ol' place."

"Thanks," Phillip said as Kurt whipped out and snapped a paper sack. Where there were usually dozens of grocery carts, Phillip found three entangled ones. Instead of dealing with that, he grabbed two hand-carry baskets and headed down a crowded aisle to some cardboard cases on the floor below a scrawled sign: LIMIT - 2 BOX POWDRD MILK. A slouched elderly man was placing his two rations into a cart.

"...drink this dog piss. Son of a bitch," the old man muttered and then glared at Phillip for some imaginary transgression.

"Excuse me," Phillip said as he reached for two boxes of milk. The man gave him another dirty look then shuffled away.

Jesus, like I drank all the real milk. He put one box in each basket and came to an upright freezer, but a lady's cart blocked the aisle as she held the door open to choose some meat. She was short and grandmotherly, her florid housedress boasting a corsage of yellow ribbons and tiny U.S. flags.

A man about Phillip's age stood behind her, jangling car keys nervously into the side of his leg. He was a foot taller than the lady, clean-shaven, with perfect blond hair; but his dress slacks, shirt, and expensive oxfords were splattered with grey mud. The man tilted back his brand-new flat-billed red baseball hat with a smudged advertisement for MUTUAL FARM on the front.

Mutual Farm is pissed — at her, at everything.

"Make up your mind, will you?" the insurance agent practically yelled, but the lady continued to ponder the frozen meat as if he didn't exist. "For God's sake," the man finally said and then leaned right in front of her to grab a package.

"I was about to choose that," she stated, impassive.

"Not sometime today you weren't," he answered, and hurried away. Not missing a beat, the lady went back to studying her remaining options.

Didn't even happen; she just wants her damn meat. He turned sideways and made his way past her cart to the cooler across the aisle to pick up a package of hot dogs. Then, dodging around shoppers and displays, he made it to the pet food section and gathered more cans than usual of Ali's favorite tuna. A tall, thin woman in her thirties looked up from deciphering scrawls on a long list and firmly poked Phillip's arm.

"Where'd you get those?" She eyed his baskets through thick glasses and pointed at them.

"Cat food?"

"No," she said, flustered, "the powdered milk."

"Aisle six." Reverting to his checker days, Phillip forced a smile and raised his arm in the right direction.

"We'd better get some right now," she informed her groceries as if they were shopping partners. The woman lugged a forty-pound sack of dog food onto her loaded cart then abandoned the stockpile, scurrying past clumps of shoppers. At the end of the aisle she stopped and faced Phillip, suspicion on her face.

No, lady, I'm not after your damn stuff. She took a quick gander at the others nearby and then disappeared around a stack of toilet paper. *What's with these people? Get it over with.*

Phillip moved efficiently around the familiar market, avoiding people as if they carried plague instead of provisions. He quickly added bread, tortilla chips and bean dip to his baskets, and then a can of green beans and some spaghetti sauce. Finding no palatable fruit in the produce section, Phillip backtracked for some canned peaches and grapefruit and decided to stock up on a jar of his favorite peanut butter. In the small hardware section he found that all the sprinklers had been sold.

At the magazine rack he took the next-to-the-last newspaper, a day-old Four Rivers Tribune with the headline: DIGGING OUT. Finally, he grabbed a half-case of cola and two candy bars, then stood at the end of Kurt Junior's long line, knowing it would be the fastest. Everyone nearby had at least one full cart; he nodded to a neighbor from Ponderosa Estates then to a bus driver from school, and noticed that people were now mostly smiling and chatting.

God, it's relief; everyone nailed their precious groceries; now they can be civil. Two fortyish women in plain summer dresses carried on a private conversation intended to hold court for anyone within earshot. He put down his full baskets and tried to read the newspaper.

"...and I see you mainly have limit items," one lady was saying in full voice. Phillip thought she sneered with superiority toward his puny selection of groceries.

The queen of all shoppingdom has a serious nose problem. God, let me out of here.

"I don't need the packaged goods," the other one said. "Our church believes in being prepared; my basement is well stocked, but as far as the fresh items, I don't think these limits are fair to regular customers."

"Precisely. Their prices are bad enough; always going up, and most of *these* people get their groceries in Four Rivers. After all, this store makes its profit from us, and we shouldn't be penalized at a time when..."

Jesus, shut the hell up. He turned his back to them and faced a very large woman draped in a flowered purple and yellow moo-moo. A dour expression on her face, she leaned over her hoard of commodities for physical support, giving the impression that she was permanently attached to the cart.

Phillip pushed his baskets forward with one foot and saw some sequined sandals moving by, snapping with each footfall. They belonged to a tall, bony middle-aged woman in a pea-green sleeveless blouse, and white culottes cinched to the last belt hole. Sunglasses peered like outsized cat's eyes from her beehive hairdo held together with a lime-colored mesh scarf. She spotted the heavy woman and halted her brimming cart. Phillip could smell some kind of fruity lotion the new arrival had basted over her taut, well-cooked skin.

Great, now the swimming pool Goddess. With the other two women yapping right behind, Phillip had no recourse but to face the new conversation.

"Lee Ann, you bought half the store," the gaunt lady commented with an affected, cocky smile.

"Didn't do so bad yourself," the moo-moo woman said back.

"This is it, you know. This is the beginning of the tribulations; He is coming. I hope you've been saved, dear."

"Tell you what, Judith, ask him to bring along the biggest damn vacuum cleaner he's got."

"You mustn't talk like that, or you will be left behind."

"Won't be the first time," she said, and the evangelist wheeled her cart away.

Right arm, two points for the moo-moo. Phillip smiled at her briefly then turned to nudge his baskets ahead. He agonized in line for another fifteen minutes.

"Phil, ya' made it." Kurt's fingers whizzed over the keys as Phillip's purchases finally took their ride down the conveyor belt.

"Man, what a zoo." Phillip made brief eye contact with Kurt Senior at the far register; they exchanged cursory waves. "Doesn't seem to bother you much," he said to Kurt.

"All the way to the bank." He shoved a straying can to the box boy.

Good ol' curt-Kurt. Phillip mused over Warren's high-school nickname for Kurt, who ignored it back then for weeks until some kid explained that it was more than an annoying repetition of his name.

"Still don't like it in here, do ya', Phil," Kurt said, not expecting nor looking up for an answer.

What was your first clue? Phillip just watched the hectic scene, observing that all the employees had tiny yellow ribbons pinned to their nametags. *Senior's idea.*

"You can get two a' these," Kurt told him, holding up the loaf of bread.

"One'll do it."

"Not stockin' up much for another wind," he said, processing the hot dogs. "Ya' see the frozen beef that come in before the volcano?" he asked, sacking the last of the purchases because his helper left for a larger order.

"Yeah." *Saw two idiots fighting over it.*

"Nothin' like a thick rare steak."

Yum, with lots of blood.

"Looks like you could use one," Kurt said. "Nineteen forty-five."

Another damn health expert. Kurt was glaring at him. "Oh, yeah, hang on." Phillip pinched two tens out of his wallet; Kurt took the bills and fingered change from the tray.

"Four bits and a nickel is twenty." He handed over the coins, moved closer and lowered his voice. "Ya' still seein' her?" Kurt pretended to write busily on a pad as he spoke.

"I guess you forgot what I told you," Phillip said. Because of Kurt's gossiping to Stephen, Phillip had already told him that Lupe was none of his business.

"Horseshit — I'm on your side," he mumbled behind his hand, checking for eavesdroppers. "Just tryin' to tell you some of the ol' biddies are talkin' 'bout you an' her."

His mom's little bridge club. "What a surprise."

"Don't matter to *me* none she's a beaner." His last words were barely audible as he figured fake numbers on the paper.

What a guy. "That's real good, Kurt."

"All I know is, she's fine," he whispered with a lascivious sneer that transformed right away into a patronizing smile for the lady in the moo-moo. Kurt began checking through her items. "So take it easy, Phil, maybe we'll double some time."

When pigs fly. "See ya', Kurt." Phillip lifted his two sacks and maneuvered around people like an adroit halfback eluding tacklers, finally passing through the doors into the first row of the parking lot.

"Free!" he said out loud, and the old man who was angry about the milk gave Phillip a disparaging glance from behind the trunk of a huge Lincoln. *Screw you; enjoy your powdered milk.* On the way back to his spot, Phillip intentionally scuffed the thin crust on the ground and watched ash rise and surround his shoe. *Like it didn't even rain.*

He put a couple items in the Styrofoam cooler in back, carrying the rest up to the seat. Phillip started the motor and exited the crowded parking lot, but traffic was sending ash into the air again and he could barely see the vehicles right in front of him. After he made his pickup creep all the way to the junction, Phillip switched on the headlights though it was hours before dark.

Doesn't help much. Turning onto the state road, he looked into his rearview mirror at what should have been the outskirts of town, but he only saw his grey wake. Visibility began to improve ahead and there were no cars, so he shifted into fourth gear at about forty miles per hour. Before he started up onto the plateau, a pickup and its dense cloud of ash came toward him. Phillip tapped the brakes, closed his window and then downshifted as they met, the soot from the other truck rolling over his windshield like dry steam.

Where in hell is the road? He was all the way down to first gear when it cleared enough to see the highway, but he maintained a very slow speed as he started up the hill. *Damn guardrail — don't stop or you'll get rear-ended.* Phillip made it up onto the mesa and wanted to cover as much ground as possible before another vehicle could approach. He shifted through the gears up to forty again and could see about a hundred feet ahead.

In a couple of minutes he passed a field of alfalfa caskets and anticipated the sighting of Ponderosa Estates when a sedan materialized from the cloud behind. Phillip looked through his left-side window and caught a glimpse of a vanity license plate, XTOPCAD, as the car pulled even to pass.

You crazy son of a bitch. Phillip removed his foot from the accelerator so the white Cadillac could get by, and then the pickup was completely enveloped by the ash cloud.

Damn, can't see again. He downshifted all the way to first; the transmission whined with the strain, and Phillip slowed to a crawl, but he felt the truck going downhill. *Shit, I'm off!* Instead of turning back up onto the steep crown, he made a quick decision to brake softly and let it roll into the ditch. The pickup settled against a telephone pole, which wasn't visible until seconds after the soft collision. He rolled down the window and stuck out his head to see if he could hear the other driver stop.

Bastard's gone. Reverse; try reverse. The rear-wheel drive truck slipped back an inch or two; then settled forward. He revved the motor and tried again. "Shit!" he yelled, and then shut off the ignition. Phillip sat for a moment; all he could see was the hood and the black pole. *I'll be goddamned.* The door, blocked by the embankment, only opened a few inches. He unbuckled his seat belt, squeezed through the narrow space and plowed his way in back to size up the situation. The pickup was settled at about a forty-degree angle, the right side of the frame high-centered into a three-foot bank of ash scrapings. The air cleared some more, and he looked at his tire tracks coming down from the road.

If you cranked the wheel, that would've rolled it, you did one thing right. Don't forget that asshole's plate—XTOPCAD. He reorganized the two bags of groceries into even weights, locked the truck, and then waded through ash up to the crown of the road and started home. When an occasional vehicle came by, Phillip had to leave the highway and wait for the ash-fog to dissipate. One guy going his way stopped to offer a lift, causing the thickest cloud of all.

It's probably somebody from Kurt's. Enough psychos for one day —it's not far. He refused the ride, shouting his thanks through the murk toward a silhouette of the Samaritan's car, and then climbed up to the road again. What should have been a ten-minute walk to the house became a half-hour trek of stops and starts.

At home, Phillip didn't remove his filthy tennis shoes, hurrying instead to the kitchen to release the groceries from his fatiguing arms. He called several towing services without success until Parnell's Garage in Ponderosa finally called back to put him on a priority list for the next morning. Even that, Mrs. Parnell told him, depended on the wind.

It was nearly seven by the time he finished with the calls, the unnatural early darkness already closing in. *This day's shot, thanks to that bastard. You could report him. Sure, Mister XTOPCAD probably owns city hall. May as well start on the house.*

Phillip started gathering trash, checking around for signs of Ali as he worked. Out in the garage he carelessly stuffed some paper into the garbage can and slit his finger. "Damn," he said, and walked back to the kitchen, sucking on the cut. He ran cold water on the small wound and applied pressure until the bleeding stopped.

When's the last time you ate? Not really hungry. He opened some beans anyway and was stirring them when the phone rang. *Don't feel like talking, not even to her.* "Hello," he said, thinking he did a fair job of not sounding brusque.

"What's with you?" Stephen asked in a composed tone.

"Nothing, where are you?" *And how wasted?*

"South Dakota. Still looks like goddamn Iowa to me." A television blabbed in the background.

Beer joint. "You got pretty far. Where you staying?"

"Motel. Expected to see Indians by now. My friend Al here says not until tomorrow."

Hang on, Al; he's only two sheets to the wind.

"You clean up in there yet?"

Got started. "Yeah," Phillip said.

"I bet. You get my car?"

"No, the highway's still closed."

"Get it tomorrow, then."

"If I can." He stirred his beans, turning down the heat.

"It's six damn bucks a day."

"Well, maybe the State Patrol will open up just for me."

"Don't be a wise-ass." His voice was still subdued, not as sharp as his words.

Wait till he hears this. "I have to get my truck first."

"What's wrong with it?"

"It's in a ditch. I was lucky I didn't roll it; this guy passed me in— "

"Leave it to you; I thought the roads were closed."

"It rained just enough to get to town for food."

"Jesus. So you went in for some junk, but you couldn't get my car."

"Wasn't time; you don't know what it's like here." Blood resurfaced on his finger.

"You're breaking my heart."

Go to hell, Stephen. With the phone on his left shoulder, he held his hand under the faucet again.

"So, is that piece of Jap-crap still running?"

Running circles around your Chevy. "It's just stuck. Parnell's going to help me tomorrow if the wind doesn't blow."

"Why tomorrow? No reason he can't take ten minutes to pull you out."

"Are you even listening? I'm lucky to be on his list; not going to argue about it."

"Just see if you can get my damn car tomorrow."

"I'll do what I can." He shut off the water.

"Jesus Christ."

Guess that's not good enough.

When Phillip didn't respond, Stephen spoke again. "I'm a couple days away, I'll make the middle of Montana tomorrow."

Depending on beer stops.

"Are you there, for God's sake?" Stephen asked, still not overly irritated.

"Yeah." He switched the beans to simmer.

"So she's going with you to the airport?"

Surprised he remembers. "I'm not sure."

"Just don't let her drive my car."

"God forbid. How was your little talk with her?"

"You already asked me."

Remembers that, too. "You didn't tell me anything."

"All right, Miss goody two-shoes called about your health. I should've said it was none of her business."

"But you didn't." *Dad didn't.*

"I told her you look like shit." His tone was matter-of-fact. *Not in those words.*

"She's roping you in. Jesus, will you ever regret it."

"That's none of *your* damn business," he said, his rancor growing. "I'll make real sure she doesn't call you again. Let's just drop it."

"You brought it up. Just don't expect me at any kike-beadsnapper wedding," Stephen said, and then laughed.

"That's one of the stupidest things you ever said," Phillip told him, but Stephen just started grumbling aside to the bartender. *What's he saying? Ordering another one — shit.* "How much more are you going to drink, *Steve*?" He said the name with loathing.

"What did you say?"

"You heard me," Phillip said, losing control. "Drink any more and you can't drive. Why don't you just use your goddamn brains and go to bed?" he shouted.

When Stephen spoke, his voice was muffled, emotionless. "Tell you what, wise-ass, you can just go to hell." He hung up on Phillip again.

I'll be a son of a bitch. The phone in his left hand, Phillip furiously swept his other arm across the sink, forcing dirty dishes to tumble into the basin. A stoneware plate and some drinking glasses shattered on the stainless steel.

"Hah! I'll just leave that for you, goddamn ol' lush." He glowered at the silent phone and then slammed it twice into the holder, not letting go. On the second blow, the casing burst open and pieces of plastic and metal ricocheted off the floor. The broken apparatus hung by wires and screws from the wall, and Phillip dropped the dead receiver onto the counter.

What a shame, fix the other one, too. He made it to the poolroom in several long strides then lifted the desk phone as if to throw it at Stephen's Korean flag, but he stopped and just switched off the ringer. *There, I'm not able to come to the phone right now.* He walked back to the kitchen sink, sighed deeply, and felt his fury begin to steal away. Though it was nearly dark, he looked toward the ponderosa, but the window caught the kitchen lights and his reflection. *What's with you, Phillip? You just start busting shit up? Maybe you can find the cat and terrorize him some more.*

He noticed fresh blood from a long gash on the back of his wrist, and his finger was bleeding again. Phillip put his lower right arm under the cool tap water, applied pressure with his other hand, and then returned to his airy image in the window.

There you are, dumb shit; take it easy, it's okay here. Stephen was so calm: ***Tell you what, wise-ass, you can just go to hell.*** *He wasn't even that drunk, so you just piss him off anyway.* Phillip lapsed into a semi-trance and by the time he came to, the ends of his fingers were shriveled like raisins.

Go to bed. He walked sluggishly through the kitchen, then down the hallway to his room and lay down on top of the blankets. *At least I got to talk to him this morning.* Tears came again, but this time they didn't stop until his cheek was cold from the wet pillow. Before ten o'clock, he was asleep.

11

Eleven hours later, Phillip woke up with a sore arm and a mild headache. He checked the spot next to his feet where Ali liked to sleep in the mornings. *Still gone — damn.* When he lifted his arm to sit up, there was dried blood on the blanket where his arm was resting. *What the—* He touched the injury with his other hand. *Lot of blood for a little cut.*

Still drowsy, Phillip dragged his work clothes to the bathroom sink and let them fall to the floor behind. He cleaned and medicated his wrist, taping it with gauze because the wound hadn't clotted well. After dispensing with minimum necessities, he put on his clothes and ambled toward the kitchen, still groggy, looking for Ali. He stopped at the hallway window, pushed the pane to the side and took in the calm morning.

The rain cleaned off my tree; looks good. It'll be there when we're all dead and buried, a hundred and fifty feet tall, unless some dickhead cuts it down. You're wasting time; should've been out there by now.

In the kitchen Phillip grimaced at the sight of the shattered dishes and the demolished telephone. He saw the light on the stove and found his beans; they had simmered all night, turning to a round, brown brick. *Good God, you could've burned the place to the ground.* He picked up the pan and rapped his middle knuckle twice on the hard beans.

Knock-knock, nobody home. How could you have done all this? Jesus, wait until he sees that phone. He put the pan down, went to the den and called the telephone company, telling them he needed an immediate repair. When the lady found out he still had service on the extension, she reminded him about the ash fall and said it could be weeks before they got to him. He thanked her and hung up.

Story time. Tell him you were screwing around in there with a basketball, wouldn't be the first time; tape a check to what's left of the phone. Not bad — yeah, he'll kill you. Phillip went back up to the kitchen, gathered the telephone innards and put them on a shelf. He cut around the edge of the pan with a dirty chopping knife and pried on the sides of the bean mold until it clunked into the trash. He put two pieces of bread into the toaster and took an ulcer pill with a non-aspirin. After spreading the toast with margarine and jelly, he took a slice with him to munch on while he walked through the house, halfheartedly searching for Ali.

Where is that stinker? He's still pissed; some asshole threw a shoe at him. He came back to the sink and removed the unbroken dishes and the pieces of stoneware and glass. His bandage was loose; he peeked underneath and found a blotch of sticky blood. *Lucky it didn't cut deeper, or on the other side.* He tightened the dressing, looking askance at the glass fragments by the sink. He picked up the largest one, a four-inch craggy shard, and placed it over his radial artery.

They slash it right here. He stared for several seconds. *Stop this crap.* As if he'd been cut again, Phillip dropped the sharp piece of glass into the sink, fracturing it in half. *Enough crazy shit, do the frigging dishes.*

He wiped out the splinters, secured a plastic bag over his cut, then squirted in dish soap and stared at the bubbles foaming out of the hot water. *You've got the house and the truck to handle, and the yards, of course. Don't forget Warren. Shit, and the damn Chevy — it can wait another day; he won't know the difference. Nothing's going to get done if Lupe comes over, just call and explain.*

Phillip shut off the water, dried one hand and left the plastic on the other. He walked down to the poolroom, made the call and looked at the ridiculous bag on his arm as he listened to the dialing pulse. *Click, click, click, frigging click — be nice, but make sure she's not coming.* He leaned back against the pool table, eying the deep footprints he made in the back yard when he fed the birds. *Probably a week's digging just right there.*

"*¿Bueno?*"

"Lupe?"

"It's Phil," she told someone, and they burst into giggles.

God. "What's with the *bueno*?" he asked.

"We're speaking Spanish while we're canning. Mom wants me to say *chabacanos*, she says my word is too fancy-shmancy."

Great. "I don't know what you're talking about."

"You helped us pick them the other day. Apricots," she said, and the two women tittered again. "We're just being silly. I called you back twice. Were you working outside?"

"Yeah, went to town when it rained — came in late and just got up."

"They opened the highway; I'm coming on over, okay?"

No. "Lupe, I, uh— " He was going to tell her about his accident, but stopped. "Lupe, the roads are still bad here."

"I'll be fine. I made you a beautiful ham."

"That's nice of you, but, uh— " *Go on.*

"What?"

"I don't eat ham." *Oh good, that's telling her.*

"Hang on, Phil." He heard her clunking around, moving away for some privacy. "So you don't like ham?"

"No, never have."

"I didn't know that. Neither does my dad."

"He's, uh, kosher?" *Okay, yak a while, then tell her.*

"No, same as you, he doesn't like it. So what kind of meat *are* you eating, besides hot dogs?"

It's a damn health test. "Uh, fish sticks; chicken patties, and, uh—" *I get an **F**.* Phillip leaned onto the pinball machine and propped himself on one elbow.

"That's horrible," she said, "and it isn't good for you."

"Yeah, like ham or a bloody steak."

"They're okay if you eat them moderately. I have an idea about why you do this. The only meat you eat doesn't even look like it came from an animal."

Phillip thought about that for a moment. *It's probably true.* "You're right, that's pretty stupid."

"What are you saying?"

"If I don't like meat, then I shouldn't eat it. Doesn't matter what it looks like."

"Do you think you could go that far?"

"Not eat any meat? Easily."

"Phil, you probably know in Genesis it says man rules over the fish, birds, and all the creatures that move along the ground. But I think it means we're supposed to look after them more than *rule* them, and no one honors that more than you do. It's one of the reasons I care about you."

"Thanks, but I think we're *all* creatures moving along the ground." He pulled off the plastic bag and began kneading the tension in his forehead with one hand.

"I guess that's where we differ a little. I believe God has chosen man to be above animals so we can care for them."

"I see, so we eat them, make dog food out of horses and exterminate half the wild species. We're doing one hell of a job."

Phillip heard static for a few moments and brought his hand down from massaging his brow.

"You're getting upset, please try to relax," she said.

Relax, my ass. He didn't respond.

"I shouldn't have changed the subject. Phil, my point is I don't think you're taking care of yourself, especially with your eating."

"Okay, maybe I'll quit the goddamn hot dogs," he said, beginning to lose his temper.

"You know I like a good discussion, Phil, but you're not even trying to tone it down."

"C'mon, so I said *damn*."

"I mean the anger more than the words."

Enough of this. "Lupe, I don't think it'll work out for you to come over today," he said, and she was silent. *Okay, you said it. Now what?*

"Phil, have you been arguing with your father?"

Shit, how does she know that?

"Phil?"

"Yes, last night on the phone."

"Where is he?"

"Halfway across South Dakota, if he didn't stop and get hammered again in some bar."

"After you two have been arguing, you're so different."

Crap. "I've told you, I usually just listen to him shoot off his mouth. This time I got mad."

"This is the third or fourth time in the last month. I can tell; you act like somebody I don't even know."

Don't tell **me** *I do that.* "That's BS, Lupe, this is how I am," he said, more vehemently than he intended.

"No it isn't; listen to how you're talking to me."

Bullcrap. Now she expects me to apologize.

"Shorty?"

Shorty's gone to the mountains. He said nothing.

"Well, you're right, I shouldn't come over," she said, almost mumbling. "I'll talk to you later, Phil."

Lupe disconnected, and he hung up his phone. *Our first damn fight, you really handled that well. Tough shit. She can't tell me I'm like him — to hell with both of them.* He looked at the ringer switch to make sure it was still off. *Damn thing can stay off.*

He walked into the TV room and defiantly sat in his father's recliner then leaned back and turned on the vibrator. *Nice chair, Stephen, but the vibrator feels like crap.* ***I*** *feel like crap.* Phillip turned off the motor and manipulated the lever to sit up. He rocked in the chair and watched his reflection in the blank TV screen. *This is okay. It's comfortable, real comfortable — just back and forth.* He became lost in his vague image for several minutes.

Jesus, snap out of it, get something done. Phillip stood and went over to the kitchen sink and looked up at the innards of the mangled telephone. *How is Putman going to call, idiot? C'mon, do it, call them.* He grabbed his address book, took it to the poolroom and picked up the phone.

What the hell, here goes nothing. He made the call and asked Putman's secretary about the status of the lynx project, but she put him on hold. *Damn, she should know. Maybe that's good. No, that means it's up in the air.* He waited in anguish, debating all possibilities with himself until the lady finally returned. She informed him there had been some reshuffling, but the project was on. She said they hoped to call soon, within a week or two, to confirm everything. They thanked each other and hung up.

"Farm frigging house!" he said, blithe and disengaged from his gloom of a few minutes earlier. *Take care of this joint and you're outta here.* He returned to the kitchen and found his other piece of toast; it was so cold the margarine had congealed. He flung it backhand like a square Frisbee across the room, curving it right into the trashcan.

"Yeah, Stark scores two from the corner." *Stop farting around. Maybe I should turn the ringer back on. No, they won't call for days, you'll get more done without it.* He put the bag back on his hand, finished the dishes in twenty minutes and told himself he would do more cleaning that night.

Phillip got his work gloves and went through the garage for the wheelbarrow and a spade so he could start on the task of removing the accumulation from below the front eaves. The ash there was two to three feet deep from roof scrapings and heavy from the runoff. The front shrubs made for some awkward digging, but he wheeled a load down to the curb and then completed a few more trips before he thought about the time. *Must be eleven, just getting on a roll. Yeah, on a roll, funny man, you have to check on the truck.*

He ran back in to call the wrecker, and Parnell's wife told him they would get to his pickup at about noon. Phillip went back out, carted two more loads, and then set out for the highway, jogging down the cleared sidewalks to the corner and then into the street. Fifteen minutes later, Mister Parnell was hooking a cable from the tow truck to the back of the pickup when Phillip approached, sloughing through knee-deep ash.

Parnell looked up. He was over six feet tall, heavy, but not stretching the buttons of his dirty chinos and red flannel shirt. Below the bill of his oily green cap, his sociable smile was shadowed by several days of spiky black beard.

"So, Stark's boy," Parnell said, "remember you on the state team." That team, regardless of its disparate personalities, was the only one since 1958 to win a game at district playoffs. Though eliminated in the round before "state," their fame endured in Ponderosa. Mister Parnell extended his hand after wiping it on his pants.

"Morning," Phillip said during a quick handshake and then reexamined the back of his truck.

"Used to play cards with your ol' man at the VFW." Parnell checked the cable as he spoke.

Let me guess, until he pissed you off.

"Haven't seen him in a while." He turned to Phillip. "What's he up to?"

"Nothing new. You think it'll come out of there okay?" he asked, nodding to the buried wheels.

"Slicker 'n snot. Winch 'er out an' tow it, if it ain't runnin'."

"It's running." Phillip reached into his back pocket, accidentally peeling off his homemade bandage.

"Pretty bad cut," Parnell said, looking at the bloody gauze and the gash as Phillip handed over the keys.

"No, my cat just nailed me." He stuffed the mangled dressing into his front pocket.

"Don't look like it."

Another citizen with a nose problem.

Parnell slogged through the ash in his huge black boots, widening the furrow, so Phillip followed easily to the front of the pickup. "How'd you get 'er down here?" Parnell called back as he inserted the key in the lock.

"Guy in a Cadillac passed me in the middle of an ash cloud — couldn't see and went off."

"Don't surprise me; half this country now is people tryin' to get nowhere fast." Parnell opened the door into the embankment then turned around. "Yup, speeders 'n drunks, my bread and butter." His expression turned solemn. "I see too much of what they do to other folks. Anyway, you could report this since another car was in on it, but there's so much goin' on I doubt they'll care. Can you get back in there?"

"Yeah, you want the hand brake off?"

"And outta gear." Parnell handed back the keys.

Phillip squeezed through the narrow opening, rolled down the window and sat in the driver's seat facing the pole. *Damn thing looks closer, bigger.* After releasing the brake and checking the gearshift, he noticed a knot circle in the creosote-embalmed tree trunk. *Hard to believe it was growing once. I wonder where?*

"Hey, you gonna get out of there?" Parnell shouted.

"What?" *Zoned out — shit.* "Yeah, right now." He grunted his way back through and stood by the cab. Parnell was resting on the truck bed as if he were in the middle of a backyard gab session.

He probably thinks I'm on drugs. Phillip looked down at his ash-smothered sneakers.

"Looks like you barely touched it," Parnell said.

"What?" Phillip lifted his head.

"What you was starin' at, the pole. Ash must've slowed you down. You're lucky; them big poles is like hittin' solid rock, no give to 'em. Seen plenty of cars take 'em on, even on purpose."

Jesus. "You mean— "

"Yup, pole like that always does the job. I seen some bad ones," Parnell added in an open-ended tone.

"That right," Phillip said more than asked. *You'd have to be pretty screwed up to do that.* He reached into the truck bed for a candy bar he lost the day before and winced when he saw the bloody cut on his wrist again.

"You okay?" Parnell asked.

What? "Sure." *Damn, snap out of it; get him moving.*

"Anyway, happens more than you think. I had a real ugly mess just last month. It was over on— "

"So it's ready to come out?" Phillip interrupted and tossed the candy through the window onto the seat.

"Sure, let's do 'er," Parnell said, raising his brows as if perplexed by his customer's lack of interest in the gory details.

Parnell had the truck out in a few minutes, and Phillip signed the form and headed off, unwrapping the melted candy. He licked off a bite, left the rest, and drove right home to start working below the eaves of the house. Before he rolled his first load away in the wheelbarrow, a road grader came around the corner.

All right, here comes progress. He watched his piles disappear into the massive blade and become part of a hip-deep ridge at the center of the street. He went back to his own work by the house for another hour and finally stopped for a late lunch. Sitting on the porch with his sandwich and drink, Phillip watched a skip loader and dump truck begin to dispose of the long pile.

Find out where they're putting it. Taking a shovel, he walked down to the curb and waved to the driver. *God, it's the disappearing fireman from the other night. He finally gets to be the driver, goody for him.*

"How're you doing?" Phillip yelled over the engine noise.

"Not bad," the young man answered from the window, his eyes droopy and tired.

"You were out here with us the other night, right?"

"Yeah, I live here. What is it you want? Burnin' daylight," he said and pushed the gearshift into low.

So now he's the big worker. "Where you putting the ash?"

"Near town, then they take it to the dump. Gotta go."

"Will it help if we put it in the middle of the street?"

"Don't give a damn where you put it," the driver said. He gunned the engine, looked straight ahead and drove away.

Bye, neighbor. Screw him, back to work. As he walked back up the front path, Phillip surveyed his next daunting project — the ash on the immense front lawn. *That'll take forever, then there's the back — good God.* He took a long swig from the tall thermos he'd filled with pop and ice in preparation for the warm afternoon.

Leaving the jug next to his half-eaten sandwich, Phillip plunged into the work again, wheeling load after load to the street. Hardly pausing during the entire afternoon, he finally finished under the eaves as the premature dusk began to descend slowly upon the neighborhood. He started on the lawn and heard the familiar staccato of a custom muffler.

Warren? He looked up from his shoveling to see a VW beetle approaching from the corner. *You didn't even call him.* Phillip let go of his shovel as the refurbished black 1956 Volkswagen with the small oval window in back pulled into the driveway. Warren stopped between the pickup and the yard, cut the engine and stayed in the car. Phillip took off his sweaty baseball cap, stepped out of the ash and jogged over to the driveway. Warren had his head bowed, avoiding eye contact.

He wouldn't be pissed; what's with him? Hat in hand, Phillip walked through the narrow opening between Warren's car and the deep embankment of ash at the edge of the lawn.

"Hey," Phillip said from a couple feet away, "I got so carried away here, I forgot to call — sorry." Without answering, Warren looked up at him, but his usually animated face was blank and long. Phillip leaned one arm on the roof of the Volkswagen.

"You stuck in there, Big Turd?" he said as he looked in, putting his grimy cap back on. Phillip noticed that Warren's freckles had thinned and his hair had turned more brown than red, changes that seemed to fit the seriousness on his face.

Geez, the overgrown kid look is gone. "What's with you?"

"Phil," Warren said, sighing, his head down again, "why don't you answer your damn phone?"

"I had the ringer off. What's wrong?"

"They've been trying to call you all afternoon."

"Doctor Putman? They said a week; how'd they get you?"

"Your sister gave them my name," Warren said, facing him again. "But it wasn't any doctor."

What the hell?

Warren exhaled as if he were winded. "Phil, your dad, there was an accident, someplace in Wyoming."

"What?"

"He's dead, Phil; I'm sorry." Warren lowered his head.

Can't be. "How?" he asked, bewildered, and sat back into the mound, ash up to his waist. A guide stick from a lilac gored him in the spine, but he was numb to the pain. Warren extended his long neck out the window, a hand on his temple as if he had a headache.

"It's pretty grim, Phil."

"Just tell me." He looked straight ahead.

"He drove head-on into a concrete pylon. The car caught fire; some guy in a camper put it out, but it was way too late. They said he could've died on impact; let's hope so."

Phillip extracted his hands from the ash, put them on his knees and stared at his dim reflection in the polished door of the car. *There it is, like the TV screen the other day. It's okay here, back and forth.* He began rocking slightly.

Warren watched him a moment then opened the door, but Phillip's glassy eyes were fixed straight ahead, where the reflection was. Warren unfolded his long body out of the car.

"Phil?" he said, but Phillip didn't move. "There were no witnesses; they can't close the case, so they want to do an autopsy. They're guessing he just went to sleep." Warren closed the door; it made the tight click of a perfect fit.

What's he saying? Asleep? More like passed out. I told him he couldn't drink any more, told him and told him. "Like solid rock, no give to it."

"Huh? Yeah, I guess. Phil?"

"He's seen some bad ones."

"Who?"

"Parnell. His bread and butter — another damn drunk."

"Phil, you can't sit here in this crap. Let's go in."

I told him, Mom, I did, but it was goddamn Stephen.

"Phil?" Warren put a hand on his friend's shoulder.

"The drunken son of a bitch killed my dad."

"What? Who? I told you they think he fell asleep."

He looked up at Warren, shaking his head. "No, no way."

"Okay, let's just go inside." He lifted Phillip's arm, making him get to his feet, ash clinging to his clothes.

"No, I'm staying here. I'm not finished, Warren."

"Jesus, Phil, I'll help you with it tomorrow."

"I'll be in at dark," he said, standing up in the mound.

"All right, whatever you say. Be right back; I have to make a quick call." Warren went in the house.

Phillip sat back down, and a couple of tears dotted the grey powder below.

Stephen finally did him in. I shouldn't have pissed him off; it's my fault. He stared at his reflection in the car door and his body started to sway again. *It's comfortable here.*

Part Two

This above all: to thine own self be true,
And it must follow as the night the day,
Thou cannot then be false to any man.

William Shakespeare
Polonius from *Hamlet*

12

Warren sipped from a bottle of premium beer and spoke with Kurt Junior behind a couple other ex-basketball players who were watching Phillip run four straight shots in eight ball. Credence Clearwater pulsed from the speakers as Phillip circled the table confidently, slapping the side of his leg to the dependable beat.

Before the wake, Warren had cuffed the sliding doors in the poolroom together with duct tape so no one would unwittingly step out for some evening air into the half foot of ash still in the back yard. Warren and Phillip also moved out the recliners and brought in folding chairs and a long table, now covered with platters of finger food and desserts from Kurt's Western Grocery. Kurt Junior had brought it all in a new panel truck he was supposedly test driving from a car dealer in Four Rivers. A few feet from the food table, Mick Lewis ran the bar from the kitchen behind a name-brand lineup of whiskey, vodka, rum and tequila.

Stephen's funeral had drawn fewer than fifty people, the wake about thirty. Some had already left and the rest were dispersed about the two rooms and the kitchen. Three of the Stark's old friends from Seattle were there, and Phillip received a few flowery condolence cards from people he didn't know who said the ash kept them from coming. Other than Phillip's ex-teammates and two teachers from his school, most of the rest of the mourners were from Stephen's warehouse in Four Rivers. The only relatives who showed were Stephen's lone sibling, Aunt May; Ellen Stark's brother and his wife; a couple of cousins; and Phillip's sister, Joann. Not wanting her two children at the funeral, she flew in from Portland alone and was sharing the guest room with their aunt.

Joann was older than Phillip by only a year, and as kids they did some things together and had a relatively peaceful relationship. She never had to deal with Stephen's serious drinking because she married and moved to Portland before her mother's cancer. Joann's husband, a Vietnam veteran who became a policeman after the war, met her in high school when they were both on the track team.

A few years into the marriage, Richard Meyers stopped visiting the Starks with Joann. Phillip despised Meyers, who sometimes boasted of "snuffing slopes" in the war. An inebriated Stephen Stark more than once told Phillip, "That animal your sister married gives a black eye to all veterans." It was a rare point of common ground between them.

Stephen's funeral was the first time Joann had been there in almost two years because of "problems at home." She offered no details until the previous Christmas when she called her brother and revealed that Richard had beaten her. Phillip had long suspected abuse, but he bristled when it was confirmed. She insisted that Richard was fine most of the time and had been under a lot of pressure at work.

Phillip asked what she was going to do about it, and Joann said she would convince Richard to go with her to counseling.

She wrote a month later saying things were better, but Phillip wasn't convinced. Though his relationship with Joann had become strained over the years, Phillip felt some obligation to check up on her, but he didn't get around to it before their father's demise.

Stephen's partially burned remains arrived by plane two days before the funeral. His brief will suggested a simple burial, but Joann held out for a church service. Phillip told her he would agree to "the stupid falderal," only if there was a closed casket and no "useless" cosmetic measures for the body. They both resented the compromise, and he stayed away from Joann as much as he could before the funeral.

To his sister's displeasure, Phillip showed up at the last minute for the late-afternoon service in Ponderosa. He entered the small, sweltering church alone in rumpled slacks and a coral-red and aquamarine Hawaiian shirt. Phillip sat dutifully in the pew for family and close friends then sulked through the clichés about his father, who was said to be both "spiritually present" and "in a much better place."

The elderly preacher began a rambling homily, saying Stephen's death was like the darkness everyone suffered from the volcano, which in turn was like the gloom of winter, a time when faith keeps people going while they wait for the light of spring. Waiting wasn't good enough, he said, God expects you to long for the light that will return, and so grief for Stephen would eventually pass as well.

Phillip whispered to Warren that the ash fall gave the old guy some new BS for his tired eulogy. "I'm surprised he can plug Stephen's name into the right places," Phillip said loud enough that a few people heard.

Lupe told him to "shush," and after the service she went to the burial and wake with her parents. The Rosendalls paid their respects and left; Phillip was supposed to take Lupe to her apartment later. By the time she arrived at the wake, Phillip had disposed of a beer and two frozen margaritas, and he cheerfully introduced Lupe to the mourners. After that, he got another drink and took on all comers in eight ball, not losing a game to any of his old teammates.

Phillip left the table with his cue, saluting toward Warren. "Sergeant Sims, hold the fort for the champ; I seek another margarita and more attractive competition." He found Lupe chatting with Aunt May and invited her to play pool, but she said there was something she had to talk to him about.

"Plenty of time for that; relax a little, like the experts say, whoever they are." Phillip smiled at a nearby couple and took a gulp of his fresh cocktail.

Never having seen him drink, Lupe was concerned but also strangely attracted to his gregarious mood. "Okay," she said, "but then we talk."

Not today, dear girl. "Absolutely; now get comfortable for the game." By the time they walked to the pool table, she had removed her black suit coat and was listening to Phillip explain the rules. She tied her long black hair into a ponytail to get it out of the way, then the members of the "state team" who never went to state pretended not to notice when she leaned over for the first shot, opening the top of her shimmering white blouse.

"Hell of a wake, huh?" Warren commented to Kurt, thinking himself clever for referring to the event and Lupe's cleavage at the same time. They were standing by a wall near one of the stereo speakers; he had to stoop for the bantam grocer to hear him. Warren hadn't changed from his dark brown suit with a tiny yellow ribbon pinned to the lapel.

"Hell of a what?" Kurt asked, his eyes fixed on Lupe. He had skipped the funeral to handle the catering and wore a new long-sleeve western shirt and crisp blue jeans with the tall boots. Kurt took a gulp from his third Seven and Seven, a burning cigarette wedged into his fingers.

"Jesus, they call this a wake, Kurt; I said hell of a wake."

"Yeah, I guess so," he answered, still staring at Phillip's girl friend. "Damn, she's loaded in all the right places," Kurt said under his breath. "Hurts to look at, part beaner or not."

"You're a good example for me, curt-Kurt."

"Don't call me that. What're you blabbin' about?"

"You're so racially tolerant," Warren said, sotto voce.

"Gotta change with the times," Kurt answered, oblivious to Warren's sarcasm as he ogled Lupe. "Man, if she wasn't Phil's— "

"Sorry to clue you in; she's *way* out of your league."

"Horseshit." Kurt took a drag of his cigarette and formulated a question. "What's with Phil, anyway?" he asked, keeping his voice just below 'Fortunate Son' thumping from the speakers. Warren nursed a sip of beer before he answered.

"Enlighten me, Kurt."

"He's actin' like she's his sister."

"He's trying to smooth over a little spat they had."

"A fight?" he said with a light of opportunity in his eyes. "Man, I wouldn't let her get close to these horny guys, couldn't keep my hands off those— "

"Shut up. Jesus." Warren's oath halted Kurt's fantasy.

"Horseshit; just said what you was thinkin'. What's your problem, anyway?" After the rhetorical question, Kurt elongated his torso because someone had blocked his view of Lupe. "Ya' know Phil got all that booze in town an' spent more 'n five hundred bucks at the store. Told him he had too much food, but he didn't give a shit. Now look around, there's enough for three times this. He's that flush?" Kurt had to bend back his acne-pocked neck to glance at Warren.

"I don't know, Kurt." He arched his brow. "It's none of my business."

"Okay, okay, but you gotta admit he's even weirder than usual."

"No he isn't, except he doesn't drink like this."

"Nah, ya' expect that. Mitch tol' me he was lookin' for a god-damn cat before the funeral."

"His cat's been gone for days."

"So?" He lowered his voice. "It's a fuckin' cat. He's walkin' around here like it's a birthday party — look at that stupid Hawaiian shirt." Kurt downed his drink, took another smoke and redirected himself for another eyeful of Lupe.

"You'd be a little bit strange if your dad kicked off."

"Yeah, not like him." He reached down to flick his cigarette in the general direction of one of Stephen's glass ashtrays on the floor. His muddled attempt resulted in the ash falling onto the rough green carpet. "I'm surprised he's lettin' me smoke; such a asshole about that. Remember we'd call him Panther pussy?" he asked with a muffled laugh.

"No, just you and Fike."

"Horseshit. How come you didn't invite Fike?"

"Don't be stupid; not even if he *wasn't* in jail."

"He's out now. That's not my point, anyway."

"You don't have a point; you don't know Phil."

"Hell I don't." He finally maintained eye contact with Warren. "Ya' know what he'd do at the store? There'd be a mouse or a big ol' spider; he wouldn't kill it, just catch it and throw it outside — crazy, or maybe just chicken shit. When we'd get a snake out back, he'd take it away before I could get the sumbitch with Dad's machete."

"Tell me this, Kurt, does it take more balls to catch a snake or to chop it in half?"

Kurt looked dumbfounded for a moment. "Horseshit; you an' your smart-ass questions." He turned toward the game.

"You've been in that damn store too long."

Before Kurt could answer, derisive laughter passed among the onlookers as Phillip shot in the eight ball.

"See, Lupe, I told you this was easy," he said toward the pocket that swallowed the black sphere. Phillip smirked as he put his cue on the rack.

"You mean it's over? I won?" she asked, not playing innocent, just not very familiar with the game.

"That's right. You took the table from me." *Nice shot — she's happy, and later for her little talk.* "So who's sober enough to play the lovely winner?"

When Phillip offered the spot, Kurt snuffed the cigarette into his palm and dropped it toward the ashtray. He dodged his way around another potential volunteer to eagerly select a cue from the rack.

"Easy, curt-Kurt," Phillip said, and everyone chuckled.

"Time to show the lady how this is done right," Kurt said, gathering the billiard balls. "We could sure use some country-western, though."

Phillip smiled. "Nope, Credence is stacked up in there."

Kurt grumbled as he put the balls in the triangle. "At least it ain't disco horseshit," he said. Lupe raised her dark eyebrows in mild disgust as she lined up the shot to start the game.

"That's good, Kurt, she loves the subject of horses," Phillip said with a laugh, and Lupe rolled her eyes good-naturedly. Empty glass in hand, Phillip grinned as he walked from the den to the bar, his dark-blond hair tousled and his fair beard beginning to show after days of inattention.

"Look at all the munchies and booze," he said, almost blustering. "C'mon folks, Stephen wouldn't want anybody to leave here sober or hungry. And feel free to dance, plenty of room at *this* funeral." His jeering comment caused people to stop their conversations and look at him, a few with disapproval, most just smiling uncomfortably.

"Another one, kid?" Mick Lewis said to Phillip, and the guests resumed their chatter. Mick had changed from his suit into khakis and a tight yellow polo shirt, accentuating both his brawny shoulders and protruding girth. Lewis's dyed black hair wreathed his bald crown, and barbed whiskers jutted from his five-o'clock shadow. Earlier in the evening, Phillip was repulsed by an up close view of Mick's nose, mouth and ears, all asymmetrically puny for his large skull.

"Kid? Talking to me, Mick?" *The Prick.* "Yup, pour me another one." Lewis had already started a new batch, and Phillip put his wide-brimmed glass on the counter as the blender whirred to a halt.

"Comin' like a two-peckered rabbit," Mick said blandly. Two nearby women overheard the figurative language and stopped their discussion to glare at him. Indifferent to their daggers, he lifted the pitcher and poured the frothy concoction into Phillip's glass. "What happened to Steve's big gook flag? I expect he'd want me to have it."

No chance. "He gave it to the V.F.W." *Not bad, Phillip.*

"You don't say. So tell me how you got all the ash off your lawn; hire a bunch of— "

Before Mick could provide a race of laborers, Phillip interrupted. "No, just Warren and me," he said, leaving out that Warren had borrowed a small tractor to help finish off the front yard. Mick slid the drink across the bar.

"Thanks, neighbor," Phillip said sarcastically, then lifted his glass and turned toward the group. "To neighborliness!" he toasted above the din of Credence Clearwater, and nearly everyone turned toward him. Several people raised their glasses, only a few repeating Phillip's words. Most of the guests took a drink and tried to go back to their conversations.

Hell, you can do better than that. He began to raise his glass again but Joann was there, holding his arm. He glared at his sister; she let go of his arm and moved in front of him. Nearly the same height as Phillip, Joann stared straight at him like she did when they were teens, knowing full well he was touchy about being face to face with anyone.

"Phillip, people are talking." Her muffled voice was cross, but she smiled toward the guests. He took another gulp of his drink, lowered the glass and had no choice but to look right at her. Their mother used to call Joann "my pretty Scandinavian," but now the veins around her blue irises intertwined like red highways on a road map, and her stiff blonde pageboy wasn't long enough to cover the beginnings of droopy skin below her jowls.

Phillip noticed her fastidious navy blue suit coat was too tight and that her hips bulged in the skirt. *Joann the jock — presto, the sagging housewife.* He finally answered her: "Shit, this is a party, of course they're talking."

"They're talking about *you,*" she said, quiet but firm, her straight teeth clenched. Phillip saw that she had powdered the circles around her eyes and a scar on her cheek.

The bastard really nailed her. "I don't care what they're saying. Maybe you could give me some breathing room." As she moved away, he said, "What's that under your eye?"

Joann kept her voice low. "I hurt myself; it's nothing."

Bull. He let her tug him over to an unoccupied corner.

"Phillip, you could've at least worn a tie to the service."

"Stephen never wore one, so in honor of the deceased, no tie; it'd look dumb with this shirt, anyway," he said, intentionally boisterous.

"Sh, not so loud." She looked around to make sure no one was watching them.

Phillip lowered his voice to a false whisper. "He always said, 'What's the point of a fucking tie? Doesn't hold anything up.' " Then, louder and with a laugh he added, "That's one thing Stephen was right about, by God."

"Hush, Phillip," she demanded softly, "Daddy wouldn't use that kind of language."

"I said *Stephen*. Nice talking to you, Joann." He turned and took the first step to walk away, but she grabbed his arm.

"Phillip, I need t-to, uh— " She paused with a sigh. "I need to discuss something, but you keep avoiding me."

"Avoiding you? It took a funeral to get you here."

"That's a terrible thing to say. I just want to talk."

"You too? How about a game of eight ball?" he said, laughing.

"What?"

Get it over with. "Forget it. Go ahead, talk."

"We need more privacy. Let's go in the parlor."

"Nope, one mausoleum a day is enough."

"Where, then?"

Crap, what does she want? "Out there." He nodded to the back door; they crossed the TV room and entered the garage. Phillip turned on the lights, put one foot on the pickup's rear bumper and began to polish off his drink. She stood next to the driver's side door, fidgeting with the hanky in her breast pocket.

"This is lovely," she said, then put on a condescending smile. "You look thin, Philly."

You look fat, Joann. "Try *Phillip*, I'm a big boy now."

"I've always called you that. All right, I don't want to fight with you." She moved away from the truck and faced him from below their father's oil-changing shelf. Like soldiers at attention, a dozen plastic quarts of oil lined the wall behind four boxed filters, a tin funnel, and a stainless steel catch basin that shone like a kitchen utensil.

"Nice and quiet out here, huh, Joann? And neat as a fucking pin, just like Stephen left it," he said, placing the glass precariously on the corner of the truck's rail.

"I don't remember you swearing so much; or the drinking."

"Well, little Philly can swear all he wants and drink all he wants, just like drunken ol' Steve." Hands in the front pockets of his slacks, he leaned back on the truck bed.

"Phillip, my God, how can you say such a thing?"

"Still having trouble with reality, Joann? How do you think he died?"

"It was an accident, of course."

"Bingo, I knew it. All they had to do was smell his mouth; they're just being considerate until this is over. Your *Daddy* died a long time ago, except for a few brief miraculous resurrections."

"What does that mean?"

"It means Stephen the booze hound finally killed both of them." *With my help.* "That's who this party's for."

"It's a wake; and I won't listen to you talk crazy about him like that," she said in her toughest big sister voice.

"Fair enough; next subject." Still against the truck, he brought his hands up and folded his arms.

"You criticize him, and look how drunk you are."

"Well, like father like son, except he couldn't stop."

"You're exaggerating." She turned away for a moment.

"And how would you know? What about you, Joann? What are you strung out on?"

"Nothing." Her shoulders drooped and she stared at the concrete floor. "I just have my stress pills."

"Sure. So, are we finished now?"

"No," she said, standing straight to regenerate her script as the levelheaded sister. "It's nice to see Aunt May." She smiled, trying to ease the tension. "Where's my elephant?"

With a reluctant grin, he pointed past her. "It's in the shop." Their aunt could pen a Sunday crossword and in her next thought send a two-foot unpainted porcelain pachyderm for Joann's birthday and have no idea it was a white elephant in more ways than one. Before May's visits it was a tradition to ensconce the tacky gift from its regular duty as a doorstop.

"She appreciates how nice you've been to her, Phillip."

"You sound surprised. I always get along with her."

"I know that, don't be so defensive."

"Get to the point, Joann. What is it you want?"

"All right." She sighed heavily. "I'd like to know about the settlement."

Phillip stopped leaning on the truck and put one hand on the back rail. "Now the important stuff," he said.

"That's not fair."

"So what do you want from me? You'll get it all from the lawyer."

"Do you know anything about the insurance?"

"Jesus, I don't know and don't care."

"If Richard leaves me, I'm worried about supporting my kids."

"It's that bad, huh?" he asked, not sounding concerned. "And you expect me to believe the bastard didn't do that to you?" He moved toward her, pointing at her face.

"I don't want to talk about it."

Phillip shook his head in disgust and reached up to the quarts of oil and pushed them out of perfect formation.

"I don't want to be crass; this is about my kids."

Back off, Phillip, that's probably true. He looked at Joann. "I don't even know them anymore. How old are they?"

"Grace is eleven and Joshua is five."

"Really. Okay, all I know is there's a few thousand in his bank account; that should hold you over. He had car insurance and probably a life policy at work, but I don't know if any of that works for drunks who splatter into a bridge."

"Phillip, you're so cold about all this. They're all talking about how, uh, unsad you are."

"Unsad? There's a new one. I tried to tell you I've hardly seen him for years; I had plenty of time to be sad."

"Please stop it," she said, her voice still low. "You're not making sense again." Two tears raced down her cheek and she dabbed them with the hanky from her suit jacket.

"Okay, tell you what: After I get back this summer, I'll sell this damn place; the equity should handle your deal."

"That's very generous, but your job's here, you should keep the house."

"Don't want it."

"Phillip, regardless of what you think, I care about Daddy."

"That's really touching, Joann. I need another drink." He started for the house.

She returned the hanky to her pocket and followed him toward the door. "Phillip, one other thing."

Now what? He turned around to face her again and saw his glass balanced on the back rail of the pickup. *Oops, better get that.* "Spit it out, Joann."

"Your friend, I didn't quite catch her last name," she said, forcing a smile. "She seems nice, she's, uh, quite striking. Do you mind if I ask?"

"Ask what?" *This should be good.*

"I told you, her name. And, well, her background."

"It's Lupe Sirhan Farouk; she's an Arab extremist."

"That's not funny."

"Okay, her name is Rosendall; she's Mexican and Jewish."

"Please stop it, Phillip."

"That's the truth, take it or leave it. Is that a problem?"

"What do you mean?"

"You know what I mean."

"All right, to be honest, I don't think biracial couples have much of a chance."

"Very nice, Joann, a genteel version of what your asshole husband would say. Jesus, what are you waiting for with him?" He pointed at her scar again.

"He didn't actually mean to do it." Joann slumped forward, her chin touching her chest.

"Yeah, some cop, maybe he was just trying to *protect and to serve.*"

"We could still work things out."

"You know, it's really none of my business, just like Lupe isn't yours. Is that it now?"

"Yes, I'm finished." Her head was still down.

"This party stinks; maybe I'll get a drink and go out and look for Ali." He started back for his empty glass.

"That old cat is more important to you than— " She stopped mid-sentence, and he turned to her from the pickup.

"More important than who, Joann — Stephen — you — those people in there?" *Damn right he is.*

"I'm sorry, I'm not being charitable." She walked the rest of the way to the door.

"Spare me your Christian charity. Jesus, you don't believe me about Stephen; you think I'm a drunk, and my girlfriend is the wrong color; you must have some more crap to get off your chest."

"You're right, I'm too critical sometimes, but I have one more thing to say: When you act mean, Phillip, it's not really you," she said, downcast as she walked into the house.

Another vote for who I really am — shit. He reached for the cocktail glass but his elbow bumped the truck's rail, and the glass teetered and fell, making a shattering *pop* on impact with the concrete.

"Oh my, Joann, how embarrassing," he said to the mess. *To hell with her.* Phillip heard John Fogerty's voice twanging from the den about "the calm before the storm." He walked toward the music but stopped and put his forehead and palms right on the door and drummed the beat with his hands until the last chorus. *Okay, John, let's shake 'em up a little.* He walked in; the few remaining guests feigned they were chatting as they watched Lupe walk over to him. Her coat was over one arm and she had freed her hair to fall over her shoulders.

"Phil, when your sister came in, she was upset," Lupe told him quietly, taking his arm. "She went straight to her room with your aunt; what's wrong?"

"Nothing, she's a damn party pooper," he said louder than he had to, and the nearby conversations ceased again as he led her toward the bar.

"Phil, please," Lupe whispered, "they're staring at you."

"Maybe they should just go home," he said to her as they came to Mick. "Another *margarita*, and one here for *Lupita*." Phillip nearly bellowed the order, saying the Spanish as best he could, accentuating the diminutives.

"See what I can do," Lewis said, his tone acerbic, and he reached for the blender and two glasses.

"Pretty good rhyme, huh, Lupe?" Phillip said to her louder than the rock and roll.

"Phil, please lower your voice, and you know I don't want any." She let go of his arm.

"Doh-say Marguh-rituhs," Mick said, pushing the drinks forward and lecherously sizing up Lupe from head to waist.

"Right, twelve should do it." Phillip laughed and then lifted a cocktail to his mouth for a long drink while Lupe stood there nervously smoothing the coat on her arm.

Mick didn't take his eyes off her until he finally turned to Phillip. "She ain't like no *Lew-pea-tuh* I ever seen, kid," he said, and then ogled her again. Lupe glowered at Mick for a moment, then turned away and saw more people gaping at them. Phillip lowered his glass and looked up at Mick.

"What's that supposed mean?" *Prick.*

"She don't count as no Mexican, believe me." Mick raised his thick eyebrows, leering to a nearby man who snubbed the attempted camaraderie by making a cheese and cracker sandwich on his plate.

Phillip took a drink and put down his glass. "So, pri—, er, Mick, that's how it works?" he asked. Lewis just nodded, ignoring or not picking up on the intentional slip.

"Lupe," Phillip said, "shall we ask my *pendejo* neighbor why he doesn't think you qualify as a genuine Mexican-American?" He hooked his arm into hers; Lupe's piercing dark eyes were riveted on him.

"How do you know that word?" she asked, her voice barely audible. "Phil, please stop this." She let go of him.

"Sure, whatever you say, *Lupita*." He pronounced her name concisely again. "I'll just change the goddamn subject."

Lupe exhaled as if his expletive had slugged her in the gut. "You need to stop drinking, now," she said.

"No, ma'am, in fact I'll drink both of 'em." He finished his margarita and lifted hers into the air. "A toast!" he shouted. While everyone looked at him, the only sound was John Fogerty philosophizing about the rain.

"In memory of the man who died years ago — my father," Phillip said and then qualified his statement with calm, implacable hatred: "And may his impostor rot in hell."

Lupe hurried away through the kitchen, face in hands. The guests watched her, perplexed about what to do.

Mick saw all eyes directed toward him; he raised his hairy arm. "To Steve Stark, my best friend," he said, swaggering, and his glass almost scraped the ceiling.

Grateful to be off the hook, most of the group responded with, "Stephen," their drinks lifted hesitantly toward Phillip.

Son of a bitch. Phillip put the margarita down.

Maybe you should stand up to him.

Phillip was glaring at his drink. *You think I can't?* He snapped out of his reverie and faced Mick. "You didn't even know my dad." His words sounded flat, factual.

"You talkin' to me?" Lewis said, not perturbed. "Me and your ol' man was peas in a pod."

"Yeah, Stephen and Mick the Prick, the shitfaced twins. You wouldn't even talk to him if he was sober," he said, scowling at Mick, unaware that some people were gathering their things and leaving.

"You're fulla crap, kid. At least Steve could hold his damn liquor." A bottle of whiskey in hand, Lewis moved from the kitchen to the end of the counter.

"Hold his liquor? You son of a bitch, get the hell out of this house." Phillip poked his finger toward the hall.

"What did you say?" Mick asked, completely unruffled, placing his glass on the bar.

"You heard me. Get the hell outta here." Phillip stepped right up to him.

"You ain't man enough to talk to me like that, little pansy." Lewis calmly poured himself a double shot.

His voice rising, Phillip nearly spat. "Man enough to kick out an ol' lush like you." The veins swelled in his neck as he bent back to look up at Mick's stubbly face.

"You're a joke, kid." He leaned down, smug, offering his grizzled chin to his much shorter adversary. Phillip coiled his arm right away to land a blow on Mick's runt of a nose but Warren was there to grab his fist before it could release.

"Stop, Phil, Jesus." Regardless of Warren's size, he had to put both arms around Phillip's chest to hold him back.

"Lemme go I'll kill the bastard." He flailed to get free, but Kurt and another ex-Panther, Mitch, joined in to pull him back near the food, where he stumbled to his knees.

"Maybe you need another drink, Phil, relax," Kurt said, laughing as they held him on the floor.

His face flushed radish red, Phillip looked up, snarling. "*You* relax, Kurt; lemme go, goddamn it." He tried to stand, but they constrained him again, and he stopped struggling.

"Let 'im go," Mick said and downed his shot with one toss. "He'd fall on his face before he could get here."

Phillip calmed down almost as fast as he'd angered. He pointed at Mick through a tangle of arms. "You two killed my dad; sure as hell," he said just loud enough to be heard.

"What? Jesus, listen to him. You're nuts, kid," Lewis said, but Phillip turned away toward the wall.

Warren walked up to Mick. "I think you better go, Mister Lewis," he said, "this deal's over anyway."

Lewis actually had to look up to talk to Warren. "You just keep the crazy little bastard away from my house." He choked a whiskey bottle with one of his simian hands. "Shit; guess you don't need all this." Mick ambled out of the kitchen to the front door.

"He's gone," Warren said to Kurt and Mitch, who both stood up, but Phillip didn't move. Warren had shoved the TV under the table earlier, and Phillip was watching the blank screen, the top of his head inches from the meat and cheese.

Easy, it's okay here. Fixated on his blurry reflection in the TV; his torso began to sway.

Deciding to leave Phillip to himself a little while, Warren turned to the guests. The dozen or so who were left pretended not to watch Phillip rock silently under the table.

"We're going to tie it up, everybody," Warren called out. "Lot of food going to waste, please take what you want, and uh, thanks for coming." He turned back to the table to gather some trash.

What's he saying? Doesn't matter, it's quiet here; you're comfortable — nothing matters.

"Damn, he's one plastered cat," Kurt said to no one in particular, laughing again.

"Just shut up," Warren told him.

Kurt pointed to himself. "*I* didn't do anything."

"Get all your crap," Warren ordered Kurt, who gestured helplessly toward Phillip's head by all the food. "Phil," Warren said, bending over to him again.

Warren seemed amorphous to Phillip, like everyone who was still there. *They're all pissed — too bad. Not their party; Stephen's.*

"Phil, you have to move so we can take care of the food."

Stephen's party; it turned out right. His epiphany made him smile, and then he laughed out loud, almost a guffaw.

"Jesus, Phil, get a grip. You gotta move." Warren leaned down to lift Phillip's arm.

"Okay, I'm up," he said, chuckling as he stood, and Kurt began pushing food off the glass platters onto plastic plates. Warren led

Phillip back to the bar, and Lupe stood in the hall, arms folded over her chest, contemplating the spectacle.

Ms. Rosendall looks ready to kill. He saw a few other guests gawking like voyeurs at a car wreck, but he ignored them and grinned at Warren.

"Tell me what's so damn funny," Warren said quietly as he screwed a cap onto a bottle of tequila.

"I realized Stephen's party turned out just right."

"Yeah, pretty exciting there at the end. He would've loved the fight with his best friend."

"That's right, he would've loved it."

"Whatever you say, Phil."

13

The next morning, Phillip was having one of his "movie" dreams, aware of the details and able to shut it off, but the vivid scenes were too compelling to interrupt. He dreamt his missing cat was mutated into an albino mountain lion, but Ali's eyes stayed blue and gold, not pink, and he was batting around people in Kurt's store like they were catnip mice.

So much for their bickering. A man in an ash-covered suit and red baseball hat ran down an aisle with stolen meat, and Ali caught him and held him down. The dream zoomed into the man's cellophane package: NEW DELICACY - WILD CATAMOUNT - $2.49 A POUND. When the shopper tried to crawl away, Ali toyed with his legs and then flipped him with massive paws, but now the man had long black hair, metamorphosed into a woman wearing a cowboy hat.

Geez, it's Lupe. No, Ali, leave her alone. She held out the saint from her necklace for protection, though Ali had already disregarded her. *Good boy.* Lupe kissed the icon, thanking God for her deliverance. *Sure, give God the credit.* Ali started for Kurt Junior's check stand, but Phillip's brother-in-law stood there in uniform, except for tennis shoes. *Good, smack him around; see how he likes it.* Ali headed for Richard, who pulled off a sneaker and cocked his arm to throw it at the white cougar. Terrified by the shoe, Ali bolted away at impossible speed to the exit.

Crap, enough of this. But he let the dream continue into the parking lot, where the puma spotted a milking bucket next to an old man opening the trunk of a white Cadillac, XTOPCAD on its plates. Ali knocked over the milk and sucked it all up in seconds, scaring the man into his car. *Serves him right.*

Phillip watched his monstrous dream-pet vandalize his way through town without assaulting anyone. *He's searching for something.* Ali ignored a group of neighbors who were trying to help an old lady clear her yard. As soon as the people scraped up a quantity of ash, it reappeared menacingly like dull, dry quicksilver.

The mountain lion was suddenly in the Stark's back yard, leaving enormous cookie-cutter prints in the ash. Ali easily leaped the six-foot fence and approached the back of a man who was leaning over the swimming pool. *He's after Mick. Good, kill the bastard.* The great cat crouched into stalking posture and twitched inch by inch toward his prey. Ghostly, huge Ali sprung into the air and the man turned, his eyes round with terror. But he wasn't the hated neighbor; it was a sober Stephen Stark. *No, Ali!* A distorted wavy version of Mick Lewis sat at the patio table with a can of beer the size of a football in one hand; he smirked at Phillip while the cougar flung Stephen around like a rag doll.

Stop this crap. The dream lost its clarity and just a few more jumbled images raced across his mind as he came to. Phillip's gut reported in with a light pang, his back ached, and a strange dullness throbbed in his head. *No hangover with tequila — sure.* He willed himself to ignore all of it and lay still a couple minutes, his thoughts fallow until a phrase came to mind. *It was Stephen's party.*

Yeah, you acted just like him. Don't think about that now — a little more sleep. An agitated slumber slowly overtook him again.

The night before, Phillip left the house a few minutes after Mick, not telling anyone. He searched Ponderosa Estates and the surrounding countryside for Ali, then came back sobered from the long walk, ready to apologize to Lupe and Joann. Warren was the only one there, napping in a recliner after finishing the cleanup with Aunt May, Joann and Lupe. He told Phillip they waited for him and then shared a taxi to the airport, where Lupe's father met her. Before Warren left, he said he'd be by in the morning to help him get Stephen's car.

Now Phillip's sleep was disturbed again when the scene reappeared of Mick grinning on the patio. *Why's he laughing? He knows you told Stephen off. That's nuts, it's a damn dream.* Phillip opened his eyes and gazed at a fly crawling on the light fixture. He thought about Mrs. Rosendall giving him the cold shoulder when he tried to call Lupe after Warren left. *What did you expect? Warren's probably the only one who isn't pissed.* He noticed his ulcer had quieted, but his back still hurt and there was something else. *Cold — how could my head be so cold? Must be the hangover.*

Phillip sat up and slowly swung his feet below, but his heels and soles settled onto his silky Hawaiian shirt, not the carpet. The garment seemed to send a shiver up his backbone and join forces with the frigid sensation already in his head. *Jesus, so cold and heavy. What is this?* He flipped the shirt aside with his toes and put his feet on the dry, rough floor. With elbows on his knees and palms on his temple, he stared at the design in the orange and brown carpet as if he had never seen it.

It's that French iris thing — what do they call it? Flor-de-lay, something like that. His eyes traced the pattern. *Strange how one figure just melts into the next — one and then another, and another — up, then down, and...*

His head and then his whole body started to follow the rhythm. *Go again. Up, then down, and over. Why are you doing this? Curve around, and up, down to the next one. Why not? It doesn't hurt anything — it's comfortable, like in the reflection. Take the small curve up then back down, and over...* He rocked for minutes with the contours of the design. *The coldness is going. Up to the top, next back down, into the middle, up, then straight, and around...* Soon, he leaned onto his side and slept yet again.

"What the hell?" Phillip said as he awoke sometime later. The sound of his own words made him more alert. *What was all that? Rocking like an idiot. Crap, it doesn't matter.* He reached for the work clothes he'd thrown across a chair near his bed. *Should be looking for Ali; it's been four days, five maybe.* As he plodded his way across the long room, he buttoned his jeans and put on the dirty tee shirt.

In the bathroom he looked at his disheveled hair and bloodshot eyes in the mirror. *The zombie walks.* He turned and lifted the shirt to look at his sore back, and at the base of his spine there was a round black bruise about the diameter of a one-inch dowel. *How'd that happen?* Phillip faced the mirror and moved a hand across one cheek, the skin of his palm hardly grating over his soft, light beard. He could see the faint contour of jawbone. *That was never there; maybe you* ***have*** *lost a little weight — big deal. Damn, didn't check the time; Warren's coming.*

Phillip finished in the bathroom and went straight to the hallway where he spotted a dark, still object up ahead on the kitchen floor. *A carcass — Ali's back!* He dashed into the kitchen and found part of a striped garter snake on the linoleum.

"Ali, you fart, where are you?" he called, returning to the hallway. He noticed that someone during the wake had left the doors to the parlor slightly open. Phillip slid one door back and there was the old white cat, asleep on Ellen Stark's red, white and blue afghan.

I'll be damned. "Hey, boy," he said, uplifted for the first time in days. Ali raised his head, and Phillip walked over, sat on the well-preserved couch and checked his pet for fresh battle scars. *No, he's okay.* He rubbed the cat's ears; Ali purred and pushed his head into Phillip's fingers.

"Wiped out, huh, *gato*? Nice snake you brought." *You should see what you were doing in my dream.* He stopped petting, and Ali put his head on his paws and returned to his own dreams. *You deserve to be pissed, but you could've come back sooner. Too many people around.*

Conditioned to remove anything that didn't belong in the room, he reached over to pick up Ali. *Wait, what am I doing? Shit, from now on—* "This room is open," he said and shoved the other door back all the way, startling the cat awake. He looked up at Phillip.

"That's right, Ali, sleep here any time you want."

Unimpressed by his human's enthusiasm, the cat, as if on cue, put his head right back down. Phillip watched him for a few moments, then went into the kitchen. He stepped over the snake and looked out front, half expecting to see the results of his labor drowned in the mercurial ash from the dream, but the yard, of course, remained relatively free of soot.

Stupid dream. Leaning his forehead on the window, he peered out; it seemed like he was looking up from inside a concrete coliseum. Above a battleship-grey horizon, an oval of blue sky had a speckled egg of a waning moon at its center.

Clearest day so far. I feel better, but what was that crap earlier? Didn't seem like a hangover. He stood at the sink and opened the bottle of ulcer medicine out of habit. Phillip took the drug and then picked up the non-aspirin. *Don't need it.* He put the bottle down and saw Warren's little car glide into the driveway. He finally checked the clock. *Twelve ten, how could that be?*

Warren parked at the garage door, turned his head sideways and extricated himself from the car. He wore a green Oakland A's cap, hiking boots, jeans, and a white tee shirt that showed muscles he didn't have in high school. Though Warren had been around for a few days, Phillip hadn't noticed his changed physique.

Man, he's huge. Phillip hurried down to the end of the hallway and opened the door. "Hey, you still talking to me?"

"Not on the phone; I suppose you turned it off again. Damned modern inconveniences."

"I think it's on." They remained in the doorway.

"I called twice; I was running some errands — you gonna let me in?"

"C'mon." As Warren entered, Phillip peeked out and caught himself checking for the dream ash again. *Jesus, forget that.* He shut the door and turned to Warren. "Where's the blue ox?"

"What?"

"Friggin' Paul Bunyan; I didn't notice how huge you are."

"Oh. Marilyn's cooking." Warren poked Phillip's side. "What about you? You're under your playing weight."

"No way."

"Yeah? I bet you didn't eat today, ya' little shit. Did you see all the stuff in the fridge? You need to eat." They started up the long hallway.

"Great. Handy health advice from Big Turd, really big turd."

Warren stopped and pointed at Phillip's jeans. "Speaking of turds, look at you. You wash those since the volcano?"

"Wear 'em to rags. It's the latest."

"Yeah, you sound like you feel pretty good," Warren said more seriously and moved ahead.

"I do now. Man, when I woke up— "

"Hangover?"

"Guess so." They neared the kitchen. "Thanks for everything last night; sorry for the hassle."

"Forget it, Rocky," Warren said with a laugh. "You were actually going to hit that jerk-off,"

"Drunk talk."

"Bull. What the hell is that on the floor?"

"Half a snake," Phillip said as if it were a treasure. He reached into the sink for a fork.

"Your cat's back?" Warren nudged the stiffening remains of the reptile with his boot.

"Yeah, he's here, crapped out," Phillip said and slipped the utensil under the snake.

"Well, farm house; no wonder you're so damn cheerful. Ready to get the car?"

"All set, after I put some food out for Ali," he said, dropping the severed carcass into the trash.

"Yeah, he's had enough snake." Warren opened the refrigerator and salivated over the meat, cheese and desserts. "Look at all this grub. What do you want?" Warren asked, sweeping his arm along the food like a TV game-show model.

"Not hungry." He brought down a can of cat food. "Where did you put the can opener, Warren?"

"Dun'no, yr' aunt dried d' dish's," he said, garbling his words on a hunk of kielbasa. "This's great, try-s'm."

"Take all that meat with you; whatever else you want." He pulled open a drawer as Warren swallowed his snack.

"Let's see if I can guess. Now you don't eat *any* meat."

"Pretty much. So?" Phillip found the opener in with the carving knives.

"Doesn't surprise me, but you have to eat *something*."

He twisted the device on the can. "I eat, damn it."

"All right, all right, I'm going to check your phone." Warren took more Polish sausage with him to the den.

Phillip leaned down to push the tuna into a bowl; Ali was already there, nudging Phillip's arm. He stroked Ali's fur as the cat simultaneously purred and gobbled fish. *Glad you're back, you ol' stinker.* He stood up as Warren came in.

"Man, he's hungry all right. You must've been wasted, Phil, the ringer's on. You never told me what happened to this phone." Warren nodded to the wires and bare bracket on the wall.

Shit. Phillip's eyes glazed over. "Busted it."

"You mean on purpose?"

Yeah, on purpose. He stared at his cat.

"Jesus, you want to tell me about it?"

"Some other time."

"Okay, whatever you say. Ready to go?"

Don't be such a drag, Phillip. He turned to Warren and tried to sound upbeat. "Yeah, just need you to move the bug."

"No, let's take it. Maybe we'll use the truck for a hike this afternoon; we could both use a break."

"I should start on the back yard. Stephen, he— " *Not any more, idiot.* His eyebrows knotted.

"Hey, it's okay. We can do that if you really want to."

"No, I don't care if it sits back there all summer. Where do you want to hike?"

"Buzzard Point, maybe?"

"Yeah, let's go." Buzzard Point was one of Phillip's favorite places for a spur-of-the-moment excursion. You could drive all the way up to an abandoned fire lookout, then take off hiking with a minimum of gear. Warren showed him the spot the summer after they graduated from high school.

Phillip retrieved Stephen's spare keys from the hall closet. He put on his soiled baseball hat and his boots, then went out through the garage, leaving the door up for later. They got in the Volkswagen, Warren's dark red hair brushing the headliner as Phillip buckled his seat belt.

Warren laughed at him. "Ready, Captain Safety Patrol?"

"Cut loose, Big Turd," Phillip said. Warren backed out, drove down the block, and they opened their windows to let in the warm, late-spring air.

"Just what I need, Stephen's damn Chevy," Phillip said.

"Any lay but a Chevrolet. You ever drive it much?"

"Some; Stephen wouldn't ride in my pickup; hated to see it in the driveway. He called this the *goddamn kraut car.*"

"Jesus," Warren said and then changed the subject to the NBA playoffs. They casually talked basketball on their way out of the development and down the state road. When they got near Ponderosa, Phillip asked him to drive through town instead of to the junction.

Almost ten days after the ash fall, Ponderosa still had the aura of a disaster zone, most people cleaning, scraping or hauling; few of them back to their routines. The two young men observed all the single-minded activity until Warren wound the Volkswagen into last gear on the four-lane highway to Four Rivers. Though the road had been cleared repeatedly, enough of the irrepressible powder was still around to keep the sporadic traffic well below the speed limit.

"What do you think you'll do with the house?" Warren asked as he settled into the right lane at about forty.

"Sell it to some Koreans, a gift for Mick since he didn't get Stephen's flag."

"No, you wouldn't be that mean to the Koreans."

"I'll worry about the house and car when I get back from the project. They said they'd be calling soon."

"Do you know when you're leaving?"

"No. After they call, I'll just camp up there and organize my gear."

"What about the cat?"

"I worked it out with Mister Beck; he'll feed him, watch the house. What about you — finished with everything?"

"Yeah, I'm outta here tomorrow unless you need any— "

"I'll be fine," Phillip interrupted. "You've already helped enough, I apprecia— "

"Damn, check this." Warren's eyes were on the mirror. "SOB must be doing seventy." The dark streak of a sedan passed them in the left lane, blowing up enough ash that Warren had to brake and downshift.

"Just like the jerk the other day, except I couldn't see my hood," Phillip said, and then napkins, straws, paper bags and drink cups tumbled from the billows behind the other car.

"Ah, look what he left for us," Warren said.

"There's your real pig. Hell, pigs are smarter."

Warren laughed. "You sure you have an opinion on this?"

"Pisses me off. Everything's his damn cesspool."

"Yeah, but he'll get his, just a matter of time."

"You're such a fatalist." He watched a tractor in a nearby field pulling a weighted-down disk, but the ash didn't seem to plow under; twenty-foot grey clouds rolled behind the harrow. Phillip broke the brief silence. "That guy's Cadillac was in the dream I had last night."

"The guy who ran you off the road?"

"Yeah, it was bizarre; realistic at the same time."

"So what happened?" Warren gradually resumed his speed.

"A cougar with Ali's face was scaring people in Kurt's store, but not hurting them much. I sort of controlled him."

"So you let him rip up the guy in the Cadillac."

"No, some old man I saw there the other day was in the car. Ali just terrorized him a little."

"Should've been Kurt. Who else was in it?"

Stephen, and Mick. "Lupe. We spared her," he said, his face glum.

"Mighty nice of you." The traffic had become steadier, and Warren's eyes moved between the mirrors and the road.

"I called to apologize after you left; her mother was pissed but tried not to show it. I get along with her, but I think she lied. She said Lupe was there, but asleep."

"Have you told Lupe the project is on?"

"Yeah, the day before the funeral. She didn't say much, but she wasn't thrilled."

"Last night she was waiting to talk to you." His next thought made him wince. "I hope Dear John isn't on the way."

Shorty could've bit the dust. "My little impersonation of Stephen last night could have screwed everything."

"Maybe, but you don't know for sure." Warren slowed for an old wide Thunderbird that inched by on the left. They watched the ash swirl only a couple feet off of the ground.

"I'll call her again tonight," Phillip said.

"Do that, see where you stand. By the way, your sister's someone who *isn't* pissed at you."

"Oh sure. What are you talking about?"

"She wanted to apologize to you about something; even paid for the taxi to wait before they had to go."

"Crap, I was the jerk last night, not her. On top of everything else, Meyers is beating her."

"Figures. I met him just that once; reminded me of a wacko I knew in basic." Warren checked the rearview again. As the ash diminished with their distance from Ponderosa, he had increased his speed to fifty. They rolled the windows part way up to continue their conversation.

"Phil, I have to tell you something, just tell me to shut up if I'm out of line." Phillip nodded and Warren continued:

"When I called you last week, you were pretty stressed out, nothing was going right."

"I guess."

"So then to have something happen like your father— "

"Joann said I was *unsad*."

"Well, yeah, it seems like you're denying it in a way."

"Believe me, Warren, I know he's dead. Remember, you asked me once why I sometimes used his first name?"

"When he was drinking."

"Yes, but it was extreme, schizo even; the Stephen side was in charge and I don't miss him. Sounds bad, I know."

"No, I think I'm starting to get it. But why are you so flat-out pissed at other people?"

"Mick? I guess I *was* going to hit him."

"Yeah, that's what I mean, you never hit anybody in your life."

"I never hated anybody so much."

"More than Fike?"

Phillip sneered at the comparison. "No contest."

"Even I usually can't tell when you're pissed about something, Phil, but now you just let it go, even over ordinary things. And it's not because of the funeral; I noticed it at Christmas. What was going on then?" He waited for an answer, checking the road.

"The fighting started with him last fall."

"Over Lupe?"

"That was part of it, everything else just built up."

"And it's still eating at you."

Told him off, and Dad's dead. Without answering, Phillip leaned his head on the window and saw the ash-covered farms and fields only as a grey blur. His temple began to sweat where it touched the glass.

"Phil, you want to talk about it?"

No, don't bum him out. "Not right now."

"All right, maybe later. If you don't fix things with Lupe, who else can you to talk to around here?"

Nobody. Crap, stop your damn violin. He sat up. "I know a couple teachers; I can always see Kurt and the boys."

"Sure, as long as the subject is tits and ass."

Phillip chuckled. "I'll be fine."

"If you ever use your phone, remember to call me, ya' little shit."

Warren switched on the radio to the Beatles singing "Hey Jude." They listened, watching the light traffic.

"Heard this a hundred times, never paid attention to the words," Phillip said, and listened some more. "What's *that* supposed to mean, give up who you are for love? What crap."

"Okay, here's the *nah-nah-nah-nahs*, no more lyrics."

To Phillip, the song's refrain drug on endlessly while he stared at the barren countryside. When they arrived at the airport, he marveled at the mere inch or so of ash in the undisturbed areas.

After arranging for Stephen's car, Phillip followed the Volkswagen into Four Rivers.

The city had recently surpassed a hundred thousand in population, due mainly to mining, lumber, agricultural commerce, and the state university. Unlike Ponderosa, the business areas were all active and clear of ash, so Warren insisted on stopping at a pizza place before starting for home. He asked Phillip to choose the toppings, and they took their drinks and plates to a table and waited for their order. When a petite but plain girl brought the mushroom-and-black-olive pizza, she flirted with Warren as he fumbled with napkins from the dispenser.

"You're so tall you must be a basketball player," she said, placing the pan between them and picking up their plastic number. Warren smiled as she left.

"She's so short, she must be a miniature golfer," Phillip said.

Trying not to laugh, Warren peeled off two pizza wedges for his plate. "Phil, that was cold. I think she heard you."

"No she didn't. Don't you get tired of that crap?" Phillip slanted his eyes toward her.

"What, girls smiling at me? No, especially since it never happened until I was twenty-five."

"You know what I mean."

"Take it easy, you're getting pissed about nothing again." Warren stretched a taffy-like string of mozzarella from the pizza slice to his mouth.

"Yeah, maybe you're right."

"Eat," Warren urged with his mouth full, already fingering his next piece. "This pizza's pretty good," he said between bites. They ate quietly for a few minutes and Warren finished his fourth slice while Phillip only nibbled on his second. "So this is how you order it if you're a vegetarian?" Warren asked.

"Don't know, maybe they order the vegetarian pizza."

"Smart ass, I thought you were some sort of vegetarian." Warren lifted another wedge off the pan.

"I'm not anything," Phillip said.

"What the hell does that mean?"

"Not vegetarian, Bulgarian or Presbyterian — name it, I'm not it." He drank some soda, pushing his pizza aside.

"That's pretty heavy, Phil, but you're wrong. You'll always be a Panther through and through, black and white, fight, fight, fi— " Warren chewed around the last *fight*.

"Right arm, Big Turd, I'll always be a frigging Ponderosa Panther." Phillip managed a slit of a smile.

"You won't even be a little shit if you don't eat something." Warren lifted the last slice to his friend, who shook his head and then sipped soda while Warren finished off the order, including what was left on Phillip's plate.

Phillip followed Warren onto the highway to Ponderosa but had to stop halfway at the rest area when his eyelids grew heavy and his head shivered a little, like in the morning. After resting a few minutes, he rolled the windows all the way down and continued the trip. When he arrived at the house, Warren was parked in the driveway, his head back on the seat.

Phillip drove by him and parked inside next to the pickup. "Want black beauty in here?" he called back.

Warren leaned out of the window. "No. What happened to you? I almost turned around."

"Got drowsy, had to stop a sec." He got in the truck and backed out of the garage. "Close up for me, okay? I'll get my stuff." He hurried to his room for his daypack, which was ready with the bare essentials though he hadn't been hiking for weeks. Phillip added binoculars, camera, an Audubon pocket book, and a thick manual for keying wildflowers. He took his red camping knife from the desk and slipped it into a front pocket of his jeans.

After filling his water bottle in the bathroom, he rushed to the front door. *Wait; check Ali.* He dropped the equipment and walked over to the parlor. Peeking in from the doorway, Phillip saw Ali had scrunched up the Afghan and was nearly camouflaged by white yarn. *Man, still asleep — he's okay. Just go.* He returned to his gear, got his windbreaker from the hall closet, and then jogged out to the truck to deposit his pack under the tarp in back.

Phillip climbed into the cab snickering at Warren, who was sitting up straight, knees above the dashboard. "Hold on, Ichabod," he said, smiling, then pulled the lever to push the bench seat back.

"Thanks." Warren adjusted his legs to the extra room, his right elbow protruding way out of the open window. "Can you still reach the pedals, Phil?" he asked.

"Funny. You know, you're too damned wide to be Ichabod. You look more like Bill Walton." Phillip was still grinning.

"Wish I could play ball like him. It's about time you laughed at something. Let's roll, wise-ass." Warren attempted to snuggle into the headrest as Phillip backed past the Volkswagen and into the street.

At the Ponderosa Estates entrance he turned right, heading away from town in sparse traffic. While Warren dozed, Phillip saw the depth of ash gradually decrease at the side of the road. In another ten miles, the pines began to show up amongst the sage, and he came to a roadside grocery with a pretentious sign: THE BLUE VALLEY INN. Two long curves after the small store, they arrived at the crest above Blue Valley.

My God. He slowed and then coasted the truck about a hundred yards down the slope before pulling to the side of the road. "Hey, check this." He coaxed Warren with an elbow until he opened his eyes to take in the scene.

"Yeah, farm house," he said then returned to his nap.

Blue Valley had overcome its thin layer of ash to become a spectacle worthy of the day it must have been named. The four-mile-long valley floor, probably a primordial lake, hosted a scattering of ponderosa pines, a few scraggly oaks and an occasional dwelling, but the rest of it that day was primarily lupine and chicory. The only divergent colors in the expanse of blue wildflowers were random dabs of burnt-orange and dark-red paintbrush. Phillip realized the colors were even more striking because they didn't have to compete with green undergrowth that was mostly blotted out by ash.

After turning off the motor, Phillip got out of the truck and took the wildflower book and the small camera from his pack. He had once been a more serious photographer but gradually decided that preoccupation with the equipment was less important than experiencing what he was trying to shoot. Nevertheless, as Phillip took a snapshot of Blue Valley he again regretted that he hadn't repaired his old thirty-five millimeter camera.

He took a second photo from a different angle, finishing the roll, then walked across the road and bent down to inspect the lupine, which seemed to be a truer blue than the purplish blossoms he was accustomed to elsewhere. Like the lupine, the unopened buds on the skeletal chicory stems were powdered with ash. He saw that most of the paintbrush had yet to bloom and surmised that in a couple weeks the floral lake would reverse into a riot of orange and red, the leftover blue wildflowers filling in as a sobering accent.

"Having fun?" Warren called from the truck.

"Yeah, life goes on. Conditions must've been perfect."

"Take your time, walk on in, that's what we're here for."

"No, I'm coming," Phillip said, and returned to the truck. "I took most of this roll during the ash fall, just finished it."

"I'll want to see those." Still groggy, Warren leaned back to snooze again while Phillip quickly checked some information in his wildflower text. He turned back onto the road and drove slowly, still enjoying the meadows, which were interspersed by only a few home sites, mostly cabins or trailers on large acreages.

Rock escarpment rimmed the left side of the valley, but the opposite ridge was thick with ponderosas and the beginning of the firs. Hop Wing's and the "museum" awaited travelers at the far end of the valley, twenty-five miles before the ski area. Phillip would be taking the Buzzard Point turnoff into national forest ten miles past the defunct ranch.

The Ski-Eden road had always been Phillip's main access to the mountains, and he usually stopped at the restaurant on the way up or back for some sweet and sour vegetables over rice. Hop Wing's was now referred to laughingly in Ponderosa as "the only sign of life at the ghost ranch," but many townsfolk were more than willing to take a scenic ride through the foothills for some passable *moo goo gai pan*.

As Phillip approached the end of the valley, the stands of pine grew closer together and most of the flowers converged toward the sunlight by the road. Without coming to a stop, a full logging truck entered the highway from the ranch.

When did that start? Phillip slowed for the semi and signaled to turn right. In his rearview mirror, the flashers of a cement truck indicated that it was also entering the old development. *What is all this?* It was over a month since he'd been to Hop Wing's; he didn't recall anything unusual.

At the entrance he slowed some more and made the turn, the cement truck right behind. The log arch was the same, PONDEROSA RANCH burned into the wood, the poles on both sides adorned with rusted branding irons. He drove by the pines that hid the ranch from the highway and discovered that the gravel road was leading to construction equipment up ahead.

Good God, they're not dumb enough to try this again. Phillip came to a two-sectioned mustard-colored earthmover, huge windows up front and a monstrous scoop of a body in the rear. It waited like an enormous sleeping insect, dwarfing a nearby faded-yellow road grader. He drove around and pulled over to the side of the road behind a car and three pickups.

After the cement truck passed, Phillip turned his head toward Hop Wing's. The restaurant appeared to be closed and the gift shop/museum was boarded up. The old false-fronted buildings had been razed, and in their place a labyrinth of wood foundation forms sprawled over the property, the rebar standing erect like wiry braids. The just-arrived cement truck waited, its cavernous drum revolving while an earlier arrival deposited its cargo down a trough. About twenty laborers worked the sloppy concrete or were occupied elsewhere in and around the foundation.

"Here already?" Warren stretched out of his slumber.

"Not quite, Sleeping Beauty. We're just at Hop Wing's."

"You hungry now? I could probably go for some dessert."

"No, take a look."

"What the hell?" Warren said as he took in the activity and equipment. Another loaded logging truck sped through the development, the timbers on top shifting precariously with each bump in the road. The rig momentarily blocked their view, and they turned away from the dust. Phillip saw an undisturbed meadow not far from the road where thousands of dollar pancake-sized bright yellow sunflowers waved in the light breeze.

Need to check out that field. He looked back at the construction and watched three men lug away a six-foot plywood red horseshoe, a relic of the old miniature golf course.

"What do you think, Warren?"

"Got me; that's a lot of foundation."

"What's with all the trees they're taking out?"

"Private land; maybe they're logging to make ends meet."

Phillip turned the wheel to the left and crossed the road, heading for two small trailers next to the work site. To get there, he drove around a maze of construction materials piled up in the parking lot. A couple dozen trucks and cars were lined up diagonally to the trailers.

"Son of a bitch, there he is," Phillip said, approaching a long white sedan. "It's my friend. Look."

"Who?"

It was the Cadillac, XTOPCAD on its Florida vanity plate.

14

"I suppose you're going back over there," Warren said as Phillip parked in some shade by the sunflower meadow.

"We need to see what's going on." He shut off the motor.

"Who the hell is *we*, you and the mouse in your pocket?"

"Come on, Warren." Phillip opened the door, got out and reached back for his wildflower manual.

"What'll you do if you find the guy, throw that at him?"

"I'm just going to check out this field and see what they're up to."

Warren leaned back. "I'll wait here; behave yourself."

"Yes, mom." Phillip closed the door and glared at the bustling site. *The prick runs me off the road to get to this mess. Later for the meadow, ask XTOPCAD a few questions.* He scraped the ground with the toe of his boot. *No ash at all.* Phillip headed across the lot for the trailers.

He came up to the side window of the extravagant white car. Soaped onto the glass in precise script there was a phone number and: FOR SALE: '77 CADDY - SERIOUS INQUIRIES ONLY. *A little **serious** justice, scratch the sucker one end to the other.* Phillip felt the thick knife bulge in his pocket. *Yeah, get real.* He stepped around a three-wheel all-terrain motorcycle and walked to the trailer with a black OFFICE sign.

The one-rail porch was the square makeshift kind they use in trailer lots; the stairs wobbled as he took each step up to the door. Phillip decided to knock, and a woman's voice called for him to come in. He entered the small office and the secretary glanced up from her typewriter, ignoring him. He let go of the door and saw a cigarette on her desk; the air was thick with smoke and sweet perfume.

Aak. He turned away, coughed, and she continued to peck at the keyboard. Phillip quickly surveyed the small room, its cheap desk and chair, two steel filing cabinets, a copying machine, and an entrance to the inner office. In block letters, a black and white plaque spelled MR. LOPES above the doorway. *Lopes? Not with a **Z**?*

Still acting like no one was there, the secretary stood to open a file drawer, her patent leather high heels clicking on the linoleum with each footfall. Below a coiffure of congealed yellow hair, she masked her milky face with pink rouge, eyeliner and crimson lipgloss. Her willowy body was encased in a synthetic white pullover and a tight beige skirt.

God, somebody's idea of loveliness, she could be twenty or forty. The woman took a step back toward her desk and finally looked directly at him.

"Excuse me," he said, surprised how meek he sounded. She peered myopically down her nose, as if to a lower species. *My grubby clothes; we disgust each other.*

"Well, can I help you?" she asked.

Thanks, oh office queen for recognizing I exist. "Sorry to bother you, I was— "

"If you're looking for work, we aren't hiring right now, but you can take an app." She pointed the lacquered blood-red nail of one forefinger toward a small rack of papers on a file cabinet. Her thin black eyebrows rose with a second thought. "I'll save you the time, he only hires Mexicans for general labor." She sat back down to her work.

No, he hires illegals from anywhere — slave wages in cash, like Mick. "Not looking for work. I was wondering if you could answer a couple questions for me."

"What is it you want?" Her bony fingers stopped typing and she looked at him again, her powdered lashes flapping once. She flicked the cigarette in the ashtray, her cold body language saying, "This better be good."

"Can you tell me what's going on with this construction?"

"First phase of Ponderosa Ridge Resort — indoor pool, cocktail lounge, everything," she said with a hint of enthusiasm, finally resigned to put up with the distraction for a moment.

"And outside? What are they using that dirt mover for?"

"For the lake." The lady took a drag of her cigarette.

"A lake? Where?"

She crushed the butt in her ashtray. "Some empty field."

"The big meadow with all the sunflowers?"

"How would I know? They start on it after they clear the trees for the bunny slope."

Good God. "Okay, so what's the lake for?"

"It's like a big fish pond. If you don't have any more questions, I'll get back to work."

"I have a question about the permits."

She picked up her phone and punched a button. "Someone to ask about your permits, Mister Lopes." The secretary said the name as if it rhymed with *ropes*. She listened a moment before hanging up, then returned to her keyboard. In a few seconds the door to the office opened and a man in a western suit, bolo tie and cowboy boots stood in the doorway. Without the heels, he was probably three inches shorter than Phillip.

"Good afternoon, I'm Xavier Lopes." With an ingratiating smile, he pronounced his surname like the secretary did. He also spoke with a light accent and ran his words together as if he were impatient for the sentence to end. In his late forties, Lopes' fair skin was rough and pocked; he had thick black eyebrows, closely trimmed grey hair and a dark, neat moustache. He began to lift his arm to shake hands, but when he got a closer look at Phillip, he held the impulse.

Mister XTOPCAD — little man, big car, shit-eating grin. "I'm Phillip Stark. Could you answer a couple of questions for me?" he asked, still near the secretary's desk.

"Please come in, Mister Star," Lopes said, his five words spoken like one, and he turned to go back in his office.

Phillip walked to the door. *Don't we sound so busy and important? Florida plates, he's probably Cuban.* He entered and remained standing while Lopes closed the door and circled his unpretentious black metal desk. It was an austere room — discount furniture and no decorations save one, a gory two-foot crucifix on the back wall. *Ah, a true believer.*

Lopes' white cowboy hat hung from a peg near the icon of Jesus. The desk was supplied with a phone, calendar pad, file rack, in-and-out basket, and a parade watcher's miniature U.S. flag. On the developer's yellow legal pad, an expensive gold pen lay next to a mechanical pencil and a silver dollar. The coin was drilled with three holes, one linked to Lopes' keys, the others to a shiny black prayer stone and a rabbit's foot.

This creep is extra superstitious.

"Please have a seat — I'm afraid we're not much to look at so far; are we, Mister Star?" he asked from his plastic chair, speaking again without pauses.

No, not much at all. "It's Stark." He sat in a metal folding chair, his book on his lap.

"Yes, of course," Lopes said slowly, and then he resumed his rapid-fire speech. "Our new office will be a bit more comfortable. Now how can I help you?" He twisted his keys and amulets around an index finger.

"Looks like you lucked out on the ash fall."

"Yes, it could've put us way behind schedule; it's a good sign when God chooses to spare someone from such a disaster."

***A good sign**, hot damn.* "So, is that your Cadillac?"

"Yes, are you interested?" He smiled at that prospect.

Something funny? Phillip shook his head.

"Yes, of course," Lopes said again before speeding his pace. "You seem to be more the outdoor type Mister Stark. Perhaps you can help me — you see, I need a car that is rugged but nicely equipped for when I'm back in civilization. Do you have a suggestion?" Lopes took a breath and grinned.

"Sure, try a Gimmy." *It'll break down in a month.* "Maybe you could tell me how you got permits for all this and why nobody knows about it?" he asked, contempt slipping into his voice. *Easy, or you won't find out squat.*

"My, my, that was a quick change of subject. We have no secrets, Mister Stark; we're just low-key for a while. You aren't from one of those environmentalist groups, are you? The public is starting to think they're destroying jobs to save a few trees, and I suggest— "

"Listen, I'm not from any group, I live here, and I, uh, have concerns about what you're doing."

"I see. Well, that's really too bad, our hundred sixty acres border private land on three sides, all zoned recreational business property; I don't have to do this but I'll show you a file with permits, deeds, everything." He paused to breathe. "Then perhaps you can go home, I imagine to a nice little cabin in the woods." With a condescending smile, Lopes lifted the file from the desk and handed it across to his unwanted visitor.

Phillip opened the manila folder. *Give him something to chew on.* "Has anyone bothered to tell you what locals call this place?" he asked, skimming the papers.

"No, but I think you're about to tell me."

"The ghost ranch; just ask around." Phillip looked up to see the man's smile fade a bit. *Spooked him a little — a babe in the woods.* "So, how did you get clearance for a ski area and a lake so fast?"

"A trout pond, Mister Stark; and the rope tow is little more than a kiddy ride for our skiers to warm up with the children before they drive up the mountain. As for the permits, Doctor Maxwell is my partner and he's one of the previous owners; we didn't have to start from scratch."

"Very convenient. These papers are all made out to Maxwell and Javier Lopez." Phillip returned the file to his desk and sat back.

"My legal name." His tone was turning blunt.

Ashamed of something? "You're from Florida, Mister Lopez?"

"Lopes. Yes, not that it's any of your business."

"Cuban background?" *Squirm, asshole.*

"Argentina, but that's also none of your business."

"True, but this development is; it affects my research up here," he lied, holding up the keying manual as if it were related to his work. "Most people in this area won't like your little project. Hop Wing's wouldn't make a dime without customers from Ponderosa."

Lopes smirked with confidence. "A dime is about what it did make; Hop Wing's will soon be The Ridge Barbecue; you might be interested to know that several other local businessmen supported my minority enterprise loan."

"Minority? You're ashamed of your own name." *Take it easy.* Phillip heard thudding footsteps outside on the porch.

"Mister Stark, my patience is at its end; you don't have any business here; I'll thank you to leave my property."

One bit of business —freak him a little. "I'd like to explain my concerns about— "

"Your concerns are of no consequence to me."

"You'd want to know that the backcountry east of here is— " Phillip stopped his sentence as Warren walked into the office. His tall, burly frame filled the doorway, and the developer's eyes opened wide with alarm.

"He wouldn't listen to me," the secretary said, whining from behind the open door.

Lopes was clutching the charms on his desk. "What is it you want here?" he asked Warren. Phillip saw his other arm reach into a desk drawer and stiffen.

What the hell?

"Easy there, big shot," Warren said, extending his palms downward in a calming gesture. "Barbie wouldn't let me in; I just came to get my friend." He walked over to Phillip, who watched the man's arm relax.

It's a gun — son of a bitch.

"I see," Lopes said, turning to the secretary. "I'll handle this," he told her, and she squinted at the intruders as she left. Lopes slowly placed his hand back on the desk then had to tilt his chair back to speak to Warren. "It's Mister Stark here who wants to argue and insult me; I want you two to leave now, and don't trespass here again." He was back to his staccato speech, but the smile was gone.

"Let's go." Warren gently pulled Phillip's shoulder.

Nail the bastard. "Just a second," he said, composing himself as he stood to face Lopes. "I started to tell you something— "

"If you don't leave now, I'll call the police."

"We're leaving." Phillip took one sideways step toward the door. "Hasn't anyone told you about the throwback cougar in this valley?" he asked, taking another small step.

"Your motive for saying such a thing is obvious; you don't frighten me; now leave."

"I admit I don't care if he scares the hell out of you," Phillip said.

"I'm out of patience with this nonsense." Lopes reached for the phone.

"I'm trying to explain that I'm doing my doctoral research up here in albinism," Phillip said, holding up the wildflower manual. "We're searching for that cougar's lair in these hills. My friend is helping me; he'll tell you." He turned to Warren, who looked puzzled for only a moment.

"He's a zoologist, specializes in wild cats. Let's get back to work, Phil." Warren sounded staid, convincing.

Lopes held the receiver in one hand, blocking the dial tone with the other. "I still doubt your sincerity, Mister Stark, but repeat what it is you *say* you're studying."

"Albinism, this puma is an albino. He's larger than normal, a throwback, we estimate more than a hundred twenty kilograms," Phillip said with a professorial air; then switched to a casual tone. "He uses this ridge to roam from below here on up to Buzzard Point into the national wilderness. I've only seen him once myself, in the moonlight for a few seconds; his white fur made him look like a ghost. He scared *me*, and I was looking for him." The developer's face blanched, and Phillip paused. Lopes put down the phone and moved his hand slowly over to his talismans.

The SOB's listening now. "Sometimes I dream about him. The other night in a dream my car was parked in the woods, and the cougar snuck up real close and, well, it was just a nightmare, but I've learned to pay attention to such things." *Right, Mister X?* "Fortunately, I do most of my research in the day." He glanced at Lopes' hand stroking the rabbit's foot. "This much is for sure: You're expanding up that ridge, smack into his territory, and I expect the lion to defend his ground. Whatever you have in that drawer won't do you much good in the dark." He nodded to the desk.

When Phillip stopped, Warren managed to keep a serious face though he expected the man would laugh at them. Lopes sat there speechless, considering Phillip's words, his fingers now fondling the prayer stone.

"So your little tale is over and now you'll leave," Lopes finally said, trying to sound like Phillip's story didn't bother him. He stood and put his hand on the phone again.

He bought it, all right. "Yeah, we're on our way."

Lopes sat back down and swiveled his chair away from the young men, facing the back wall and the crucifix. His elbow stuck out as he crossed himself.

Yeah, ask God for a sign, you bastard. Phillip followed Warren out the door.

"You better get off this property now, or I'm calling the cops," the secretary said, but Warren had already pulled the door open and was ducking through the entrance.

"Go file your nails; we're gone," Phillip said with a snarl and walked out behind Warren, who was negotiating the wobbly stairs. Phillip grabbed the railing with both hands and vaulted himself over the two-by-four all the way to the ground, just a few feet from the white Cadillac. His face felt warm, flushed; there was a high-pitched hum in his ears, and his neck throbbed.

Man, buzzing like crazy. "Warren, I think I'll lower the price on this junker." He took out his Swiss Army knock-off. "If he can pull a gun on us, I can decorate his car."

"Put that damn thing away," Warren said, but Phillip flipped out the corkscrew and extended his arm to a back door. Just before the knife touched the paint, he pivoted around.

"Gotcha!" Phillip yelled, laughing as he lowered his arm.

"Shit, Phil, that's enough." He turned toward the office to be sure no one was watching them.

"C'mon, you knew I wouldn't do it."

"Jesus, just be quiet." Warren took the knife, and pushed him toward the pickup. "After last night, I wouldn't put anything past you."

"You mean Mick? That's different; he's fair game. Ya' know I've wondered if dog turds would float in his swimming pool; I think it's time to find out." He took several quick strides as if they were the first steps to carry out his plan.

"Good, keep moving." Warren checked the trailer again.

A shudder crept up Phillip's spine, his exuberance waned and he walked slower. *What the hell?*

"Your keys," Warren said, catching up at the gravel road.

The coldness was settling into Phillip's head; he put his hand to his temple. *That weird chill again.* "What, Warren?"

"Give me your damn keys; I'm driving."

"Okay." He handed them over. *It's colder.* "Let me get my coat." Phillip walked to his pack in the truck bed, then climbed stiffly into the cab with his windbreaker. He zipped on the coat and pulled the flimsy hood over his head. Warren drove off, tossing over the knife. Phillip picked it up and focused on the white shield imbedded in the red plastic.

So cold. Hunching away from Warren, Phillip began to trace the knife's emblem with the tip of his forefinger. *That's good, do it again; it might help.*

Warren turned right at the gate, drove a few miles, then pulled off into a wooded turnout and killed the motor. Phillip still stared at the knife, his finger moving over the design. Warren looked at him but waited before he spoke.

"Phil?"

"What?" He sat up, the knife in his palm.

"Are you okay?"

"I'll be all right." The chill had subsided but he felt drowsy.

"Then put that damn thing away."

Phillip gaped at the knife. It seemed incongruous in his hand, and too heavy for its size. *Why was I doing that?*

"You look like you need some rest, Phil."

"Yeah." He slid the knife into his chest pocket.

"I could use a few more Z's," Warren said, pretending to start another nap. He saw Phillip put his head down, close his eyes and fall into an agitated slumber. Warren watched the forest until Phillip woke up about twenty minutes later.

"Phil, let's bag the hike and start back."

"Whatever you think." He stared at the trees as the pickup turned around and headed for town. After a couple minutes, Warren asked if he felt better.

"I'm fine." He was sitting up straight and had removed the hood. The knife in his shirt pocket seemed to weigh on his neck; he moved it to his jeans. "I guess that was pretty weird at the ranch — sorry," he said, looking at some mountain daisies by the road.

"No skin off my nose, but it *was* off the wall. So what was the deal with the albino mountain lion?" Warren asked, shaking his head.

Yeah, what was it? "I was only trying to scare him a little at first, but the gun thing pissed me off."

"I'm not so sure there was a gun."

"I'd bet on it. I got carried away after that; you backed me up pretty well," he said with a hint of accusation.

"You knew I wouldn't let you hang, even if it was nuts."

"The truth is a cougar wouldn't come anywhere near a busy place like that. It wasn't all BS; there really are albinos. They've been spotted in the Sierras, near Reno."

"Sure, Phil, just over the hill. What I don't get is why he didn't laugh right in our faces; he ate it up."

"Remember those people in Sageview a few years ago who swore the devil was at a church dance; said they saw his cloven hoofs? This guy's that superstitious." His gut gnawed as Warren slowed for a logging truck leaving the ranch. "Speak of the devil," Phillip said, glaring at the semi.

"Yeah, well, you're confronting people left and right. It isn't like you."

Phillip noticed his loose seat belt, pulled it across his lap and buckled it. "Maybe it *is* like me," he said quietly. *Tell him about Stephen?*

"I don't buy that, Phil, but when you tell people off this is how it is; they get pissed; you have to expect it. So you scared the living crap out of him, serves him right, but was it worth it?" He passed an old war-surplus Jeep and shifted into fourth on the straight stretch into the valley.

"What do you mean?"

"Your revenge didn't change anything, so it better feel pretty damn good."

"It did then, but now it feels like I scared some little kid who thinks a tree is a monster or something."

"I knew it. When he finds out you jerked him, he blows it off and you have all this regret; he wins. Before you take on somebody else, decide if it's worth it. If it isn't, then *you* blow it off before you say anything. End of sermon."

"Yeah, you're right." Phillip looked out at Blue Valley, flush with wildflowers. *I should've stayed here.*

"You want to stop here again?"

"Yeah, thanks, maybe a couple minutes at the other end."

"Phil, when we talked about your confrontations this morning, you held back; you want to give it a shot now?"

Go on. "I told Stephen off again right before he died." He spoke slowly with pauses. "Like you said, I didn't think first. The last thing he told me was go to hell, and I busted the damn phone. He wouldn't have tried to drive if I— "

"Wait a minute, you can't blame yourself for that."

"I told him straight out to sober up; he drove off to spite me. I shouldn't have pissed him off." Phillip's ulcer constricted a little.

"It wasn't your fault, Phil. Look, it's not as simple as you make it out. You couldn't know everything that made your dad tick, and like you said last night, Mick made things worse. You have to stop feeling guilty about it."

"It's not a feeling. I did it — cause and effect. I don't feel anything."

"You sure as hell feel the anger. When you're up at your project, you can mellow a little; sort some things out."

"Yeah, maybe I will. Another reason I'm ready to go."

15

Leaning on the Chevy's trunk, Phillip watched Warren drive away. A light ash cloud trailed the beetle like grey exhaust, as if the perfectly tuned little engine were burning oil. Before he left, Warren asked again if he was going to be okay, and Phillip reassured him, promising to call before leaving for the mountains.

Warren's car disappeared around the corner. *There he goes. So? He's got his own life; you can't bleed him dry.* Phillip left the pickup in the driveway and started across the lawn. As he walked, he saw the grass had hardly grown above the ash residue. *Needs water.* Nearing the ponderosa, he noticed something glistening on its trunk and was about to make a close inspection when he heard a faint ring through the open kitchen window. *Looks like sap — get the damn phone.*

Phillip ran to the door and opened it. *Slow down, you're not going to make it, anyway.* He dropped his pack in the hallway and walked to the den; the phone was still ringing. Ali followed him and jumped up to stretch out on the cool glass of the pinball machine as Phillip lifted the receiver.

Probably the lawyer. "Hello," he said, his tone surly.

"Mister Stark?" a high-pitched woman's voice asked.

"Yes." *What are you selling?* He massaged Ali's ears.

"Good, I caught you, I was about to hang up. You're hard to reach," she said, sounding annoyed about wasting the time.

"I've been out a lot. Who is this?"

"Sorry. Phyllis Meisner, I'm an instructor in Doctor Putman's department; she asked me to call."

Phillip stood straight. "Uh, right, sure." *This is it!*

"I'm calling to update you on the status of the proj— "

"Status? I thought you were calling about arrangements."

"Not yet, but we're still planning to go ahead."

"That's great!" he said with more zeal than he intended.

"We appreciate your enthusiasm, Mister Stark."

You're a dipshit, Mister Stark. "Sorry uh, I, it's Phillip."

"Yes, as you know, we'll be in the northern range away from the ash, which is why we've been able to hang on this long. But we've had some movements of staff to help other departments with zoological issues related to the volcano. Unfortunately there will be a delay, and then we'll probably have to cut it to six weeks. I'm sure you understand."

Damn. "Of course. How long of a delay?"

"We hope only about a month."

Early July, that cuts it close. "When will you know?"

"We'll try to contact you within three weeks, one way or the other. Sorry I don't have better news right now. So that's it, unless you have other questions."

"No, I'll be expecting your call; I'll have my phone on."

"Excuse me?"

Dumb. "Nothing, thanks for calling."

"Thank you, Phillip. Good-bye."

"Bye." *Your amazing volcano is screwing the project. Still a chance for six weeks; that's extra time for Lupe. First apologize, then tell her about the delay; it's what she wanted; maybe it'll get you out of the doghouse.*

He called Lupe's parents and got the machine, so he tried the apartment and she answered.

"Hi, Lupe; I'm surprised I caught you there."

"Just got back; I was about to call you."

"Lupe, I'm sorry for how I spoke to you last night."

"Thank you, Phil, I appreciate that."

"I'm not going to use booze as an excuse; I knew what I was doing, I was wrong." *Not about Mick.*

"Don't be too hard on yourself. I obviously had no idea of the intensity of what was going on between you and your father. I'm not sure I can even begin to understand the emotional trauma you experienced."

Geez, pretty heavy. "Uh, that's old news now. I have something else to tell— "

"I don't agree that it's old news, Phil. I think we both need a little time to process everything."

What? "Go on." *She* ***is*** *dumping me.*

"Well, I never did talk to you yesterday, so here goes: I'm taking an opportunity that came up. Dad has some business in Central America; he asked me to interpret for him, and I'll get to see my other family in San José."

Yeah, and your ***brother****, Enrique.*

"Phil?"

Whose idea, hers or her dad's? "When do you go?"

"Day after tomorrow, but I'll be back in three or four weeks. Since you'll be in the mountains anyway, it'll be a good break for both of us."

"You'll get back about when I'm supposed to leave."

"What do you mean?"

"The research was cut back and postponed until July."

"I'm sorry to hear that, Phil."

"Isn't that what you wanted?"

"No, why would I want that?"

"Messing around this summer sounded real important."

"Do you think I'm that selfish? You weren't listening, and neither was I. We need this time to think."

Bull. "Why don't you just admit you want to break up?"

"I'm not saying that. Listen, Phil, you know I care— "

"Okay, then before you go, maybe I can see you a minute."

"I don't think that's best right now."

"You aren't being straight with me, Lupe."

"Yes I am, but you obviously don't believe me."

"Then let's deal with it. I'll meet you downtown."

"No, Phil, this isn't getting us anywhere."

"That's such bullshit, I don't see why you can't— "

"Phil, I'm sorry," she interrupted, "I'll write to you."

"No, don't, I already know what you're going to say." He dropped the phone to its cradle. "Shit, shit, shit!" he said, each expletive louder and more intense. *Goddamn her.* Phillip kicked a leg of the pinball game with his heel, startling Ali.

Don't take it out on him. He petted the cat, Ali started to purr, and Phillip led him to the kitchen. He put a few kibble treats into a bowl then stood up to rub his aching eye sockets; he heard Ali crunch on the food.

She didn't mess everything up; it was you, jerk-off. Think about something else. He looked down at his cat. "Guess it's just you and me and this damn house, Ali." *Nobody left to piss off.*

Phillip turned and stared out of the kitchen window at his well-scraped front yard. Though the wind hadn't blown for days, the dun-colored air still screened out much of the sunlight. A tinge of the strange cold sensation crept into his head; he saw his reflection. He put his finger on the glass and traced the shadowy image, his body moving slightly back and forth. The coldness didn't get stronger, so he kept moving his finger over the window.

Minutes later, Phillip's trance was broken when he saw his tree glisten again. Oblivious to what he was just doing, he rushed out the front door and into the yard. Parting two of the larger middle branches, he looked in at the trunk of the young tree. Just below the main fork, the bark was encased in thick ocherous sap and some kind of white ooze.

What is this? After checking the rest of the trunk and finding no more of the sticky mess, he hurried back into the den and looked up the number of Ponderosa's only nursery.

"Nora's Greenhouse, this is Chipper," a man said with the perky demeanor that probably earned him his nickname.

"This is Phillip Stark, I have a— "

"Stephen Stark's boy, sure. Sorry I couldn't make the funeral, son..."

You weren't the only one.

"...want you to know I don't pay no mind to gossip. Far as I know, your dad was always sober in this store, yup."

***Yup**, more like hung over.*

"So what can I do ya' for today?" Chipper asked when he realized Phillip had nothing to say about Stephen.

"Something's wrong with my pine tree."

"What kind is it?"

"Ponderosa."

"That's likely your problem right there."

"Why is that?"

"Nobody bothers with 'em much anymore. I'll stop selling Ponderosas eventually. Mainly we sell Austrians now. So what's wrong with the tree?"

"Globs of sap and some white stuff."

"Right where some main branches come apart?"

"Yes."

"Pine borer; he's right in the crotch of that tree, happy as a clam. The white stuff is his waste; you got all that sap 'cause it's like the tree is bleeding. I've dug a couple of 'em out with hangers, but that's not a real fix."

"Then what can you do about it?"

"Chop it down, especially if you've got other pines."

"It's the only one I have."

"I'd still cut it down."

No way. "There must be something I can do."

"Austrian's more resistant to the pine borer; a few young Austrians would cost less than fooling with a sick Ponderosa." Chip waited a moment for a response but didn't get one. "You have one shot, and there's no guarantee it'll work."

"I don't care. What do I do?"

"The co-op in Four Rivers has this fancy insecticide that kills the moth that makes the grub..."

How toxic? He stroked the cat once; Ali didn't move.

"...doesn't even look like a moth, more like a wasp. That stuff kills it before it can lay eggs."

"Is it toxic to animals?"

"Not sure. The B.I.A foresters on the reservation dust all that timber there. It's pretty nasty stuff; I'd keep your animals in while you're spraying and get yourself a good mask. See what the co-op guy says. Five pounds is probably the smallest he's got, you'll need to ask how to cut it way down."

"What's it called?"

"Don't recall, not much need for it when the Austrian..."

It'll brown up and die — twenty bucks.

Try and collect it. I'll stop the sonsabitches.

"You still there, son?"

Damn. "Yeah, sorry. The co-op's on Fifth, right?"

"Yup. When will you be goin'?"

"Right now."

"That grub's got an enemy, I see that. I'll call and tell 'em you're coming and what you need. Good luck with it."

"Thanks." Phillip got his checkbook and was off for the city again, driving with determination, much faster than earlier in the day. He bought the insecticide and the clerk told him he could apply it as often as he wanted, but once a week was more than enough. He said it wouldn't harm animals or people as long as there was no direct contact.

From the time he called the nursery until he turned off the highway coming back to Ponderosa, Phillip was thinking mostly of saving his tree. He stopped at the feed-and-seed; bought twelve feet of chicken fence, steel poles and a heavy-duty mask. He left town and drove up onto the mesa, passing some fields that had yet to be plowed under. The stark countryside reminded him of Xavier Lopes running him off the same road.

Seems like a month ago. He came to about the same spot where he went off before. *I think that's the pole.*

Solid as a rock; always does the job.

You'd make everything so simple; nobody but Warren would even give a damn — doesn't even scare me. That's crazy shit, Phillip. He drove on home, scraped off the ponderosa, watered it and then sprayed.

Phillip finished erecting the fence around his pine before dark, then ate a banana and some tortilla chips while he did a load of wash and watched TV. His eyes began to droop and he was in bed by ten, trying not to think about anything that had happened or what he would do the next day.

A new nightmare kept him from any sound rest. It wasn't a lucid dream like the night before, only a hazy image of a Stephen-thing stalking through the yard, axe at the ready, in search of the ponderosa. The zombie returned again and again, like a continuous TV rerun with bad reception. The repetition eventually weakened the dream's ghastliness, it faded, and he fell into an uneasy sleep.

In the early morning he was conscious but didn't open his eyes. *Why don't you get up? And do what, scrape the back yard?* He felt the beginning of the cold heaviness in his head and avoided it by going back to sleep again. Later, when Ali pounced on the foot of the bed, Phillip sat up slowly, eyes open and fully awake. The old cat minced gracefully across the lumps in the covers.

"Hey, *gato*." Glancing at the clock on the bookshelf, he patted Ali on the head. *God, it's after eleven, more than twelve hours.* "Almost lunch time for you, no wonder you woke me up." The nightmares and everything else out of his mind, he stroked Ali's fur. "Let's get you some food, boy."

In briefs and tee shirt, he followed the cat down to the kitchen. As Ali devoured his brunch, Phillip looked out at another wan morning that should have been awash in sunlight. The dull day didn't bother him, but he glared at the hunks of sap, now dark yellow offal in the grass below his tree.

Get rid of that crap when you spray. He saw a branch of dry pine needles he didn't notice before. *The tree's probably had it.* The ulcer bit at his gut, reminding him to take the medicine. By the time he swallowed the drug with water, Phillip felt the strange coldness in his head again so he chased the first pill with a non-aspirin. He walked back down the hall to his bathroom sink and looked in the mirror.

Why does my head get cold like this? Maybe you can get rid of it here. Phillip traced his reflection with one finger several times. *Still numb; this isn't working. Just get moving, that'll stop it — go on.* He went back in the bedroom, picked up his work clothes and sat on the end of the bed, holding his shirt and jeans. *No, it's too cold. The carpet worked before.* Phillip wrapped both arms around his middle, the dirty clothes wadded between his forearms and stomach. He leaned forward and saw the pattern below.

Yes, here; you can get rid of it here. He followed the lines of the *fleurs-de-lis* again, looking down his nose. *Down and around, up again, in and then out, now down...* The chill persisted, but he continued to outline each bend and curve. His body began to dip with the motion, and soon his entire torso swayed. *...up and over, back* *and down — yes, that's better. Stay here — up again and...* The monotonous movements continued for several minutes, even longer for all he knew.

It's gone; get dressed. No, still tired. He dropped his clothes on the floor and crawled back under the covers. *No way you can sleep any more. It's okay, you're finally comfortable, just rest awhile.*

After some relatively solid sleep, Phillip finally got up after two o'clock in the afternoon, put on his clothes and shoes and walked through the house. *Blew half the day, now what are you going to do?*

He sat on the edge of Stephen's recliner, looked up at the blank TV screen and saw his reflection again. *Jesus, don't look at that.* He focused instead on the old framed photo of Ingemar Johansson above the TV. He walked over to inspect it. *Black shoes, little gloves, short shorts, smug look on his face — the tough Swede, Stephen's hero.* Phillip backed up and sat down again. *That picture's been there forever — why does it seem like I've never really seen it?* He surveyed the familiar room, not sure what he was looking for. *What's left of him? This damn chair, shop tools, the Chevy, Mom's pictures, and Ingemar up there — maybe something in his room.*

He got up, retrieved the key from the hall closet, and walked over to the door across from his own bedroom. Since Stephen kept the room locked, Phillip couldn't recall being in there more than a couple times since they used it for storage. He turned the key, entered and found everything in military order. The single bed was perfectly made next to an uncluttered dresser; a high-back wooden chair stood flush to the wall. On the nightstand by the bed there was only the reading lamp and a thin coffee-table book. The shade was drawn exactly halfway over the window, which faced the prevailing breeze and had been left open a couple inches. All of it was just as Stephen had left it, except it was filthy. A thin layer of fine ash covered every horizontal surface.

He'd shit a brick if he saw this. Phillip closed the window, walked over to the closet, then turned and saw the trademarks from the bottom of his sneakers imprinted in the tracks on the carpet. He slid back the closet door and found only a dusting of ash on his father's organized shoes, shirts and pants. His army uniform and one old suit coat were hanging in dry-cleaning covers. Phillip lifted the plastic from the brown dress uniform and touched the corporal's chevrons and then the rectangle of colorful honors emblems above the left pocket.

Thought he got rid of this; could've put it in his casket. He had provided only one item for burial — Stephen's enormous, enigmatic South Korean flag to use as a shroud. After Mick asked for it at the wake, Phillip was gratified he had the flag buried with his father.

He shut the closet, then searched the dresser drawers, finding only socks, shirts, underwear, and shoe polishing paraphernalia. *Crap for Goodwill.* Phillip approached the nightstand and sat on the double bed, noticing that the pile ribbing in the bedspread's chenille design had mostly resisted the ash, and it snaked like a banana-colored maze over the smudge-grey background.

Phillip stared at the cover for several mesmerizing moments. *Follow the yellow brick road.* With the end of his index finger he slowly traced the curves of the soft piling until the track led his hand over the side of the bed. *Stop this — now!* He shook his head, trying to clear it, then reached for the book on the nightstand and brushed off the ash. *DECKS AND PORCHES STEP BY STEP — still interested.* The binding was stiff and it cracked as he opened it to a picture of some redwood planks. *He hardly even looked at it.*

Phillip replaced the book, pulled out the top drawer and found four items: a box of tissue, a face-down envelope, an old revolver and a box of cartridges. *What the hell?* He lifted the gun and checked the chamber. *Loaded — Jesus.* Phillip placed the firearm gently on the bed, then flipped the envelope over and found his name printed on the other side. He opened it and took out a one-paragraph handwritten letter.

My God. From him or Stephen?

Dear Phillip,
I wish you didn't have to deal with this...

It's Dad — deal with what?

...but I know I'm no use any more to you or anyone. It's hard to go through with it...

Kill himself, dear God.

...but since you're reading this, I guess I finally got up the nerve. I've hurt you again, I know, but this is the only way. Mostly I'm sorry for how I treated you since your mother died. I think in the long run this will be best for you.

Dad

Though he'd finished reading, Phillip glared at the note. *No, Dad wouldn't go through with it — Stephen just passed out.* The chill crept gradually up his back.

Sorry for how I treated you. *How much was he aware of Stephen?* Phillip dropped the letter back into the drawer, returned to the door and crossed the hall. He went directly to his bed and sat on the edge, his face partially covered by one hand. *If he could write that, he could've talked to me.* Shivers pressed into him between his shoulder blades.

You'll believe any ol' bullshit.

"Shut the hell up," he said, tears bulging in his eyes.

Aw, are we going to cry about it?

Bastard. The coldness moved quickly to the top of his spinal cord and into his head. *At least I'm ready for it this time.* He wiped his face with his sleeve, then leaned forward to follow the contours of the pattern in the carpet. Phillip began rocking back and forth and was soon asleep.

The short nap ended when part of the Ali dream came back to him — the image of Mick sitting on his patio, laughing as Stephen was attacked. *Mick the goddamn prick.* He opened his eyes. *Like Warren said: remember, it wasn't* ***all*** *your fault.*

Peas in a pod — me and your ol' man was peas in a pod.

Too bad I didn't hit him, hard. Phillip sat up. *The chill feels close, like it's waiting. Crap, get up.* He stood, moved slowly out of his room and saw he'd left Stephen's door open. Phillip walked in and stared at the pistol on the bed.

Peas in a pod.

Yeah, you should ***be*** *in his pod.* He picked up the weapon and tested its heft, his finger on the trigger. *What the hell are you doing, Phillip?* He put the gun right back down, dropping it the last couple inches; ash puffed up from the bedspread. The chill started to kick in, and Phillip returned to his carpet again.

16

Wielding its axe in search of the tree, the Stephen-zombie haunted Phillip every night. The recurring dream vanished and reappeared so often that it became a dull respite between other nightmares. Sometimes images returned of Ali and the people in the store, or of Mick laughing at Stephen's slaughter, but Phillip was especially agitated by a new dream of Ellen Stark in the intensive care ward, asking him if he was taking care of his father.

Bizarre variations of those dreams and others prevented sound sleep most nights. He would finally catnap from about two A.M. to dawn and then wake up for a few minutes, waiting to see if the coldness shuddered in his head. It was always there, but he was able to go right back to sleep to avoid it. Phillip would wake at around noon to feed Ali, convincing himself each time that he was up for good. But he was soon at the foot of his bed ridding himself of the chill and then sleeping into the afternoon.

Days after he found Stephen's note, Phillip awoke as usual in the very early morning, but this time he couldn't go back to sleep. He sat up in bed, and the chill was there, stronger than the one he fought off the previous midday. *This one's a damn glacier — c'mon, you can sleep.* He started to lean back, but Ali came in and meowed, though his lunchtime was hours away.

"What's with *you*?" Phillip asked the cat. *Man, it's so cold.* He struggled to get up, tossed out the cat and closed the door. *Now sleep it off.* He got in bed, covered up and closed his eyes for a few minutes, but he stayed awake and his head still trembled. *Crap, there's no choice.*

He sat on the edge of the bed and assumed his usual posture for expelling the chill — elbows on knees, forehead in both palms. Phillip concentrated on the design between his feet and began to trace it. *Curve up, now down, and around. Curve out, to the base, now up. What's wrong with me? In to the other side, small curve — it's not getting better. It will — just shut up and do it. Around, straight into the slit, out, and back to the top, curve out, and down...* The chill eventually withdrew, and he finally went back to sleep.

Phillip woke up before twelve with mild ulcer symptoms. *At least the coldness is gone. That one counts, by God; the noon chill can go to hell.* He got up and walked confidently to the kitchen to put out the cat's brunch. Standing at the sink in his underwear, he watched Ali eat, but a cold tinge crossed his nape. *No, fight it; don't think about it.* He tried petting the cat and then looking at some bills, but the icy pall gradually descended upon him again. *Didn't the first one mean anything?*

He dispatched an ulcer pill and a non-aspirin, but before he could return to his bed he had to stop in the bathroom. Phillip started to touch his reflection in the mirror. *That won't work; take your dump and get out.* He lowered his underpants, sat on the toilet, and looked down at the plain linoleum for something, anything, to trace with his eyes. *Nothing there. It's stronger — cold and heavy like this morning.* He draped a bath towel over his head for warmth, but it was so clammy he let it fall to the floor.

Phillip finished going and saw the dispenser was empty. *Damn.* He fumbled with the ends of the chrome holder, but it was jammed. *Still colder, can't wait, you need the carpet now. No, idiot, wipe your ass.* He tried to separate the tube again, but it burst in his hands. "Shit!" he yelled as both pieces and the spring rolled across the floor. *Easy, just get some paper.* He reached for the cupboard by the sink, but his arm seemed to move in slow motion. *Hurry up. There, open it.* Phillip pulled the glass knob, but the door didn't give. *It's stuck; pull harder. God, I'm so cold.*

The cabinet opened after two more tugs; he found the toilet paper in a new cellophane four-pack and picked it up. He was momentarily impressed by its unexpected bulk and then considered his next step. *Rip it.* He tried, but the plastic seemed tough as hide. He jabbed with his forefinger; it just bent at the knuckle.

Damn weakling. Can't wait, freezing. He leaned up for the tissue box on the sink and managed to sweep it back onto his lap. Only two thin sheets remained inside, and even they seemed too heavy. He reached under himself and did the best he could. A couple tears welled up in his eyes.

You're so pathetic.

Shut up, bastard. Phillip stood slowly, pulling up his briefs, though he wasn't completely clean. *Just get to the carpet.* Everything was blurred and moving slowly again as he made his way to the side of his bed. Staring at the pattern, he began to rock and swerve. *...around and in, now straight out of the slit — straight outta hell. Easy, this is the only way, keep going. Down and over, all the way to the top. This is where you need to be. Around the curve — that's better. Good, nothing else matters. Back down to the base, and up...* When the chill was finally gone, he was asleep again.

He woke up in the afternoon and lay there, anxious and still, staring sideways at the wall. *It's gone, whatever it is. Frostbite in the head — chilblain — no,* ***chillbrains****. Great, you named it, now get up.* He noticed the slight odor of excrement.

"Shit," he said to the wall. *Got that right — how could you be any more disgusting?* Phillip got up, walked into the bathroom, shed his underwear and turned on the shower. He waited for the water to get scalding hot. *Chillbrains — Jesus. What if you couldn't stop it?*

What Phillip couldn't stop that day or the days that followed was the routine he settled into: the early chill, the Ali-feeding chill, and then by his third waking of the day, usually after two o'clock, he could make himself get up. He would dress in his work clothes and head straight for the garage to prepare insecticide. If Ali was around, Phillip put him in the house, the cat door bolted. Next, he'd shake up what was left in the gallon sprayer, pump it up and then open the garage, heading for the ponderosa, nozzle at the ready. Sometimes he'd forget his mask and have to put his tee shirt over his face while he coated the branches.

A telemarketer called one day and interrupted his spraying preparations. Before Phillip got far from the phone, it rang again and the lawyer asked to come by for a signature. An hour later, he signed the document and asked the lawyer to use the mail next time. After the man left, Phillip went to the phone and turned off the ringer.

When he finished his spraying each day, he neglected the lawns but sometimes filled the bird feeder in the back yard. After the chores, Phillip would walk to the street for the mail and newspaper and then retreat to his recliner in the TV room. Except for bills with threats on the envelopes, he just tossed most of the mail onto a pile next to the recliner. When he bothered to open the newspaper, he'd read the main stories, then nap until he took a meal of sorts in the late afternoons. It was often cereal, or beans with cheese; sometimes he had spaghetti with plain sauce, or his favorite, some variation of a peanut butter sandwich.

He spent evenings in front of the TV, usually for nature or news programs, or he would read *All Things Wise and Wonderful,* the Herriot novel he was struggling with. Phillip paid attention to the TV or his book for an hour or so, then napped on and off until about eleven. He intended to watch the news but would only make it through the sports and then wake up in the middle of the *Tonight Show*. After Johnny Carson signed off, Phillip went to bed and dreamed fitfully most of the night, followed at dawn by his singular method of exorcising the chill; then he slept again before dealing with the midday chill and sleeping into the afternoon.

The tedium was interrupted only by an occasional early-evening trip to Kurt's market in town. He dreaded the outing and soon decided to stock up on cat food, powdered milk and other staples so he didn't have to go so often.

Phillip fiddled with the accumulated mail one evening and found a letter from Doctor Putman's office near the top of the pile. *Never saw this. So? You wouldn't be any use to them anyway.* The two-page form letter was "to clarify information already given to staff in person or by phone." The field research, it said, would begin in September, pause for winter and start up again in the late spring. The letter described project details and there was a printed note at the bottom. It said they assumed Phillip had a conflict with the new schedule, but to call if he could somehow participate.

Yeah, no problem, I'll just quit my job. What job? How are you going to get your ass out of bed when school starts? Take it easy; there's time. It isn't getting any worse; maybe it'll start to back off.

In the days after he read Putman's letter, Phillip continued to have no dominion at all over the mornings, and his afternoons and evenings remained a sluggish progression of napping, chores, TV, reading, and nibbling at his food.

One afternoon after his post-chill slumber, he looked out the kitchen window at his tree. *Still alive — time for the bug juice.* By the time he gathered the equipment and opened the garage door, the wind started to blow. The ash was airborne again, but visibility wasn't as limited as before. *So skip a day; won't hurt.* He put the sprayer away and went into the TV room to pick up two tardy bills.

Phillip walked back outside, wrist over forehead to keep the particles out of his eyes. Down at the curb he extracted the Four Rivers paper from its tube then opened the mailbox and exchanged his outgoing mail with a typically meager delivery of advertisements and one bill. He discovered a small envelope, the kind used for thank-you cards, wedged into a thin glossy catalog.

What's this? Probably my Dear John from Lupe. Using the other mail to cover his eyes, he checked the letter. *From Joann; she has a new address. What's she want?* He hurried to the garage, discarded the ads into the trash and went in.

Phillip dropped the bill and newspaper onto the pile by the chair and walked down to the poolroom with the letter. He drew open the curtains and leaped back on the pool table, his slender rear end nudging ash-dusty billiard balls that hadn't moved since the wake. They rolled together and clicked behind him as he looked out at the wind. Thistle and tumblemustard skeletons swirled across the yard, and the deep rut he'd made out to the bird feeder was barely visible.

You're stalling; get it over with. He opened the yellow envelope and took out a card printed with bright sunflowers.

> ***Dear Phillip, I've been trying to call you since the lawyer told me you didn't go to the mountains.***

The nosy bastard.

> ***I hope you're okay and there's nothing wrong.***

Everything's just ducky, Joann.

I need to discuss what you said about the house. I don't need the money after all, but I want to explain things.

Her reconciliation with Richard the Nazi.

As you can tell by the address, there have been some changes here. Please call me as soon as possible.

Love, Joann

PS- my new phone number below -

Crap, may as well be done with it. He slid off the pool table, moved over to pick up the phone receiver, then poked the number buttons. Instead of listening to the clicks, he checked to be sure the ringer switch was still off. *Be civil; you could even apologize. Maybe she won't even be home.*

"Hello."

No such luck. "Hi, Joann."

"Phillip?"

No, it's Elvis. "Yes, Joann."

"You got my note, thank God; I've been calling for days."

With her big news. "Been busy. So you moved?"

"Yes, I'll tell you about it in a minute. How are you doing, Phillip?"

He scratched his hairy cheek. *Obligatory question.* "I'm growing a beard. I look like a Civil War general, maybe Stonewall Jack— "

"Phillip, what happened to your project?"

"Postponed to the fall." He lifted the base of the phone to the pool table so he could watch the wind.

"I know it meant a lot to you, that's a shame."

Thanks for your sincere empathy. He said nothing.

"So what's been going on?" she asked, trying hard to be cheerful.

"Just catching up on things."

"What are you doing to keep busy?"

Nothing. "Let's see, thanks to Carter I won't be watching the Olympics; there's still ash to clean up; I read a lot and take care of Ali." *And the goddamn chillbrains.*

"I'm glad to hear he came back. Are you hiking a lot?"

Out to my tree, every day. "Is there something you *want* me to do, Joann?"

"No, just asking, I don't mean to be nosy."

Well, you are. He jumped back onto the table, bumping the billiard balls again. Joann broke the silence.

"Are you taking care of yourself, Phillip?"

"Yes. You sound like Lupe."

"How is she?"

"Fine, I guess." *Yeah, like you don't miss her.*

"What do you mean?"

"She's with her father." *And Enrique.* "On a trip."

"Aunt May and I chatted with her while we waited for the taxi. I like Lupe, Phillip, but even if I didn't, it was wrong to say what I did in the garage."

What? He didn't respond.

"Have you spoken with Warren?"

"No, he thinks I'm in the mountains."

"You sure you're all right? The lawyer said you didn't look well when he dropped by."

Crap. "I'm fine; the lawyer's a damn snoop."

"It wasn't his fault. I asked him to check on you."

Why all the sudden concern? "Joann, did you need to tell me something or not?"

"Yes." She paused. "Since Daddy died, I've learned a few things about myself. I treated you and Daddy like, uh, well, terribly — all those years in my own little world."

Phillip heard her cry softly. *Good God, what **is** this?* "What do you want me to say, Joann?" He saw the wind dying down; the bleak back yard was nearly unveiled.

"Nothing. My behavior with you two was a big part of who I was; I regret it so much now, and I'm sorry."

Don't be so brutal, Phillip. "It's old news, forget it."

"I can't. And I'm sorry for the other things I told you at the funeral," she said, still sobbing a little.

"I remember what I said; I owe you the apology."

"Some of it I needed to hear. I'm the one who—"

"Okay, Joann, so we're both sorry. Tell me about your move." *And how dear Richard isn't really so bad.*

"I will, just a sec."

While she gathered herself, he watched a robin flutter down to perch on the fence. The chubby orange and grey bird took one look at the unpromising yard and then flew off for Mick's place.

"Phillip, I still think you should keep the house. Like I wrote, I'm not worried about the money. Richard and I— "

"So you worked it out with the bastard," he interrupted. "Don't expect congratulations from me."

"You've been right about him all along. The kids and I moved into a small duplex just inside city limits."

"You did?"

"Yes. I finally came to my senses when he hit Joshua. My counselor helped me see I was fooling myself, thinking he'd be a good husband if I kept hoping and waiting. It was like I didn't see the bruises on my own face."

Jesus. "Jesus." *As if you cared, Phillip.*

"I didn't call to have you feel sorry for me. I've started divorce papers," she said, her tone now intrepid. "I want it to be quick and amiable for the kids' sake, but he's stalling; the SOB."

SOB? My, my. "Has he bothered you since then?"

"No, there's a restraining order. He's almost broke from his gambling so I don't depend on him for anything except medical insurance. He doesn't have visitation rights yet; there's no reason for contact."

"Good. If he shows up, call the city cops, not his county buddies."

"Right. I have something else to ask you, Phillip."

Here it comes. "Go ahead."

"I want a new start with you. I'm building a new life for myself and my kids and I want my only brother to be a part of it."

Why? "I don't know what to tell you."

"I'd just like to give it a chance. We could begin maybe by calling at a regular time. Can we just see what happens?"

What the hell. "I guess."

"How about every other Saturday morning?" she asked.

Fat chance. "I can't do that; I have men's league basketball then." *Good one, Phillip.*

"That's wonderful, I'm glad you're playing again. Let's see, Sunday evenings maybe?"

"What'll we talk about?"

"I don't know. I don't think it matters."

"All right."

"Thank you, Phillip."

Change the subject. "So how are the kids adjusting?"

"Naturally they're upset, but I'm very proud of them. Grace has helped so much and little Josh is adjusting better than I expected. Guess what? After they're in bed, I have a sitter and I'm playing four hours a night at a piano bar. And I'm taking a class at the college; if I finish my degree someday, maybe I'll teach music. You're my inspiration."

Some inspiration. "You'd be good at it, Joann; you like kids, and your subject."

"That's such a sweet thing to say." She sniffled again.

Brother. "So you're surviving financially?"

She didn't answer right away. "Yes. It's funny, we've been living simply — no frills, and we're making it on much less than I thought, even with all the inflation. Some of the so-called necessities don't mean much anymore. We're like the Flintstones — you know, washing dishes by hand, opening cans with dinosaur teeth."

He chuckled. *A joke no less. Tell her what's happening to you. No, this isn't about your little problem. You didn't help her with that creep, now's your chance.*

"Phillip?"

"I'm here. Sounds to me like you need some money."

"Between my job and piano lessons we're making it, really. And the bank already sent me half of Daddy's savings; that's our emergency fund. You got your half, didn't you?"

"Yeah." *I guess.* "You sound good, Joann. I'm, uh, glad you're doing okay." *You* ***are*** *glad for her, jerk.*

"Thank you, Philly. It's like a new life."

Philly *again. So what?* "Joann, I'm still going to sell the place and send you half, more if you want it. It'll be ready to go after I finish the ash and a few repairs." *Look at that damn yard.*

"All I really want from the house someday is the piano."

"It's your piano." He put one hand around a billiard ball. "Uh, Mom would be impressed you're playing."

"Yes, bless her heart."

God, like she's still alive. "I can't believe how much has happened with you in just a couple weeks."

"It's been over a month since the funeral, Phillip."

How could that be? He rolled the striped yellow ball into a pocket.

"Can we talk about Daddy a little bit?" she asked.

No. "I don't have anything to say." He watched a dime-sized jumping spider jitter across the ceiling.

"At the wake you tried to tell me how bad his drinking was. You made it sound like he was two different people."

"You still don't believe it?" he asked defensively.

"I do now; it was just another lie I was living. I'm sorry you had to deal with all that without any help from me."

"Forget it; more old news." He leaned back on the table.

"Yes, that's why I'm hoping we can have a new start."

Such drama; you think you can trust her? The arachnid stopped right overhead; he saw its red thorax.

"Phillip, did you see the autopsy report?"

"No. Why bother?"

"Daddy was sober at the time of the crash."

"What do you mean?" He looked down, trying to stifle his exasperation. "You just told me you understood how he was."

"Yes, but they said he wasn't legally drunk."

No way; it had to be Stephen.

"They tried to call you after the wake, Phillip; I told them you were gone. An investigator wanted to know Daddy's doctor, but I said he hardly ever went — right?"

"Never; but get to the point."

"He asked me if we thought he was ever suicidal."

Jesus. "What did you say?"

"No, of course. Their final decision was he just went to sleep. It's all in there."

My God, it was Dad. He looked up and saw the spider skitter away. *Pissing Stephen off had nothing to do with it.*

"Are you okay, Phillip?"

"Yes. This isn't what you think, Joann."

"You don't believe the autopsy?"

"I believe it. Hang on." He hurried through the house, retrieved Stephen's letter and came back to the den.

"I'm back," he said, sitting on the desk. "Listen." After a deep sigh, he read the grim note; then they were both quiet a few seconds. "There was a loaded gun with this."

"My God," Joann finally said, weeping as she spoke. "It must have been awful — for years." She paused. "Give me a sec, please."

"Take your time." *Did he have something like the chillbrains, something worse? You were a big help.* He waited several more moments before Joann came back.

"Phillip, can we talk about this more on one of our calls?"

"If you need to."

"Thank you, Philly. Now don't get upset, but I'm still worried about you. Promise to take care of yourself?"

"I'll be fine."

"I hope so. I'll get going now; I saw the kids coming. By the way, my little bird watcher, Grace, wants to know you better. So does Josh."

"One thing at a time, I guess."

"Yes. Call you Sunday after next, about eight, okay?"

"All right."

"Bye, Philly."

"Bye, Joann." *Do you buy all that? What the hell, just sell the place for her, gives you something to do.*

Phillip got off the desk, looked at the phone and decided to switch on the ringer. He went right out and gathered his ash-scraping implements, tossed them in the wheelbarrow, and rolled everything toward the back yard. After opening the back door of the shop, he crossed a perfect line of soot that had built up on the weather stripping. As in the front yard weeks before, the six-inch mass of ash and the imposing mounds below the eaves seemed to dare him to begin.

No time like the present. At first, he fell easily back into the rhythm of the work, rolling each load through the shop and the garage and then down the driveway to start new piles near the curb. After his third trip, he had to stop out front. *What the hell? My arms hurt, and my back —just stop a couple minutes.*

He walked over to the front porch, sat down and surveyed the yard. *What a mess.* The walkways were dusted with ash from the wind, and the straw-colored lawn had two survivors — his pine and the ginkgo tree. The lilacs and the arborvitae looked to be dead or dying. *Can't sell it like this.*

Phillip grabbed the front hose and set up the sprinkler at the far end of the yard, next to Mister Beck's adjoining lawn. He watched the water splatter onto the dry turf, a tiny puff of ash bursting from each drop. *Wonder if it'll green up.* He stared until the ground was wet; his eyelids grew heavy. *You can't be sleepy; get back to work.*

Phillip made himself trudge to the back yard for his push broom, then came back out front and began to lethargically sweep up the wisps of ash on the front walks and driveway. *Move it, you slug.* As he labored with the simple task, he recalled the boundless energy he had while hosing the ash off the streets with his neighbors. *All night long.*

When he finally finished, Phillip looked at the withered lilac bushes he freed from the ash weeks before. *Take me forever to dig them out.* On hands and knees with a trowel, he unearthed one broken bush and was surprised to find it still had supple roots. By the time he reburied the plant, dug moats around the rest and flooded them, it was early evening. *Plenty of light — do some more in back. Too tired, you'll put a big dent in it tomorrow.*

Phillip returned some tools to the back yard, then went in for a shower. After that, he fixed some cereal, carried the bowl to a TV tray and turned on the set, hoping for a nature show. He settled for a *Taxi* rerun, ate some of his skimpy dinner, then leaned back in the recliner and was soon asleep. He woke up after one and shuffled to his bedroom. As was now his habit, he intentionally closed the door to keep Ali out.

17

At dawn the next morning, the chill was there, but for the first time in many days Phillip went back to sleep without having to fight it off. When he got up at noon to feed Ali, he wondered about the early-morning reprieve, but the icy prostration descended upon him before he could even go out.

That afternoon he woke up feeling some of his old energy as he walked over to the bedroom window and looked out at the calm day and the deep ash. *Should've been working. The morning chill was weak; maybe it **is** starting to back off. Get up earlier tomorrow or you'll never be ready to sell the place. You're wasting time; move it.*

After dressing, he went straight to the garage and then the front yard to spray his tree. Finishing that, Phillip checked the salvaged lilacs and turned on the sprinkler. He started on the back yard again, stopping frequently to stretch his sore muscles. After an hour of hard work his stamina was gone, so he took off the gloves and rested on the patio step where he'd first watched the ash fall back in May. Not even half the ash below the eaves was removed, and the yard itself was still buried.

Great. Maybe I'll finish by Christmas. He managed another half-hour of on-again, off-again work. That night, pledging to get up earlier, he set his alarm for nine A.M.

Phillip woke up groggily around six with the chill and had to use the carpet to get back to sleep. He was out of bed when the alarm sounded three hours later.

All right, you did it; now get moving. He put on his clothes and went right to the kitchen, looking for the cat. *It's only nine, dimwit; he's out.* After a few steps toward the garage, the phone rang. *That's what you get for leaving it on.* He walked to the den and gruffly answered the call.

"Stark?" It was his six-year nemesis, the principal.

Great. "Yes."

"I just got back and heard about your father, my condolences."

"Thanks." Phillip fidgeted with the phone chord.

"I need to touch bases with you, Stark."

So much for condolences. "Okay." *He wants something.*

"Varsity basketball camp was postponed to mid-August; they want you to help out. I also happen to know they're sniffing around for a new assistant. The camp will do you some good, considering everything; a few bucks in it, too."

Thanks for thinking of my welfare — no frigging way. "Thanks, but I'm still dealing with some family things."

"I understand, but there's time to think about it."

"I won't be able to do it."

"I already told the varsity coach— "

Shit. "Afraid that's your problem; I can't do the camp."

"Can't or won't? Ya' know, Stark, you'll never coach at that level unless you're more of a team player."

Team player, my ass. "Not interested in high school."

"I suggest you think it over; I'll send the schedule. The other thing is I don't have your commitment letter."

Must be in my pile. "Haven't seen my mail in a while."

"Okay, send it in; we want them by next week."

"Are negotiations over with the association?"

"No, they haven't quite settled, but they will soon."

"I'll send it when there's a contract."

"I didn't think you were the union type, Stark."

"I'm not, but I won't break ranks on that."

"I'll overlook your attitude because of the situation— "

"Is that all you have for me?" *I've got grass to water.*

"Think about things, Stark. I'll be in touch."

Phillip heard the call disconnect then hung up and turned off the ringer. *Try calling me now, asshole.* He started for the kitchen, but his stomach reported in with a biting pang and the chill shuddered up his back.

No, it's too early for the second one. He placed two non-aspirins and his ulcer pill on his tongue and took them with tap water. Standing with his back to the sink, Phillip covered his face with both hands for several seconds, but the cold pounding moved to his head. He made it down to his room, stopped the chill and slept until twelve fifteen.

All right, now stay up; you've done your time — two's the limit. A couple hours head start is better than nothing. He got up and walked down the hall toward the kitchen, Ali flanking against his legs.

"Lot to do today, *gato*." He puttered with the dishes then put down Ali's food and reached for some cookies to take outside. The slightest hint of the chill moved up his spine, and he put his arm down. *No, it doesn't get to come three times; think about something else.* Phillip stood at the sink, closed his eyes, and for some reason recalled an insipid TV commercial for air-conditioners. He remembered a caricature of a dog with a sweaty human face sticking his upper torso into a freezer; the dog pulled out his head and it was transformed into a blue ice cube with a big frown.

Crap, this is real helpful. He looked at the floor; the chill strengthened. *Come on; hold it off or you'll be asleep again.* He scooted the footstool over, sat down and stared at the flecked linoleum, trying to find a pattern he could follow, but his vision clouded and his head pulsed as if he'd been eating ice cream too fast.

Just get to the carpet; but you're going to stay awake this time. Steadying himself with one hand along the wall, he walked to his room. *I'll only need a few minutes.* Like so many times before, Phillip traced the whirling lines of the *fleurs-de-lis. Yes, this is good — around the curve — this is what you have to do — over and around, up to the top — what you want to do — then down and...*

He woke up on his back and touched his chin to his flannel shirt. *Still dressed, you just dozed. It's gone; now get to work.* Phillip turned to the clock on the shelf. *Two ten; it can't be.* He started to re-tie his shoes. *Frigging chillbrains — you can't fool with it.*

Over the next days Phillip was locked back into his rut, but he kept trying to work in the yard when he could. One afternoon he got up to stay after two and walked into the bathroom and stood in front of the mirror. He preened through his long, dark-blond hair, then palmed both hands over his beard. *Behold, the hermit. Not funny.* He went down the hall into the kitchen and looked out at the yard; there was a green tinge to the lawn. *Finally, it's coming back. What day is this?* He checked the calendar on the kitchen wall. *The last week of June?*

He walked to the TV room and unwrapped the top newspaper from the pile. *July ninth. What happened to the Fourth, friggin' Rip Van Winkle? Seven weeks until school — good God. Should I explain the damn chillbrains to somebody?* He went back to the kitchen and started to peel a nearly black banana. It was so disgusting he discarded it, brought down some cereal and opened the fridge.

Call Warren, I guess. What'll you tell him? Hey, Warren, my head gets cold; I stare at my carpet and I sleep a lot. He took out the milk and found there wasn't enough for cereal. *Make some powdered. Sick of that crap; guess I'll go to the store tonight. Talk to Kurt — about what? You could talk to Senior; he was almost a pharmacist. Don't be stupid.* Phillip made and ate half of a peanut butter and pickle sandwich, then went out to spray his tree before returning to the back yard.

By five in the evening he finally finished the mounds under the eaves but was too weary to start on the lawn. He came in, showered, and then put on a light flannel shirt and some relatively clean jeans. Phillip sat on his bed to put on socks and noticed the *fleur-de-lis* below. *Up, then around — no need to call anybody — and down — then over — what are you doing? Stop looking at it.* He tied his shoes, went to the kitchen and stared at the barren telephone bracket.

Lupe could be back; wonder if she'd talk to me? Maybe she could help. Screw that; I just want to see her. What if she told you to get lost? You'd deserve it. Maybe write a letter; apologize again. Great, get on your knees and beg while you're at it. Do ***something****; this place is getting to you. Call Kurt — a little beer and BS can't hurt.* He called the store and waited, holding the clicks away from his ear again. *He might not be on tonight.*

"Kurt's Western Grocery, this is Senior."

"Hi, Mister R., it's Phil." *Can I talk to you?*

"Hi, Phil."

"Uh— " *Something's wrong with me.* "Can Kurt get away?"

"Sure, he's just over in produce. How're you doing?"

Like shit. "I'm fi— "

"Good, I'll get him."

"Thanks." *How are* ***you*** *doing? Just empty words.*

"Kurt," Kurt Junior said, aggravated by the interruption.

Good ol' curt-Kurt. "It's Phil."

"Phil, he didn't say it was you. Glad you called, been wantin' to talk..."

This was a dumb idea; think of a way out.

"...off at eight. Let's go for a brew."

Let's see, save me some fruit. "Uh, I don't know."

"Why not, you doin' somethin'?"

"Just tired; been working on the ash all day."

"Still? Thought you'd be the first one done."

"I haven't had time."

"Horseshit — you're on vacation. C'mon, it's Saturday night; have a little fun for Christ's sake."

What the hell. "Where do you want to go?"

"That's better. There's a party at Tom's Tav."

Washed up Ponderosa Panthers — I'll pass. "I need some things at the store; I'll just be over when you get off."

"That'll work. Hold anythin' for you?"

"Yeah, some fruit. Any good bananas left?"

"Sure, what else?"

"Half of a Hermiston melon, if you've got it."

"Yup. That why you called, to have me hold fruit?"

"Yeah, thanks, see you in a while."

"I'm buyin' the beer. See ya'."

Phillip hung up. *Kurt's buying; there's a first — he's up to something. Farm house — you had to talk to somebody.* He had an hour to kill, so Phillip opened some Spanish peanuts, turned on the TV, leaned back in his chair and realized he was sitting on something. He pulled his baseball hat out from under his rear, smacked it on his knee and watched the ash dissipate before he put it on. He half-listened to a special about Afghanistan and the boycott of the Russian Olympics.

Sixty-five countries out. We didn't even boycott Hitler's games. The moderator introduced two senators and they began a droning debate for and against the policy. In a few minutes, Phillip was asleep.

He woke up and looked at the clock on the bar. *Damn — eight twenty.* When he snapped down the recliner, the peanut can toppled off the armrest and rolled toward the kitchen. Scores of brown nuts ricocheted all over the linoleum like tiny billiard balls after a break in eight ball.

"Damn it," he said, and then got up, stumbling to the kitchen, peanuts crunching under his shoes. *Son of a bitch, sleep through ev-*

erything. No phone in here, idiot. He walked to the den, made the call, and Kurt Junior answered this time.

"I'm sorry, Kurt; I'll be late."

"Still finishin' up; no problem."

"Fell asleep in front of the TV — I'm sorry," he said again, as if he'd committed some serious transgression.

"Jesus, Phil, everybody does that."

"I, uh, I— " *Do it all the time.*

"You all right?"

No. "Yeah."

"Come on; we'll put down a few in back, unless you want to go out."

"No, that sounds fine."

"Good, I got your fruit right here."

"Thanks; be right over." He hung up and started for the back door, crushing more peanuts as he crossed the TV room. *Clean that up before Stephen — shit, you expecting the zombie?* Phillip hurried into the garage, lifted the door, and then got in the pickup. He turned the key; there was no response. *Son of a bitch.* He tried again — nothing. He groped for the knob and found he'd left his lights on.

"Goddamn it!" He heard his loud oath reverberate in the steel frame of the small cab. His stomach clenched and he reached into a pocket for his vial of emergency ulcer pills and took one dry. Phillip yanked the keys from the ignition, got out of his truck in the semi-darkness and slammed the door so hard that Stephen's metal funnel fell off its shelf and clanked onto the concrete floor. *Tin piece of crap.* He made a half-turn toward the noise, swept his leg like a field-goal kicker, and the funnel took off straight out of the garage door and landed without a sound in the lilac bushes.

The kick is good, into the crowd; keep the damn ball. "What a frigging madman," he said, and then walked over to the Chevrolet and got in behind the wheel.

Is that piece of Jap-crap still running?

Still running circles around this junker.

Then what the hell are you doing?

"Shut up; not going to drive it, just suck its juice." He popped the hood, then got out and turned on the interior garage light. Phillip took his jumper cables out of the truck bed and soon had the pickup running. "Take that, bastard," he said and backed down the driveway and into the street.

As he made the turn around the first corner, Phillip was aware of the chill beginning to rally at the back of his head. *Not this late; not here. Turn around.* He pulled over to the curb and leaned back on the headrest for a couple minutes until the mild onset was gone. *Backed it off without the carpet — just go.* Focusing all his attention between the headlight beams, he drove slowly out of Ponderosa Estates, down the highway and into town.

18

There were only four cars in the lot as he pulled into Kurt's. Phillip got out and approached the store's front doors; they opened for him though it was after the nine-o'clock closing time. He walked through the entrance where he found Kurt Senior in his green apron counting cereal boxes at the first display in the nearly deserted store.

"Hi, Mister R.," he said, though most people called him *Senior*. Kurt Raihofer was a bit taller than his son, about Phillip's height; his face was pocked with old scars from the same skin problems that still plagued Kurt Junior.

"Hi, Phil. Kurt's finished; he's in back."

"Got a little shopping to do, if the till's open."

"Sure, take your time; I'll be here a while."

"Thanks." Knowing what he needed and exactly where to find it, he shopped quickly and soon returned to the front of the store. Kurt Senior met him at the one open check stand.

"Pretty quiet night, Mister R?" *Can I ask you something?*

"Yeah, for some reason. Good time for inventory."

"Uh— " *Maybe you could help me.*

"Something on your mind, Phil?" he asked, but Phillip shook his head. "He left your produce right here," Senior said, pointing to a bulging gunnysack.

As his groceries were being processed, Phillip checked the sack and found a bunch of bananas, six ears of corn, some peaches, oranges, grapes, and a whole watermelon. "This is more than I really needed."

"Yours is nine even, Phil, the produce is on the house — *he* paid," Senior said, skeptical of Junior's largess.

What's Kurt after? "Uh, thanks." He gave him a ten.

"Thank Mister Generosity." Senior handed back a dollar.

"Yeah. I'm going to put this stuff away." He went out to the pickup bed and put the milk and cheese in his Styrofoam cooler, then left the produce and other groceries in the cab. He walked back in then down an aisle to the swinging doors at the rear of the store. Phillip pushed with his palms; the louvered doors creaked and swung open like the entrance to a cantina in an old western. He'd forgotten the stark contrast between the bright, cheery market and the dingy concrete walls and stacks of boxes in back. *Same cruddy place.*

He turned left past carts of produce, made another left at the bathroom and approached the break room. Phillip saw it still had sheetrock walls, no door or ceiling, and a bare hundred-watt bulb hanging down from the steel beams above. A collapsible table and wooden folding chairs took up much of the space, and he could see the old avocado-green refrigerator and a rusted white stove, its surface caked with overflow from years of employees' meals. On one wall behind a pile of soiled laundry, a perpetually inoperative time clock endured next to a corkboard with fading notices. He saw new additions by the doorway: a scarred end table, a black phone, and a yellow directory scrawled with numbers and doodles.

Phillip walked all the way in, and at the far end of the long narrow room Kurt was intently focused on a magazine, his fingers holding it flat. The secondhand primary-school table was a tight fit even for the squat grocer, who had one leg sideways, his boot propped on a chair. Kurt's other hand was around a glass filled with brown liquid. There was a taller empty glass, then four cans of cola, some unopened corn chips, a small sack of ice, and a bottle poorly disguised by a paper bag. Kurt's cigarette smoldered in a fired-clay green ashtray, a crude project from somebody's forgotten art class. The smoke accumulated around the beams above.

"Hey," Phillip said, and Kurt looked up.

"Phil, you go back to sleep?" He sniggered and returned to his magazine.

Not funny, asshole. "Dead battery."

"Le' me finish this joke. Sit, have a drink," he said, eyes on his reading. Phillip grabbed the chair opposite Kurt, pulled it a couple feet back and sat down.

"What's hiding in the bag, Kurt?"

"Rum," he answered, his head still down.

On the page opposite Kurt's joke, Phillip saw a nude photo of a thin redheaded woman. "Rum n' Coke — pretty rank," he said.

"Horseshit. I don't get it," Kurt muttered at his magazine, closed it, and saw Phillip hadn't served himself. " 'Stead a' beer, thought we'd get a little shit-faced. Relax, Phil," he said in the ingratiating grocer's voice he could turn on and off at will.

He's almost wasted. "What about your dad?" Phillip waved smoke out of his face and tossed his dusty hat on the next chair.

"He puts up with it now I'm his partner. I'll pour." He smiled and dropped a handful of ice cubes into the empty summer tumbler. "A little Coke with your rum?"

"Lotta Coke, a little rum." He coughed from the smoke.

"You got plans or somethin'?" Kurt gurgled the liquor into the glass; it ran over the ice like thin maple syrup.

"No plans. That's enough," Phillip said, but was left with at least a double shot. "You gonna finish smoking that damn thing or just let it burn?" He nodded to the ashtray, and Kurt reached over and crushed the cigarette.

"There. Christ's sake, Phil, think you can relax now?"

"Maybe after you stop telling me to relax."

"Jesus, you do it." Kurt handed over the unopened can of cola. Phillip pulled the tab and filled the tall glass to the middle, leaving the half-empty can at the edge of the table.

Back to a soft-soaping tone, Kurt grinned and said, "Drink up; I'm way ahead of you." He stood for a moment, undid his grocery apron and threw it on the laundry pile. "I got chips here. Need anythin' else?" He sat down, wiped a palm across the tormented blotched skin on his forehead and then checked his hand as if he might find blackheads.

"I'm fine." Phillip took a drink. *Aak — like rotten candy.* "Thanks for all the fruit, Kurt, that's a real good melon." *What'll it cost me?*

"Sure. Man, you wanna see melons, check these," he said, pleased with his joke as he pulled an advertising card out of the magazine. He turned the glossy page around and spread it flat.

Phillip glanced at the voluptuous blonde. "Nice," he said, watching the cigarette resurrect with a curl of smoke.

"Nice? Horseshit, they're wicked."

Barely looked at her. Phillip leaned over the table to show more interest. The buxom model was on her knees, head back to her heels. *She must be a damn contortionist.*

"Not so exciting after the beauties you've been around," Kurt said, clicking his tongue as he leered at the photo.

What? Ah, Lupe. "That's quite a shot all right," he said, nodding to the magazine as he sat down. *God, haven't been hard since — don't know.*

Kurt mixed a drink and downed two full gulps. "Word is you two are breakin' up."

"The *word* might be right for once; I don't want to talk about it." He took another swallow. *This crap is terrible.*

"Hell, I know your problem. Price is way up, but Bonnie's in town." Kurt smiled and raised his brows.

"Inflation strikes again."

"Horseshit; a seventy-dollar blow job won't set *you* back." Kurt laughed at his gibe. "So what's with the hair and all the fuzz on your face?"

"Growing a beard." He stared at a rusted mousetrap by the door.

"I can see that. What's the deal?"

"Nothing, just felt like it."

"Man, you could use some meat 'n potatoes. Not turnin' into a damn hippie, are you?" Kurt grinned and drank again.

God, what the hell am I doing here? He picked up his glass and took a small sip.

"You hear about that jet crash in a big city in Poland?"

"Warsaw?" Phillip asked, looking at his glass.

"That's it; crashed into a cemetery. They can't get a body count because the Polacks keep countin' the skeletons."

Fell into that one. "Real funny."

"It *is* funny; you're so fuckin' serious. Shit, tell me what you've been doin' with yourself."

Phillip sipped again. "Been busy." *I feel this crap.*

"Doing what?"

"Getting the house ready to sell."

"No shit? Where you gonna live?"

"Don't know. Probably rent a small place."

"Four Rivers?"

"No, probably out here, closer to the mountains."

"Christ's sake, you'll get big bucks from that house."

"What's your point?" Phillip held his glass on a cork tavern coaster as Senior walked in. The storekeeper put a doughnut box on the table then took off his apron and tossed it on the pile.

"I'm finished, Minnie. It's all locked up, just need you to wrap the laundry; kill these lights when you're done."

"Got it," Kurt said, pouring another drink.

Senior looked at the table. "I see you two have an exciting evening planned."

"Just shootin' the bull, Dad."

"Stay in the apartment tonight or your mother'll have my hide." The apartment was a small trailer they kept hooked up behind the store.

"Okay." Kurt rolled his eyes.

"Couple of good apple fritters left in there," Senior said to Phillip, pointing to the white box on the table.

"Thanks Mister R.," he answered, trying to smile.

"Well, good night." Senior moved to the door. "Don't drive, Minnie."

"Yeah." Kurt shook his head with contempt as his father disappeared around the portal. He waited for the squeak from the swinging doors. "Treats me like a goddamn kid."

Treats you like a son. "Why does he call you Minnie?"

"What's it to you?" Kurt's eyelids were getting heavy with the oncoming stupor.

"Just wondered; you'd never tell anyone." Phillip let his drink wash up to his lips, not ingesting any.

"Guess it don't matter no more. My smart-ass brothers started it. When I was little, my gram sent me a stuffed Minnie Mouse; she thought it was Mickey. I'd take the damn thing everywhere, sleep with it, all that. Pete and Al called me Minnie from then on. My parents still think it's cute."

Fool doesn't know what he has. Holding the pop can, Phillip pushed his mixed drink away from the edge of the table with the back of his hand. "If it's so bad, why don't you move out again?" he asked Kurt, then drank some plain cola.

"Alimony. Hey, we could room together in Four Rivers and commute; split the rent and shit. Man, think of the tail we'd get with our own place. What do you say?"

Over my dead body. "No, I'll be out here somewhere."

Kurt bristled at Phillip's refusal. "Man, you're nuts, don't even know how lucky you are," he said, dribbling rum on his chin as he nearly polished off the drink.

"Tell me how lucky I am, Kurt." *This should be good.* A diffuse sense of the chill tingled his neck and temples. *No, it won't come now. What's he saying?*

"...got independence, steady job, cash comin' outta your a-hole; then you can't hold on to the finest tits in the whole goddamn valley." He wiped his face with the sleeve of his western shirt.

"Yeah, that about sums it up — all the important stuff." Phillip crinkled the top half of the aluminum can.

"Don't pull that shit with me." Kurt poured straight rum over ice, sneering as he lifted his glass. "You and your fuckin' cats," he said, and downed half his drink.

Asshole. "Dogs and horses for you, right?"

"Yup. I can take or leave the rest, or shoot 'em." He laughed without smiling.

Nail him. "The fact is, Kurt, any cat could survive in the wild if it had to, and every little pussycat is smarter than that ugly pure-bred dog of yours."

"Horseshit; can't train a fuckin' cat to do anything."

"I thought you admired independence."

"In people." Kurt took another gulp of rum.

"Oh. You ever see a cat chase a car, or walk up and eat shit right off the ground, or just roll in it like your dog does every day?" The chill began to creep into the back of his head. *Damn, should never have come here.*

Kurt was finishing his drink. "So you hate dogs."

"No, I'll get one after I move." *It's colder.*

"You make no goddamn sense. Why the hell am I arguing with you?"

*Why am **I** fighting with another damn drunk?* "Beats me, Kurt." His ulcer twisted; he took out a pill and held it, watching Kurt put down his glass and push it away.

"Fuckin' rum makes me pissed; I better slow it down," Kurt said, feigning regret. "I, uh, want to ask you, uh..."

Ask what? Screw him; this chill is for real. He took his pill with the soda.

"...uh, I know you don't want to talk about Lupe, but— "

It's stronger. Phillip couldn't focus on Kurt.

"What's wrong with you? You hardly drank nothin'."

"I'm not feeling good; I have to go."

"Hear me out," Kurt said. "I mean if, uh, I— "

"What do you want, Kurt?" He put the pop can down but lost hold of it and it rolled across the table. Kurt stood to trap the can, but liquid sloshed on his magazine.

"Shit, Phil." He snatched a towel from the laundry. "Fuck, it's ruined — damn things ain't cheap." Kurt dabbed at the photos as if they were precious documents.

"Sure, like you bought it," Phillip said, wincing from the chill as he stood. He took out his wallet and dropped a bill in front of Kurt on the table. "That'll cover it; I'm leaving." He put on his hat.

"Thanks; that'll buy a fuckin' newspaper." Kurt flung the towel away.

What? He saw the bill was a one. *Shit.* Moving stiffly, he took out a five and put it on the one. *It's worse; get to the carpet.* He took some wobbly steps toward the exit.

"Wait a minute, forget the damn magazine," Kurt said, putting a hand on the money. "I started to ask you, uh— "

Phillip stopped at the end of the table. "What the hell do you want?"

"If you break up, you think she'd go out with me?"

"Lupe?" he said. "Fuck you, Kurt." He made the last step to the door, his vision blurring more. *Damn, so cold.*

"Jesus, you don't have to get all pissed. I was just askin' in case," Kurt said from the doorway as Phillip staggered away, moving along the wall to steady himself. He heard Kurt shout, "Horseshit, fuck you, too."

Phillip made it out the back door, through the dark alley, then around the building into the dim lights of the parking lot. He got in his pickup and sat behind the wheel, his head pulsing. With the small flashlight from the glove box, he tried to find a pattern to follow on the dashboard.

This won't work — get home; there's no other way. He started the motor, buckled his seat belt out of habit and drove to the store's back driveway.

Take it easy; you'll make it. Two cars sped by in the dark and there was plenty of room, but he hesitated. *Idiots are going too fast, now the air has to clear.* He waited for more cars to pass until he was convinced there were no more in sight. He pulled onto the highway.

It's even colder — Jesus. Hunched over his steering wheel, Phillip drove so slowly that a young couple taking in the late-evening air gawked at him as if he were an old farmer struggling to make his way back home. He finally made it to the junction and turned onto the state road.

Phillip passed the city limits sign and squinted at the rearview mirror, his head freezing. *Nothing there, just blowing ash — go.* At the incline, the engine whined for the next gear, but Phillip kept it in second. After he made it onto the mesa, he shifted and picked up some speed. Through his clouded vision he tried to read the instrument panel, but the numbers didn't come into focus.

Slow down, you're making a big cloud. He braked without down-shifting and the motor seemed to lug in time with the shivers in his head. *It's too strong; I can't make it.* On the opposite side of the highway he saw the back of a pedestrian walking toward the mountains. Surprised to hear the sputtering pickup, the hiker looked around the side of his frame pack, assuming there must be engine trouble.

Maybe he could help me. Sure, Phillip. His body writhed and he bent forward, hunching his shoulders again to ease the pain. He was looking at the road through the steering wheel when some headlights flared behind. He managed to sit up.

Can't pass me in this crap, not again. The driver of the other vehicle pulled into the left lane to go by. *Not this time, Mister X.* Phillip bit his bottom lip, shifted and then accelerated. He didn't realize his truck was off the crown of the road until he saw a utility pole straight ahead.

There it is. God, my head is so cold.

Always does the job. He stepped on the gas and collided dead center into the pole. On the other side of the field fence, Phillip couldn't see that one of his pickup's headlights haloed an ash-entombed bale of hay. The beam faded in the clear air and went out like a stage light.

Part Three

<u>*Church*</u>

You exhort me to worship Him
In your gilded cathedrals,
But my temple is palisaded basalt
Where I see Her
In blue lupine, brown lizards, summer rain
And the searching eyes of a curious child.

From the collection, "Hell"
By T. Lloyd Winetsky

19

Below a white ceiling and fluorescent lights, Phillip was aware of two objects on the wall in front of him: a two-foot terra cotta Madonna and a small off-duty television connected to a movable black steel arm.

The hospital again, Mom's going to ask about him. Why's the Virgin Mary up there? Dumb dream. My head itches. Thinking he was about to lift his left arm, he saw it was splinted and that an IV line pulsed into the other arm. *This is real, Phillip. Jesus, Four Rivers — Saint Lourdes.* A dark face stretched partway into his field of vision.

"So you are awake, Mister es-Stark?" the lady asked, almost whispering. "Do not be es-cared," she said louder in her gentle voice, "and please try to not move the head."

The chill at Kurt's — had to get home. Blowing ash, then frigging Mister X. Again? No way.

"*Cálmate*," she said, straining to get her face to the center of the elevated bed; but he still couldn't see her well. "I am *María*, Mister es-Stark."

So the arm's busted, my head is sore; feels like I've been slugged in the gut. He also felt a brace constricting his neck. "Do you know what happened to me?" he asked her.

"A car accident; they bring you here in the ambulance. It is good you talk now, but please be calm." Maria straightened up, disappearing from his vision. "*Momentito*," she said, then came around to the other side of the bed and put her hand on his shoulder. When she touched him, he felt some of the apprehension leave his body. She pushed a button somewhere, the bed lowered and he could see her from the waist up by just moving his eyes.

Phillip guessed she was almost fifty and barely five feet tall. Like his girlfriend, she had brilliant black eyes, but Maria's were almond shaped, and her sienna brown skin was shades darker than Lupe's. Maria's jet-black hair, braided into a thick pigtail, hung down out of his sight. She wore a yellow bow, the kind sold for gifts, on the collar of a snug pastel-green uniform that made her look chubbier than she was.

"Do you know what's wrong besides this?" He lifted the plaster of Paris cast and saw band-aids and some scratches on his upper arm.

"You have a bad hurt on your head; that is all I know," she said, her soothing palm now near his elbow. "But you will get better, they tell me this, Mister es-Stark. Now I must call the nurse to say you are awake."

"Aren't you a nurse?" His peripheral vision detected dim light from a window beyond the small woman.

"No, I help her today." Maria reached over his shoulder to press a call button pinned to the bed, and he noticed her hand was calloused.

Hard labor, but her hands are soft. Why is she so nice to me? "Uh, Maria, did they say anything about this thing on my neck?" *Doesn't even hurt.*

"It is precaution." Her word sounded like *precaución.*

The IV aches; why do I need it? He separated his dry lips. *Aak, like cotton.* Maria put the back of her warm hand on his forehead. *Mom checked me like this.* She lifted her hand; he turned toward her, ignoring the neck brace. Maria's cardboard nametag spelled out: MARIA N. HOUSEKEEPING in black label-maker script, as if the last word were her surname.

"It does not hurt to move your head, Mister es-Stark?"

"No, Maria. May I have some water?"

"I am sorry, I only can give you the ice." She scooped frozen chips from a water jug on his table and then carefully lifted the plastic cup to Phillip's lips.

"Uhm, thanb youb," he garbled, trying to smile.

"*Seguro que sí.* More?"

He nodded, and she shook in a few chips. As he sucked on the ice, she gently parted Phillip's dark blond hair from his forehead. "You're very nice, Maria, thank you." His temples and cheeks flushed.

"*No es nada*, Mister es-Stark."

Though the only physical similarity between Ellen Stark and Maria was their short stature, Phillip again thought of his mother. A couple of tears swelled in the corners of his eyes. *Stop, you're embarrassing yourself.*

"You have much pain?" she asked.

"No, you just remind me of, uh, somebody — a good person."

Her head downcast, she tucked at the blanket, though the bed was in perfect order. Maria's eyes moistened a little.

You've upset her. "Sorry," he said, trying to curtail his emotions.

"No, do not be sorry, Mister es-Stark." She whisked out some tissues from a box on the small chest of drawers next to the bed. "Sometimes crying is good for us. You see?" She dried her own eyes, then dabbed a single tear that had curved down to Phillip's ear. "Before, you look es-cared. Now you look better," she said, placing her hand on his shoulder.

Phillip smiled. "I'll take your word for it. Thank you, Maria." He closed his eyes and rested.

After a few minutes, a nurse hurried into the room and stopped bedside to assess her patient, who opened his eyes and lifted his head. About Phillip's age, she looked trim and athletic and hid her face behind severe black glasses. Impeccably ironed creases lined the skirt and sleeves of her starched white uniform, and one of those stiff winged hats was bobby-pinned uselessly to the top of her short auburn hair, making her look six feet tall.

Ah, little miss professional, except not so little.

"Nothing wrong with your neck. I'll be right back," she said. Before he could talk, she left without a second glance.

"Will that nurse answer my questions?" he asked Maria as if he'd missed his only chance.

"Yes, soon, Mister es-Stark." Her palliative touch was back on his arm. "*Cálmate por favor.*"

"Yeah, I'll try. Do you know when I got here, Maria?"

"Last night, late." She moved the television to the side, revealing a round black clock on the wall.

After ten. God, think. You couldn't see. It was the coldest chill ever; that jerk came from behind. Tried to keep him from passing — bad move. Then what? The pole — it must've stopped me. The truck's probably buried.

Maria walked over to the window and opened the drapes. Hazy sunshine streaked through the glass into the small private room. She twisted a handle and the louvers separated, admitting a slight breeze that barely jostled the bunched drapes. She looked at him with a buoyant grin. "Some fresh air, Mister es-Stark," she said.

He smiled. "Thanks. Is your bow for the hostages?"

"Yes, I pray for them, and for the family."

The prim nurse returned, pushing a small metal cart so fast that the wheels made two loud reports when they rolled over the metal rails embedded in the doorway. "Okay, take your break," she said, ordering Maria. The nurse gave Phillip a disparaging glance, then began checking the IV.

What's your problem, Florence Nightingale?

"I will be back soon," Maria said to them on the way out.

"Thanks, Maria," he called, since she was ignored by the nurse, who was busy manipulating Phillip's arm like he was a machine with broken parts, making the IV hurt even more. He noticed a miniature yellow ribbon on her collar and that she wore little or no makeup, an apparent attempt along with the heavy glasses to downplay her attractive symmetrical features.

Phillip looked away at the glistening sink and mirror, the closed bathroom door and a small table with a phone book but no phone.

"Maria's a pretty good girl — at least she works," the nurse said grudgingly as she inspected the neck brace.

"Girl? She's a lot older than you."

"You know what I mean." The nurse pulled back his sheet.

*Ah yes, the **help**.* "No, I don't know."

After his snarling answer, she plunked a thermometer into his mouth. "Whatever," she said, then began to roughly knead various parts of his upper torso and kept asking, "This hurt, Phillip? That?" He shook his head to each inquiry; then she went to his arm again and jostled the IV.

"Tha hurs," he said, and she extracted the thermometer. He felt breeze on his bare skin when she lifted one side of his hospital gown.

"Quick little procedure here, won't hurt," she said.

What? That's my dick! "What the hell are you doing?"

"My job; disconnecting your catheter."

He felt tugs and a jab and then a release of pressure.

“There, that’s all there is to it,” she said. “When you’re ready for the bathroom, we can roll the IV in there, or you can start out with a bedpan.”

Not while you’re here, lady. He lifted his head and looked at her. “Don’t you warn people before you do something like that?”

“I did warn you.”

“Not until you got there, you didn’t.”

“Maybe you should just relax, Phillip.”

Yeah, shut up and behave — ***relax****, my ass.* He turned away again as she started pumping up a blood pressure band above the elbow of his broken arm. When she finished and ripped apart the Velcro, he acted like it didn’t hurt.

The nurse moved over to his abdomen, pressed firmly, causing a sharp pain. “Tender there,” she said.

No shit. He watched as she continued the once-over. Her Dutch-boy hair-do bounced like a bobble toy and settled with each step, its perfectly square notch framing her scrubbed waxen face. The nurse’s official-looking security badge had a likeness of the hospital building, her mug shot with a forced smile, and M. VAN DE GRAF, R.N. in quarter-inch bold letters.

I’ve seen this angel of mercy before.

“Any other pain you’re experiencing, Phillip?”

Just you, Florence. He lifted his right arm. “This IV aches more than the broken arm.”

“They do that sometimes; your pain med was backed up. I took care of it.”

“Maybe you can take off this neck brace; don’t need it.”

“No, doctor must okay that.” She eyed him with even more disdain. “Maybe you want to shave that stuff off your face. I suppose we’ll need to find you some toiletries.”

“Don’t bother, I won’t be here that long,” he said, and she smirked like she knew better. “Do you know anything about what happened to me?”

“Doctor knows the details of your, uh, incident.”

"Great. What about when I got here?"

"They said you were out when you arrived, then semi-conscious when they worked on you. You've been sleeping ever since, like you hadn't slept for days. Do you have insomnia?"

"No. How bad is my arm?"

"Broken, obviously. When he comes— "

"Yeah, yeah — *doctor* will explain it all."

"He's making a special late round just for you." After she scowled and started adjusting the drip line again, he turned to the window and stared at the floating particles in the light. She left the IV and stepped in front of him, her garish diamond ring refracting in the sun.

Lucky Mister Van de Graf.

"The IV stays until you start eating. Will you eat?"

"Of course I'll eat. What kind of a question is that?"

"Just following instructions. Your lunch has been ordered. For now, we need to fill in what's missing on the admission forms."

"Can I write like this?" He lifted his right arm and the attached tubes.

"Most of the forms just need your signature; I'll fill in the rest. They opened your wallet for I.D., insurance and— "

"Fine, just show me where to sign." *Maybe it'll get rid of her.* She raised the back of the bed and rolled the patient table over him from the side. He rested his right arm on the white Formica while she retrieved a brown clasp envelope from her cart and slid out the papers.

"So you still live in Ponderosa, Phillip."

"Still?"

"High school, senior year — Marsha Wilson?"

God, pageant queen Marsha — dumped on Warren half his life. I knew I'd seen her. "Yeah, I remember now."

"Small world."

Too small. "Why did you wait to tell me?"

She moved a chair between Phillip and the sink and sat down with the patient chart and clipboard to record the information. "I was curious to see if it would dawn on you."

"You've changed a lot." *Changed uniforms.*

"Short hair. And you, still quite the individual."

And you, still quite the priss.

"Why didn't you and, um, Warren come to the tenth reunion? Almost everyone was there," she said, her tone intimating they feared humiliation.

"I think I was doing something important like washing my clothes. Warren was probably in Japan or France on business; he's vice-president of a computer company." *Put that in your alumni news and smoke it.*

"Impressive," she said, unimpressed. "Okay, they didn't locate any relatives; who's your next of kin?"

"My sister, Joann, in Portland."

"Phone?"

"Don't know it. *When was she going to call?* "She's in the book under Joann Meyers, maybe Stark — best I can do."

"Do you want her advised of your condition?"

"No, I think I'll survive."

"Anyone else?"

"I need someone to call Parnell's and have him tow my truck to the house." *Damn, what about Ali?*

"I'll have them arrange that." She asked more questions to complete the form and went on to the next one. "This is a list of your clothes and the contents of your pockets. Read it to be sure it's right." The nurse handed over the sheet; he skimmed it in a few seconds.

"I had ulcer medicine; it's not on here."

"Confiscated; it's procedure. Doctor will discuss that."

"Of course. Why am I in a private room; is this joint trying to make a little extra cash?"

She didn't answer. "Now medical history, Phillip."

Mister Stark to you. He answered negatively to the first maladies on the long list; then she continued, stopping to note Phillip's ulcer, his mother's cancer and Stephen's death.

"How did your father die?"

None of your business.

"Well?" She tapped her pencil and glared at him.

"Ran into a bridge."

"Auto accident?"

"What do *you* think?"

"Whatever." She made the notation, then finished the medical background and explained two other papers. Van de Graf quickly perused everything and asked a couple of missed questions. She put the papers in front of him and he signed them as fast as he could.

Good, now get lost.

"There's a good boy," she said with a facetious grin. He turned away, scrawled something on a napkin and folded it over. A sudden stab from his ulcer made him wince.

"What's wrong?" she asked, looking suspiciously at his napkin. The nurse took away the pen and inserted the papers into the envelope.

"My medicine. What am I supposed to do about my gut?"

"You'll have to wait for Doctor Lang. I can get some crackers to calm your stomach." She lowered the bed.

"Don't want any damn crackers; it's not a stomach ulcer. I'll eat something when I get my medicine."

She peered over the rims of her glasses. "Now let's not be uncooperative."

"You can help with one lousy pill. Who's uncooperative?"

"I'm not going to argue with you." She nearly sang the last three words, making them sound like a warning.

"When will he get here?" Phillip asked.

"The doctor?"

"No, the Pope."

She frowned. "You do know this is a Catholic hospital."

"You don't say? That must be why Mary is bigger than the TV." He directed his eyebrows toward the Madonna on the wall.

"No need to be sacri— "

"Look, you won't help me, and you don't have anything else to do. Why don't you just leave?" He turned his head toward the window; his intestines seized again.

"Phillip, I don't appreciate your attitude."

"I don't appreciate yours. Make us both happy and go."

"When Maria's back. There has to be someone here."

There does? He turned to her. "Why?"

"Doctor Lang will expl— "

"Bullcrap, more damn secrecy."

"I'll ask you to please stop the swearing, Phillip."

"Okay, then I'll ask you not to call me Phillip."

"Whatever," she said again, rolling her eyes as she began reorganizing her cart.

A hint of the chill rippled across Phillip's forehead. *It's coming. Now what'll you do?*

Maria came in and was immediately interrogated.

"Where have you been?" the nurse said.

Leave her alone.

"I am early, it was my break of thirty minutes." Maria sounded obedient but not intimidated.

"Okay, okay, keep a close eye on *Mister* Stark here; he's not cooperating."

Screw you, lady. The chill strengthened.

"Doctor will be here any time," Van de Graf said halfway out the door. Maria came to him and put her hand on his arm.

"Mister es-Stark. What is wrong?"

"Hi, Maria. Nothing — we were fighting a little. I'm glad you're back."

"You look es-cared again."

"No, I'm not scared. There's something trying to come back into my head. I just have to keep it away." She soothed his forehead with the back of her hand again. *Yes — thank you.* He started to close his eyes, and she lifted her hand.

"You want to rest, Mister es-Stark?"

Not ***Mister.*** He looked at her. "No, please stay here."

"It is a bad dream you have?" Maria held his shoulder.

"Sort of like a dream, except I'm awake; it's real." *It's already starting to fade.* "But you're helping me."

"What do you mean?" She parted his long hair again.

"You're helping me by just being here."

"I am happy you think I help you, Mister es-Stark." She put both her hands around his lower arm, above the IV, comforting him with a pat.

You're overmatched, chillbrains. He stared at the window a minute or so before speaking. "Maria, have they told you why you're here?"

"No. They just say to watch you, call the nurse when you wake up." She closed her eyes a few moments and when she opened them, crossed herself. "I just pray for you now, Mister es-Stark. You are going to be better, I know this."

A prayer'll do it. Shut up, the chill's gone, isn't it? "Uh, that's very nice of you. Will you do me a favor, Maria?"

"If I can, Mister es-Stark."

He handed her the napkin. "That's my neighbor in Ponderosa; could you call and ask him to leave cat food by my back door? Oh, and please tell him the garage is open."

She nodded willingly then hid the note in her pocket as if she had broken some rule. Phillip realized Maria was reacting to the arrival of Van de Graf and the two lab-coated doctors who shuffled in slowly behind her.

20

The physicians chatted by the door then moved to the foot of the bed. Maria backed away while Van de Graf stood at attention by Phillip like she was the one to be inspected. One doctor, much younger than the other, smiled in Phillip's general direction as he reached for the clipboard. He was clean-shaven, towheaded, well over six feet tall, his plain face showing no wrinkles or stress.

"Doing okay, Phillip?" he asked, seemingly in charge, as if he had decades of experience. Unaware that his patient nodded to the obligatory question, he skimmed the data. "I'm Doctor Lang; this is Doctor Mortinson," he said, attentive to the chart.

I'm over here, doc. "Hi," Phillip said.

Lang attached some papers to the clipboard as the nurse moved the table out of the way and raised the bed again. Phillip eyed the older doctor, who wasn't much taller than Maria. Instead of a shirt and tie like his counterpart, Mortinson wore a tweedy green sweater under the lab coat, though the day was warm. Skin drooped below his eyes down to a bushy white moustache, and Mortinson's straight silver hair touched the back of his collar. He squinted as if his silver-rimmed glasses were the wrong ones.

What's Einstein doing here?

Doctor Lang took a couple of long strides up to Phillip and finally looked right at him. "Does sitting up bother you?" he asked. The other doctor was scribbling notes.

"No, but my ulcer's been checking in."

"Yes, we'll discuss that in a moment," Lang said. He briefly examined Phillip's abdomen and torso then spoke again when he began to gingerly knead the trapezius muscles on both sides of the brace. "No pain here, then. Good, I think we can get rid of it." Doctor Lang turned to Van de Graf.

Phillip sent an *I-told-you-so* scowl toward the nurse as she took two rigid steps forward to remove the plastic device. She finished quickly and held the brace behind her back.

"I understand you're a teacher in Ponderosa," Lang said, giving the broken arm and cast an inspection.

Ah, bedside manner. "Yes." Phillip looked over at Maria, and again she reminded him of his mother, smiling proudly over some ordinary accomplishment.

The physician dispatched a cursory examination of Phillip's heart and lungs then began to remove the dressing from his head injury. "What do you teach, Phillip?"

"Junior high — science; P.E."

"Must be challenging." Lang removed the gauze from Phillip's head. After a few slow steps forward, the second doctor took a glimpse at the gash. Phillip saw a tiny yellow ribbon like the nurse's pinned to each doctor's lapel.

A company gesture, except for Maria's big bow.

"Before shift change we'll need a new dressing on the wound, Mrs. Van de Graf," Lang told her as he replaced the bandage.

"Yes, doctor," she said, standing now in front of Maria. Lang asked Phillip to hang his feet over the side.

Geez, see if you can keep your ass out of the air. He bunched the gown behind, swiveled to the side knee-to-knee and dangled his feet below. Lang shined a pocket flashlight into his pupils then wheeled the IV pole to the side and conducted a hasty neurological exam. When Phillip started to get back under the covers, the physician held him by the shoulder and gently pinched the skin under his upper arm, then did the same to his stomach and upper leg. After that, the doctors left him sitting there and took a few furtive steps away, mumbling to each other.

What the hell? "Can I get back in?" he asked, indignant.

"Yes, please go ahead," Lang said, then spoke to his colleague before coming back to the bed to begin a rapid-fire diagnosis. "Phillip, it seems there's no serious damage from the blow to your head; no concussion. It bled considerably, but five stitches shouldn't leave much of a scar; the swelling will last a few days. The contusions on your abdomen are from the seat belt, which saved your life, I believe; and you were also fortunate to avoid whiplash and deeper lesions. Your abdomen will be sore for a week or so.

"The arm has a relatively clean break in the lower radius, about here." His finger darted over to the cast, just above the wrist. "You'll be in the cast for several weeks; the arm will eventually be good as new. I'll show you the x-ray next time, and by then we'll have you up for a more thorough neurological exam. Do you have questions so far?"

"So far?" *There's more?* "I'll wait until you finish."

"All right. Doctor Mortinson and I have some items to discuss of a private nature." He picked up the chart and then approached Maria to read her nametag. "Maria, is it? You may leave now; please wait in the hall," Lang told her in a direct but cordial manner, and she left right away.

Just a damn minute. "I need to speak to *you* privately," Phillip said, twisting his forehead toward Van de Graf, indicating she had to leave. Though the doctor hadn't expected this interruption, he turned to the nurse.

"Mrs. Van de Graf, for just a moment please." She arched her brow and walked out, stiff as a soldier.

"Thanks," Phillip said. "If you're going to discuss something private, I object to *that* woman being here."

"I'm sorry you feel that way; Mrs. Van de Graf is one of our most efficient nurses." He seemed more disappointed than surprised by Phillip's comment. "You do understand it is part of her job to confer with us on what we're about to discuss?"

"Fine, just not here, but you can bring Maria back."

"I'm afraid that wouldn't be professional."

Professional *— give me a break.*

"She'll be back soon," Lang said, and came around to the side of the bed, the old doctor behind him now, writing again.

"All right, so what's the big secret?" Phillip asked.

"How long have you had the prescription from Doctor May?"

"He's written it for years; since his partner died."

Lang didn't hide a disgusted sigh. "Okay, we'll come back to the ulcer later. Phillip, you arrived here with your weight and body fat below normal. How did that come about?"

Crap. "I don't know; maybe I need to reconsider my diet a little. My father used to do some of the cooking."

"Yes, we were sorry to hear of your loss. Do you mind telling us the circumstances of his death?"

What is this? "He was a drunk. He ran into a bridge, like I told the nurse."

"You didn't tell Mrs. Van de Graf he was an alcoholic." He glanced at Mortinson.

And watch her gloat? "None of her business."

"Why did you tell her you wouldn't eat?"

"I didn't. I said I'd eat when I got my medicine."

"Is the ulcer bothering you now?"

"Since she left, it settled a little. You know how it works, sometimes they flare up when you're aggravated; she aggravates the hell out of me."

"All right, I get it," Lang said, tiring of Phillip's opinion of the nurse. "What do you remember about the crash?"

"Not much. The ash was blowing everywhere; I was trying to get home." The doctors consulted their documents, so Phillip stopped. "Did I say something wrong?"

"No, please go on."

"Okay, so this jerk passes me, I couldn't see, and my truck was off the road. I don't remember exactly what happened next, but I was off that road before, after the ash fall, when I almost rolled it. I'm sure it was in the back of my mind that you can't brake hard or crank the wheel on those steep crowns." Phillip paused because Mortinson eyed him suspiciously.

*What's **his** problem?* "And I remember a pole; it must have stopped me. Should've braked a little more, I guess."

Mortinson stepped forward, squinting again. "So, you decided that hitting the pole was better than rolling over, Mister Stark?" he asked, hardly disguising his doubt.

Einstein speaks. "It happened fast; I think so. Why do I have two doctors?"

"I'm sorry," Lang said, "Doctor Mortinson is a psychiatrist; I should've mentioned that sooner."

"Why's he here?"

"After you finish your version of the collision, he has some questions for you."

*My **version?*** "I *am* finished."

The doctors changed places, Lang acting more deferential than before. "Please tell us how you're feeling emotionally, Mister Stark, after such an experience." Mortinson said, his eyelids sagging as if he was bored.

Already starting his thing — don't need this. Phillip ignored him, looking up at the ceiling until Lang intervened.

"Phillip, we both have other patients; we'd appreciate your cooperation."

Tell them; then Maria can come back. "All right," he said, grumbling. "How do I feel? Confused and pissed."

"At what or whom are you angry?" the psychiatrist asked.

Doesn't matter. "I don't know." Phillip turned away and saw Mortinson reflected in the blank TV screen above.

"Mister Stark, what do your supervisors say about your work, if I may ask?"

"My work? All my supervisor cares about is if I make trouble for him, and what *you* really want to know is how I get along, right?" Tubes and all, Phillip lifted his cup and shook a few ice chips onto his tongue.

"Yes, something like that." Mortinson rubbed his chin.

Einstein thinks he's Freud. "Okay, I'll cut the crap for you. I like teaching, but not the stupid system. That's about it." *Calm, Phillip, like she says.* He turned away and imagined Maria's pleasant face in the spot where it belonged, but the psychiatrist took another step forward into that space. He was so short and the bed so high that he and Phillip were almost face to face.

"Mister Stark," Mortinson resumed, "do you feel like you don't belong in education?"

"I don't know. Maybe education doesn't belong with me."

"I see. We'll follow up on that later." As if he were onto some grand insight, he raised his grey eyebrows to Lang.

Freud knows all. "Is that it?"

"Last night there was a witness, a hiker; his description isn't consistent with what you just told us." The psychiatrist nodded with self-assurance toward the papers held by the other doctor, who had taken another step back.

"I remember him. So what, why would I lie about it?" A hint of the chill crossed his back, between the shoulders.

"No one thinks you're lying," Mortinson said with a brief condescending smile. "You're telling us what you remember, but your condition has likely affected your memory. For example, he said visibility was good."

"Bull, that's one thing I'm sure of; I couldn't see."

"More importantly, Mister Stark, the witness and the officer suggested your crash could have been intentional," he said, his tone still placid.

Intentional? *Jesus.* "You think I tried to kill myself?" He felt the chill try to rally in his spine. *Easy.*

"We haven't made any firm conclusions."

Liar. "That's why somebody's here all the time?"

"Just a precaution. Tell me about that scar on your wrist, Mister Stark."

"What? That's the wrong side of my wrist, doctor. For God's sake, it's from an accident with a broken dish. You can just forget it, I didn't try to kill myself."

"Very well. Have you had any problems with alcohol?"

"I wasn't drunk."

"We know that, but we want to know— "

"Listen, damn it, I probably drink less than you do." The chill hesitated in his back, as if it were deciding what to do. *Shit, don't get messed up in front of them.*

"Mister Stark, please try to relax," Mortinson said.

The magic word again, thanks for the professional help.

Doctor Lang stepped forward. "How often were you taking the ulcer drug, Phillip?"

"I lost track. Every time my gut hurt, three times a day, maybe more."

"Mister Stark," Mortinson said, reclaiming their side of the conversation, "have you had difficulty sleeping?"

Ha, you're dead wrong. "No, I sleep a lot."

"More than you're accustomed to?"

He trapped you —just tell him. "I guess, but I'm always up late in summer. When I wake up in the morning, I have this coldness in my head." *It's waiting there, right now.* He stopped, expecting the psychiatrist would ask him to describe the sensation.

"And the sleeping?"

Guess the chill isn't important. "I go to sleep to get rid of the coldness. When I wake up, it comes a second time, then I go back to sleep again. I'm up by one." *Or two.*

"Any of that later in the day?" Mortinson asked, jotting in his notebook.

"No. Well, not usually. A couple times when, uh— "

"When you were stressed or angry?" Lang asked with some eagerness, and his cohort turned to him with a sneer.

Uh oh, Einstein, he's on your turf. "I don't know, you two argue about it." His nape trembled a little. "Finished now?" To keep the chill at bay, he closed his eyes.

"Perhaps we'll take a short break, Phillip." Lang sounded sheepish after committing his transgression.

"Yes, excuse us," Mortinson said.

Phillip opened his eyes and saw them walking at Mortinson's slow pace until they were gone. He started to rest but heard Maria come in and watched her return to the bed. *Thank God.* "Hi, Maria, please take a chair; I bet you didn't sit down all morning."

"Thank you, Mister es-Stark." She comforted his shoulder. "I cannot look lazy to the nurse."

You're twice the nurse she is. "Maria, even *she* knows how hard you work. Please sit."

Maria smiled then lowered the bed and scooted in a chair. She sat and moved her hands to his arm. Phillip closed his eyes again.

The royal treatment; you don't deserve it. After a couple minutes, he knew the threat of the chill was gone and he looked at her.

"Mister es-Stark, it is good you rest. I bother you?"

"There's no way you bother me, Maria. Did I get you in trouble with Van de Graf?"

"She is angry with you. You do not like her, why?"

"I knew her in school, we never got along."

"I see," she said, and then paused. "It is wonderful you are a teacher." Her dark eyes glistened. "Your mother and father, I think they must be very proud."

Of what? That's how she sees it, Phillip. "They both died, but I do have a sister who wants to teach."

"She knows you are in the hospital? I am sorry; I must, uh, be minding of my business."

"No need to apologize, I'll give her a call." *When I'm out of here.* "What about your family? Do you have kids?"

"Oh yes, three boys. My Ernesto, he— " Before she could go on, the two doctors returned, moving the rolling table over to the bed. Maria got up and exchanged smiles with Phillip on her way out.

"You look more at ease." Doctor Lang put a small packet on the table.

"Yeah, Maria's your best medicine."

"Well, yes," Lang answered, glancing awkwardly at Mortinson. "Phillip, we need to change your ulcer drug, the one you've been taking is contraindicated. Taken excessively, it can have serious side effects. I'd like you to start on this." He opened the sample into a miniature paper cup and then poured water over Phillip's ice. Both men stared at him.

They want to see if you'll behave. He picked up the pill cup and swallowed the medicine without water.

"Okay," Lang said, raising his eyebrows. "Phillip, your old drug is known to exacerbate depression, which you've been living with for some time, it seems."

"Depression? That's your big conclusion?"

Lang pulled the table aside and the psychiatrist spoke up with an air of serene authority. "That's what your symptoms indicate, Mister Stark. After losing a loved one, depression is, of course, normal for a while, but— "

Big deal. "That's good, isn't it?" Phillip said to Lang, intentionally ignoring the psychiatrist. "Except for my arm, a little bump and a few pounds, there's nothing really wrong with me."

The young physician turned to Mortinson, who resumed his slow spiel. "Mister Stark, what you seem to exhibit is beyond the normal grieving process. With prolonged clinical depression, the patient often denies he is profoundly ill, or is unaware, either of which can lead to tragic results."

Back to suicide. "Listen, I don't know exactly what happened and neither do you, but I didn't attempt suicide," he said, and Mortinson raised his eyebrows toward his colleague.

"We hope that's true," Lang said, "but we'd like you to stay a couple more days, start your prescriptions, eat regularly and regain some strength. We want to be confident about your frame of mind when you leave here. Doctor?" He bowed his head slightly to the psychiatrist.

"You've told us, Mister Stark, that the symptoms come with your anger, and I— "

"You don't get it," Phillip broke in. "I know my anger has become a problem, but I'm not angry when I wake up, and that's when I usually have *symptoms*. Explain that, doctor."

"Well, I was about to tell you I'd like to have a short session with you right now, if you feel well enough."

"I feel fine. What kind of session?"

"I suspect you're going to need long-term psychoanalysis. For now, we'll just have a preliminary discussion."

Farm house, analysis, I knew it. "Would it save time if I told you I hated my father?" Phillip said with a laugh.

"Mister Stark, it's a complex process to get to the underlying causes of serious depression."

Screw this. "I thought the drug was the big problem." He ignored Mortinson again and looked at the other doctor.

"It likely made things much worse," Lang said. "Your new ulcer medicine won't affect mood, and we also want to start you on an anti-depressant, which is most effective when used in tandem with therapy. It's important you understand that." He directed a patronizing smile to his colleague.

Want outta here? Do what they want — for now. "Can I assume you know there's no interactions with the new drugs?"

"Fair question — no known contraindications."

"All right, get on with it."

"Good, Phillip," Lang said, starting to touch Phillip's arm, but he thought better of it. "Since you're about to eat, we can stop the IV and drop the twenty-four-hour watch."

Hold on. "You're going take Maria and leave me with that nurse? I should've said I was going to jump out the window."

"Come now," Mortinson said, "Maria helps you that much?"

"Yeah, maybe she can give you some pointers," Phillip answered with a wry chuckle, but Mortinson ignored him and looked at his notes.

Stifling a grin, Lang cleared his throat. "Phillip, she can finish the day here. I trust you'll be okay tonight?"

"I'll manage. Thanks, doc."

"You're welcome. You'll also have a new nurse with the next shift, but Mrs. Van de Graf will likely be with you again in the morning. Please give her a chance. I'll leave you with Doctor Mortinson for now and see you bright and early tomorrow. Take care." Doctor Lang headed for the door.

"Don't wake me if Nurse Ratched is here," Phillip called to him. "I'll be trying to sleep through her shift." Lang pursed his lips with mild disapproval, then Phillip saw him meet Maria in the hall. They spoke a moment; she stepped forward to smile at Phillip and then closed the door.

Great, now it's me and Einstein.

21

Doctor Mortinson moved a chair a few feet away from Phillip, turned it toward the window and sat down.

What's he doing? "Why did you turn your chair around?"

"Allow me to explain. I— "

"Hang on a sec, is Maria still right outside?"

"Yes, to prevent intrusions," he said, facing the dull sunshine. "Now, I prefer to work like this, Mister Stark, so body language doesn't interfere with our communication."

"Whatever you say. Over."

"Pardon me?"

"So you'd know I was finished. Over."

"I see. If it's very uncomfortable not facing me, I— "

"Just joking, let's get it *over* with."

"Yes, humorous." He coughed before beginning again. "Mister Stark, do you mind if I address you as Phillip?"

"Knock yourself out." He turned from Mortinson to the white ceiling overhead.

"Okay, Phillip, please fill me in a little on the history of your relationships, a couple of the best and worst."

This is such crap. He gave Mortinson very sketchy descriptions of relationships with his mother, Warren, and Lupe. "Last but not least," he said, "my father." *The part he's eagerly awaiting.* "Actually, we're talking about two people, my father and Stephen." After a terse summary of his conflicts with Stephen, Phillip finished with, "You're going to love this: he haunts me in my dreams. Interesting, huh?"

"Well, yes, I'd like to go a little deeper with him."

What a surprise. "Weren't we going to keep this short?"

"Another ten minutes or so, Phillip. Maybe you could tell me whatever comes to mind about him from your childhood, and then move forward. Try not to self-criticize or edit what you're about to say. Let your thinking flow, and verbalize whatever comes to you — just your early memories about him and wherever they take you."

He must think I'm an idiot. "Free association."

"Well, yes."

"I did have to take psychology to become a teacher."

"Of course, all the better. So just let it go, don't stop yourself. If you like, I'll put your bed all the way back and you can close your eyes."

"I don't think so." He stared at the blank TV.

"If you're comfortable, please begin."

This is stupid — so tell him, he wants to hear it all. "This is stupid." *Good boy — what the hell.* "Okay, let's play your little game. My father, my real father, he was, I guess, pretty ordinary, quiet, puttering with things all the time. I'm not sure what made him so content, being with my mother I guess. They were pretty close, only argued a little when he was plastered, which was maybe once a week back then. He wasn't violent, just a jerk, not himself, and I'd stay away from him.

"Anyway, we did some things together, especially woodworking. He bought me a kid's carpentry set and had me using real tools in no time; we made things other kids envied, like a big fort we put up." *So I miss him, big deal.* He felt pressure in the corners of his eyes. *Don't cry, twerp, just say it.* "I miss him, that's all, even though near the end I could hardly ever reach him."

What a load of crap.

Shut up. "Bastard," he mumbled.

"Excuse me, Phillip?"

Damn. "Not you."

"Then who?"

"Talking to myself, it's nothing."

Mortinson waited, and then asked, "Do you hear voices?"

"No, I just remember things people said. Don't you?" Phillip looked at him, noticing that his white hair almost touched his back.

"Who do you remember?"

"A few people, mostly Stephen; things he repeated."

"And you speak back to him?"

"Usually not out loud. So what? I know it's not him."

"If you're not too tired, please go on."

Now he thinks I'm schizo. "There's nothing else to say."

"M-hm."

"What's that supposed to mean?" There was a slight tremble in his lower back. *No, don't let it come, look at something.* He tried to concentrate on the tiny holes in the ceiling tiles. *What's Einstein doing? Waiting me out.*

"What are you thinking, Phillip?" Mortinson finally asked.

"That you're waiting me out. This is a waste of time." He could feel the chill move up his back. *Damn, it's coming all right. Easy, you can hold it off.* He searched for a pattern in the soundproofing holes overhead.

"Phillip, from your description of the relationship and your recurring dreams, I'm sure you'd agree that you seem to harbor a remarkable amount of hostility toward your father."

That's it? He looked back down. "That's my feedback?"

"Did you expect something else?"

"News flash: I don't agree with your learned conclusion."

"Please explain."

"Okay, I told you about my *hostility* for Stephen, and then I told you about Dad. Did I sound hostile toward him?"

"It seems you're exhibiting what we call resistance. As you approach memories that could reveal the root of some of your problems, you resist talking about them, perhaps skipping painful details. You seem to deny the difficulties you must have had with him when you were younger."

"Hate to burst your bubble, but I wasn't a miserable kid." *It's colder; forget this. No, nail him.* He turned to Mortinson. "Okay, you want free association? When I told you about Stephen your face must have lit up, but I don't know, since I can't see it. You thought you were peeking into my uh, subconscious. Let's see if I remember this BS. Uh, repressed deep-seated aggression toward my father — right?" He shivered between his shoulder blades.

"But you don't get it," Phillip continued, "I'll tell you again. Before he started drinking a lot, I loved him. Then I still loved him when he wasn't drunk with his buddy Mick, the world's two biggest assholes. How could I repress aggression toward Stephen when I hated his guts and knew it all along? Nothing hidden, nothing harbored — I hated him for what he did to my father. So how am I doing with my *flow*?" Phillip waited; no answer. "I just called bullshit on you, don't you have anything to say?" The chill had nearly settled at the back of his head.

"Well, you seem to be transferring your anger toward me."

"From Stephen to you? It doesn't have anything to do with you, doctor. What I care about is what's wrong now." *So cold — now what'll you do?*

"Go on."

"With what, painful subjects from my childhood? I have something painful in my head right this moment, but that doesn't seem to matter to you."

"I'm not quite sure what you mean, but I believe I'm pretty aware of your condition."

"That's a contradiction if I ever heard one." *To hell with it.* In order to concentrate on the ceiling, Phillip moved his left hand to his temple to block the fluorescent glare, but he grazed himself on the forehead with his cast. "Shit," he said and put his arm down.

Only those little holes up there. Wait, just connect them. Over, down, back, up — first square. Now back and down, over and up — the second one. Good, over and down, back again, and up... His head moved with his eyes in the making of squares until he heard Mortinson talking nearby.

"...not aware you could be this incapacitated..."

...over and up — don't bother me, it's working. Let's see, that's square ten — a whole section. Start again — connect the dots, boys and girls. Down and back...

After a few minutes, Phillip heard the doctor speaking again.

"...and I have a recommendation..."

...and over, leave me alone — then down and back...

"...we should consider ECT..."

...that's better. Over and up — what's he want? "What are you talking about?" Though the edge was off the chill, Phillip held his place up in the tiles.

"Electroconvulsive therapy, ECT, along with analysis."

ECT my ass, Doctor Frankenstein. "Listen," he said, his eyes still directed above. "Nobody's going to put any goddamn electrodes on *my* head." The chill kicked right in.

Cálmate.

She's right. Start again — back, down, and over...

"Phillip?"

Screw you. "Leave me alone." *And then up, close the square and back — calm — down and over again...* Phillip continued until he was drowsy, but he saw Mortinson by the bed, watching him.

"Are you all right, Phillip?"

It's still close. "I'm okay," he said, his eyes heavy.

"You should know ECT is the most immediate way to ease symptoms of severe depression, and it's relatively harmless."

BS. Now more alert, he looked right at the doctor. "I read somewhere it destroys brain cells and memory."

"It's rare for memory loss to be severe, and a regimen of ECT in conjunction with long-term analysis— "

"It's rare? That's reassuring? What's more depressing than losing *any* memory?" *Calm, Phillip.* "Please go."

"Very well, I'll leave for now."

Thanks for nothing. He slept nearly an hour, waking when he heard Doctor Lang come in to ask Maria to wait outside. Smiling at Phillip, she let go of his arm and left.

Didn't even know she was here. "Why are you back, doc?"

"Well, Doctor Mortinson called and said you weren't very receptive to his recommendations."

"Now wait a minute, he wanted to— "

"Phillip, I don't want you to get upset; please hear me out." The doctor was friendly but serious. "Do you feel well enough to talk for a minute?"

Phillip checked the ceiling tiles to reassure himself that his refuge had not somehow vanished. "I'm fine; go on."

"There are other options for therapy besides analysis."

"Yeah, tell that to your buddy Einstein."

"I'm going to be honest, Phillip; I'm looking for some cooperation here so I can let you go in a couple days." His voice was now stern. "We have to agree on a treatment plan and you need to show me you're going to follow it."

He thinks I'm a basket case. "Go ahead."

“As I told you, anti-depressants aren’t enough; it’s crucial you begin therapy, perhaps with a younger therapist. Will you agree to that?”

“Do you have one who isn’t obsessed with potty training?”

“All right, Phillip, I get it. I have a list of reputable therapists who are not analysts, but you have to agree to stick with it. I want you to take it easy here for a couple more days; a day or two at home, and then begin therapy. If it doesn’t seem to work out, then you try someone else, that’s the deal.”

Or what? He sniggered. “Okay, I see you’re serious.”

“You have a serious illness, Phillip; I expect *you* to be serious about it. I’ll make an appointment for about four or five days from now. Are mornings okay?”

Fat chance. “No, I can’t do it in the mornings.”

“You have a commitment?”

With the damn chillbrains. “Yes.”

“Afternoon then?” He turned to the door, ready to leave.

“Late afternoon is good.”

“Okay then, if there’s nothing else, we’ll talk about this again tomorrow.” The doctor smiled and walked out; Maria returned right away and moved the table back over the bed.

“Hi, Maria, I won’t sleep through your watch this time.”

“Rest is very important, Mister es-Stark. They say you will get better soon?”

“Sure, could be a lot worse.”

“Good. Oh, Mister Beck is happy to care for the cat.”

“Thanks, Maria. Can I ask you another favor?”

“*Claro que sí.*” She comforted his arm again.

“Would you call me Phillip?”

“It would not be right near the others I think. When nobody is here, maybe I call you *Felipe*, the name of my *tío*.”

“Felipe, sure, Felipe.”

The shiny cart clattered through the doorway, a frowning Mrs. Van de Graf guiding it from behind. Ignoring Maria and Phillip, she put a pill cup on his table.

She's not **too** *pissed; tell it to the shrink, lady.* He watched her fool with the IV and rip off some adhesive along with his arm hair, but he anticipated the pain and tried hard not show it. *No satisfaction for you, Florence.*

Van de Graf spoke to him through clenched teeth. "Take that pill. Your private helper can find a straw. Lunch is here, and you'll eat or I won't disconnect the IV." She turned to leave.

"Would you be so kind to tell me what the pill is?"

"I've had enough of your sarcasm. Doctor just told you what it is." She turned to leave and looked at Maria. "*Your* job is to tell me if he doesn't take it."

"Bye, Florence," he said, but she just walked out.

A puzzled look on her face, Maria got a flex-straw from the small chest of drawers and put it in his cup. "Ready for the pill, Mister es-Stark?"

"Not *Mister Stark*, okay, Maria?"

"Oh, yes. *Sí, Felipe.*" She smiled, moved the cup closer, and he took the drug.

"Your boss is not too happy with me."

"Yes, she is angry, but she knows this work. I think she will learn how to be with people."

When pigs fly. He sipped more water. "I'll try to get along with her." *And keep her off Maria's case.*

"*Está bien, Felipe.*" She comforted his arm again, then Van de Graf came back in with a food tray. She put it on his table and glared at him. The tray held a carton of milk, a navel orange, raisins, and a slab of some kind of chopped meat with two buttermilk biscuits lathered in thin yellow gravy.

Aak — try not to be a total jerk about this. "I'll take the milk and fruit, but I can't eat this," Phillip told the nurse in the most cooperative tone he could muster.

She started dismantling the IV. "Well, let me guess, Mister Stark." She yanked off a band-aid; he pretended again it didn't hurt. "You don't like biscuits and gravy."

"I don't eat meat anymore." He kept an eye on her and readied himself for each little burst of pain as she removed the rest of the adhesive and the needle.

"So, you're a vegetarian," Van de Graf finally said, securing cotton over his vein with tape.

"No, I just don't like meat."

"I believe that makes you a vegetarian. It's obviously done wonders for your health," she added, putting the materials on her cart. "What about eggs and dairy?"

"I just told you I'd drink the milk." *Easy.*

The nurse picked up the food tray and smacked the milk carton and the little red box of raisins onto his table; then she dropped the orange so carelessly it rolled onto the bed. "You'll have to wait until five for a vegetarian meal." She disappeared around the doorway with her cart, and Phillip looked up at Maria.

"Well, I tried," he said with a grin.

"Yes. She hurt you, Mister es-Stark?"

"No, I'm fine, Maria."

"Tomorrow, maybe she forgets. Please try your milk." Maria pried open the carton, inserted the straw, and put it in front of him. He sucked in some long gulps. "On my next break, *Felipe*, I can find juice and cookies," she said.

"Thanks, I'll be okay, but I'll need help with this orange in a minute." He palmed the fruit in his right hand, enjoying the sense of having some physical control again.

"Please tell me why you do not eat the meat," she said, furrowing her brow slightly.

"No big deal. It just doesn't feel right to me anymore."

She waited and looked at him, encouraging an explanation.

Okay, make it quick. "Maria, you've probably heard about cultures where they eat dogs?" He sipped more milk.

"Yes, I think it is horrible."

"Well, I feel the same about dogs as pigs or cattle."

"I see. What if a big animal, if it tries to hurt you?"

"I'd kill it if I had to, but humans are more dangerous." *Enough of your deal, Phillip.* He sucked on the straw until air bubbled in the carton.

"Some of what you say is like the old ways in Mexico."

"What do you mean?"

"We are *indígenas* — Indians. My grandmother and my grandfather always believe the old ways, not very good Catholics. *Mi abuelita* talk the old language today, not much es-Spanish. When they kill for food, she believe the es-spirit is everywhere, in the animal, and the plants. Some people they laugh at her and *mi abuelito*." At the mention of her deceased grandfather, she crossed herself. "But for them it is religion; I have *respeto*, um, respect for this."

"I'm sure you do, but you're a good Catholic, right?"

"*Pues, sí.* Sometimes we say a true *Mexicano* is also *Guadalupano*. I can fix the orange for you?"

"Yes, please, but will you explain what you just said?"

"*Sí, Felipe.*" She picked up the fruit. "*Juan Diego*, he was *Chichimeca*, he see *La Virgen de Guadalupe* long time ago, and then many people change to be Catholics." As she spoke, long strips of peel spiraled down into the garbage can. "One day, we hope *el Papa* will make *Juan Diego* a saint." She let one hand go from the orange and crossed herself again. "Last year, I see *el Papa — en México*; he bless *La Virgen de Guadalupe* and *Juan Diego*."

The Pope — thank God she didn't hear me before. "You went to Mexico for his visit?"

"Oh yes, my family from here and *México*. It is a great honor for us." Maria paused to consider what she said, picking off the last bits of peel. "I am *Guadalupana*; it is even part of my name."

"It is? Would you tell me your whole name?"

Her smile broadened. "*María Guadalupe Martinez Prieto.* I am *María* only here. To my family, I am *Lupita.*"

Good God. "You're called Lupe?"

"Sometimes. This is a surprise to you?" She placed the sectioned orange on a napkin in front of him.

"My girl friend— " *You wish, Phillip.* "Her name's Lupe."

"Yes? She is *Mexicana*?"

"Half, from her mom."

"*Guadalupe* is um, common, but to have the name is also an honor." Maria washed her hands at the sink and smiled at her thoughts. "My husband, he is a quiet man; but he is angry with Mexican movies of *La India María*, because she is *payasa*, a clown with my name." She finished the sentence with a self-effacing titter and dried her hands on a paper towel. Maria looked up at Phillip, who was swallowing a section of orange. "You look sad when you talk about her, *Felipe*," she said.

"About Lupe?" *It's that obvious?* "We're having a few problems."

"I hope she knows you are a good man. Have more orange."

"I will. You see the good side of everyone, Maria; I tend to assume the worst until people prove differently. But you're a good teacher, you've shown me I can at least be more neutral."

She was listening carefully, but didn't comment.

Maybe she didn't understand. "Is *neutral* a new word?"

"No, it is almost the same in es-Spanish, but you learn this not because of me." She placed one hand on her chest, just below her neck. "It is because you are good."

"Thanks," he said, trying not to scoff. "Maria, do you know they're letting you stay here all day?" So as not to discomfit her, he didn't show how much that pleased him.

She nodded and smiled. "Yes, they tell me."

"Where's your regular job?"

"I clean on this floor and two others."

The right people doing the wrong work. "When you go back, I'm going to miss talking to you."

"I can visit on my break?"

"Of course, if you promise to sit and rest."

She grinned at his reminder. While Maria reached for a chair, he looked at the holes in the ceiling. *Phillip's little squares; at least you've got some backup.*

Maria slid the chair up next to him and sat. "You will get better and maybe come visit my family. I make you *tamales* with beans, no meat," she said, the corners of her eyes narrowing with the quip.

"Sounds great." He patted her once on the arm. "Maria?"

"Sí, Felipe."

"If it's not too personal, may I call you *Lupita* when nobody's here?"

"*Claro que sí, mijo*," she said, her nurturing touch around his wrist again.

22

Waiting for his cab at the emergency entrance, Phillip felt foolish in the wheelchair, a male orderly standing at his side. Maria had removed some of the grit from his hat, and he was glad he had it to hide the dressing on his head. She traded addresses with him before he checked out and promised to pray for his health. He reminded Maria to sit down more often, and they hugged each other like parting relatives.

Phillip's disturbing dreams decreased during the three days in the hospital, but the chill was still there, strongest in the early mornings when he had to make his squares in the ceiling to escape back into slumber. Maria visited on every break, and he nearly forgot about the chill in the afternoons, except when it surfaced once after an acrimonious exchange with Van de Graf. He ignored her as much as he could and got along okay with the other nurses.

Now he scanned the well-kept hospital grounds and saw no ash, but the sky was flint grey. *Traffic's blowing around what's left.*

Though the sunlight was filtered, the afternoon was very warm; he pulled down his brim and stared at his battered tennis shoes. He felt perspiration begin to accumulate on the inside facing of his cap.

"Could we please wait in the shade?" he asked, not looking up.

"Of course, sir, thought you might want some light after being cooped up," the orderly said as a florist's van parked in the lane.

"Thanks anyway," he answered, and the man pulled him under the wide awning at the entrance. A taxi pulled up in front, not fifteen feet away. It was an old four-door Bel-Aire with a fresh white paint job, a phone number stenciled in black on the side. Phillip could tell that the cratered bodywork was finished in somebody's back yard with Bondo and a ball-peen hammer. He was surprised to hear the Chevy's motor run smoothly.

"Mornin'," the cabby called to them as he circled around the front of the taxi, a lit cigarette between a thumb and forefinger. His slightly stooped frame betrayed his actual height of almost six feet, and he was so thin that his belt was pulled into its last hole and threaded back into the front loop of his tan work pants. A yellow ribbon curled from the collar of a white polo shirt tucked deep into the trousers.

The cabby combed his free hand once through his straight, slick grey hair, incursions of baldness showing only on his temples. He rattled out a deep cough as he came to Phillip, who was repulsed by the old man's cigarette stench, bloodshot eyes, and the liver spots on his face.

"Where to, bud?"

*He's gawking like **I'm** the one who's kicking off.* "To Ponderosa," he finally answered.

"Okay. Can you walk over— ?"

Phillip was already up from the chair, stepping off the curb and reaching for the cab's rear handle. He got in, closed the door with his right hand, then reached across the cast and put his plastic bag of meager belongings on the floor. Holding the seatbelt clamp with his elbow, he shoved in the metal slot from the other strap. Phillip coughed from the stale, pungent smoke odor then rolled the two half-open windows all the way down. He tilted back his sweaty hat and watched the man come to the front door, take a last drag, and then hack a couple more times.

The driver extended his lanky arm through the window and dropped the cigarette into a soda can that was secured in a black plastic holder on the driveline hump. The can apparently contained liquid since the butt gave off only one wisp of dying smoke. The cabby opened the door and sat down.

"So, were you in a traffic accident, bud?" he asked, turning down his dispatch radio before he shut the door.

No, it's bubonic plague. "Yeah."

"Thought so; the patch is about where you'd hit a windshield."

Not to mention all the scratches, Sherlock. Phillip pulled the brim back down far enough to cover his head injury. The driver put the automatic transmission into gear and then reached out to start the meter, revealing a faded red and blue tattoo of a patriotic anchor on his upper arm.

Great, I'm riding with Popeye.

"Feelin' all right, bud?" He pulled away from the curb.

"Fine, thanks."

"Well, that's good. Anybody else hurt bad?"

"Just a pole."

"Must've been a pole in the ground, hardly any Polaks in Four Rivers."

Except the old rummy driving this cab.

" 'Sides me, that is. Frederick Stankewicz at your service." He smirked into the rearview mirror, showing his crooked, tar-stained teeth.

Got any more Kurt jokes, Phillip?

The driver turned out of the lot and onto the city streets. "My uncle changed our last name to Stanky; I'm Freddy Stanky, almost like Eddie Stanky, the Dodgers ol' second baseman."

Never heard of him. So? Lighten up, for God's sake. "Hi, uh, Freddy. I'm Phillip Stark."

"Pleasure. So, I imagine that pole's left in better shape than your car, Mister Stark?"

"Guess so, but I'd prefer not to talk about it."

"Sure; don't mean to pry. Lotta folks climb in wantin' to tell all." He stopped talking to cover a deep cough with his fist. "Kept my own bar twenty years, then I started up this hack thinkin' I wouldn't hear everybody's problems so much. Not so; I've heard just about everything from up here."

Good, then there's nothing for me to add. Phillip just nodded and began to check out the scant amounts of ash in the tidy neighborhoods, mostly middle-income stuccos and ramblers built in the fifties. *Looks like it never hit here.* Freddy jabbered some more, glancing at his passenger in the mirror, but Phillip smiled weakly and looked back out the window. When the talking from up front ceased, Phillip counted the curbs of thirty front yards and felt drowsy as the cab entered the highway.

"Not too long now; you doin' all right?" Freddy asked.

I must look like crap. "Yeah, I'm still fine."

Out in the country, the traffic moved just below normal speed, each vehicle followed by a filmy wake of ash. Phillip scanned the checker-boarded green and grey fields, discovering details he'd missed before. Next to a well-preserved turn-of-the-century farmhouse, he noticed a mound of earth with a wooden door. *An onion cellar? There's still ash on top; no reason to move it I guess.*

At the next farm Phillip watched the wooden blades of an old-fashioned windmill rotate in a slight breeze. *Why haven't I noticed these things?* He went on observing the countryside without hearing from the driver. When they neared Ponderosa, Phillip saw the haze still formed a dingy grey three-hundred-sixty-degree horizon with a ring of blue sky at the middle.

Freddy called back to his rubbernecking passenger. "You stayin' out here with someone?"

"What? No." With three of the four windows down, they were practically shouting to each other.

"Saw you checkin' around. Usually that'd mean a stranger or a camera bug, somethin' like that." The yelling made Freddy expel an especially rough cough.

The third degree. "No, neither one. I live here."

"Sorry, I can be a nosy ol' coot sometimes."

Got that right. Phillip watched a white sports car speed by way over the limit. *Idiot.* He grimaced, anticipating a thick cloud, but Freddy hardly had to brake for a light fog of ash. *It was worse that night; there must've been some wind.*

"Okay back there?" Freddy called.

Get a grip, Phillip. He just nodded.

"That fella's probably got one of those radar detectors."

"Should be against the law." They were still shouting back and forth.

"They are. What part of town?" He slowed the taxi.

Phillip saw him in the mirror fumbling around for the cigarettes in his chest pocket. "Ponderosa Estates."

"Got it." With the reduced speed, Freddy didn't have to speak so loud. "You mind if I smoke?"

Mind if I fart? He's just asking, don't be a jerk. "If you don't mind, uh, Freddy, the smoke gets to me."

"You bet; won't kill me to wait for one of the buggers." He let go of the pack and slowed some more for the light up ahead. " 'The devil hath power to assume a pleasing shape.' My wife used to say that about her Kools."

She split, or she's dead. "The Bible?" Phillip asked, now in a normal voice. He wasn't really interested but doing his best to be friendly.

"Sounds like it, but nope, it's from Hamlet."

"Was she an English teacher?"

"Just a big reader; the Bible and Shakespeare were her favorites."

"Isn't Hamlet one where they all die at the end?"

"Yup, it's a gloomy tale, but it was the words she loved. She'd always spot Shakespeare in everyday conversation; she taught me some of the famous lines." Freddy cleared his raspy throat as he left the highway at the junction, turning on to Pine Avenue. He nearly stopped to avoid a fellow senior in a Chrysler who exited Kurt's parking lot without looking.

Honk at the ol' blue-hair.

Freddy's face turned momentarily solemn, then he drove by the retail strip onto the mile of countryside before downtown, well below the speed limit of forty. "Man alive, even with all this ash, the air is better here."

"Fewer cars," Phillip said.

"I like that; hope to live not far from here some day."

"That right?"

"Yup. I know some folks out here, but main thing is to be closer to those mountains; been thinkin' about some land."

"You a hunter?" *Shakespeare-quoting, no less.*

"Not anymore. Stopped after my kids grew up."

"How come?"

"Didn't need the meat, but I still enjoy scoutin' the animals. I think they somehow know when you aren't after 'em. Seen twice the deer and elk since I stopped huntin', and plenty of goats, sheep, bear, even a big cat."

No way. "You saw a mountain lion?"

Freddy grinned as he saw Phillip's interest heighten. "Matter of fact, seen her twice, the same one I'm pretty sure, up on Raging Creek. You know where that is?" He drove slowly by the old school into the center of town.

"Yeah, I've been in on that trail head, pretty busy there. You saw it while you were what, hiking?"

"More like bushwhackin' with my grandson; he's twelve." He looked out at some imaginary traffic problem. "His daddy, my youngest, was in the navy like me; died on a ship comin' back from

Vietnam." Freddy paused again, his face grim. "I try not to think about it too much, but it's one thing to die in combat, another from somebody's negligence."

Jesus.

"Enough of that." Freddy reduced his speed even more for the residential neighborhoods.

"Sorry about your son," Phillip said quietly. He watched two magpies waddle around a yard like chesty waiters in black tuxedos. On every block he saw someone still removing ash in one way or another. *Ask about the lion, but don't be pushy.* "You were telling me about your grandson."

Freddy coughed from deep in his chest. "He's a fine boy. My son actually named him on account of his mom's love for Shakespeare — William S. Stanky."

They didn't. He arched his brow toward the mirror.

Freddy laughed when he saw Phillip's expression. "Just the *William* part, middle name is Samuel. I sort of took over best I could with Willy; help Kate out when I can. Me and the boy even got snowshoes for winter." Freddy cleared his throat again. "Don't know how long I can keep up that part. I'd have more time for him if I semi-retire; get some land up there a ways; go right out my door into the trees when we feel like it, cut down the travel." He passed the last houses and turned onto the state road.

Phillip rolled his windows over halfway up so they could hear. "What holds you back, if you don't mind me asking?"

"Nah, don't mind. Been over two years now since my Myrna died, but it's still hard to think about sellin' the place. Forty years there with the same ol' gal; still got a lot of her stuff."

"Yeah, my dad kept a lot of my mother's things."

"Does he live here?"

"After she died, he went downhill — died this summer." *You're telling him all this? The lion, Phillip.*

"Sorry for you, Mister Stark. The *downhill* part is some food for thought."

Damn. "I didn't mean— "

" 'Course not. Were you pretty close with him?" He passed the LEAVING PONDEROSA sign and started up the incline.

In another life. "Just when I was younger."

Freddy looked up in the mirror, stifling another cough.

He's waiting for more, or for me to shut up — just tell him. "My mom died of cancer when I was in high school, then, well, he never adjusted and started to— " *That's enough.* Phillip stared at the ash-cloaked scrub pines on the ridge.

"Sorry to make you think about it," Freddy said.

"It's okay."

"Y'know, we're all runnin' out of time. Myrna had one for that, too: 'Golden lads and girls all must, like chimney sweepers come to dust.' Don't recall which play that's from. Point is, I better get on with it."

"Get the land?"

"Yup."

"I hope you do." *Pipe dream.* Phillip kept to himself as the taxi made it onto the mesa. The telephone lines next to the road caught his attention. *Is that the pole? Maybe that one. Crap, doesn't matter.* He stretched his neck to see how much ash was in the road ditches, but he couldn't see any.

"Somethin' wrong?" Freddy asked.

"Hm? No." He settled back in his seat. "So where might you be looking for land?"

Freddy spoke to his side mirror. "It's all yours, bud," he said, slowing for an empty logging semi that rumbled by on the left, leaving a faint trail of ash. "Another big hurry. Anyway, I can't be as far up as I'd like. I've been eye'n some property near Blue Valley, maybe I could afford to put in a small cabin and a garage."

"You might want to re-check land values there."

"Why's that?"

"Have you seen the old ranch?"

"The Ponderosa? Don't pay attention much to that place."

"It's being re-developed, very quietly, last I saw."

"You don't say?" Freddy turned into Ponderosa Estates.

"I saw the new foundations — left at the third street."

"Sounds like you know Blue Valley pretty good."

"I sometimes hike or ski up there." *Used to, anyway.*

"When did you see this construction?" Freddy started making his turn at the corner by Mister Beck's house.

"It's been, uh..." *How long?* "...a few weeks — second house on the left. They plan on a hotel, all the comforts; they were even clearing land for a bunny slope and a lake. I think the developers greased some palms and used old permits."

"Sounds like somethin' s rotten again in Denmark."

"My God, there's my truck." The wrecker had parked it by the curb; Freddy stopped and they both viewed the damage. At the center of the front bumper the indentation staved so far into the engine that the fractured headlights were inches closer together, making the small pickup look cross-eyed.

Jesus, it's totaled.

"Man alive, you hit a pole all right," Freddy said. "You're lucky it didn't catch fire. Did you fall asleep?"

No. "Yeah, they said the seat belt saved me."

"I guess you're livin' proof they work. You have insurance?" Freddy asked, and drove on.

"Just liability."

"Then she's junk now." He turned into the driveway.

"Yeah." Phillip checked the yard as the taxi came to a stop. *Brown needles in my tree — summer shedding — I hope.*

"Mister Stark, could I ask you somethin'?"

"Sure." *What the hell, already told him half my life.*

Freddy reached over to stop the meter then turned back toward Phillip, the motor idling. "I saw your eyes light up when I told you about the lion."

"Yeah, I'm interested in wild cats. I had a couple questions for you, too."

"Figured as much. Are cats related to your work?"

"Sort of. I teach science at the junior high here."

"A teacher, good for you." Freddy shut off the engine and covered a raw cough. "I bet your dad was proud of that."

God. "You're the second person who said that to me recently. He didn't care about much of anything, except drinking." *Crap, don't leave anything out, Phillip.*

Freddy's neck had stiffened so he spoke through the mirror. "I shouldn't have brought him up again."

"It's all right."

"So, you been interested in wild cats a long time?"

"Yeah, I was supposed to help with some field research this summer, it's postponed for now."

"That a fact? Can you tell me what the research is?"

"Sure." *He's just being friendly; don't bore him to death.* "We were supposed to be studying the lynx up north. Some of them have radio collars, so I had a fair chance of seeing one."

"Never come across a lynx. She's small next to a cougar, little doohickeys on the ears?"

"That's right." He paused to gauge Freddy's interest.

"Any chance seein' one here in our mountains?"

"Very rare this far south."

"What's her highfalutin' scientific name? I'm sure you know it." Freddy smiled at his fare through the mirror.

"Felis lynx canadensis." *Show off.* "Canada Lynx."

"Canada Lynx. Tell me more about what she looks like."

*He always says **she** and **her**.* "Like you said, smaller than a cougar, forty pounds tops, but very long legs for its size; lives mostly off snowshoe hare; black tufts on its ears and a black tip on its short tail, and— " *What the hell — **her**.* "And her paws, they look oversized like a puppy's — huge and furry for moving in the snow. Her face looks something like a grey tabby."

"You paint a picture of a beautiful animal, Mister Stark."

"Yeah, she's beautiful." Phillip smiled at him. "Forget the *Mister*, Freddy; sounds like school. It's Phillip."

"Okay, Phillip. I imagine the research is because there ain't many left — I mean *aren't*." Freddy chuckled. "That's the only word Myrna ever got on me about. So how many lynx?"

"The population is still pretty healthy in Canada and Alaska. You really want to know all this?"

"Yup, real interestin' to me."

"Okay, there's probably less than a hundred in the Northeast, a few hundred way up in the Rockies and maybe two hundred here, mainly up north in the fir and lodgepole pine."

"She must be pretty shy."

"Yeah, wants nothing to do with us."

"Less forest and more people; survivors go further up."

"That's about it. The study is supposed to come up with more accurate counts to qualify them for threatened or endangered status."

"Ya' ask me, it's plain dumb they're not on the list already. So when is this study?"

"They're going to try to start up in September."

"Well, you do some important work..."

I don't do anything.

"...a teacher; scientist. I wish you and the other professors good luck with it."

"Thanks, but I was just a gofer on the project. The timing is all off for me now because of Saint Helens."

"Maybe it'll still work out." Freddy cleared his throat, fondling his cigarette pack. "Volcano changed a lot of plans, that's for certain, but how often do we get to see somethin' like that? You folks really got the brunt out here. What was it like?"

"It was pretty amazing." *Stop; he wants his smoke, not your little ash story.* "You want your cigarette?"

"I'm okay for now. So how was it here?"

"Like Four Rivers, I guess, except more intense. I'll never forget going out, pitch dark in the middle of the day, totally quiet, no engines, no people, nothing. The birds were silent, no sign of life except this mouse. I saw him for a couple seconds, and then just his perfect little tracks. The ash didn't slow him down; he was out there looking for food, trying to survive. Then my neighbor came out, cussing about ash in his precious swimming pool. Right then, if I had to choose between that mouse and the neighbor for a spot on the evolutionary scale, no contest."

Freddy thought about Phillip's comments a few seconds before he spoke up. "I think I get the drift of what you're sayin'. A lot of my fares complain about the ash; I just listen. The way I see it, we've got nothin' to gripe about. Any of us could've been campin' or workin' over there when it blew. It was a tragedy those people died, but if you pay attention to what else is happenin' it changes how you look at things." Freddy paused, looked at the yard and coughed.

Where's he going with this? Ask how he found the lion.

"Like the heat wave in the South this year," Freddy said. "Hundreds of people already dead, most of 'em my age and older, because they couldn't afford to get out of the heat."

Good God. "Heard something about it, but not much."

"Not spectacular like a volcano, but I see it as damn shameful; it could be prevented," he said with an atypical frown. "All those old people sufferin', just wasted; I guess *expendable* is the word. Suppose that's why we don't hear much. When I think about them, I don't have much truck for people who gripe about the ash. I figure the least I can do is send a few bucks to help out through the Red Cross."

What about you, Phillip? Too busy staring at your damn carpet? "I'm glad you told me; I'll send something, too. I see you have a yellow ribbon on your shirt."

"Don't want to forget them either. Some make it all political, but I see those folks as our neighbors caught up in the middle."

I pray for them, Mister es-Stark.

Freddy probably does, too. "I see what you mean."

"Afraid I'm just prattlin' on here, professor."

Professor; *there's a joke.* "No, not at all." *How long are you going to BS with this ol' guy?*

"I got us off track; was gonna tell you about the lion."

Okay. "So when was the last time you saw her?"

"Two summers ago, fishin' with Willy. I bet he'll remember it his whole life."

"Yeah. It's amazing you've seen the lion twice."

"Mostly luck. There's a pool on the creek there, fair fishin', but it's a drinkin' spot for all kinds of critters, tracks all over. First time I saw her, must be five years ago, I came to the spot and there she was, just slurpin' away like a kitten. Now every time I go up there I give it a try..."

God, maybe he'd let me tag along.

"...sneak in through the woods, downwind and such. Best chance is a hot day; a drink is about the only thing that'll bring her out in the daytime; but you already know that."

"What makes you think it's the same lion?"

"Mainly size, maybe a hundred pounds, a female. I think I could tell her from another."

"How long were you able to watch?"

"This last time with Willy, maybe five seconds. Had my dogs that day, they spooked her; she was gone like a ghost..."

Mister Lopes would love this.

"...but the first time, well, it was like a gift. I sat maybe thirty yards away, behind some trees and bushes on the opposite side of the creek watchin' her drink. Darned if she didn't climb up and stretch out on this big ol' boulder and take a nap in the sun. I watched her maybe a half-hour, her ears flickin' off flies like a house cat. I could count her whiskers through my binocs until she just strolled away like it was too hot." His story forced out another scratchy cough.

"Man, did you take her picture?"

"You'd need a fancy lens. Watchin' her meant more to me than a photo anyway." Freddy reflected a few moments. "Only bothered to tell a couple ol' friends and the boy; I think he was the only one who believed me. That made the second time real special too, but now the kids tell Willy he's crazy as his ol' grandpa."

"Does he bring a camera now just to prove it?"

"Yup, he does. Might not ever see her again, or maybe we will, but I don't have nothin' to prove." He grinned, revealing a jagged incisor, and Phillip was sure Freddy was confident he would see the cougar again.

Ask to go along. No, you don't even know him. You want a chance to see the cat? "Uh, Freddy, do you think I could see the spot some time, if I promised not to blab about it?"

"Why, you bet, we'd be glad to have you," Freddy said, genuinely pleased by the request.

Geez, just blurt it right out. "I wouldn't be imposing?"

"Not at all, but seein' her could take ten times or— "

"I know, but I appreciate any chance. It must've been a little scary being that close; did you carry a gun?"

"With Willy I pack a big ol' pistol in case I have to chase somethin' off. I'd be plenty scared if she came after us, but I heard the last fatal cougar attack was way back."

"The last one in the state was in the twenties."

"Shoot, we had two, three fatal attacks by yard dogs in Four Rivers just the last couple years."

"Right. What kind of dogs do you have?"

"Two ol' mutts. Weren't much at huntin' birds, just good companions. What's your take on huntin', professor?"

"They have the right if they follow the game laws, but the only thing I ever shot was a can with a twenty-two."

"That could be awkward for a young man in these parts."

"Yeah, I'm used to it. Every fall someone asks when I'm going out, and I say I'm doing something else. A few times I got pestered and I told them I don't hunt. Then you get the *he must be queer* look."

Freddy cleared his throat again. "A few years ago I told some buddies I wasn't huntin' anymore; they thought it was my health. When they asked, I told 'em I didn't need the meat. Like with you, a couple of 'em kept at me until I said I never did care much for the killin' part anyway. Funny how I found out who was a real friend — the ones I still bowl with; the others avoided me." Freddy chuckled and coughed.

Good riddance.

"Spent too much time doin' things because it's supposedly what men do," Freddy said. "Take wildflowers; you'd think they're not a man's business. I bet you know all about 'em."

"I've studied animals more, but plants are a hobby."

"Myrna and I learned some wildflowers before she passed; the boy likes 'em too. You can be our guide when you come with us."

Phillip smiled. "I bet you know more of them than I do."

"Don't think so, professor."

That's me, Professor Stark; this is embarrassing. "Guess I better get going." Phillip picked up the plastic bag, undid his seat belt and opened the door. He walked around the taxi, the bag dangling from his cast as Freddy started the motor. Phillip took out his wallet as he approached the window.

"Your money's no good today," Freddy said.

"Come on, you can't make a buck like that." Phillip held the wallet to his side with the cast and maneuvered out a twenty-dollar bill with his free hand.

"No sir, I appreciate the tip on the land; I'll probably have to look somewhere else. It was a pleasure talkin' to you." He reached out and they completed a firm but comfortable handshake.

"I enjoyed talking to you, too, Freddy. I have an appointment in Four Rivers on Friday at three. Are you available?"

"Sure am, this makes it official," he said, handing out a dog-eared business card. "Ol' fart Freddy's cab. It has dispatch and my own number, but no need to call this time. Pick you up about two?" he asked then began writing the time in a loose-leaf notebook on the seat.

"That's fine. Are you sure about the fare?"

"Yup. And when you're feelin' better, you give me a call and we'll go on up to Ragin' Creek before the snow flies."

"Thanks, Freddy, and uh, good luck with the land." He awkwardly jammed the card and the twenty into his billfold.

"You take care, professor." He released the hand brake and backed out. Phillip waved once as the taxi passed the wrecked pickup, Freddy lighting up his smoke.

Nice ol' guy, and you had him nailed. After watching the cab disappear around the corner, Phillip went over to the ponderosa and picked out a handful of dry needles. *This is normal, but it needs attention. Yeah, spray the tree, feed the cat and dig the ash — what a great plan.* He turned to the house. *You forgot the mail. Later, just go in.*

Mister Beck had lowered the garage door, but it was ajar because of the brick Phillip always left at the base for Ali despite Stephen's objections. He walked over, lifted the door and glowered at his father's Chevy. *Sell the damn thing and buy a truck, easy as that.* At the back door there was a bowl of hard cat food on the step, and a note taped to the knob.

Phillip- Have checked each day, no sign of the cat. Hope you're feeling better. Gil B.

"Shit," he said out loud. *Take it easy, Ali'll figure out you're here.* Phillip reached into his pocket for his keys, then discovered he'd left the door unlocked. *Stephen would've freaked.* He entered the house and found mashed white nutmeat, papery brown skins and scores of whole peanuts all over the floor. *Knocked them over that night — seems like a month.*

Indifferent to the crunching under his shoes, he came to his recliner, sat down, dropped the bag and looked at the blank TV. *Lupe must be back. What would you say to her? They think I'm nuts, Lupe, but I start therapy soon — so how was your trip? Shit, stop staring at that damn screen.* He walked down to the den, sat at the desk and glared at the phone. *Wait a few days; settle in. Joann was going to call — last Sunday, I think.* He switched on the ringer. *The doctor said to rest; maybe leave it off.*

He debated with himself about the phone, then stood up and lackadaisically pushed all the billiard balls but the eight ball into the pockets. *Guess I'll spray the tree; look around for Ali.* He tried a few times to ricochet the black ball across the far corner and back into the pocket where his cast rested on the rail. After several more attempts, he finally banked it in and retrieved the ball to go for two in a row. The phone rang, startling him, and the hard sphere dropped from his hand to the carpet, clanking on the floor without bouncing. He reached for the receiver and answered with a quiet "Hello."

"Well, I'll be. Where've you been, Stark?" It was the principal again.

Damn. "Uh, I've been sick, the phone was off."

"So I guess that means you're better. Okay, there's a settlement with the association, your contract is in the mail along with a supplementary for the camp in August."

Bullshit. "I told you I'm not doing the camp." He felt a shudder at the small of his back.

"You better think about what's good for you, Stark— "

"Don't threaten me." The chill rallied at his neck.

"I wasn't threatening you. What's your problem?"

***You**, asshole.* Phillip hung up and flicked off the ringer. "Keep in touch, *boss*," he said with a laugh. On his third or fourth stride toward the TV room, his momentary glee gave way to the chill's onslaught. His head frigid and pulsing, Phillip staggered to his room, sat on the bed and swayed to the design in the carpet. *...then* *up and over, back and down again. Up and into the slit, around and back — home sweet fucking home...*

23

Phillip relapsed the next day into a double bout with the chill, but Ali's return in the afternoon helped him disengage from the dull gloom of his morning. After lavishing attention on the cat for a while, Phillip decided to make a few calls. He thanked Mister Beck, phoned in a pledge to the Red Cross for the heat wave, and then called Parnell to come for the truck. Phillip salvaged maps, tools, gadgets and parts from his pickup, then an hour later he watched it get hauled away like a dead animal, staring cock-eyed down at the street.

On Friday it took all his resolve to get up and be waiting for the taxi at two o'clock. He sat up front and buckled his seat belt, noticing a long cigarette butt stuck in the soda can under the dashboard. Freddy had on brown work pants, black loafers and a polo shirt, this time a tan one, no cigarette pack in the chest pocket. He backed down and pulled away from the house.

"Freddy, I might drift off on the way in."

"Rest if you need to, professor. Still early," he said, turning the corner. "Want me to pull over a few minutes?"

"I'll be okay; thanks." Phillip leaned his head back and watched Freddy take a peanut from a plastic bag on the seat, crack it deftly with one hand and toss the nuts in his mouth, the shells into a paper sack on the floor.

"Goober pea?" Freddy asked.

Curious about the term, Phillip wrinkled his brow.

"My folks called 'em that back in Virginia. I read once that *goober* comes from an African language." Freddy made the turn onto the state road and pushed the bag toward Phillip. "Help yourself."

"Thanks, maybe later." They watched a red Mustang pass the cab, leaving behind a fine veil of ash.

"I'll clam up so you can rest and not be bothered."

"You don't bother me, Freddy." He smiled then looked out the window; they were both quiet on the short drive to Ponderosa. Staring at the passing telephone poles, Phillip fell asleep before they got to the main highway and didn't wake up until Freddy slowed down to drop him off in Four Rivers. They were in one of the city's older neighborhoods at a two-story house converted to medical offices.

Phillip thanked him and took the stairs to a short porch, looking down at the new tennis shoes that had been in his closet for months. He also wore clean jeans, a sport shirt and had replaced the ashen Ponderosa hat with his red-orange Portland Trailblazers cap. The Herriot novel he still hadn't finished was wedged under his arm above the cast.

He walked into the remodeled living room, a waiting area for six health providers; five with academic alphabet soup listed after their names. The last one on the directory was Phillip's therapist: R. GIRARD, M. ED.

Deciding not to claim insurance, he paid the secretary for a session then sat to fill out Girard's form in one of the black office chairs that lined the walls. He finished, then peeked at the other people waiting: one was asleep; the others flipped through *Business Week*, *Golf Digest*, and *Women's Day*.

What a lineup. Phillip put the form in his book with Doctor Lang's letter then looked at the ocean-blue walls, each with two large framed prints of impossibly quaint forest cottages. He noticed that a graffiti artist had enhanced a nearby bland sculpture of some ancient goddess by supplying red Magic Marker nipples to the siren's white breasts.

A realist; right below a cheesy cottage. He opened his novel, but an endless instrumentation of "Moon River" droned in the background. *Aak, MUZAK.* He tried to read until the therapist came out, fifteen minutes late, and announced with a smile: "Phillip?"

He was less than ten years Phillip's senior, had a full head of neat dark-brown hair, protruding ears and no sideburn vestiges from the seventies. His most remarkable feature was a steadfast smile that etched permanent creases in his deeply tanned face. The counselor was slender, an inch or two taller than Phillip, and conservatively dressed foot to waist in black oxfords, pleated charcoal slacks and a black leather belt. Tucked neatly into his trousers, however, he sported an incongruous turquoise shirt, brightly patterned with prismatic streaks and blossoms. The silky Hawaiian garment, buttoned near the top, covered most of a gold chain on his neck.

"I'm Roger," he said.

Cool shirt, but stuffed into the pants? He stood and gave the form to the counselor. "Phillip Stark."

They shook hands and Roger asked about his teaching assignment as they entered an inner office. Phillip just said, "Junior High Science," then Roger enthusiastically shared that he left school counseling a few years earlier to strike out on his own.

Phillip was vaguely aware of the brightly decorated room as they sat down opposite each other in matching overstuffed chairs upholstered with chartreuse cotton ticking. *Like sitting in a damn marshmallow — at least I can see his face.*

Roger checked his plastic yellow clipboard. "So, you were referred to me by Doctor Lang?" he said with a blithe smile, his raised eyebrows eclipsed by his dark skin.

What a shit-eating grin. "Yes, here's a copy of his letter." Not hesitant to be free of the cloistering chair, Phillip stood up to extract the envelope from his book. He handed it across then stepped back and sat on the wide armrest, crossed right ankle to left knee, his shoe only a few feet from Roger's face.

"Snappy looking sneakers, Phillip. A new purchase?"

"M-hm." *He's worried I'll stay here.*

"So are these chairs. Aren't they comfortable?"

No. "They're fine."

As if opening a prize, Roger's eyes widened as he unsealed the envelope. "I'll just have a look, if you don't mind," he said as if apologizing, and attached the letter to his clipboard.

He must be high on something. "Keep it; I have a copy."

"Of course, please make yourself comfortable."

Placing his book on a small glass coffee table between them, Phillip saw Roger look askance for a fleeting moment at the red cap on his head. *He wants me to lose the hat too.*

Roger brought out a plastic orange hammer from behind his chair, put it on the table then began to read the material.

Phillip saw the word MELLOWMALLET molded into the handle of the toy. *What's the hammer for?* He scratched at his dark-blond beard and spotted a yellow smiley-face poster near Roger. *How charming.* He finally lowered his backside into the roomy flaccid chair, resting the cast over his waist, right arm at his side. He removed the hat and placed it on his book. Roger glanced up at the patch on Phillip's head and gave him a quick approving nod.

Oh what a good boy am I. He took a closer look at the windowless, oblong office. Framed posters and prints of rainbows, flowers, blue skies and cutesy animals adorned the walls, all spotlighted by track lighting that encircled most of the room. Below a rendering of seraphic sunbeams breaking through fleecy clouds, some unabashed wisdom declared: AS WE CHOOSE LIGHT OVER DARK, WE CHOOSE HAPPINESS OVER UNHAPPINESS.

So Roger is Mister Happiness and Light — like the preacher at the funeral. This is going to be just ducky. He spotted another smiley face on a second door, EXIT painted in precise black calligraphy above the top molding. His eye for carpentry detected that the exit was an addition to what was once probably a storage room. *An escape into the alley for his nut cases. Look at this place; you could be next.*

While Roger still examined the papers, Phillip saw a wide maple desk at the end of the office. Bouquets of white daisies in lavender vases garnished three lacquered bookcases that covered the wall from the desk to the entrance. The shelves were jammed with all sizes of books, some close enough to read the jackets. The two gaudiest titles were FEEL GREAT NOW! and NEVER A NEED FOR THE NEGATIVE! *Never? That should be a good one.* He saw some embossed volumes, including *The Holy Bible.*

So what? Even you have a Bible. The closest shelf had at least a dozen inch-thick books with pastel yellow covers: EIGHT STEPS TO JOYFUL LIVING. *That must be his guru.*

Roger moved the papers under a light-blue writing pad and then scribbled notes with a gold-plated ballpoint pen. Still beaming, he looked up. "Phillip, let me start by apologizing for running late, I was on the phone with a client in crisis."

Client? What's this guy selling, insurance? "No problem; I had my book."

"I appreciate your flexibility, it's been a very busy summer. It seems to be that doggone old volcano, especially the ash fall."

"How is that?"

"Well, I think of it as widespread cabin fever from those horribly dark days and the cleanup, so many interruptions to daily life;

the ash never seems to go away. It's been very challenging for all of us." The broad smile didn't waver with his complaint.

***All** of us?* "Sounds like it bothered you a lot."

"Well, I've tried not to let it. A week of vacation in the islands was our best decision." Roger's voice lilted when he said, *best decision*, as if everyone had the same option.

Good God. Easy, Phillip. "So you escaped the whole thing."

"Yes, for a while anyway, and we even missed the dreary monsoons; it was so sunny, warm and beautiful. How about you? My gosh, Ponderosa, did you find refuge?" The therapist seemed exhilarated by what they were sharing.

"I had some plans ruined, but the ash fall was amazing."

"Oh? Good for you, Phillip, I applaud your ability to choose the positive side of *that* experience."

"I didn't choose; that's just how it was for me."

"Well, that's wonderful. Phillip, before we get going, I noticed you were looking over my festive little gallery. I'm happy to report this dark old place is now temporary, but I've tried to brighten things up as best I could."

Farm house. Phillip nodded, trying to act neutral.

"My wife and I just bought a home with a separate apartment..."

Blah, blah, blah. As Roger spoke and gestured, Phillip saw a Milky Way of crumb-sized diamonds sparkling from his wedding band.

"...private entrance for clients; we've started our remodeling and..."

Yeah, big bucks rolling in, thanks to the **doggone old volcano.** When Phillip didn't hold back a sigh, Roger paused.

"I get a bit carried away with my plans; sorry."

You're sorry, all right. Phillip just raised his brows.

"After all, I'm supposed to be the listener," Roger said, trying to jest. He checked his notes, then looked up with animated anticipation. "So, Doctor Lang says you started on medicine for, uh, clinical depression. I guess that's the phrase *a la mode.* I prefer the old word, melancholia."

Sounds like syrupy old music.

"How do you feel about taking the drug, Phillip?"

"Who knows? Maybe the crap will help."

Roger moved his fist to his chest, showing discomfort.

What was that, a repeat from lunch?

"And so you have hopes the medicine will work for you," Roger stated more than asked.

I just said that. "Yes I do," he answered.

"Perhaps it will; I hope so, too." Roger's tone was vacuous. He jotted on his pad then continued. "I don't know a lot about these new drugs yet, but I do know you've made a choice to be here; that's a very positive step in coping with your daily challenges..."

Like clogged drains and cat barf? Still ***coping*** *with those.*

"...to be congratulated." Roger crossed his slim legs.

Three cheers for me.

"Doctor Lang referred you to an analyst. How was that?"

"Didn't work out." *I'll spare you the details.*

Roger waited a few moments. "How do you feel about this diagnosis of *suicidal tendencies*?" he asked, reading notes.

Crap. "I *didn't* try to kill myself."

Phillip's surly reaction seemed to startle Roger. "Well, that's good enough for me," the counselor said in his practiced supportive voice. He was about to continue when there was a loud knock at the exit.

What the hell? There was a second knock.

"Excuse me, Phillip." Roger got up and walked to the back door, peered out, and opened it all the way. A gaunt man in casual clothes, perhaps in his sixties, stepped right in. The therapist backed up then stood his ground in front of the visitor, who peeked around Roger to gawk at Phillip.

Yup, this is where they keep the screwballs, Egbert.

Phillip made "big eyes" toward the intruder, who then turned back to Roger. The two men gabbed for a couple minutes until Roger finally sent him off with "Have a nice day."

Nice day my ass.

Roger returned to his chair, but didn't settle all the way back. He spoke up, chortling. "You just never know when things will come up," he said, expecting Phillip's empathy.

Bullcrap. "While you were having your nice little chat, he stood there looking at me like I was a freak."

"Gosh, I'm sorry. Mister Nugent is the owner; I managed to discourage him from checking the electric panel." Roger sat back and crossed his legs again.

Phillip looked directly at him. "Does he always walk right in or does he know how to use a damn phone?"

Roger pursed his lips, but the smile endured. "Again, I'm very sorry, Phillip. Please try to relax."

Another jerk telling me to relax.

"I wouldn't be concerned; Mister Nugent's a nice man."

Sure. "That makes it okay?"

"Perhaps we weren't quite ready to communicate, anyway."

My God. Phillip shook his head and looked down at the light-brown pile carpet. *Easy, or you'll be staring at* ***this*** *damn rug.* "Can we just get on with it?" he finally said with as much courtesy as he could summon.

"Certainly, Phillip." Roger took a few seconds to regain his thoughts and his cheery demeanor. "Okay then, first I want to say that I like the way you speak so honestly..."

I like the way *Johnny sits down; same phony BS as student teaching.*

"...were telling why it didn't pan out with the analyst."

No I wasn't. "Let's just say he was looking for all of these repressed problems from when I was a little kid."

"So you feel your challenges are more immediate than some mysterious complex from your childhood?" A sardonic sneer momentarily replaced Roger's saccharine smile.

"Sounds like you're not a big fan of psychoanalysis."

"Well, it's not really for me to judge."

Gee whiz, Roger, you ***did*** *judge. So what?*

"So, Phillip, what happened next?" he asked with a half-smile as he made another notation.

"After I crapped out," he paused, "with the analyst?"

"Yes, please."

He cringed again; ***crapped out*** *is too vulgar — thought so.* "I was told to try someone younger; you were elected."

"Well, I'm glad you're with us and..."

At these prices, I bet you are.

"...hear you saying you want to focus especially on the here and now, and I want to reassure you we'll do just that. If you're ready, please start with how you're doing now; then only go back as far as *you* think is important."

Something's screwy — get on with it. "The truth?"

"Yes, please."

Let's see what he really wants. "Okay, right now I'm fine, but it takes me half a goddamn day to get this far." Phillip stopped when the counselor's smile receded. *That did it; the shit just hit the fan.*

"Phillip, this will probably be the only time I'll interrupt." Roger put down his fancy pen. "I need to share this with you; it's not a judgment, but how I feel about something that makes me uncomfortable." As he leaned forward to put down the clipboard, the necklace disengaged from his shirt and a solid gold icon of some saint hung momentarily in front of Phillip.

Holy moly. "You don't like swearing."

Caught off guard by Phillip's perception, Roger's eyebrows went up. "It's just a personal preference really, a strain to my comfort zone." He waited for a response.

Even Lupe wouldn't buy this. "Well, I can't guarantee I won't swear again, Roger, and if you're not comfortable with that, then maybe we should just bag it."

"Phillip, we can easily work this out. All I'm saying is I appreciate it when you can hold off." Roger sounded like he was begging. "I understand completely you might slip."

"Why don't you tell me why it's such a big deal for you?"

"Well, the negativity of it tends to distract me and— "

"Even a word like *crap*?"

"A word like that makes me envision, well, *stuff*, coming from the person's mouth."

"My God, that image is more profane than the word."

Roger's head jolted back, his face blank; then he forced a perky smile that didn't fit his bewilderment. "Phillip, I stopped swearing many years ago because I discovered it was just another obstacle that kept me from being in touch with how I really feel."

"Sometimes it helps me express *exactly* how I feel."

Roger stiffened, uncrossing his legs. "We could continue without your compliance if necessary."

"That's mighty nice of you."

"Do I sense you feel some dissatisfaction?"

"Whatever you sense, I don't see why we should go on."

"Please say more about why you feel that way."

"Because I don't buy your explanation. You're laying your sanctimonious morals on me."

"You think I'm trying to influence your beliefs? I'm only asking you to respect my personal preference when you can. I don't think it's related to my beliefs or yours."

Phillip turned his head toward the cloying visuals on the walls. *Just find out what the rest of his deal is.* "Okay, I'll try to tone down my *vile* language, but no promises."

Roger resurrected his smile. "Thank you, but it goes both ways — if somehow I make you uncomfortable, please let me know."

"Deal. So, are you ready for my little story?"

Roger raised his brows, and Phillip began with an understated account of his life with Stephen, the therapist nodding to every statement. He took no notes and responded occasionally with affirmative rephrasing. After a few minutes, Phillip thought Roger's eyes were drooping.

Yeah, this is boring; let's make it more fun for him. He told a little about his mother, making a point of her religion; the counselor perked up and jotted a note. *Thought so; I'll hear about that.* "So, is that enough background?"

"We can always go back when you think it's important. Perhaps you can tell me more about your day-to-day situation."

As Phillip superficially described his sleeping/chill rut, Roger's grin seemed to grow until he couldn't hold himself from chiming in with: "So you're saying in the afternoon you seem to control things better."

More of his parrot act. What's he so enthused about? "I have a question, Roger. From the letter and what I've told you, do you think I need therapy?"

"Yes, but I'm already confident of your improvement."

"How's that? You know next to nothing about me."

"You're saying that I don't have enough background?"

Another frigging echo. "Yes, that's what I said."

"If there's more you wish to share, please go ahead."

"No, you've heard enough to ask a relevant question."

"Well, my first job is listening, but just let me reassure you that we've had wonderful success with similar profiles as yours."

Phillip glared at a rainbow butterfly. *Let's see, a profile — depressed offspring of dead alcoholics. That's D-O-O-D-A — doo-da.*

"Phillip? Will you expand upon how you feel right now?"

"I told you, I'm fine now, and I told you about when I'm not fine." ***Doo-da.*** "I don't know what else to say unless you ask me something."

Nonplussed but maintaining congeniality, Roger said, "Please give me a moment, Phillip."

As the counselor scrawled on his pad, Phillip's right arm went to sleep. He stretched it out and read two more slogans on the walls. *Hm — HAPPINESS IS A CHOICE. MAKE LEMONS INTO LEMONADE — how sweet.*

Roger looked up, buoyant again. "Phillip, maybe we can move on from how you feel in general to how it felt to tell all that."

"Didn't feel like much of anything, like with the analyst. So far, the experience hasn't been much different."

"You're saying it was similar with him? Interesting."

Hard to believe, huh, Rog? "Yeah, he sat there and said almost nothing, and you just paraphrase everything I say to death. I think it's starting to upset my, uh — What did you call it? My *comfort zone*. You said to let you know."

"If I may explain; paraphrasing is how I try to clarify."

"It's rewording; you aren't clarifying anything for me."

"The idea is for us to be on the same page; to validate your statements and— "

"I don't want your validation," Phillip interrupted, and Roger's face went blank again. "If I'm going to cut back on swearing, you can do the same with the paraphrasing."

"Okay, Phillip, I'll try not to clarify, but I'm sure I'll slip. Maybe we can forgive each other's trespasses."

"Ah, so the Lord's Prayer is part of your therapy?"

"Just an expression, but I see you're familiar with it."

"My mom was big on that one, too. Okay, now what?"

"Where you go from here is what really matters," he said, thinking Phillip was showing signs of cooperation. "From now on, attitude is everything."

"My turn to paraphrase. You're saying my crappy attitude made me sick. Oop, I said *crappy*, I didn't last very long."

Roger ignored the taunt by scribbling a quick note. "It's not for me to judge your old attitudes, Phillip, but I will be asking you to refocus your decisions and choices through a fresh attitudinal framework." He broadened his smile, hoping for some affinity in Phillip's reaction.

Gobbledygook. "A better attitude." *Who defines that?*

"More like positive attitude. We believe every action is preceded by thought, so let's make it a good ol' positive one," he said as if he expected agreement with the platitude.

What about reflex, instinct? He has zero questions and all the answers. Without comment, Phillip covered his brow with his right hand, peeking through the gaps. He crossed his eyes and transposed the smiley face from the poster to Roger's head. *That's perfect.* He grinned as he lowered his hand, prompting Roger to continue with even more exuberance.

"Phillip, one example is to replace a word like *sick*, which you use to refer to yourself, with a positive one."

How about ***Stark raving mad?*** He chuckled uneasily at the private pun he and his mother shared a few times.

"Did I miss something?"

Everything. "What's the point of just changing words?"

"Do I hear you say that thinking of yourself as healthy rather than sick wouldn't be of some benefit?"

"Yes, but that's another paraphrase; we're even."

"With positive thinking we believe it's possible to find some good in the worst situations."

"Oh really? Tell that to a rape victim, or somebody whose kid was killed by a drunk driver." When Roger didn't respond, Phillip read a poster that said: I'M POSITIVE ABOUT THINKING. *What this is about is* ***no*** *thinking.*

"Perhaps we need to get back to you, Phillip. Could it possibly be that you've decided to let melancholia have the upper hand, instead of seeking the brighter side of things?"

"So it's something I can just change my mind about? I have some news for you. I don't control it; if I did, I'd get rid of it. I think I can get better, but from what I've seen here so far, you don't even understand what I'm fighting."

"I believe I do understand, Phillip, and our methods can help you with what you said — a way to control your mind, but positively. Will you hear me out on what we have to offer?"

*Warren would say **we** must have a mouse in our pocket.*

"Phillip?"

Made it this far. "Yeah, go ahead."

"Good," he said, eager to explain. "Each week, we'll work on a strategy from our book, EIGHT STEPS TO JOYFUL LIVING." He nodded to the stack on the shelf. "You'll also receive exercises and some tapes to take home to help you develop your positive attitude."

"How much more do I pay for this positive attitude?"

"Excuse me?"

"The book and tapes."

"Well, the materials are well worth the price."

"Of course they are."

Roger didn't seem fazed by Phillip's sarcasm. "The first step is to concentrate on the present and avoid the pervasive negativity that's all around us in places like television or the newspapers. You begin your positive decisions and choices from this point forward..."

With my head in the ground.

"...first we'll have you concentrate on the afternoons, when you seem to be doing better. With every thought you'll choose the positive alternative, and I believe your afternoons will soon change from disagreeable into manageable; then enjoyable. Then we take on the mornings."

Just like that, white man's magic.

Roger picked up the MELLOWMALLET. "This is a fun reminder. If those negatives jump into your mind, you can smack 'em away." He struck the side of his own head with the accordion end of the toy hammer, causing a muffled squeak and a goofy look on his face.

Good God all mighty.

"Here, this one's for you," Roger said merrily, handing the toy across, but Phillip didn't lift his hand to take it.

"No thanks. I assume there's more to your program."

"Just getting started," the counselor said, trying not to show discomposure as he put down the hammer. "One of our main strategies we call *affirmations*. These are positive statements you make about yourself. You repeat them out loud or silently; put them on your mirror, your dashboard, on— "

"I get it, let's hear an example."

"Certainly; here's a basic affirmation: 'I will be happy; I will dwell on positive thoughts; if clouds fill my mind I will chase them away and fill myself with sunshine.'"

Hogwash.

"Sometimes they are much more specific, like for an avid golfer who's having a difficult day. He reminds himself, 'I am a good golfer and I'm relaxed and skillful enough to play at this level.'"

"And he wins the match."

"Win or lose, he plays with less anger, frustration, and more concentration, improving his chances. Why don't you try one? For starters, try to speak positively about something in your everyday life you think is causing you difficulty."

"Let's skip to the big stuff. How's this? 'I'm not sick or screwed up.'"

"Yes, but we want to couch our words positively. Perhaps like, 'I am joyful that I feel more healthy each day.'"

Phillip laughed. "Do I recite that before or after I thaw myself?"

"I'm not quite sure I understand."

"You told me you *do* understand. Look, that couldn't budge my, uh, *melancholia*," he said, trilling the last word.

"Which is why we start with the ordinary and graduate to the more serious. Perhaps you can try one that might work at school."

"Maybe you'd better help me out." *This should be good.*

"I have a whole list of teacher's affirmations. You could simply start with 'I'm very proud to be an educator.'"

Bingo. "No can do, Roger."

"Explain, please."

"Okay. I'm *not* proud that we 'educators' are mostly about rote memory, grades and useless testing, instead of exploration and curiosity. Let's see, I'm *not* proud when a teacher gets nailed for molestation, and then my union pays court costs and my district helps the creep teach in another town. And I'm *not* proud that our training is a farce and I have to disguise my teaching because I don't use the crappy curriculum. More?"

"Do I hear you saying you feel isolated in your work?"

"I don't know. My point is that repeating your affirmations with one foot in a pile of *you-know-what*, Roger, won't stop the stink. I'll take a rain check."

"I see. Let's put affirmations aside for now; we have many other techniques." The counselor paused with another half-smile. "One of your assignments would be a forgiveness list where you're asked to identify three people who've hurt you in one way or another. Perhaps you can think of one person now who you think has hurt you somehow."

"Easy — my neighbor. I'm supposed to forgive him? I can honestly say I hate the bastard."

Roger winced at the profanity. "What we use here is visualization technique. You visualize reconciliation by— "

"Nope, I'd never forgive him; and I'm sure he won't forgive me; call it the opposite of the Lord's Prayer."

"I believe you'll eventually be able to let go of what you think he did. Please trust me, we will be making progress right away," he said, hanging in there with another smile.

Wasting my breath. Phillip closed his eyes a moment to tone down his contempt. "I don't think you can help me."

"Please tell me why you feel that way."

Do it, but don't let him get to you. He looked right at Roger. "We're clueless about each other, we're both wasting our time because we perceive reality so differently."

"Say more about that, please."

"Okay. I see some things you value as illusion — like your ring. Diamonds are controlled by a cartel that spends millions to convince us they're rare. The truth is they hoard the diamonds in huge piles like Scrooge McDuck."

"Interesting," Roger said, not interested. "Would you give me a more personal example of how we see things so differently?"

"The volcano. You saw yourself as a victim of the ash fall and ran away. Now you're still moaning about it, and I'm still fascinated. So who's negative?"

"You seem to say that positive thinking for you is tied to deep experiences. I wonder if it's possible to depend on such experiences to go through each hour of the day."

"Don't know, but I'll take two or three of those instead of pretending that everything is rosy. Since I don't buy this hocus-pocus, maybe it's time for me to go."

"Phillip, I'd like you to know that studies have shown that clients who practice positive thinking describe their lives as happier and more successful than do those from other therapies." Trying to sound informational, partiality slipped into Roger's voice. "We also believe they live longer."

"Yeah? For what, a fancier car, a bigger diamond? So they can watch Lawrence Welk with the *right* kind of people at their condo on a golf course in Arizona? I don't want to be one of your happy successful people." *Easy, Phillip.*

"I wonder how that perspective has worked out for you; if sometimes you don't feel cut-off, even lonely?"

"If I am, it's not because of how I define success."

"Phillip, it's my belief we can handle life's challenges much better if we emphasize things like the beauty of a rainbow, the warm sunshine or some fresh flowers." With a beatific grin, Roger gestured with his arm toward the daisies on his bookcases.

More BS. Phillip lowered his head slightly, sighed, and closed his eyes a couple seconds. *Leave — Freddy should be here soon.* He picked up his book and put it on the armrest.

"You seem to disagree, Phillip. I'd like to hear why."

"Fine." He sat up straight and looked directly at Roger again. "Your mother nature comes right off of a greeting card: sunbeams, rainbows and pretty dead flowers. You worship light and sunshine, but the rain, cold and clouds are the scary bad stuff. Our religions spell it right out — evil and darkness go hand in hand."

"So you're saying that religion encourages us to worship the light and fear the dark and— "

"Yes, Roger, if winter, darkness and stormy weather are enjoyable to someone, maybe *they* are thinking positively."

"Interesting," the counselor said again. "May I ask if you don't enjoy a beautiful, warm and sunny day?"

"Of course, but I like rainy days just as much. Maybe we should take weather for what it is and stop whining about it."

Attempting to disguise that he felt personally affronted, Roger summoned another smile. "Phillip, would you agree that judging others is a challenge for you?"

"I agree judgment can get carried away, but it's also true that we've both been judgmental since we met."

"May I hear an example of how I was judgmental?"

"Sure, let's see, you judged the analyst and my attitude, and you judged me when I didn't buy your idea of success."

"I see. And how have you judged me?"

"You have an axe to grind; you're trying to sell me something. Whatever your deal is, positive thinking, religion, non-judgment, it's your business and I'm not buying."

"From what you said before, it seems your mother had a positive perspective toward life and her faith." Roger's sanguine facial expressions finally showed signs of sagging.

"I thought you'd get back to her. There was a lady in the hospital who reminds me of my mother." Phillip described Maria's acceptance of the indigenous religion of her grandparents. "...people like Maria and my mother can enjoy their spirituality without being hustlers. But most religions operate aggressively on the premise that everybody else is wrong — if it isn't a mission to convert the heathens or infidels, it's a holy war or flat-out genocide to destroy them. Now *there's* some judgment for you."

Roger checked his watch. "Phillip, do you believe the anger you seem to be feeling now serves you well?"

"Anger has its time and place. Did you hear about the hundreds of old people who are dying in the heat? It's not in India or Africa, it's right here, right now, in the South. An elderly man I know told me about it."

"That's certainly tragic, but sometimes we invest ourselves so much in the world's difficulties and unpleasantness that we— "

Phillip spoke right over him. "My friend says their lives are expendable because they're poor and old. I think he's right; nobody gives a rat's ass." His tone dared Roger to disagree.

"It sounds like it causes him considerable anguish."

"So? He doesn't dwell on it, but he's not afraid of the *unpleasantness*, as you call it. In the real world there are nuts like Hitler and Manson, and, of course, the good reverend Jones leading his flock and all those kids into annihilation."

"Well, I don't believe anyone wakes up in the morning with an intent to do harm to others."

"Be careful where you sleep, Roger. Inhumanity has to be judged and sometimes it takes anger to stop it." A tinge of the chill pulsed at his nape. *No, not in front of him.*

"Well, I try to deal peacefully with what I can control."

"Yeah, that's what the good Christians of Berlin said while their neighbors were exterminated. What you do, Roger, is see no evil, hear no evil, and say no evil. How can you affect inhumanity if you're not even aware of it?" *Take it easy.*

"I hope my work is my contribution. At some point," Roger added, his tone pious, "perhaps we have to make a leap of faith to believe in something positive and uplifting."

Screw you, Roger. "That sounds like a judgment that I don't believe in anything. I do; maybe you just didn't listen." A shiver reported at the back of his skull. *Damn, get out.* He got up, sat on an armrest and looked down to gauge the strength of the chill. "I'm leaving."

At a loss for words for a moment, the counselor's felicity completely disappeared. "I didn't say you don't believe in anything," Roger said, sounding defensive.

"You sure as hell implied it." *It's colder.* Phillip stood to grab his hat; the chill shuddered and made him sit right back in the soft chair. He sank into its depths and pulled the cap down over his eyes.

"Are you ill, Phillip?"

"Just a headache." *Get rid of him.* "I'd appreciate it if you'd check for my cab outside. It's white and black."

"Of course, I'll take a look."

Phillip heard him go out the door. *It's not that strong; see if you can lick it before he gets back.* He tried counting backwards slowly from five hundred and was almost asleep when the counselor returned.

"Sorry to wake you, Phillip."

He pushed up his hat. "Just resting my eyes."

Roger started for the exit. "I asked this, uh, Stanky fellow to come around back," he said with a hint of derision.

Why don't you just say ***Stinky****? Non-judgmental my ass.* Phillip got his book and stood up.

"He's here now," Roger said, looking out. Phillip ambled slowly toward the door as Freddy walked in.

"Let me help you a little, professor." He came over as if to take Phillip's arm.

"I'm okay, Freddy," he said, but walked beside him to the exit. The counselor was waiting there, his grin wide as the smiley face taped to the door.

"Remember, we always keep this open," Roger said.

Phillip scowled at him. "Yeah, so I noticed." *Calm; it's just waiting back there.* They all stepped into the alley; the cab was parked there, its motor running.

"Whether you decide to come back or not, Phillip, please know that I care about you."

God, his trump card. Phillip stopped walking and looked at him. "Tell you what, Roger, maybe you should stick with *clients* who buy into your presumptions. Adios."

"I mean it unconditionally, Phillip, I— "

"Listen, bud," Freddy said to Roger, "I think that's about enough from you."

"Right arm, Mister Stanky. Let's go." He walked with Freddy to the old Chevy.

24

Phillip sat in the rear, opposite the driver's side and put his head back. *Forget that jerk; just take it easy.* He tipped his brim over his forehead. *Freddy will understand.*

Freddy drove off and asked if he was okay. Phillip muttered back he was fine and discovered a pattern like argyle socks woven into the front covers. To make sure the chill wouldn't return, he peered down the end of his nose and traced the design. He dozed and then slept until Freddy jostled the car while rolling up the front windows.

Phillip looked out and saw they were already at the outskirts of Ponderosa and the wind was bending the poplars. Though two months had passed since the eruption, the ash was rising again from the nearby forests and unplowed fields. As before, only the ghostly outlines of the roadside businesses were visible in the unsettled grey soot.

Man, it looks like the day after. He rolled up his window, sat back and established eye contact with Freddy in the rearview mirror.

"It's a real shale lifter, professor, but it's drivable." He was glancing back and forth between the traffic and his passenger. "Looks like the ash is still with us for a while."

"Yeah, it does," Phillip said.

Freddy came to the junction, took the state road and settled the cab at about forty. "How you doin' back there?"

I must look wasted. "Good." *After that little scene, he thinks you're wacko.* "Uh, back at that office— "

"There's nothin' you gotta explain, but I take it you're finished with that guy."

Screw all of them. "That's right." *New subject.* "Freddy, what do you hear about that heat wave?"

"They say over a thousand dead now, more each day," he said with a rare frown, and started up the incline.

"Terrible." *Hear no evil, Roger? Forget him.*

A car approached and Freddy had to slow for the oncoming ash, but it dissipated in seconds. He resumed his speed and then cracked a peanut.

"That cleared up fast," Phillip said.

"Just blow-over, nothing like before," Freddy said around a swallow. "I'd like to ask you somethin' that's probably none of my business. You mentioned you have a sister in Portland; she know how you're doing?" He tried to contain a guttural cough.

She doesn't even know I was hurt. "No, you're right, I need to give her a call. You're a sentimental guy, Freddy."

"Myrna told me that sometimes; then she'd scold me a little if I got embarrassed about it. Guess I'll just have to live with it," he said as the cab made the ridge.

Phillip smiled toward the mirror then watched the silhouettes of telephone poles by the road. In the intervals, the wires were hardly visible in the whirling dust, and each obscure pole looked like a forlorn bare tree. *Which one was it? Crap, say something.*

"What's the deal with the cigarettes in your soda, Freddy?" Phillip pointed to the can below the dashboard.

"After a puff or two I dunk my coffin nails in there."

"You mean you're cutting back? Good for you."

"You're a good example for this ol' piece a' work."

Yeah, great example.

"That's Willy Shakespeare again, see if I can get the words right. 'What a piece of work is a man,'" Freddy said without pretension. "Hamlet again, that's my favorite."

"I think you did more than just listen to your wife."

"Oh, I studied some. Anyway, a story in my magazine said even ol' smokestacks like me might add some years by cuttin' back. Figured what the heck, really would like to see Willy grow up; that's a motivation." Freddy covered a croaking hack, chuckling because it came on cue. "Right there's another motivation, but it still ain't easy — *isn't* easy," he added, laughing and coughing at the same time.

"I think you'll do it."

"These goobers help, keep my mouth busy." Freddy ate one as if for demonstration and then slowed for some tumbleweeds gusting across the road. He bent his neck sideways and peered up through the windshield. "This wind's leadin' in a storm. I do enjoy a good rain," Freddy said.

Of course he does. "Yeah, me too."

"Seen a lotta nice days in seventy years; the best are when it's crisp and clean after a good rain."

"Not many people make that connection; most can't stand anything about rain."

"Yup. Took me some years to decide that. I'd sell more booze on a wet day, and now in the cab most folks gripe when it rains. Never have figured it out."

"I have a little theory. I was just arguing about it with that jerk back there."

"Run it by me, professor." Freddy passed a ramshackle farm truck overloaded with shucked corn.

"Nothing profound — I think hating rain sometimes is related to fear of darkness. The shrinks have a two-dollar word for it: nyctophobia." *He doesn't want to hear this crap.*

"Sounds interestin'," Freddy said, his eyes on the road as a few raindrops dotted the windows.

"I found that term after the preacher at my father's funeral blubbered on and on about light and dark. You know, how darkness is evil, conquered only by the light of God. It bothered me."

Freddy thought for a moment. " 'When darkness and evil are upon us, fear not,' " he recited.

"There you go, they're synonymous, and most of the other religions push the same idea."

"And the rain?"

"It wipes out daylight; people associate it with darkness. They want their sunny days. A few days of rain, then a credit card gets them to Hawaii or Mexico, and if it's raining there — the ultimate downer. The ash wasn't the biggest problem here with the volcano, it was the darkness; it interfered with the light of spring." Phillip stopped his rant. *Oh great philosopher, let him say something.*

"See if I get you," Freddy said, then released the gas pedal and honked at some ravens that wouldn't leave a road kill ahead. "So the dark and light, they just *are*, they're not good or evil. Same with the rain, the night, and the ash fall," he said, the taxi regaining its speed.

"Yes, exactly. It's unfortunate people die in storms and volcanoes, but that's all the more reason to respect them."

"Takin' nature as she comes," Freddy said. "Like those ol' scavengers we just passed, a lotta folks hate ravens, but they do their part, and they fly like hawks when it suits 'em. One of the smartest animals I've ever seen."

"Yeah, and they get branded as evil, like a black cat."

"Not real surprising that darkness is paired with evil so much; it's all through books and scripture. What I have no truck for is when they use it to scare kids and ol' folks into the fold," Freddy said seriously.

"Yeah, me either."

"Don't need anybody botherin' me about mortality; already care enough to try and squeeze in a few more years." Freddy smiled, popped in a single peanut and thought for a moment. "I was actually raised a good Polish Catholic; let it go in the navy. Went to Myrna's church once in a while, but mostly we studied the poetry of the Bible like we did the Shakespeare." The strain from his narrative made him stop for a short coughing fit. "Guess I'm most likely to see God in the things you and me talk about, like the wildlife." He raised his grey eyebrows, looking solemn. "And I see Him in that boy. Seems to be enough for me."

"And you aren't selling it to anybody."

"Not even to a friend." He smiled at the mirror. "Myrna was like that, never pushed anything on me or anyone."

"She must've been something," Phillip said. "I'd like to hear more about her, if you feel like it."

Freddy cleared his throat. "Hardly mentioned her to anybody since she passed, even my daughters. Maybe it's time I did." He checked his side mirror. "Go on, bud," he said, slowing for a pickup to go by. "Must've been about your age when I decided it was time to leave the navy. I was no bargain, real squirrelly, always messin' with motorcycles n' guns; drank too much. I took it all for granted before her. She was a clerk in the county offices; I went in there for a permit one day and came out smitten — I'll skip that part." Some larger drops splattered the windows; they both looked out at the gathering bruise-colored clouds.

"Here she comes, professor." Freddy started the wipers. "Anyway, we were poor as Job, and she had his patience. After we settled, it was our kids and her animals. She'd bring home strays, and the kids and I started helpin' out until half our back yard was a pen for dogs, cats — even a few wild critters. She found good places for most all of 'em. We had some stray kids mixed in there, too.

"No dust gathered under her, always helpin' folks. She loved all the seasons — practically cheer for a storm like this." Freddy swiveled his wind wing open to sniff the cool air. "And there was one religious woman who didn't think evil crawled around in the dark. Sometimes we'd go up in the mountains, talk and watch the stars till we fell asleep — some of our best times."

Freddy coughed and looked in his mirror at some imaginary traffic problem. "I'm just runnin' on here, professor, but one thing seems to ring true: Comes to likin' rain, guess it's just you and me an' ol' Mister McGee."

Phillip smiled at the rhyme. "I guess so, but you left something out: Myrna cared about somebody else as much as the kids and the animals."

"Yeah, *now* who's the sentimental one? But you're right — I've been a lucky man." Lost in thought a couple minutes, Freddy drove on until they were a few hundred yards before Ponderosa Estates; he turned onto a gravel driveway and rolled into an alfalfa field. There was no view, just solid green hay and thick mouse-grey mist above. He stopped and then cranked both front windows down a few inches; they heard the thunder rumbling outside. The rain had settled the dirt and ash, pushing a wave of fresh oxygen into the car.

"Take a whiff of that," Freddy said. "You mind if we sit here a sec and watch 'er roll by?" he called back.

"No, not at all." Dollops of rain thickened on the windshield, and Phillip lowered his window a little more and inhaled. "Man, you can breathe it all the way in."

Freddy turned off the engine, and the rain sprinkled their faces as they listened to the downpour pelt the roof. The lightning snapped over them twice, a minute or so apart, followed by cracking thunder; then the storm began to let up.

"That was quick," Phillip said. He opened the window all the way and drew the ozone into his lungs. A slit of azure sky opened in the clouds above.

Freddy rolled his window down. "Yup, we're just on the edge of 'er, but we'll take what we can get, right?"

"Absolutely." He stuck his hand out into the light rain.

Freddy looked at Phillip in the mirror. "I'm probably bein' too nosy again, professor, but I made up my mind to ask if you've got somebody else to go to for some help."

Phillip brought in his arm. "You saw what that place was; do I seem like a wacko to you?"

" 'Course not. But if you got a problem and don't do somethin' about it, now that wouldn't make any sense."

"I'll just lay it out to you, Freddy. They told me I'm clinically depressed."

Freddy waited in case Phillip wanted to explain. "If I understand it right, that's when depression takes over your life; people can't stop it and can't do what they usually do."

"That's about it. How do you know all that?" Phillip asked, turning his head to face Freddy's reflection.

"A couple articles I read; knew it was true from keepin' bar; had some regulars just like that. They'd change and finally shut down, like cuttin' off a motor, even to people they were close to." His lower jaw moved up and his lips tightened with the difficult memories. "Sometimes I remember them like it was yesterday, thinking I could've— " He stopped talking and lowered his head a little.

"Helped them?" Phillip said, completing Freddy's thought.

"I guess so. Some of 'em never came back from it; drank themselves to death."

Stephen. "I'd bet my dad's house that you helped." *More than I ever did.* "These so-called professional therapists — I've had two now — they could learn a lot from you. You're the only one who helps me sort things out."

"Glad if I can help a bit, professor, but I'm just an ol' fart set in his ways. Who started you with the therapists?"

"My doctor has a whole list; probably all crackpots."

"Guess it can't hurt to try again."

The hell it can't. "The doc has me on some fancy new drugs; I'm going to try to deal with it myself."

Freddy cranked the ignition, then looked up. "If I'm not around town, is there somebody you can call in a pinch?"

"Yeah, some school buddies." *Like Kurt, fat chance.* "I could drive my dad's car if I had to."

"Sure you could, but I wouldn't rush the one-arm driving. You ever need anything, not just a ride, you're welcome to call me." He backed into a "y" turn and started out the gravel lane, wet alfalfa bent to the ground on both sides.

"You don't have to feel obligated, Freddy."

"Not an obligation; I take it as an honor when you call me, somebody who does the kind of work you do. You and me, we just sort of hit it off; we look at some things the same way. It pleases me if there's somethin' I can do for you."

"You've been a lot of help today, I appreciate it."

"That's what friends are for, professor."

25

The day after the ride home with Freddy, Phillip had what he thought was a pretty good day. The early chill was the usual, but after the second one he was up to stay before one o'clock, figuring out a way to work on the ash in back.

He started by jamming a heavy-duty snow shovel under his right armpit to push the ash into piles. After making two good mounds, he realized that one-armed wheelbarrowing was out of the question. Phillip went to Stephen's shop and in less than an hour built a makeshift hauler out of scrap plywood and an old wagon they used for moving trashcans.

He devised a procedure to drop the cart on its side near a pile then shove in as much ash as possible before righting the box and rolling the load down to the street. Repressing any thoughts of his mental state, Phillip concentrated on the labor into the late afternoon, ignoring the mail and leaving the phone off again. That evening he felt that maybe he had taken some first steps in dealing with his situation, hopeful that the drug was starting to help a little.

On Sunday, after nightmares about Stephen and two rough stands against the chill, he sat up in bed and checked the clock. *Crap, it's two thirty, so much for progress, didn't even get up for Ali.* He walked idly into the bathroom, looked in the mirror and removed the dressing from his forehead. The swelling was gone and the gash had crusted over at the center of a yellowish-purple bruise almost the size of a tea saucer. He put a long band-aid over the stitches, making a diagonal line across the injury like a no-parking symbol.

Phillip relieved himself and got dressed; then he walked straight to the TV room to look for Ali. The cat had staked permanent claim to Stephen's recliner and was curled up there sleeping, though he hadn't eaten. Phillip sat in his chair and stared at the blank TV until he began daydreaming of passing the telephone poles on the road from town.

Stop this; you didn't do the tree today; the ash is just waiting. He petted Ali, but the cat didn't stir. *Must've eaten out last night.* He went to the garage for the sprayer, opened the double door and walked out front. Phillip stopped as soon as he saw the yard. *Son of a bitch.* Someone had driven across his and Mister Beck's property in the night, making deep ruts in their adjoining lawns. The small fence around the ponderosa was run over and the tree bent halfway down, cracked in the middle.

In front of Beck's place, a county sheriff's officer shooed off some gawking kids then got into his squad car and drove up the Stark's driveway. Phillip stood there, sprayer in hand, as the cop looked out his window from beneath the flat brim of a brown "Smokey" hat, his face fresh and eager; cheeks the color of bubble gum.

"Mister Stark?" the young sheriff asked, and Phillip nodded. "Something wrong with your phone, sir?"

It's off. "Didn't hear it, I guess."

"Your neighbor filed the report on this mess. You didn't happen to see or hear anything unusual after one A.M.?"

"No, nothing," Phillip said, glaring at the ponderosa.

"Anyone have a grudge against you, Mister Stark?"

Kurt maybe. Fike? He shook his head, still facing his tree. "Find who did this," he mumbled. *Don't tell me the bastard's name.* "I'd kill him," he said under his breath.

"What did you say, Mister Stark?"

He looked at the cop. "Nothing, talking to myself."

"You seem pretty angry about this, sir. We'll do what we can, but it's just a dead lawn and a scrawny tree."

Bullshit. Phillip turned away again. "Yeah, it's no big deal," he said, trying to sound agreeable.

The officer got out, surveyed the damage, then double-checked Phillip's phone number. When the squad car pulled away, Phillip inspected the tree more closely and stared at the globs of sticky sap oozing slowly onto the ground.

Got all that sap 'cause it's like the tree is bleeding.

He lifted the top of the ponderosa's trunk back in place then let it go; it fell even closer to the ground. *Damn it to hell.* Trying to decide what to do, Phillip walked slowly around the tree two or three times.

Screw that dying piece of crap; water my lawn.

The corner of his eyes moist from anger, Phillip walked to the garage for cloth tape, then came back to the lilacs and yanked up a plant stake. He secured the long dowel to the trunk of his tree. *Shit, now we're both splinted. It doesn't have a friggin' prayer.* The chill began to overtake him so he went inside to his carpet.

When Phillip got out of bed to stay the next afternoon, it was almost four, the latest he'd slept since high school. He decided there was no choice but to call Doctor Lang, who arranged an appointment with a therapist for two days later. Phillip left a message with Freddy's dispatcher, then didn't go outside the rest of that day or the next, spending most of his waking hours with the TV, his cat, and the chill.

On the ride into Four Rivers late Wednesday afternoon, they talked about the damaged yard then mostly about cougars, and Freddy repeated the invitation to visit the creek when the time was right. Phillip was feeling better by the time he had to get out at the building downtown. He stepped alone into a fusty elevator the size of a bedroom closet, and his dread for the appointment deepened floor by floor up to the fifth.

Phillip found room 508, a plain door with a COME ON IN sign on the knob. He knocked anyway then entered and shook hands with the new therapist. Bill Rhodes was in his mid-forties, clean-shaved; his curly light-blond hair circled a sunburned balding pate that was radiant as a pink tea rose. His clothes were informal but neat: a light-blue short-sleeve dress shirt, black khakis, no tie, a thin black belt, and dark-brown Hush Puppies. Bill's husky six-foot frame and very light complexion reminded Phillip of Sam Fike, and the similarity bothered him.

They sat on opposite ends of a curved, firm living room sofa; Phillip left his hat, book and flannel shirt on a cushion between them. Bill inscribed notes on five-by-eight cards as Phillip studied a photo enlargement that papered most of the wall above a simple metal desk. He transported himself into the poster's window-sized image of a subalpine meadow, wild with bright flowers. *Lupine, tiger lilies — fantastic. Penstemon and paintbrush — just stay here.* He enjoyed the forest scene another minute or so before checking out the rest of the small square office.

The other three walls, laminated with mock wood grain, lacked decoration except for a cork bulletin board by the door that overflowed with happy snapshots of family trips to the mountains and shore. A four-foot-long fluorescent light illuminated the whole room, and a rumbling air conditioning system rattled the floor registers intermittently, leaving the air too cold, even for a warm day at the end of July. Hazy sunshine filtered through a single shut window that faced west overlooking downtown.

Feeling an ordinary chill, Phillip put the flannel on over his dark-blue tee shirt while the therapist continued to take notes from Doctor Lang's letter. Below the giant poster, Phillip noticed a spray-painted twelve-by-twelve garden block serving as a book-end for a small desk library. He realized the molded form in the white brick was a *fleur-de-lis.*

That's two good omens, one bad. What crap, Phillip. A desk phone and a large Webster's blocked his view of half of Bill's books, but to the right of the dictionary he made out the titles of *African Genesis*, *The Third Wave*, *Chesapeake*, *The Dead Zone*, a thesaurus, and about a half-dozen pocket editions of poetry.

The crackpot books must be on the other side. As if it had fallen from the wall, a framed diploma sat crookedly on the books. Phillip squinted to read it. *Ph. D. —probably not an official shrink. Doesn't mean he's not into it.* He focused on a lacquered redwood burl on Bill's desktop, the works of an electric clock protruding from its carved out middle. *Ugly.*

"Phillip?"

"Yeah, I was, uh; that's quite a clock."

"It's one of those well-meant gifts, but it's starting to grow on me. I saw you looking at my wall. That photo's a favorite; some-times for a break, I think of it as my view."

And just take off, like I did. Phillip was close to the narrow win-dow and got to his feet to check the real view of drab buildings and rush-hour traffic. "I can see why," he said and turned back to the meadow. "Is it your own shot?"

"Yes, near Mount Hood." Rhodes handed back the doctor's letter as Phillip sat on the couch.

"You don't want a copy?" Phillip put it on his book.

"I wrote what I need, and he gave me a brief report on the phone. He said you wanted to talk about the other therapists. Up to now they're anonymous, and I'd prefer to keep it like that if you still want to discuss them."

"Fine, I just want you to know why they were a waste of time." *Maybe it'll cut some of the crap.* "You're not into analysis, are you?"

"No, I'm not. Any other concerns?"

"Yeah, try not to tell me to relax while I'm here."

"That's not helpful I take it."

"Not when it means get with the program."

Bill thought about Phillip's comment. "I think I see what you mean. Shall we begin?"

Can't be worse than the others. "What about your fee?"

"No charge unless you make a second appointment."

"Sounds fair." Phillip crossed his leg, ankle over knee, glaring at his boot. He remembered putting them on with a vague notion of going on a hike somewhere. *Stupid idea.*

"That's quite a bruise up there," Bill said, looking at Phillip's head. "How's the arm?"

"Child's play." He did fake calisthenics with his cast.

"Good." Bill smiled at Phillip's silliness. "Okay, maybe you can fill me in. I'd like you to go back to when it seemed like you more or less had things together; further back if you think it's relevant. Then, of course, the march of events leading to now, including what you want me to know about your previous therapy. Are you up for all that?"

Déja vu. "Why not?" he said with a slight sneer.

"Okay. I might interrupt for an occasional question."

"And to paraphrase what I said?"

"No, assume I'm with you unless I say otherwise."

Two points for Bill.

The therapist's phone rang. "Sorry," Rhodes said, miffed by the call. He stood and took one long stride and a short step to his desk. "This'll only take a second," he added.

Sure. Phillip groomed his fair beard with his hand.

"Hello," Bill stated firmly and waited for a reply. "Pam, I'm with my last appointment; I didn't forward the phone, my mistake." He listened a moment. "Thanks, Pam, I'll call after five. Bye."

So Bill scores another two.

Rhodes pushed buttons to disconnect then opened the nearby door and reached around to display the other side of his sign. He returned to Phillip. "That should take care of it," Bill said with a touch of exasperation as he readjusted himself on the couch. "Okay, Phillip." He picked up his thin stack of cards.

Haul out the ol' thumbnail sketch. In about twenty minutes, he divulged a brief autobiography and an account of his recent life, including blunt, critical summaries of his two experiences in therapy. Rhodes asked for clarifications, concentrating on how the chill emerged and Stephen's avowed dual personalities. Phillip responded succinctly, and the therapist continued his questions.

At least he wants to know something.

"...said after you called your sister there was some brief improvement. Would you give me some details on that?"

"Yeah. The next morning the first chill wasn't as bad, and when I finally got out of bed, I was all psyched to work. Selling the house gave me something to do, I guess. The next day I actually got up early, then my principal called and gave me trouble about not sending in my commitment letter."

"Are you thinking about leaving?"

"No; I don't know. He also volunteered me for basketball camp. Normally, I probably would have done it, but not like I am. I lied that I couldn't do it for family reasons, but he didn't back off. I was pissed; the chill came back in spades, and the next day I was back to square one. He called again right after I got out of the hospital. Same argument; this time I hung up on him."

"Isn't there someone in administration you can talk to?"

"The assistant superintendent, but she's powerless, they make sure of that. What would I tell her, anyway? You can't say you're being treated for depression to an employer."

"Explain that to me," Bill said.

"I remember the stigma when it leaked out about a guy at work, as if he was goofing off. People think it's just a downer; this happened, that happened; you get depressed, it's lousy and it passes. But this crap isn't anything like that; it's regular, it's relentless; it completely takes over."

Aw, poor baby, get a goddamn grip.

Go to hell.

"Did you finish your point, Phillip?"

"Sorry. Most people think you should just get a grip, especially a man. I tell myself the same thing sometimes." He finished with an agitated sigh, rotating his ankle nervously, the black sole of his boot toward Bill.

"As far as what people are thinking, Phillip, we can only guess, of course. But in general, not only do most people not know about serious depression, they don't care to find out. 'Depression is too depressing,' is a comment I hear often. You're right about the stigma, too. It's socially acceptable to have, say, liver disease, but it's somehow shameful to have severe depression, which kills a lot more people."

Suicide. "Is that right?" Phillip was unimpressed.

"Yes, and psychology has a deficiency of scientific knowledge on the disorder, though we often lack humility on the subject. Genetics and chemical imbalance in the brain seem to play a part, but what we know for sure is that one source is intense personal trauma. Someday we'll understand more about how the mind shifts from grief or dejection, which we all have to deal with, into extreme depression and loss of control, like the chill you've described, or even worse, self-destructive behavior." He searched for a card.

Suicide again.

Bill looked up. "What you said about men and depression reminds me Hemingway supposedly wrote the only real sports are bullfighting, mountain climbing and auto racing. I think we're wrapped in so many layers of that kind of macho nonsense that the idea depression can be such a killer is laughable to some people, especially men. Extreme depression..."

More damn suicide; don't lay it on me, Bill.

"...disproportionate between women and men because so many men are ashamed to admit it, let alone seek treatment." He paused to consider the statement then scribbled on another card. "Excuse my little speech. Phillip, is it fair to say that acting on anger is relatively new for you?"

Sounds like Roger's bull. "You could say that."

"When did you first notice it?"

"I started telling Stephen off a few months before he died." Phillip sighed audibly. "So my anger is the problem, right? I just need a positive attitude; forgive Stephen and Mick, and then see the holy light — I'll be all set."

Bill waited to see if he'd exhausted his sarcasm. "Well, attitude is important, Phillip, but I don't subscribe to the old saw that attitude is everything."

"That's good, because the chill is there twice a day, every day, like clockwork, regardless of my attitude." He was emphatic, but not vehement.

"How often has it shown up outside of the regular onset?"

"Five, six times maybe, but those are the *only* times anger could've been a factor. I argued with the other therapist that being angry about a blatant injustice, like Freddy's old people I told you about, was sometimes necessary. I told him that kind of anger was unrelated to my problems."

"I agree. A commitment against inhumanity seems more like caring or passion to me." He looked down to jot a note.

Is he patronizing me? Calm, Phillip. He waited for Bill and gazed up at the meadow again.

"Phillip, one of those times anger *did* bring on the chill was at the store that night, before the crash, right?"

"Yes." *I let the pissant get to me.*

"Can you tell me a little more about the crash itself?"

"It's pretty simple. That jerk passed me, I couldn't see; I went off and hit a damn pole. Doctor Lang makes such a big deal out of it, but that's all there is to it."

"Was it just your friend who angered you?"

"That driver." *And Stephen.* "And my father, I guess."

"Explain that, please."

"Not sure I want to; the shrink was convinced I talk to little green men. I recall things Stephen said; I did it that night; I did it a minute ago. Sometimes I react in my mind, but I know it's not actually him. Once in a while I tell him off out loud — that makes me schizo?"

"No, it doesn't." He paused. "Phillip, I'm not clear on your father's accident. I assume he'd been drinking?"

"No, Dad was driving." *He's going to love this.* "He left me a suicide note, but don't start laying any genetic crap on me."

"I won't. Have you told the authorities about the note?"

"I think my sister did after I told her."

"How did you react when you first read it?"

"With a damn chill, what do you think?" *Easy.*

"It's a normal reaction to be angry with a loved one who commits suicide."

"I was pissed at myself, too. I should've helped him."

"I disagree with that. I think you kept the promise you made to your mother; you hung in there, tried to communicate, and to get him to seek help. It seems to me you cared for him as much as anyone could."

"Yeah? The shrink said I repress aggression toward him."

"You didn't buy that and I don't either; we're not all doomed to tragically hate our fathers. I think you also did the right thing to call the analyst on the ECT, but I don't need to go into that now." Bill paused again to get back on track. "I believe the truth is you loved your father."

"Sure I loved him, but I hated Stephen."

"I won't minimize how difficult it was to live with him, but drunk or sober, he was still one person, and I don't believe you hated him." Bill halted his discourse so Phillip could evaluate the comment.

He doesn't get it; nobody does. The floor registers vibrated and Phillip felt another unnatural wave of cool air that mimicked the chill.

"Phillip, you seem to have distorted him into this Jekyll-and-Hyde personality. It's my guess your father wasn't so oblivious when he was sober, nor was he quite so evil when he was drunk. It was black and white to you, but like most of us, he probably lived his life somewhere in between."

"How do *you* know?"

"I don't for sure, I'm going by what you said. It also appears you've distorted your thinking in some other ways."

"I don't have any idea what you mean by that."

"I'm talking about assumptions not based on reality; they're sometimes twisted, exaggerated or irrational and often build upon themselves, which deepens depression, in my opinion. They're called mental distortions."

"That sounds nuts all right. Listen, I do have my own way of doing things, my own interests and opinions. It doesn't mean— "

"Phillip, excuse the interruption, but I'm not talking about your individualism or independent thought. You've been under intense personal stress, especially the long-standing environment with acute alcoholism, then his death and other issues related to it. In dealing with *those* things, you seem to have distorted some of your thought processes."

"Like seeing him as two different people."

"Yes. Another distortion I think you're struggling with is unfounded self-blame. It appears you've convoluted your thinking into excessive amounts of guilt, convincing yourself for years you were responsible for your father's behavior, but it was his life, not yours." Bill flipped to a card in his pile. "Your best friend, uh,

Warren. He was on the money when he told you the accident wasn't your fault. And that goes for the rest of what your father did."

"Just more words, I can't accept that out of the blue."

"Of course not, it'll take time. What I do is help you pinpoint thinking that was possibly distorted; but it's your decision whether or not the idea holds water." Bill stopped when he saw interrogation in Phillip's face.

"So *decision* is the big buzz word. The other guy told me more or less that I *decided* to be depressed. He said every action follows a thought, so you can always decide on a positive one, something like that."

"That's an extreme proposition in my opinion. Real decisions and choices are often difficult, unhappy, or have tough consequences. So-called *positive thinking* can sometimes be beneficial for people who seek a prescription for life, but you wanted no part of it because you thought it was doctrinal as well as contrived."

Bingo. "And your distortion deal, isn't that doctrine?"

"In a way. It's an approach with some structure developed by psychiatrists disenchanted with psychoanalysis for some of the same reasons you mentioned. But identifying distortions is one of several techniques I use for both normal and extreme depression, because no approach has all the answers. I've also found that distortions overlap, so I de-emphasize the labeling from the approach."

Bill the maverick. Just shut up and hear him out.

"Nevertheless, Phillip, I think this technique can be especially helpful for you because you seem willing to examine your thought processes. Your sister's situation illustrates what I mean. It appears she figured out she hadn't been telling herself the truth about her husband for years. She was personalizing his abusive behavior, seeing herself as the cause, an unfortunate but common distortion. I'm sure you've heard Shakespeare's famous line, 'To thine own self be true.' Your sister learned that, as does anyone who untangles a distortion," the therapist said earnestly, but Phillip snickered. "What is it?" Bill asked with a smile.

"Freddy's a fan, he has half of Shakespeare memorized."

"Ah. He seems to be a remarkable person."

"Yes, he is."

"Phillip, a distortion is to thine own self be *false*, which is what I think you did when you told me Warren's friendship is the only one you have left. The improving relationship with your sister, and the new ones with Maria and Freddy, say a lot."

"They don't know me."

"You don't give yourself any credit, Phillip."

"Like the way I handled Lupe?"

"We all make mistakes; what matters is if you still care for each other. It's possible she's tried to communicate; you've been isolated a lot."

"She made things pretty clear when she left."

"I wouldn't burn that bridge until you know more. If it *is* over, then you can go on."

"Yeah," Phillip said, his face downcast. "So, is that all of my *distortions*?"

"Well, I'm very concerned about whether you've been honest with yourself about one more thing: Have you really tried to examine your thoughts from just before your crash?"

Shit. Phillip looked up. "So you think I tried to kill myself, too? You know, the other therapist was a complete sap, but at least he believed me." He shivered and buttoned up his shirt. *No, it isn't coming; it's just cold in here.*

"What I asked is whether or not you've tried to deal with exactly what happened. You're the only one who knows."

Son of a bitch, that does it. He picked up his things.

"Phillip?"

"I don't want to get pissed and turn into a mess on your couch." Phillip stood and put on his cap.

"Are you having symptoms now?" Bill got to his feet.

"Not yet, but I'm leaving."

"Are you sure that's what you need to do?"

"Yeah, that's what I need to do." He walked to the door.

"I think maybe I overdid it for the first day, Phillip. Please call me if you want to continue."

"Nothing personal, but I don't think so." He left the office and took the stairs, galloping down the flights recklessly without looking at his feet. *None of them can help.* He walked through the small lobby to wait out front where someone had planted flowers in the oval island formed by the drop-off lane. Bunches of black-eyed Susans survived the warm summer there shaded by red and pink cosmos and some desiccating sunflowers.

Phillip sat on the curb and shivered again, though the early evening air was balmy. He put the appointment with Bill out of his mind by concentrating on a goldfinch that perched on one of the drooping sunflowers. To get at the seeds, the dainty little bird stretched all the way over and upside down, and Phillip mused that the finch's two main colors were about the same as ash and yellow ribbons. He watched it lean and nibble several times, but the therapy session came back to him. *He did make more sense than the others. Screw it; you're on your own —face it.*

26

When the cab arrived in the lane, Phillip felt a hint of the chill as he climbed up into the back seat. "Hi, Freddy." *I don't want to talk.*

"Hey, professor," Freddy said and drove off.

To keep the chill at bay, Phillip leaned back, closed his eyes and dozed fitfully for most of the trip. Freddy kept to himself until he passed Ponderosa and settled his taxi well below the speed limit on the Ski-Eden road. When Phillip's eyes flickered, Freddy cleared his throat and spoke up.

"Feelin' all right?" he called into his mirror.

"I'm fine." Phillip straightened his spine, but the chill stirred between his shoulder blades. *No, goddamn it, not after all that sleep.* The frigid tingling advanced to the back of his neck.

"You sure you're okay, professor?"

Professor, my ass. "Maybe you could ease off on the *professor* thing." *And get this heap moving.*

"Okay, uh, Phillip."

God, Phillip the prick. Easy, we're almost there.

Freddy slowed even more to make it a relaxing ride.

What's he doing? "Could you step on it, please? I need to get home." *To my carpet.* The taxi accelerated, but to Phillip the last mile seemed endless as he tried to hold off the chill by focusing on the diamond patterns in the seat covers. *No good, it's worse.*

Freddy hacked out a cough as he turned off the state road. "Your appointment go okay?" he asked in the mirror.

"What?" Phillip asked, annoyed by the interruption. He had one hand over his eyes. "Maybe you'd be better off if you didn't worry about me." *Crap, stop barking at him.* Freddy made the turn down Phillip's street and sped up to the garage.

Just get out. He climbed down, every muscle seemed to ache, and he walked stiffly as if it were his leg in the cast.

"You need anything, call me," Freddy offered from behind, but Phillip was already moving slowly toward the garage.

All I need is my damn carpet. He wanted to hurry, but the house seemed to be agonizingly distant, and he forced himself to make one step at a time through the garage and into the kitchen.

When Phillip finally got to his bed, he tried to rid himself of the chill. After tracing the design scores of times, he fell into an agitated slumber that brought back the caricature of Mick laughing again at Stephen's slaughter.

Me and your ol' man was peas in a pod.

Shut up, prick. The images faded and Phillip opened his eyes, realizing right away the chill hadn't completely subsided. *Get rid of it.* He sat up, stared at the carpet again, but found only slight relief. *Damn, now what?* Phillip staggered out of the room and tried Stephen's door. It didn't open; he dug into his jean pockets with his good arm, but his sluggish efforts were fruitless until the third attempt. The keys hefted like iron, blurring together in his hands until he finally opened the door.

He approached Stephen's bed. *Maybe here.* Phillip sat on the edge, leaned sideways and drew his index finger slowly along the pile labyrinth in the yellow chenille bedspread. *This has to work — down, around, to the right, out, and in...* On his knees and one elbow, he traced the thin pathway until the chill receded some. He became drowsier with each loop; a murky vision of Mick materialized again. *Screw him; keep going — up, over, around, and in...* After several more seconds, his finger came to an obstruction, the old revolver. *I shouldn't have left this thing here.*

Phillip picked it up to get it out of the way, but he held on to the loaded weapon and stared at it. *Never shot one of these. Just pull the trigger, idiot. He'll be out there sometime today, half-hammered, fooling around in his yard nonchalant as hell. I wonder how cool he'd be if I—* The chill rallied at full strength; he put the firearm behind and returned to his course in the bedcover.

...up and over, around, and back again. Keep going — left and down again, back and around... In a couple minutes, the track brought him back to the gun. *There's an omen for you. Such BS, Phillip. No, no it isn't; find the prick.* He grabbed the pistol and left the room. The chill was there, but somehow he moved more quickly than he had for hours.

"Where do you think you're going?" he asked himself out loud in the kitchen. *Just go.* Phillip crossed the poolroom, opened the sliding doors and stepped down onto the patio slab. *You can't do this.*

Can't stand up to him?

I'll do more than that, Stephen. He waded through the deep ash to the crab apple tree then hopped onto the makeshift riser to peek over the top of the fence. *Bastard's not there.* He took a longer survey of Mick's yard. *What did you expect? Wait for him.*

Like a seventy-eight RPM record switched to forty-five, his thinking stalled. His temple chilled again and Phillip slouched onto the steppingstones, wrapping the cast around his waist. He bent forward, head between his knees, and saw a bush surrounded by worm tracks in the crust. As if stalking an ant, he aimed the pistol down to follow the tiny arcs and segments made by the worms that once slithered over the ash.

...around and up, curl and over, spiral down and over, then up and — How did worms get up here? Across and around — Tunneled up through the ash? Why do you even care? Still cold, keep going — over and down, another curl and back up...

He swayed for several minutes and then paused. *That's better — now around and up...* After a few more seconds, Phillip heard a weed-eater start up in Mick's yard. *There he is; move it before the chill rallies. What if you do this? His word against yours — hide the gun in the ash. Doesn't matter; nothing matters except scaring the piss out of him; see if Mister Nonchalant's eyes get real big.*

He climbed up onto the bricks and peered over the fence, but the yard was out of focus. Halfway across the huge lawn, Phillip saw Mick's back, his arms swinging the trimmer side to side. *He looks small — crap, do it. Wait for him to turn.* He tried to raise the gun but its weight increased tenfold as the chill revived. Phillip struggled to lift the weapon high enough to direct it across the yard. He heard the trimmer stop and watched the blurred neighbor kneel sideways to fix it. *It's colder — you're out of time.*

Phillip steadied the cast and his other arm on top of the fence, both hands on the gun. *Go on.* He saw the dull image of Mick yanking on the starting cord. *You'll hit him. That's the idea. No, you were just going to scare him. Bullshit, he took Dad; you take him. Hold still, prick.*

His brain trembled but he moved his index finger slowly to the narrow steel on the outside of the trigger guard. Phillip started to move his finger into the trigger, but for endless seconds it didn't respond, frozen to the metal like a kid's tongue on an icy monkey bar.

...your actions just before the collision.

What?

Have you really tried to examine your actions just before the collision?

Shut up; you're no help. He tried to concentrate on the neighbor, who was tinkering again. *Now — do it now.*

To thine own self be false.

Leave me alone.

Just before the collision, just before the collision, just before the—

Shit, be quiet.

Distorted thinking.

No.

A distortion, Phillip.

It's the chill; I can't stop it. It's so cold the speedometer's out of focus. Why's that guy hiking in the ash? He can't help you, idiot. God, headlights right behind — not again. The bastard can't pass me this time — hit the gas. Damn, can't see anything — off the road — there's the pole.

Always does the job.

Step on it. Looking down the gun barrel, Phillip saw the dim target begin to turn in his direction. *Yes, step on it.* His finger finally touched the trigger.

Step on it? The neighbor almost faced him. *You did it, Phillip, you did it on purpose. Jesus.* Tears swelled and ran over his face. *My God, stop this now.* He tried to pull back the gun, his arms hardly budged; he looked into Mick's yard. *What the hell? He **is** short.*

Phillip blinked to see better, but the top brick slipped; he wobbled back, catching the top of the fence with his cast — all in slow motion again. His knee struck a plank, the pistol flipped up, misshapen, floating above him as if supported by helium. *He'll see it.*

Reacting to the noise, the neighbor had spotted Phillip, who regained his footing and watched the Daliesque gun tumble interminably through the air and descend into the crust below, expelling a small-scale eruption of ash.

"Can I help you?" the man shouted, sounding puzzled.

He didn't see it. Phillip looked at him; the chill reverberated back and forth from his head to his spine. "Uh, where's Mick Lewis?" He thought he had yelled, but the neighbor barely heard him and then smiled.

"Oh, Mister Lewis? We rent from him. I'm Ron— "

Phillip ducked down right away, but he still saw the man say his name. *Mother of God, you could've shot him, you fucking madman.* Shuddering throughout his body, he stumbled off the riser. It seemed to take an hour to plod back to the patio, ash up to his shins. Phillip shuffled to the door, but it slid open like bank vault steel. He fell into the den and collapsed on the floor, squinting at the carpet. *Useless green crap. Stand up — too cold. Damn, crawl then.* On his three good limbs he dragged himself up to the TV room and crept across the kitchen, peanuts fracturing under his knees.

Ali showed up, arched his spine at first and then sat back on his haunches. His curious blue and gold eyes watched Phillip crawl closer and sit up, legs spraddled on the floor, back against the wall. Ali walked right onto his human's lap and settled there, purring loudly.

"Hey, boy." Distracted from the pulsing cold, he scratched Ali's ears, and the cat turned to rub the plaster of Paris cast. The chill subsided a little more as Phillip petted the old feline's white fur.

That guy didn't see the gun; nobody even knows what I did. ***You*** *do, Phillip, you completely lost it. And you tried to hit that damn telephone pole.* He cradled the cat back to him and looked over at the peanut mess on the kitchen floor. *Frigging chillbrains, do your worst; I think I'm on to you.* Phillip stroked Ali in the hall until they were both asleep.

He dealt with the chill at dawn the next morning and again at about eleven thirty, but he was up and dressed in his work clothes before one o'clock. It was Saturday so Freddy was off; Phillip called him right away and he answered.

"I'm calling to apologize, Freddy. If I talk to you like that again, just tell me to shove it."

"Nah, you were in bad shape; I felt bad just leavin' you. You sound pretty good now; you doin' all right, professor?"

Long way to go. "I'm doing okay."

"That's good to hear. Say, I've got somethin' to tell ya'. Last week I talked to Myrna's ol' pal at the County about that Ranch project, asked her to keep an eye on it for me. She called today and said they're selling out to a local who plans to scale it way back and re-open Hop Wing's."

"Really? Does she know why?"

"She thinks they bit off more than they could chew."

Farm house. "It's a done deal, then?"

"Close enough that I'm ready to check out Blue Valley some more."

Adios, Mister Lopes. "Good for you, Freddy."

"Thought maybe you might go up there with me this week."

"Definitely." *You'll be with Bill.* "Uh, except I'll probably have a couple appointments back downtown again."

"With the new guy? I thought things didn't go— "

"I didn't give him a chance. Maybe he can help me."

"Now that's real good, professor; we'll just schedule our trip around it." They chatted a few minutes and Phillip said he'd give him the appointment times on Monday. After the call, he made peanut butter and jelly toast and turned on the radio. While he ate, Phillip heard a forecast for higher temperatures so he prepared some ice water to take outside.

He left the water jug, a tube of sun tan lotion and his transistor radio by the patio door and started working on the ash behind the house. After rolling a couple of loads to the street, Phillip came back to the patio for a drink and to remove his hat and tee shirt. He spread lotion on his face and upper body and listened to the Eagles on the radio fretting about "wasted time." He heard a car door slam somewhere out front then returned to his one-arm pushing until he sensed someone was standing behind him.

He pulled the snow shovel back and started to turn around. Phillip's jeans, grey with ash up to the pockets, sagged from his hips; vertebrae showed through his bare chest, and his once-sinewy arms were thin and rubbery. He hadn't showered since before the appointment so his dark-blond hair and beard were unkempt and gritty.

"Nobody answered the doorbell, so I came through the garage," Lupe said, standing there in her riding clothes — boots, jeans and a short-sleeve madras shirt. Errant strands of long black hair from her ponytail flowed over one shoulder. Lupe's eyes, always huge to Phillip, widened even more as she approached and took in his appearance from a few feet away.

"My God. Hi, Lupe," he said, but she just stared, her mouth slightly open. Her vacant expression made Phillip look down at himself; it dawned on him he could pass for a survivor of a bombed-out hospital. "Uh; pretty dirty stuff." He sounded meek. "You look great. How long have you been back?" He leaned on his snow shovel.

"A few days; I've been trying to call." She moved closer and Phillip saw a couple tears course over her cheeks.

Jesus. "Lupe?"

She dried her face with the back of her hand. "What happened to you, Phil?"

"Totaled my truck; it's just a bump and a broken arm."

Shaking her head in disbelief, Lupe looked down at his gaunt glistening torso. "You don't look well at all."

"Yeah, I've been to a doctor; I'll be fine." *I hope.*

Lupe sniffled and said, "Give me that damn shovel."

A crease of a smile crossed his face. "Geez, nice language." He chuckled, handed it over and she dug out a full scoop of ash.

"Well, where do we put it?" she asked, her mien still somber as she held up the shovel.

"In my cart." He pulled over his homemade contraption.

"Fine." Lupe heaved the load up and into the box; a grey cloud mushroomed right back out and powdered her clean hair.

Phillip grinned at her. "Uh, you have to drop it in there a little easier."

Lupe waved at the soot floating around her face. "I see that," she said, finally with a smile. "C'mon, Phil, let's get all of it."

They cleared away ash and talked quietly until early dusk closed in again.